Lesson Learned:

It is What It is

Portia A. Cosby

DISTINCT | Publishing

Portia A. Cosby

DISTINCT Publishing
PO Box 1034
Beaver Falls, PA 15010

Copyright © 2009 by Portia A. Cosby

PUBLISHER'S NOTE
This book is a work of fiction. Names, characters, places, and incidents
are either the product of the author's vivid imagination or are used
fictitiously, and any resemblance to actual persons, living or deceased,
business establishments, events, or locales is entirely coincidental.

ISBN 13: 978-0-9823013-1-9
ISBN 10: 0-9823013-1-6

Cover designed by Marion Designs
Printed in the United States of America

For information regarding special discounts for bulk purchases, please
contact DISTINCT Publishing at the above address or
ordernow@ portiacosby.com.

To everyone who has believed, this is for you.

Acknowledgements

God has smiled on me! I am covered in His favor, and though I can describe almost anything, no words would do His blessings any justice. I am grateful to Him for opening doors I thought would always be closed.

Mom, thank you for your sacrifices. I don't take what you do for granted. Your time with Amari and your patience (sometimes *wink*) with me staring at my laptop screen for hours at a time is much appreciated. Amari, Mommy loves you. I smile every time you say, "Mommy's book!" Like we've discussed, I truly do believe you will write your own book some day. Glenn, thanks for tagging along with me to signings, promoting my book to strangers, and sharing advice (that I tend to reject on the wrong day *smile*). I appreciate your support.

To my aunts, uncles, and cousins: Thank you for spreading the word about my books. I've heard many stories from other writers about unsupportive family members, and I can gladly say I can't relate! I won't list names because I may forget someone and never hear the end of it, but you know who you are.

Oh, Advisory Board! What would I do without you? Ericka, Rosie Shirletta, and Cleveland…thank you for taking your valuable time and devoting it to reading my drafts. Ericka, I also thank you for your contributions in every other aspect! DeVawn, my cover consultant, thank you for sitting on the phone with me, clicking thumbnail after thumbnail, and coming up with detailed analyses of why one concept would work versus another. In a few months, we'll be doing it again! Jamie, my marketing advisor, thank you for all the ideas. Just when I think I'm thinking outside the box, you come up with something that reminds me I'm only peeking through the top of it! April…I know your schedule didn't allow you to read the work-in-progress, but I value the ongoing support you've shown from the first *Too Little, Too Late* chapter allotment. Janice and Shandra…along with 1 and 6, you personify what it means to be D.I.S.T.I.N.C.T. We're all in this together.

To my beautiful sorors of Zeta Phi Beta Sorority, Inc. and phenomenal brothers of Phi Beta Sigma Fraternity, Inc., the Burk PT book club, Ms. Lucille Nesmith, Chris Hinson, and everyone else who has undoubtedly been in my corner…thank you, thank you, thank you!

Special thanks go to my editor, Carla Dean, and my cover designer, Keith Saunders. Shunda Leigh, thanks for helping get my name out there. Regis Bolden and Wayne Warner, thank you for making sure my website is on-point. Tracey M. Lewis-Giggetts, Erica N. Martin, and Vanessa Miller...thank you for sharing your wisdom about the business. I've learned so much just by talking with you all.

To the readers who have emailed me and left feedback on my website: Understand that you keep me going. I am touched that *you* are touched by my writing. I create these characters and their stories in hopes that someone will not only be entertained by them, but that they can also relate to them. Because of your words, I know my purpose has been met.

To anyone I forgot; charge my head and not my heart. And to those who exited my life for reasons unknown, thank you. You've taught me a valuable lesson.

So it continues for some & begins for others…

November 2003

Portia A. Cosby

Prologue

Jacqueline's Surprise

Jacqueline popped up and looked around the living room.

What time is it? How long was I sleep?

With the help of the flickering light from the television, she located her glasses on the coffee table and glanced at the clock...10:56 p.m.

Why hasn't Shawn called? He's been gone since 5:30 this evening.

She checked her cell phone and saw she had three missed calls, but none of them were from Shawn.

"Where are you?" she said aloud as she pressed the speed dial button for his number. Immediately, she got his voicemail. "You better not have your phone off, idiot," she mumbled while redialing the number. Again, she reached the voicemail. "Shawn, it's Jackie. Call me."

She then checked her voicemail and returned some calls. As she gossiped with Melinda about the possibility of the school hiring a new principal, she made herself a martini and returned to the couch.

"Girl, I'm just glad we don't have to deal with the drama of those damn inner-city public schools. The 'hood is an afterthought. I worked too hard earning my degrees to go back to that world. All those—"

"Gurrrrl, turn to channel five! I missed this story earlier," Melinda interrupted.

Jacqueline sipped her drink as she casually turned to the news. "What now?"

The words "Top Story" flashed on the screen, and the inset showed a familiar neighborhood. After setting her glass down, she turned up the volume. As the broadcast went live at the scene, the newscaster reported the horrific story of a ruthless rapist and murderer seeking revenge on an innocent woman.

The usual peace and quiet of Crescent Park Condominiums was interrupted at approximately seven o'clock that evening, when shots rang out at 715 Bluewater Lane. The camera zoomed in on Jacqueline's ex-boyfriend's condo as she raised her trembling hand to her mouth.

"Isn't that where Craig lives?" Melinda asked.

Jacqueline listened closely to the details, bracing herself for tragic news about her ex. To her surprise, he was not involved. Instead, it was that bitch, Tameka, the mother of Craig's son. She was in a shootout with the man who raped her a year and a half prior. The intruder, identified as Rashawn Carter, allegedly broke in, sexually assaulted

Tameka again, and shot her four times. In the midst of the commotion, she was able to shoot back. At the time of the report, Rashawn Carter was pronounced dead at the scene and Tameka James was in critical condition.

Melinda sighed. "Wow. All that with Thanksgiving being tomorrow." She paused before continuing. "I know you don't like her, Jackie, but that girl's been through a lot. I hope she makes it. She seemed like a nice person."

"How would you know?"

"We chatted at a few of the district parties when she was with Craig."

"Well, for the record, I hope she makes it, too. I don't wish death on anybody."

"That rapist deserved to die, though. Justice was finally—"

"I gotta go," Jacqueline said hurriedly. She hung up the phone and clenched her hair. "No, no, no! What the hell is going on? Rape?"

They had to have the wrong person; maybe someone with a similar name. Her brother wasn't capable of doing that to anyone. Sure, he was rough around the edges and had been to jail a few times, but that was for drugs. And as much as he loved women and they loved him, how could he possibly force himself on one?

Jacqueline convinced herself that the police had to be mistaken and reached for the phonebook. As she opened it to search for the nearest precinct's number, another image on the screen caught her eye: the black Acura believed to be the car Rashawn was driving. She felt lightheaded as she watched her car being showcased to the city.

It was confirmed. Her younger brother had gotten himself in a mess he couldn't get out of. Or did she get him into the mess? No. Absolutely not. They had a plan, and evidently he didn't stick to it.

When she began stalking Craig after their breakup, she didn't mean any harm. She was just curious to see what was so great about Tameka. Why would he choose to get back with a girl who had HIV and a ton of emotional baggage?

What was supposed to last for a couple days turned into a month-long regimen that dubbed as Jacqueline's second job. Every day, she would follow Craig to Tameka's house after work and watch their activities through her binoculars. On Mondays, Tuesdays, and Thursdays, she was at the gym at 5 a.m. sharp, staring at him from under the low-riding brim of her hat. Sundays were devoted to church, where sometimes she could get as close as three pews behind him. She simply wanted him to miss her—to somehow feel her presence—but she soon realized they didn't have that kind of connection.

10

Feelings of pure hatred grew within her the day she witnessed Craig visit four different jewelry stores, browsing at what appeared to be engagement rings. That man was supposed to be the one…*her* one. During their relationship, he had her convinced that he was going to take care of her and her two children, so the ring should've been hers. On that day, reality had bitch-smacked her in the face, and she knew Craig was truly in love with the glorified hoodrat.

The time for being mad was over. It was time to get even. Coincidentally, Shawn had come down from New York a few weeks prior and stopped by Jacqueline's to say hello…and to borrow her car. Of course, she refused. Her brother was far from trustworthy, and she did not want to pay for the car to be detailed after he spilled alcohol on the rugs and implanted the smell of marijuana in her upholstery. She had a reputation to uphold.

Although they were only three years apart, Jacqueline Randolph and Rashawn Carter's personalities were as different as the daddies who created them. Jacqueline was all about appearances. The economics teacher was too ashamed of the truth, so she lied about her past. Her "deceased" husband of five years was actually living in New Mexico with his new family, and the exclusive Regale Frontier subdivision she boasted of living in as a child was really the Regal Wood Projects.

Rashawn kept it real—sometimes too real. He studied the street game thoroughly and practiced what he learned as if he were an eager intern longing for a top-notch position. He rarely stayed in one place, bouncing from New York, to DC, to Michigan, to Florida at any given time. Whenever he did return to Texas, he would stop by his sister's house to make sure she was all right.

It was a rare event, but Jacqueline had called Shawn on the 23rd, asking if he still needed her car. He knew there were stipulations, which he learned of once he arrived at her house. He could drive the car for a week, but first he had to scare her ex…bust some windows, trash his place, maybe even whoop his ass if he was home. All was fair in love and war, and Craig had unknowingly declared war when he prepared to move Tameka into his condo under Jacqueline's watchful eye.

She took Shawn on her surveillance run the next day. As they drove by at five miles per hour, she pointed at Craig through the tinted windows. She hated that he looked so happy. Her skin crawled as she witnessed a host of people unloading the U-Haul truck packed with Tameka's belongings. When Tameka appeared in the doorway with Darius in her arms, Jacqueline made it clear to Shawn that he was not to do *anything* if the baby was home.

Shawn couldn't believe his luck. He could barely stifle the grin on his face when he saw Tameka. It was like Jacqueline had placed her in his lap; the poor thing had no clue what she had just done. As he cupped the bulge in his pants, he laughed silently at the irony of the situation. He and his sister somehow wound up with the same circle of enemies and were about to taste the sweetness of revenge.

"That's why you looked like that," Jacqueline said aloud, after replaying the day in her head. "You already knew her. You were looking for her, and I led you right to her!"

She fidgeted in her seat and tapped her fingers on her knee. Tameka's blood was just as much on her hands as it was her brother's.

Tiffany's Discovery

It was 6:10 a.m. and still a little foggy. Tiffany sped through the ritzy subdivision in her Escalade, trying her best to ignore the vibrating cell phone on the passenger seat. Her aunt had been bothering her ever since she left the hospital. Aunt Retha knew it took a half hour to get to her place from Collins Memorial, so there was no need to keep asking how close she was to her house. In two minutes, she would be in the driveway, ready to pick up her kids.

She knew the three children were driving her fifty-seven-year-old aunt crazy. She was only supposed to keep them for about five hours, and they had been there almost twelve. Tiffany understood Aunt Retha's frustration, but she wanted some understanding in return. She was tired as hell. After being at the hospital all night with Alexis, she was drained. Her textbooks never taught her how to console her best friend after her only sister dies. All she knew to do was be there, and she still would've been there if she didn't have to get the kids.

Almost every driveway she passed housed cars with out-of-state plates. It was the season for visitors, the season for family. It was Thanksgiving Day. Sadly, she didn't feel like celebrating. Although she wasn't close to Tameka, she sympathized with Alexis. Morgan was Tiffany's only sister, and she knew she would be a wreck if something tragic happened to her.

As Tiffany neared her aunt's residence, she was alarmed to see two police cruisers parked in front of the neighbor's house. When she got a little closer, she saw two officers standing on the neighbor's doorstep. She slowly pulled into Aunt Retha's driveway and almost ran into the bushes when the neighbor greeted the policemen.

Though sleep-deprived and somewhat delirious, Tiffany was sure the widowed schoolteacher with two kids and delicious banana bread was Jacqueline Randolph. The minor details had come from her nosey aunt six months prior, but she never cared then. Aunt Retha always had a mouthful of gossip to share about everyone on her block.

Equipped with the "nosey" gene herself, Tiffany pulled up to the garage and parked the truck. She exited, barely closing the door, and crept over to the side of Jacqueline's house. The muffled voices couldn't explain what was going on, so she inched forward until she could hear clearly.

"Ma'am, do you own a black 1999 Acura Legend?" the Hispanic officer asked.

"Well, I own that and a '02 Jaguar, as well," she said with a haughty but uncomfortable laugh. "Is there a problem?"

"Do we have to stand here and play the game, or would you like to tell us how you know a Mr. Rashawn Carter, Ms. Randolph?" the black officer asked. "The vehicle was found at a murder scene, and we learned that it's registered to you."

After a long pause, Jacqueline replied, "Shawn is my brother. I let him borrow my car yesterday evening, and I haven't seen him since."

"And did you know Tameka James?"

"What do you mean *did* I know her? She didn't make it?" Her tone was filled more with desperation than concern.

"Guess that's a yes," the Hispanic officer said to his colleague, while pulling out his handcuffs.

"Wait a minute. What is this? I had nothing to do with the murder. Why are you questioning me? I need to call my lawyer." As she turned to go back in the house, both officers grabbed her arms.

"You can do that at the station, ma'am. Right now, I'll let you get out of your pajamas and put on some real clothes before we leave," the Mr. T lookalike said. "And make it fast because I don't have to do you that favor."

Jacqueline immediately became hysterical. "Am I under arrest? You're arresting me on Thanksgiving?"

The same officer reassured her. "It's only questioning, ma'am. If you haven't done anything wrong, you'll be home in a few hours."

Aunt Retha opened the side door just as Jacqueline and the officers went inside. "Girl, what you doin' over there?" she asked, squinting.

Tiffany put her finger to her mouth to silence her aunt and then ran into the house. "You can't be yellin' like that when I'm tryin' to be sneaky, Auntie."

Aunt Retha put on her glasses and peeked through the blinds. "Those are police cars at Jackie's? What in the world is going on?"

"She had somethin' to do with Meka's murder," Tiffany replied.

"Oh, no. Not Jackie. She's got more sense than that."

"Well, her brother sure doesn't."

"Huh?" Aunt Retha asked as she took the turkey out of the sink and put it in the roaster.

"Nothin', Auntie. Why are you about to bake that bird at six-thirty in the morning?"

"That's how you do it! I was supposed to start it last night, but that dern Tony wouldn't stop cryin'."

"Unfamiliar surroundings," Tiffany replied. "If it's not his bed, he can't sleep."

As she talked with her aunt in the kitchen, she kept thinking about Jacqueline. She couldn't believe the connection between her and Smoke, or Rashawn, or whatever he was going by. It was news that Alexis needed to know, but Tiffany didn't want to jump the gun. She didn't know enough information to go off and run her mouth. What if Jacqueline was cleared and had no fault besides being the unfortunate sibling of a rapist? Something told her that she was more of a contributor, though, and she'd rather Alexis hear it from her than some random gossiper on the street. With all of the stress Alexis was under, Tiffany decided to wait until after Tameka's funeral to share the news of the prissy princess' suspected involvement.

Alexis' Mourning

Tameka looked beautiful. Her makeup was flawless, her lips were traced with her favorite lip liner, and I could've sworn the corners of her lips were slightly turned up. I knew she was happy...satisfied. She was fly as usual, wearing the lavender suit and matching scarf I picked out. Her manicured hands rested just below her belly button with her fingers intertwined. That's how she held them when she was deep in thought.

The diamond on her left hand sparkled for nothing. It wasn't a ray of hope or a symbol of her bright future. It was a heartbreaking reminder that Craig's last effort to keep her alive was too little, too late. Real life didn't have the same endings as most Hollywood creations. Tameka was on her deathbed when he proposed, and that's where she remained after she accepted. We weren't gathered at the church for her wedding. We were mourning at her funeral.

14

I couldn't believe the sea of people that was spread across the huge sanctuary. For somebody who could count her friends on one hand, there sure was a hell of a lot of spectators. Don't get me wrong. Many of them were probably sincere in their attendance, but I knew damn well some of those shiesty bitches were just there to get the gossip on what really happened so they could spread it around town.

As I briefly scanned the crowd during the choir's second selection, a few faces stood out. Isaac Gray, the ex-waiter-turned-nurse who met my sister at a little jazz and poetry spot called Smoothies, sat five pews behind me on the opposite side. Though they were just friends, we had come close to being more than friends at one time. I was surprised to see him because I thought he couldn't take off from work. Jacqueline Randolph thought she was incognito, slouching in the very last pew in the back. I saw her ass, though. She looked like Mary J. Blige in her "Not Gon' Cry" video, wearing a scarf and some Queen Bee sunglasses as a disguise. Little did she know, if she was at a Halloween party in full costume and I had glaucoma in both eyes, I could still spot her with no trouble. That bitch had struck a chord with me the first day I met her, and its vibrations were still lingering in my bones. I made a mental note to make sure I asked her why the hell she showed up at Tameka's memorial service.

My former best friend, Daphne Thomas, better known as Dap, was in view just as I looked over my right shoulder. She looked spooked, staring at the pearl casket that held her number one enemy—"the bitch who wouldn't leave Tyrone alone." Funny how Tyrone was the farthest thing from Tameka's mind since high school and the farthest distance away from Dap at the funeral. He dumped her after hearing how her immaturity interfered with Tameka's justice. She kept up more shit with Tameka every chance she had, and when she could've given the cops information to help with the rape case, she tightened her lips out of spite. Although she had no business being there, I knew she would come. She felt guilty and thought that seeing my sister would give her closure.

After the obituary was read, the program called for a special guest to sing a selection. Tielle was supposed to handle that part of the service. She said she could call in a favor and get a local artist named Niecy to sing at least one song. Everybody said she was comparable to Alicia Keys, but I always caught the end of her song when they played it on the radio. To my surprise and everyone else's, Randall Austin, the hottest new R&B artist out of Dallas, entered the choir stand as the musicians played the intro to Kirk Franklin's "The Storm Is Over Now." I was comforted by his mellow voice and secretly ashamed that it was the first time I'd paid attention to the lyrics of the song my sister loved so much.

When it was time for the female's part, a familiar voice hummed into the microphone, but she could not be seen. A couple bars later, you could hear everybody in the sanctuary gasp. Kelly Rowland joined Randall, and they brought the house down. Their rendition sent chills through my rarely moved soul. If Tameka would've risen up from her casket just to lift her hand and say, "Amen," I wouldn't have been surprised. The best thing about their appearance was that they weren't there to showboat. It was still my sister's day and they paid their respects as humbly as everybody else did.

Next came the eulogy. The pastor encouraged us to move on with joy in our hearts—the same joy Tameka is feeling now that she's dancing with the angels. He reminded us that God has His own plans for our lives and that maybe He was tired of seeing my sister suffer so much. I thought about how happy she was before she died, and wondered if God waited until she experienced contentment before He took her away. It hit me that if I had my selfish way, she could've ended up worse off. The HIV could've taken over her body. She could've gotten full blown AIDS. Darius could've grown up to only remember his mom as a pill-popping, scrawny, sickly woman who practically lived in the hospital. I zoned out and sat with my thoughts, missing the rest of the tribute to my sister.

The final viewing of the body was the toughest experience for me. I coached myself, concluding that I needed to be the strong one among the host of my broken-down family members and Tameka's closest friends.

My dad was the first to approach the casket. He stood over Tameka and stared down at her. I'm sure he was wishing there was some way to bring her back. He was always our protector, and it troubled him that he wasn't around to save his oldest daughter from such a terrible ordeal. Daddy felt helpless for the first time in his life, and there was a sense of failure lurking in every tear that rolled down his face.

Mom could barely walk to the casket. My cousin, Jermaine, escorted her. She tried her best not to be "that crazy mom" at a funeral, but her relationship with Tameka was much too complicated for her emotions to remain tamed. Their love-hate bond was mostly full of hate until a few months before. Mom had finally apologized for setting her up with a job at a strip club to help pay for college. I wasn't sure if Tameka ever forgave her for her past malicious ways, but they were definitely in a better place before she passed. Still, the demons that my mother had abandoned came back to haunt her, as we all witnessed. Despite Jermaine's grasp, she fell to the floor and sobbed aloud. I bit my lip to fight my tears, knowing the pain she was in.

"Meka! I never meant to hurt you, sweetheart. I wasn't a real mother to you, baby. I'm sorry." She slid down the front of the casket and patted it as if it were Tameka in the flesh. She stroked the metal and rested the side of her face on its cold surface. "I never wanted you to hurt. You were too special to hurt like this. Please forgive me."

Before my father and Jermaine lifted her from the floor and guided her back to the pew, she kissed the casket. Her body trembled and her face was flushed. The only color evident was the redness of her eyes.

It was my turn. I remained tear-free as my boyfriend, Robert, tightly held my hand and led me to my sister. He was the one who had separated us many times when we were on the verge of throwing blows. Now it was time to say goodbye to the phenomenal woman I'd once wished to be out of my life for good. All of our arguments and the terrible things I'd said seemed ten times worse as I watched my big sis sleep peacefully. A month before, you couldn't have told me that I would ever touch a dead person, but I held Tameka's hand and shook my head in disbelief. Then I couldn't help but chuckle, thinking about what she would say if she could speak: "Look at the hard-ass touchin' a corpse, but still won't cry in front of people."

Robert probably thought I was about to crack when he heard me laugh quietly, but that wasn't the case. I'd never admit it to anybody, but at that point, I really felt Tameka's presence, as if she were still around; and I had a feeling she would keep talking to me here and there to ease my mind.

I leaned over and whispered in her ear, "Thank you for everything."

My forehead lingered on hers for a while as I took a deep breath to gather myself again. When I returned to my seat, I felt overwhelmed and out came the tears. I broke partially because I couldn't watch Craig and Darius view Tameka's body.

Craig was a wreck throughout the whole service, so I knew he would take it hard, but Darius' reaction really got me. He was fighting to get out of Craig's arms, leaning towards his mommy. I wasn't sure if he was crying because he sensed what was going on, or if he was just frustrated at Craig for not handing him to Tameka. Either way, it messed me up because he was too young to understand. There was no rationalizing with a five-month-old about why Mommy couldn't hold him anymore.

After the service ended, we went to the cemetery to bid a final farewell. There would be no more complaints about my weed smoking and cursing; no more late-night talks about our sometimes troubled relationships with Craig and Robert…no more anything. Too often, I used to wish that she would just shut up, but as I watched her casket descend into the hole, I would've given anything to hear one more of her lectures.

You need to act like you got some sense, Tameka's words resounded in my head. *Why do you act so ignorant? You can at least show that your vocabulary spans far beyond four-letter words while you're in public. Most people don't even know you're actually intelligent.*

A lot of her gripes were valid, and I made a promise to myself that I would take heed to most of my sister's preaching. I wanted to make her proud and pay homage to her memory. She wouldn't want me to act like a knucklehead and tell someone I'm her sister. I used to say she was stuck-up for feeling that way, but she only had my best interest in mind.

I felt like I was changing already. I'd learned the hard way that I had been more passionate about bullshit than about things that really mattered. I spent more time kicking it with my friends than hanging out with my sister. I didn't want to be remembered as the girl who couldn't hold a job to save her soul, but could smoke a blunt with the best of them, make a sailor blush with her language, and tear the club up every Friday and Saturday. I had some growing up to do.

The first thing I wanted to work on was my language. I knew I had a cursing problem for sure when I was talking to the pastor after the funeral and had to keep apologizing for casually saying "damn," "hell," and "shit". He prayed for me on the spot just before I joined everyone in the church reception hall for repast.

We left the church at four o'clock. I couldn't wait to get home and change clothes. The thought of getting some rest sounded nice, but I knew it wouldn't happen. All of Tameka's friends and our family were right behind me and Robert, waiting to share old stories, play a few games of spades, and munch on the desserts and side dishes random people had brought over. The hardest part of the day was over, and it was time for life to go on.

"It is the Law that any difficulties that can come to you at any time, no matter what they are, must be exactly what you need most at the moment, to enable you to take the next step forward by overcoming them. The only real misfortune, the only real tragedy, comes when we suffer without learning the lesson."
-Emmet Fox

Portia A. Cosby

1

Alexis:
The Storm is Over Now... or is it?

Our two-bedroom apartment was crowded; however, I didn't mind. Our only other option was to go to Craig's roomier condo, but none of us would've been comfortable there. Although the carpet had been replaced and the walls were repaired and repainted, it still dubbed as the crime scene. Because he wasn't big on having company, Robert had an attitude, but tried his best to act like he didn't and sucked it up for the occasion. I thought he would stay cooped up in our bedroom. Instead, he surprised me by pulling out extra chairs and helping to make room for everybody.

As Earth, Wind & Fire's greatest hits blared through the speakers, the makeshift family reunion began. My mom manned the kitchen because she can't stand when people touch food without washing their hands or taste food from the serving spoon. Aunt Kathy helped as she bopped around the kitchen singing every lyric to "September". The evening was going to be about fun and fellowship, not sadness and sniffling. That's what Mom tried to keep in mind when her big-hipped sister forced her to do The Bump in the small space. She didn't even get mad when Aunt Kathy got a little too excited and bumped her across the kitchen, into the stove. Instead, for the first time in about five years, Regina Clifton-James shared a genuine laugh with her sister, as if they were teenagers again.

My daddy made his home at the spades table on the patio. He partnered with Jermaine, and they vowed to beat the brakes off of Isaac and Dallas, my cousin Yari's fiancé. We could hear them talking shit through the patio door, bragging about how many books they had. All the smokers were out there with them, resting against the railing as they made up stories about their life experiences. Their game was to see who could tell the most believable bullshit.

After a few drinks and too many slices of pie, cake, and whatever other snacks were available, we all sat in the crowded living room and socialized. Craig tried his best to look like he was in high spirits as he joked with Robert, Marlon, and Romeo in the corner by the window. I knew how he was really feeling, though. He was looking for anything to make him smile, and even Robert's pitiful jokes would work for the moment.

I felt the exact same way. With a little help from my friend, Martel, I was able to enjoy myself for the evening without breaking down in front of everybody. No, alcohol wasn't the cure-all, but it sure helped me for the time being.

I sat on the arm of the couch, talking with Nicole, Tielle, Yari, and Tiffany.

"Tielle, how in the hell did you get Kelly to sing at the funeral?" Nicole asked. "That guy was good, too, but I don't know him yet. He was probably cheap, huh?"

Tielle laughed. "Neither of them charged me. My boy from the station called in a favor and it worked."

"You couldn't get Beyoncé?" Tiffany asked, keeping her eyes on me.

All the girls laughed. They always got a kick out of taunting me with Jay-Z and Beyoncé jokes.

"Tielle knows better. Y'all laughin', but I'm serious when I say I don't like that chick. She's causin' problems in me and my baby's relationship." My imaginary love affair with Mr. Shawn Carter seemed like a joke to all my friends, but I was convinced that if we ever met, it would be curtains for him and Miss B.

I took another sip from my glass. "But y'all know what's crazy as hell? How messed up is it that him and Smoke damn near have the same name? I just realized that shit the other day when I was reading an old newspaper clipping."

"That's right," Nicole recalled. "*Ra*shawn Carter."

Tiffany chimed in. "That's okay, girl. The similarity only means y'all destined to be together."

I gave her the finger and gulped down the last of my drink. She was always my devoted cheerleader. I could rob a bank and get caught, and she would tell the cops to leave me alone because I just needed some pocket change. Some stupid shit like that. It was nice to have such a supportive friend, but sometimes she got on my nerves with her exaggerated loyalty.

Tiffany and I had been homegirls since she transferred to Winfrey High in the middle of our freshman year. Her family had moved from North Carolina, so I took her under my wing and tried to make her transition to Texas a smooth one. She was a cool girl, but was sometimes too fragile for my taste. Even in her adult life, when she faced a little too much adversity, she still wore the same apprehensive expression on her face that made her stand out nine years ago.

I almost felt obligated to be her peer mentor of sorts, being that I was "the new girl from Ohio" just a couple years before and knew how awkward it could be to try to make friends without seeming desperate. Right away, we found we had a lot in common. However, my personality had always been crass, while hers was more refined. I rubbed off on her in some areas, though. She was much quicker to put people in their place now and didn't fall for the okie-doke when somebody mistook her for a dumb ass. And even when she found herself in a crazy predicament fooling with me, she played the role like she was down for whatever, even though I knew she was 'bout to piss on herself.

Her lack of identity in high school and struggle to maintain one as an adult was a result of her childhood. Her family always moved around. The locale-specific culture, slang, and clothing style that the rest of us naturally acquired growing up were things Tiffany had to learn. She was a chameleon of sorts, hanging with the 'hood chicks on Friday and effortlessly blending in with rich white folks on Saturday. When she met somebody new, she soaked up their personality like a sponge and could instantly imitate them from their mannerisms to their accent, with ease and unknowingly. She was lucky I was around to let her know when she was being a copycat.

Tielle and Nicole were Tameka's best friends. Nicole grew up with us in Ohio and still lived there. Tielle and Tameka met in high school and were inseparable after they did their first group project together. They were both my adopted big sisters from day one. Their concern for me and tendency to get on my damn nerves was deeply rooted—not a fly-by-night obligation because my sister wasn't alive anymore.

Yari made eye contact with me and motioned for me to follow her down the hallway. We stopped near the guestroom.

"You alright?" she asked. I shrugged. "You remember what I said, right?"

When Yari arrived in town the day after Tameka died, she witnessed a full-fledged hollering match between Robert and me. She

23

heard much more than she would've liked to and could tell that I harbored a lot of anger toward him about a number of issues. Bottom line, she knew I wasn't completely happy.

The following day while we ran errands and made arrangements for the funeral, she gave me a proposition. She and Dallas were relocating to Atlanta in February, and she invited me to join them if I decided Robert wasn't for me. She felt a change of scenery could be just what I needed. I couldn't really argue with her. I was already under enough stress from the murder, and Robert's mess was causing unnecessary stress. Knowing I wasn't ready to close that chapter for good, I promised her that I'd think about her offer and put the Accord on the road if it came down to it.

Yari was doing her thing. Her purpose for moving was career-related. She went on a random casting call with her best friend while she was visiting her in Atlanta the previous month. Just for fun, they auditioned to be extras for an upcoming movie, but Yari was too gorgeous for the casting director to ignore. He asked her if she had any acting experience and she told him yes. He didn't know her only experience was in church plays and one high school musical. Long story short, she read for a supporting role and got it. Her natural abilities landed her a thick-ass script and tons of lines to remember. That meant saying "Goodbye" to Columbus, Ohio, and "What's up, Shawty" to the A-T-L, where *One Minor Detail* would be filmed.

Proud was an understatement to describe how I felt about her venture. Yari had been through a lot. She had Paradise when she was seventeen, which caused static between her and Aunt Kathy. No real mother is happy when her perfect teenage daughter gets knocked up by her twenty-year-old boyfriend. Their relationship was strained even more when Uncle Roy was killed in the line of duty a year later and left ninety percent of his money to Yari. She was his pride and joy, and I guess Aunt Kathy was just his wife. Because of her experience with the death of someone close to her, I kept her coping advice closest to my heart and shared most of my grief with her.

"I remember, girl," I said to Yari, tracing the rim of my glass with my index finger.

She lifted my chin so I would look at her. "Don't stay because you're comfortable. Leave when you're not."

I playfully rolled my eyes. *She always has something deep to say,* I thought.

She snatched the glass from my hand. "And you need to stay away from this stuff. You're supposed to be making changes, right?"

I threw my hands up to signal my surrender. "I don't need no more anyway," I replied, repeatedly yanking the collar of my shirt to create a breeze. "I'm hot as hell! You hot?"

I stepped outside to get some air. The cool breeze that swept across my face reminded me that I should've put on a jacket, but I knew I would manage. My body probably needed the shock anyway. The alcohol was running warm through my veins and causing me to sweat beyond my ladylike allowance; and the feeling that was supposed to be a notch above tipsy was quickly transforming into a notch below faded. I paced in the breezeway in an effort to sober up, but decided to sit my dizzy ass on the step after three laps.

I needed a little time alone. I was tired of putting on a social front in the crowded space. Even though we were supposed to just be chilling inside, someone would occasionally come over and whisper what they thought were reassuring words in my ear. I reacted as expected thanking them for their kind words, but my face was beginning to hurt from withholding tears and forcing fake smiles.

"It'll be okay," was the annoying mantra that everyone's lips chanted to me throughout the day. No one really believed it. It just sounded like the right thing to say. Being raised in church, I knew I was supposed to be encouraged and remember Tameka is in a better place, but I'm human and that wasn't enough for me at the time. My feelings about her murder were black and white. That bastard terrorized and shot her. He took her away from her son. I hated him. I hated that I wasn't there to see him die his miserable death and maybe even put a few extra holes in his perverted body. He took my only sibling away from me, and that wasn't okay.

Isaac exited the apartment and saw me sitting on the step with my head between my knees. "Everybody's wondering where you are," he said as he leaned against the railing.

"I just needed to breathe. Need some time alone."

"I understand," he replied, cautiously resting his hand on my shoulder.

Isaac was like a character straight out of a black romantic comedy. He definitely looked the part—a real chocolate Casanova. Morris Chestnut had nothing on him. His facial hair was so neatly groomed that it looked drawn on. What was once a baby afro on his head was now hair neatly twisted, making his gorgeous face stand out even more. He looked like one of those sexy neo-soul brothas with a style all his own. No smedium shirts and tight jeans; but loafers instead of sneakers, a button-down instead of a t-shirt, and jeans that didn't fall below his ass. Normally that wasn't my thing, but I could tell he was comfortable in his own skin and looked damn good in it, too. He was getting his grown-man on and I wasn't mad at him.

I became a little soft on Isaac a little over five months ago when I went to Columbus for Darius' birth. He was different—into poetry and jazz, knew how to sing a little bit, and ate foods other than pizza and wings. The mystery in his eyes intrigued me, but the openness of his words impressed me. It was clear that Isaac wasn't into games, so I put my player card away. I knew I wasn't ready to leave Robert and try a relationship with him, so I remained friendly and toned down the flirtatious comments I showered him with when we first met. We'd talked a few times since June, but kept the conversations on a "play cousin" level. Who knew that when I saw him again I'd feel a little more than what I thought was curiosity?

"Thanks for comin' out to check on me." I patted his hand, then quickly pulled mine away when I realized it was lingering.

"You know you don't need to be out here by yourself. I know you need space, though, so I won't crowd you. I'll play bodyguard and chill in the background to make sure nobody jumps out of the darkness," Isaac said.

I laughed and gave him a look of contemplation.

"Or I can go inside and get Robert. It's just not safe for you to be alone. You don't even have your purse with you," he joked, knowing that I keep my gun in the Coach bag.

"Fuck Robert. He didn't come out here to see about me." I started down the stairs, then paused. "I need to take a walk, bodyguard. You comin'?"

Isaac smiled. "After you, Madame."

We strolled around the apartment complex in silence. It was a golden silence. The crickets chirping and the whistle of the wind were sounds that specified where we were, but our lack of dialogue and limited eye contact proved who we were. Isaac was a real friend and a real man. He never tried to hold my hand, spit game, or stop somewhere to talk. And as the wind picked up, he didn't have one complaint, even though I knew he was cold as hell. The alcohol had warmed my body, not his.

When we returned to my doorstep, people were leaving. I waited for the large group to file out, hugging each person. I felt like I was in the receiving line at a wedding. Once the coast was clear, I went inside.

"Where you been?" Robert asked.

"Walkin'."

"How long you been gone?" he followed up.

Isaac softly touched my arm. "I'm heading out. Take care of yourself, *Whitney.*"

"You too, *Kevin.* Thanks again," I joked, playing along with his *Bodyguard* analogy.

Before he left, he made sure he shook my dad's hand and hugged my mom.

I turned back to Robert. "Long enough for you to notice I was gone and call to see if I was okay, but you didn't. Excuse me."

I pushed past him and joined Tiffany in the kitchen, where she was fixing plates for her, Marlon, and the kids.

"Why are you movin' so fast?" I asked, laughing. She looked like she was on a game show trying to win a million dollars for fixing five plates in under thirty seconds.

"Girl, you already know." She looked at Marlon, who was sitting on the couch, and blew him a kiss.

I shook my head. She was the horniest thing walking when she had more than two drinks. "Don't y'all make no more babies. Y'all already got three too many."

She mooned me, revealing the birth control patch on her right butt cheek. "Naw, we ain't gon' do none of that. I'ma wear his ass out, though. Look at him, sitting over there in all that fineness."

She exited the kitchen and summoned Marlon to join her at the door. He laughed, acting like he was embarrassed and somewhat uninterested in her blatant display of affection.

"You stay strong, lil' mama," he said as we hugged.

"I will," I replied.

Before they left, Marlon turned to me again. "Hey, I already know how you gon' receive this, but I promised to relay the message. Dap said call her. It's on you what you do with that information."

Marlon knew how I felt about his sister. I didn't believe we could ever be close like we were before. I always knew she had a shady side and I didn't judge her because I had one of my own. But when she turned the shade on my sister, putting her in harm's way, I was done. She was lucky I hadn't choked the life out of her ass yet.

Finally, everybody was gone except for my dad, who was asleep in the guestroom. Mom usually stayed with me when she came to town, but even after a few years of divorce, they couldn't be in the same vicinity for an extended amount of time. Robert put away the extra chairs and straightened up the living room, while I loaded the dishwasher and put the rest of the food away.

By the time I finished, I could barely keep my eyes open, so I headed down the hall to the bedroom. Robert was checking the

Indianapolis Colts' schedule on the internet. No surprise. If he was gay, I promise Peyton Manning would be his celebrity crush.

"You comin' to bed?" I asked, hoping he'd say yes.

"In a minute. I'm just lookin' at some stats."

I lay in the bed, wearing only my bra and panties, struggling to stay awake for Robert. As tired as I was, I knew I'd have the strength to move my hips a little bit and arch my back the way he liked. We had our best sex when we were beefing, so I knew I was in for a treat.

I dozed off and woke up at 2:47 a.m. I flung my arm behind me. No Robert. I didn't have to wonder where he was much longer. The bass in his voice carried down the hallway, even though he was trying his best to talk quietly. This was the fourth time in two weeks I had awakened to this shit.

Ever so carefully, I tiptoed to the door and tried to hear what he was saying. I also wanted to make sure he wasn't out there talking to my dad or something. Daddy hadn't been sleeping well, so I considered they might have been spending "guy time" together.

Wrong. Robert's conversation was with somebody on the phone, and it had to be a female. If he was talking to a dude like that, we would need to have a "down-low" discussion to see if there was something he needed to share. Really, he didn't have any business snickering and whispering to anybody during any time of day, and he knew I didn't tolerate that kind of disrespect.

***

"I'm not in the mood for your attitude this morning," Robert said as he checked his email.

I laughed. "I bet you're not."

"What's that supposed to mean?"

"It means you ain't got time for shit lately. No time to talk, no time to fuck, no time for me, huh?"

"I thought you were workin' on not cussin'."

"Yeah, well, today is my off day, dammit. And don't try to change the subject," I snapped.

I was tired of him acting funny-style, and it was time to call him out. His latest forms of communication were starting to look suspicious. All of a sudden, he was Mr. Technology and couldn't live without his phone or the computer. For a guy who would barely check his email when I met him three years before, he sure had learned the ins and outs of instant messaging and using a webcam pretty quickly. He even installed the messenger on his phone so he could get his emails and engage in frivolous chats when he wasn't home.

The only reason it took me so long to say something is because he was such a defensive person. No matter how I would spin it, he would catch the undertone of my questions. It would seem like I was accusing him of being sneaky or cheating in some way.

Cybersex wasn't his style, nor was it my concern. I just knew that his new habits had caused me to raise more than my eyebrows. If all late-night activity didn't cease, the next thing on my agenda was to raise hell. I'd been taking Tiffany's advice to stop cussing him out and punking him every time he pissed me off, but he was starting to mistake my calmness for weakness.

"I've had plenty of time for you, but all you do is push me away. You don't talk to me about nothin'. You'd rather stay on the phone with Tiffany all day. Y'all act like y'all in love or somethin'."

Tiffany was always his scapegoat. Like most men I know, whenever he needed a comeback, someone to insult, or someone to take the pressure off himself, he chose my closest friend. When we first got together, Dap was supposedly my boo.

"So I guess you and Romeo are sweethearts, too, huh?" I asked. "And how do I push you away? Is it because I want to talk about somethin' other than Meka bein' dead? I'ma never get over it, fuckin' with you. What happened to havin' fun and shootin' the shit about who makes the best Ramen noodles or chasin' each other around the house for the hell of it?"

Robert signed out of his account and clipped his cell phone onto his belt. He then walked into the kitchen and took a banana off the counter. "Baby, I'm already runnin' late. I'm through with this conversation. It is what it is," he said.

He was brand-new in every way because he was far from being a nonchalant person. Up until that moment, I had refrained from being the smart ass I'm notorious for being, but since he was trying to dismiss me, I got one last thing in—the thing I should've said long before that day.

"If you'd stop whispering on your phone at 2:47 in the morning, you might get enough sleep to get yo ass up on time."

He paused at the door and cut his eyes at me. I stood my ground, waiting for a response. Five seconds later, Mr. "I'm-so-pressed-to-make-it-to-work-on-time" couldn't close the door fast enough. For once, he had a real excuse to cut an argument short and he took it. He knew me well enough to sweat all day, wondering what would happen when he returned that evening. The poor thing didn't even realize that if he kept playing, he'd walk through the door and find all my shit gone.

29

Portia A. Cosby

2

Tiffany:
High Maintenance

"You know what, Marlon? I don't have time for this mess today. If you have any more questions, comments, or concerns, write them down and leave the tablet on the kitchen table," Tiffany said, while transferring the last item of her red Fendi handbag into her emerald Marc Jacobs one.

"Excuse me?" Marlon replied, stepping closer to her.

Although she was barely 5'2" and he was every bit of 6'1", she wasn't even close to being intimidated. Marlon was a good man and she knew he would never put his hands on her. They'd had this argument too many times...she needed to stop spending so much money. Why did she have to get her nails and hair done every week? Why does she have all the movie channels but doesn't watch them? What's wrong with wearing "regular" clothes instead of the high fashion designers'?

Tiffany gave the same answer every time: She grew up with the best and wasn't settling for anything less. Her kids were fed, clothed, educated, and happy, so it wasn't like she was depriving them because of her luxurious habits. Marlon was just a simple guy who grew up with simple things, and he expected Tiffany to convert to his frugal lifestyle.

He often forgot that they were from completely different worlds. She was a military brat, so she'd seen many places and had lived around as much diversity as Michael Jackson's children. She was born in Alaska and could recall maybe eight or nine of the other states and countries she has lived in. Her style was exquisite. The finest threads housed in her two walk-in closets fit her petite frame perfectly. She had a pair of shoes to match any color outfit, along with sunglasses, necklaces, earrings, and any other accessory stores sold. If she wasn't so jazzy,

31

people would probably call her a "label ho", but her sophistication kept her out of that category.

Marlon knew nothing about travel. He had only left the state of Texas once, and that was when he went to Florida to help his cousin move. His idea of stepping out involved wearing a Phat Farm polo or button-down, freshly starched jeans, and a splash of Curve cologne on his neck and chest. He always looked good, though, and never had a wrinkle on him.

Since hip-hop clothing was his thing, Tiffany worked with him, refining his look with matching money clips and cuff links bearing his favorite company's logo. She'd been trying to convince him to wear a sweater for about a year now, but he still had the mindset that it was a nerdy look.

Despite their differences in taste, she accepted Marlon for who he was just as he accepted her, except for that one time every month when he was on his period. That's when he bitched about her weekly appointments at the nail shop. He knew good and well there was only one man in her life just as important as him, and his name was Steve Wong, the owner of New Nails. Tiffany could always be sure that her nails would be flawless by the time he got through with them. If it wasn't for his unique skills, she wouldn't be caught dead on the raggedy end of 9th Avenue.

She flung her purse onto her shoulder and smacked Marlon on his thigh. "Listen. I'm gonna be late if I don't leave now. Don't forget to give Bryant his medicine when he wakes up." She turned on her heels and hurried out the door.

While Tiffany was driving, she called Alexis to see if she wanted to meet her at the nail shop. She figured she could treat her to a manicure and pedicure to lift her spirits some. Robert answered.

"Is Lexis home?" Tiffany asked.

"Naw."

"Do you know where she is? She's not answering her cell."

"Maybe she's busy. She ain't gotta pause every time you call."

"You are so ignorant."

They tried to hang up on each other, but wound up doing so at the same time. She couldn't stand Robert's ass, and he couldn't stand hers. They had a Martin-Pam relationship, except they weren't acting. She was the "evil-best friend-who-needs-to-mind-her-business," and he was the "no-good-boyfriend-who-thinks-he's-slick."

Tiffany knew Robert's problem. He didn't like her because she was onto him. It was like he was walking around with shitty drawers on and she smelled them, but Alexis couldn't smell them yet because she had a cold and her nose was stopped up. He didn't like that Tiffany cleared Alexis' congestion when she needed it; and he knew one day Alexis' nose would be clear enough to smell his filthy behind.

She continued the day's schedule without her friend, making her usual stops at the mall and a few specialty stores in Chamberlain Village, a classy shopping complex on the south side of town. While out, she took a moment to inspect the new daycare center located downtown. Everybody was raving about its state-of-the-art equipment and friendly staff; and if she acquired a job in the area, it would be perfect for her children.

***

Morgan called during Tiffany's drive home that evening. It had been a week since they'd talked. They caught up on family gossip, then shared their personal updates. Morgan was the model aunt and loved to hear the hilarious stories about her niece and nephews' antics, so Tiffany gave her an earful. Tiffany's enjoyment came from hearing about her big sis' latest addition to her dating circle. Morgan kept a team of men who wined and dined her, took her on luxurious vacations, and performed great sex. With a steady team of three, there was always one for each category. Her newest contestant was Ryan, who took over Christian's position of wining and dining her. Tiffany smiled and shook her head as Morgan ran down the list of exclusive restaurants Ryan had taken her to in New Jersey and Philadelphia.

Tiffany and her sister were like night and day. While Morgan preferred to taste love's variety, Tiffany stayed true to one man and was intent on keeping it that way. Her only temptation was Aaron McCloud, an average-looking guy with a body of steel. She met him a year ago at Fit Club, the gym Marlon managed. There was something about his eyes that she instantly found mesmerizing, so she knew she had to stay away from him. Unfortunately, he didn't stay away from her. He was determined to have at least one night with her and sweet-talked her every time they ran into each other. Flattered but uninterested at first, her interest piqued when Alexis heard from a trustworthy source that Aaron had a tongue that should be dipped in gold and placed on someone's mantle.

That was the area where Marlon was beginning to falter. Their lovemaking had become predictable and came in three varieties: the works, the essential, and the quickie. If she was lucky, she would get the works, complete with oral sex, three to four positions, and a hearty orgasm. She still would have liked a little more variety, but Marlon wasn't into toe licking or massages. It was better than the essential, though, which was nothing more than the basic in-and-out with a little hip rotation and kissing. The quickie? Not even worth elaborating on.

As Tiffany pulled into her garage, she said goodbye to Morgan. Careful not to damage her nails, she hung two large shopping bags on her left wrist and carried four plastic grocery bags in her other hand. Eager to see her mommy, Bria greeted Tiffany at the door and carried the bag of bread inside.

"Hey, Poochie!" Tiffany said as they entered the kitchen. After she set the bags down, she hugged her bright-eyed princess. "What you do today?"

As Bria rambled on about watching *Blue's Clues* and seeing a new commercial for a dollhouse she wanted, Tiffany daydreamed about her life. New things were about to happen—things that would practically bring her life full-circle at a very young age. By New Year's Day, she hoped to have her master's degree, a bread-winning job, and a marriage proposal from Marlon. She felt confident about all three, especially after she saw Marlon flipping through a Gordon's Jewelers ad when he thought she wasn't looking.

Most twenty-three-year-old ladies would cringe at the thought of being bogged down with three kids, a husband, and a full-time job, but that was the life Tiffany yearned for. She loved to sing to her children and read them a story before tucking them into bed. She didn't mind cooking a full-course meal, ironing everyone's clothes, and picking up random toys in the living room. Growing up, she saw how happy it made her mother and how happy her father was in return.

She wanted that same happiness and relationship longevity. So, after she baked orange roughy and prepared red potatoes and broccoli with cheese, the normal routine began. She loaded the dishwasher, picked out clothes for the next day, and then sang "Jesus Loves Me" to the kids as they lay in their beds. Halfway through *Goldilocks and the Three Bears*, the twins were knocked out and Tony was sucking his thumb, determined to fight sleep.

By ten o'clock, she and Marlon were cuddling on the couch, watching reruns of *A Different World*. After a little fooling around, he led her to the bedroom.

Great, Tiffany thought. *As tired as I am, he'll probably want the works.*

She stared at the ceiling as Marlon mounted her and did his thing. Suddenly, it hit her. Her final was the next day and she still hadn't finished writing her notecards. Determined to speed up the process, she rolled her hips a little harder, squeezed her walls more frequently, and exaggerated her sounds of enjoyment. What was supposed to be

34

"the essential" turned into "the quickie" when Marlon climaxed three minutes later.

Mission accomplished.

***

The sound of the garbage truck woke Tiffany up. She raised her head from the kitchen table and pulled a 3x5 notecard from her cheek. It was 7:30 already. She stared at the open psychology book, pile of notebook paper, and study guides, and realized she must've fallen asleep while studying.

When she tiptoed into the children's room, she found them still sleeping soundly. Instead of utilizing her time to cram some more, she laid in her bed to get some real rest. Before she knew it, it was 10:30 and she was running around the house like a wild woman, trying to gather everything for her test.

She arrived on campus at 11:22 and pulled into the last spot near the psychology building. She figured if she walked fast, she could glance at her notes one last time before her exam. She was confident that she knew the information, though. Analyzing mental states and processes was almost natural for her.

The heavy oak door creaked loudly as Tiffany eased inside the lecture hall, where Mr. Finnell was passing out tests to the second row. She hurried to her fourth-row seat and plopped down. In almost one uninterrupted motion, she opened her messenger bag, pulled out her lucky Bic mechanical pencil, and crossed her legs.

School was finally about to be over. This would be her last final...ever. That was, unless she decided to get her doctorate. But Tiffany knew it would be a while before she did that. She wanted to devote some time solely to her family. The kids barely received attention from her during the week because she was busy writing research papers, attending her internship, and reading fifty-page chapters; and the weekends were only productive if she woke up in time to watch cartoons with the rowdy bunch. Poor Marlon needed a break, and she was well aware of that.

The test was twelve pages long—ninety-six questions and three essays. It was almost like taking the SAT again! The Scantron bubbles seemed to blend together after the fiftieth question. Tiffany blinked repeatedly to refocus her eyes. She could've sworn the bubbles had formed a smiley face on her answer sheet, and it was messing up her concentration.

An hour and twenty minutes later, she handed her test and Scantron sheet to Mr. Finnell. Unofficially, she could now say that she had her master's degree in psychology. She hugged her plump professor.

"Congratulations, Ms. Price. I know you did just fine," he said softly.

"Thank you," Tiffany replied in a whisper, then added, "and you know I'm gonna be asking for a letter of recommendation."

They laughed quietly and he gave her a thumbs-up sign.

On her way out of the building, she saw her classmate, Frenchie Carlson, standing near the glass doors. Frenchie was a walking stereotype of an eclectic, spiritual, fist-in-the-air kind of sista. Her fuzzy dreadlocks were always pulled back with a headband or scarf, and their copper-red color was as bold and shameless as her personality. A light-skinned sista, tiny brown freckles decorated her butter pecan face and made her look extremely innocent, but her blackberry lipstick and narrow eyes told a story that she was not ready to share.

"It's over, girl!" Frenchie exclaimed. "That was easier than I thought it would be."

"I know," Tiffany agreed. "Now I can focus on what's really important." Frenchie looked confused. "My birthday party, girl! Don't act like you forgot. You still comin'?"

She laughed. "Yeah, I'll be there. I have never seen an adult so excited about her birthday. You've been talking about this party for weeks."

"That's because I throw unforgettable celebrations. I don't half step, sweetie. And remember you can bring somebody. No more than two people, though."

Tiffany's phone rang. Alexis' name glowed on the blue screen. She turned to Frenchie. "I gotta take this. Call me for directions."

As she ran to her truck to escape the heavy wind, Alexis ranted on the other end of the phone.

"I'm about to quit this damn job. I had to leave early. Charlene's got one more time to say somethin' smart before I blast her in the mouth. And Ginger's little country ass is gon' catch one, too. That little passive-aggressive heiffa keeps takin' shit off my desk—" She stopped abruptly and breathed slowly. "I'm not supposed to be cussing. Forgive me, Lord. I'm trying to stop, but these folks keep takin' me there."

Tiffany laughed as her friend coached herself. "Is it my turn to talk now?"

"Yeah. What you doin'?"

In her happiest tone ever, Tiffany boasted about taking her last final and asked Alexis if she wanted to join her at the party supply store. She was eager to see if they had any more plates and cups to go with her fiesta theme. Alexis agreed to meet her since she had no plans of returning to work.

"Why do you need more stuff? How many people are comin'?"

"Well, Frenchie just confirmed that she's coming, and she'll probably bring two people with her," Tiffany replied, bracing herself for Alexis' response.

"Frenchie? That gay chick from your class? Aw hell. And she's bringin' her little lesbian crew?"

"She doesn't just hang with lesbians, fool."

"They all hang together. If one of 'em touches my ass or says some crazy shit…"

"What makes you think they'll be attracted to you? And even if they are, they can usually tell who's down with that and who's not. They won't bother you."

"Just keep 'em away from me," Alexis replied.

Tiffany laughed. "You are the most homophobic person I know."

"I ain't got nothin' against gay people. Frenchie's just weird. She always looks like she's undressin' me with her eyes. I'ma tell you now that if she brings her little buddy who looks like Carl Thomas, I'm leavin' early. Every time I see that chick, she stares at me. I already threatened her manly ass once," Alexis said. "I'm in the parking lot. Bye," she finished as she exited her car and walked toward the store.

It was all Tiffany could do to keep her composure in the balloon aisle as she doubled over from laughter. She knew exactly who Alexis was talking about, and her description was extremely accurate. Kelly could easily be mistaken for a man, right down to her mannerisms and texturized fade.

She ignored Alexis' reaction to the new additions on her guest list. Frenchie and company would be the farthest thing from her mind once the party got started. If there was any possible guest of concern, it would be Dap. Although Tiffany didn't invite her, she knew Dap would assume she was welcome to come just because Marlon was her brother. With her recent attempts at reconciling with Alexis, she would definitely come to see her former friend, even if she simply played the background and never said a word to her. That was the scenario Tiffany hoped for, because if any words were exchanged, trouble was likely to follow.

3

Alexis: Moonlighting

Robert sighed from exhaustion as he rolled his sweaty body off mine. "Damn, girl. You gon' kill me."

"You gon' kill yourself. I didn't tell you to do all them acrobatics," I replied. I moved my damp hair away from my forehead. "You owe me fifty dollars, though. I just got this perm two days ago."

We laughed, and I playfully punched him in the chest before running into the bathroom. It had been almost a week since I confronted him about the late calls on his cell phone and we hadn't had any more problems. He admitted that the person on the other end was a female, but it wasn't what I thought. It was his sister's best friend, Jamie, who needed advice about a situation with her boyfriend. Even though she was a little nineteen-year-old airhead who lived all the way in California and thought of him as a big brother, I told him to inform her of appropriate counseling hours. Anything after nine could wait until the next day. I could care less about the time difference. Quiet as it was kept, he was the wrong one to ask about that kind of shit anyway.

Once we were on the same page about that, life at the apartment was pleasant again. I had enough sex, attention, and affection to last me a couple months. I was praying that he would give me a few days to rest, because I was sore in places I never knew existed.

After I washed up, I walked back into the room. Robert was already asleep, so I nestled beside him and joined him in Dreamland. The journey was interrupted when his phone vibrated loudly on the wooden nightstand. We both sat up and he looked at the screen.

"I gotta take this, baby. It's Brittany." When he showed me the number that started with a 404 area code, I smirked at the thought of him taking extra measures to reassure me. He knew he'd better get his shit together if he wanted to keep me around. My satisfied expression vanished, though, when he walked into the living room to answer the call.

My first thought: Brittany called from Atlanta on three-way with Jamie on the line in California. It would be extreme, but definitely possible. And if she was going through that much trouble to talk to my man, what the hell were they talking about?

Robert slipped back into bed at 3:05 a.m. after having been on the phone for a half hour. Even though I was lying there with my eyes closed, I was far from being asleep.

"What did she want at this time of night? Is she okay?" I asked.

"What do you mean? She's my sister. She can call me whenever she fuckin' feels like it."

I rolled over and faced him. "Are you cussin' at me? I just asked a simple question, and you comin' at me like you crazy."

I never got a real answer, so I saved the incident on my mental hard drive, preparing to open the file at just the right time. Something wasn't right. Robert only snapped when he was hiding something or when he was guilty of something. The more I thought about his response, the more restless I became.

I got out of bed, walked into the living room, and sat on the couch. For the first time in our relationship, I had a gut feeling that Robert was up to no good. When he showed me the number on his caller ID, the area code fit his explanation, but only the number popped up. Brittany's name should've been on the screen, too, since her number was stored in his phone under "Lil' Sis." And why did he have to leave the room to talk? Why was he so irritated when I asked him what his *sister* wanted?

I was pissed and needed to talk to somebody. I was on the verge of shedding angry tears and knew I wouldn't let them fall if I wasn't forced to be alone with my thoughts. I may seem hard and unemotional to strangers, but a select few people can tell you I'm a softie at times. Robert could attest to that. When I love, I love hard. When I'm hurt, I lash out in pure, unforgiving anger. I claim my tears are from frustration rather than pain, but that's a lie. Fortunately for Robert, he had only made me cry one time.

I was usually the one messing up the relationship with my unladylike habits and my occasional wandering eye. Don't get it twisted, though. Whenever I decided to share my goodies with somebody other than Robert, I placed our relationship on hold until I was ready to return. It was a dangerous game because there could come a time when Robert had moved on, leaving no room for reconciliation. At least I was honest with mine, though. I'd rather take that risk than be a cheat. I'm a lot of things, but you'll never be able to call me that.

Maybe Robert had developed a wandering eye of his own. He was almost too good at ignoring the stares and comments he got at work and at play. He was a delivery guy for American Parcel Express, and there were offices all over the city with women who were in love with him, more interested in the package that wasn't in his hand. He was fine as hell and he knew it. He used to play football in college, so his body was on point from his sexy pecs to his powerful thighs. He even had those creases that ran from his abs to his pelvis. I think Tielle told me they were called inguinal creases or something. Whatever they were, they looked good and made me wanna run my tongue down each of their well-defined lines when he walked around with no shirt on.

When I first met him, I felt the same way those chicks must feel. I wondered if his butterscotch skin tasted like it looked. And for the record, it did. I almost wouldn't blame him for wanting a change, but he could at least have the balls to tell me so.

It was late as hell, but I knew my girl would listen to my theory about Robert's infidelity. I let the phone ring twice, then moved it away from my ear to hang up. *I'm not gon' call her this late.* Before I pressed "End", Tiffany answered, sounding like an eighty-year-old man with emphysema. I apologized for interrupting her sleep, and after ten minutes of me running down the latest update to the Robert saga, her voice was as clear as mine.

"He's up to no good," Tiffany said. "You've been feelin' it for a while and you can't keep ignoring your intuition."

"It's beyond intuition now. He's layin' the clues right in front of me. I almost feel like this dude is tauntin' me."

"You said it, not me," Tiffany passively agreed. "Now you know what you've gotta do."

After we hung up, I passed out on the couch. Before I knew it, it was 6:30 and Robert was tapping me on the shoulder. When he asked why I slept on the couch, I ignored him and walked straight into the bathroom to get ready for work.

***

I looked at the two bins of mail sitting to the right of my desk. *They can't be serious*, I thought as I locked my purse in the bottom drawer and set my juice on the desk. What a way to start a Monday morning.

"Who put this here?" I asked Teesha, my coworker who dubbed as my partner in crime at times.

"Ya girl," she replied, referring to our supervisor.

41

"So she expects me to do this shit on top of everything else?" I examined the box more closely. "By the end of the day? That bitch done lost her mind."

Teesha shrugged. "If you don't have time to get to it, ain't nothin' she can do."

"You damn straight! And I won't have time. Why didn't she give this crap to the little intern? Ain't she still here?"

Someone cleared their throat behind us. Teesha turned to see who it was while I jotted down the number for the Tom Joyner Morning Show contest I'd heard in the car. In ten more minutes, I could call in to win some cash.

I knew who was behind us. It was Charlene's high-strung ass. She cleared her throat again, this time louder and stronger, three times in a row.

"Whoever that is, you need to be gettin' a drink of water instead of standin' in here."

"I'm fine, Ms. James. I'm just letting you know I'm here before you open your mouth again. I don't want you to end up sticking your foot in it," Charlene replied.

"Oh, okay. I thought maybe you had a hairball stuck in your throat from one of your twenty-five cats. And thanks for lookin' out for me, but I know where my foot is at all times. If I stick anywhere, it won't be in my mouth."

***

"Lexis, you can't just say whatever you want to everybody," Tiffany chastised after I told her about my day.

"Today was not the day, Tiff," I replied as I sped down 40th Street.

"I understand, but you can't take your problems to work."

"I didn't take 'em to work. They followed me."

Tiffany laughed. "Smart ass. So how many times have you been written up?"

"I think this is the second time. I don't even care. I don't like the job anyway."

"So what's next on the list? Lifeguarding? Taming lions?" Tiffany joked.

"They didn't fire me, ho!"

"Yeah, but you won't be there long. You're either gonna quit or be dismissed in a couple months."

Although she was right, I told her I had to go before I cussed her out. I was only calling to confirm the restaurant anyway, until she asked how my day was and got me started on Charlene's ass. We were

42

supposed to meet for dinner, but she remembered Marlon couldn't watch the kids.

"Oh! Before you hang up, did you hear Gary's other baby mama showed up at Kaelin's house while he was there and busted the windows in both their cars?" Tiffany informed me.

"What? I didn't even know she lived here."

"She doesn't. She drove all the way here from Virginia after she heard he was thinking about marrying Kaelin."

That was one thing I could say I hadn't dealt with—baby mama drama. I refuse to deal with a dude who has a kid. If I ain't the only one calling him "Daddy," he can keep it moving. If my windows were to get busted like that, I'd be in a cell, the bitch would be dead, and ol' boy would be at home chillin' with a new broad. No, thank you.

***

It was apparent Robert and I had reached a fork in the road. We had our problems before, but his fidelity was never in question. I didn't like what I was feeling, but I was trying not to run since everyone said that's what I did when something didn't go my way. It was hard, though, because I don't tolerate liars—especially those who go out of their way to keep lying to my face.

All in all, you never know what the truth is. You just go by a person's version of the truth until something happens to make you believe otherwise. To say someone is trustworthy is relative. A person is only as trustworthy as their least revealing secret. It's human nature to only reveal a piece of ourselves because we're afraid nobody will like the real us. We pick and choose what we share, and that's okay…until someone finds out you shared everything with them except what was important. There were only two people I trusted completely: Tameka and my dad. I trusted my mom based off of matters concerning me, but she had a shady reputation with quite a few others.

When I say I trust, I don't question.

When I question, I expect answers.

When I get answers that sound like bullshit, I investigate.

What does all that mean? I never trusted Robert completely, but I was close until he began his love affair with his cell phone. With the affair getting hotter and his lies becoming more bogus, it was time to find out the truth a different way. Since he wouldn't be straightforward, I chose to go along with the program and act like I was as stupid as he thought I was. I'm competitive as hell, so he had picked the wrong bitch to play games with.

43

A lot of people don't know this about me, but I moonlight as a detective. I didn't have to go to the academy for my knowledge. I have natural instinct, common sense, and plenty of hands-on experience with doing people dirty. In Robert's case, if there was anything to be found, I was sure I could find it, and when I did, somebody needed to be praying for his careless ass because I was going to kill him.

***

Friday had come and I was so happy. No, Robert and I hadn't made up—we were far from that—but I was off work and the only thing I had to do was help Tiffany get ready for her party.

It was 8:30 and I was up for no reason. Since I was wide awake, I made breakfast...for myself. Robert was running late again. Maybe another late night convo shortened his sleep time. I wouldn't have known since he'd been sleeping in the guest bedroom all week. He came out the room, buttoning his shirt. He glanced at the skillet, wishing he could ask for a piece of sausage, but he knew better.

On his way out, he turned and looked at me. "You not goin' in today?"

"Nope."

"Is Tiffany's party today?"

"Nope."

"So how long you gon' have this funky attitude?"

"Until you deserve better."

He stared at me for a few seconds and then exited the apartment, slamming the door behind him.

I took the sausage out the skillet and started toward the fridge to get the eggs. As I grabbed the handle, I heard something buzzing. Over and over, the noise continued. I could tell it was coming from the guest bathroom. Something was on the counter, vibrating.

Hot damn! I hadn't even come up with a solid plan, and evidence was already falling into my lap. Robert had left his cell phone, and it was begging me to look through it. I looked at the screen; *4 text messages.* I was one button away from retrieving them when the front door opened. *Shit!*

In ten seconds, he was in the bathroom getting his phone, and I was in the guest closet, pretending to search for something to wear. I wasn't trippin'. My chance would come again, and I couldn't wait to see who was texting him at eight in the morning.

After he left again, I ran to the door and locked the deadbolt. I then returned to the closet to rummage through the boxes he had packed away. If I could find a clue amongst the random pictures, receipts, and bills, I'd have something to start my portfolio.

The first box I pulled out was full of old family photos. I couldn't help but laugh at the ones of him naked in the tub, splashing with his rubber ducks. The second box wasn't his. It was a box I forgot I had, full of Tameka's journals. I opened the first notebook.

> *September 4, 1993*
>
> *Okay. I just heard the craziest argument between my mom and dad. They were talking about Darryl again. Turns out, this Darryl guy and my mom have been knockin' boots!!! I thought Daddy was just jealous because they spent long hours together at the office, but it looks like he had a reason to be. I can't wait to tell Lexis that goody-goody Mommy has been sharing her cookies with Mr. Darryl. All that crap she tells us about being virtuous women like her is garbage. She ain't no better than the next hoochie out there. She's just old and married, which makes it ten times nastier.*

I laughed as I read the slang we used back then. *Knockin' boots?* I still couldn't figure out how that phrase ever made sense.

I remembered that day vividly. We couldn't believe our "saint" of a mother was creeping. After that day, we never looked at her the same. The respect we had for her for years was gone after one argument we were never meant to hear. Funny…what we mean to happen and what actually does happen are complete opposites, especially when lies and deception are involved.

4

Tiffany:
From Your Lips to Mine

Tiki lamps lined the walkway to the front entrance and lit the entire yard. Island tunes filled the air, as well as the traveling scent of herbal pleasures that some party guests were enjoying in the backyard. Red, yellow, and orange streamers swung freely above the front door, inviting everyone to feel festive and party as if they were on vacation. Tiffany's birthday bash was definitely the place to be, and even the introverted neighbors down the street couldn't help but peek out their windows to enjoy the celebration from afar.

The screen door flung open, and Tiffany stepped onto the back porch. "I know y'all heard me say there is no smoking at this party. This is not the 'hood. Y'all should've done your ghetto ritual at home," she said to the three men passing around a Swisher Sweet. She picked up its packaging. "Peach flavor. Am I supposed to be smelling peaches, 'cause I'm not?" Her face showed nothing but disgust as she returned the box to the patio table.

"Stop trippin'," one guy said before he inhaled.

"Oh, you must think I'm joking," she replied, snatching the burning cigar from his hand and throwing it on the ground. All three mouths dropped as she smashed it beneath her foot and confiscated the remaining cigars. "Now I said, NO SMOKING. If you don't like that stipulation, follow that brick path to the front of the house and go home."

She didn't flinch as she reentered the house, leaving the angry men speechless. She could talk that talk because Marlon was only a high-pitched holler away, ready to come to her rescue if the wannabe roughnecks got out of line.

It was 9:30 p.m., and the house was starting to fill up. Her plan worked: Tell everybody the party started at eight, and they'd be there at the real time—nine.

She two-stepped into the kitchen to check the food. The cocktail shrimp were still neatly arranged on the serving tray, although it was obvious that a few people had already sampled them; the stuffed finger sandwiches sat untouched beside the half-eaten pan of wing dings; and the container housing the plain chips had been invaded by a few stray nacho chips.

Marlon approached her from behind and kissed her shoulder as she surveyed the table. "Everything straight?"

"Yeah. As long as I don't smell any more weed, I'll be fine."

He rolled his eyes in response to his bourgeois girlfriend's comment. It was only five months ago that she'd stopped smoking Black & Milds with Alexis. "Just make you a drink and calm down, boo. I'll make sure nobody gets outta line."

Before she could say another word, R. Kelly's "Fiesta Remix" sounded through the speakers. She couldn't help but smile as she sang along to her favorite song and danced with Marlon near the refrigerator.

"I knew you'd be in here, gettin' it," Dap said, entering from the living room. "Happy birthday, Tiff!"

Uh oh, Tiffany thought. *She showed up.*

They made small talk, long enough for Tiffany to make another drink before she went to mingle with her other guests. As she chatted with a friend from Marlon's job, Frenchie rushed over with a small gift-wrapped box and a card.

"Happy birthday! Told you I was coming," Frenchie said after handing the items to Tiffany.

"Thank you so much. You know you didn't have to do this, though. No gifts required. Just bring yourself, have a good time, and don't throw up on my carpet. That's all I ask. Oh, and don't clog up my toilet."

Frenchie laughed. "I'll remember that next time."

Two other women navigated through the growing crowd and stood next to Frenchie. The light-skinned one smiled softly at Tiffany, her nonverbal way of saying hello. Tiffany couldn't help but laugh to herself, though, when she realized who the other guest was.

Alexis is gonna have a heart attack.

Frenchie initiated the introductions. "These are my friends, Venni and Kelly. Oh, wait. You met Kelly before, right?"

"Yeah. She picked you up from class a few times."

Just then, Aaron walked past and Venni grabbed the bottom of his shirt, pulling him toward them. "You don't see nobody?" she asked with a hint of an attitude.

"Aw, my fault. I didn't see you there." They hugged, and he whispered something in her ear.

Tiffany felt awkward. Evidently, the man who'd been persistently flirting with her was involved with this Venni chick in some capacity. Small world.

"What's happenin', lady?" Aaron said to Tiffany, then kissed her hand. "Gotta make sure I speak to the queen of the night."

She prayed her smile appeared casual, because she was trying very hard to stifle the large grin that would really express how she felt. She glanced at Venni, searching for any sign of jealousy or disapproval. Nothing.

"I'ma need a dance with the birthday girl before the night is over," Aaron whispered in her ear. "We gon' have to sneak away since Marlon's here."

She couldn't believe how disrespectful he was being toward her man—his acquaintance. But why couldn't she check him? Was the alcohol making her want to take his tongue for a test drive to see if he really deserved the acclaim for his talents, or was she really just that intrigued by him? For a moment, her mind wandered to a special place where she pictured herself sexing Aaron and holding onto the ends of his cornrows for dear life.

The sound of Frenchie's distinct cackle helped her regain her composure. After she blinked a couple times, Alexis came into view. She yelled for her friend to join her.

Alexis took one look at the company Tiffany was keeping and gave her the finger. Just as she expected, Carl Thomas, Jr. had shown up, and she didn't want to be within ten feet of her. If she wasn't concerned about disappointing her homegirl, she probably would've left the party.

☒ ☒ ☒

Two hours and a whole lot of people later, the party was jumping. There were people all over the house and in the backyard, and more people were still arriving.

"Don't y'all be spillin' shit all over my carpet," Tiffany barked as she sashayed through the living room with her glass filled to the brim.

"You need to direct that to your damn self," Alexis replied, pointing to the liquid that was one false move away from decorating the floor.

Tiffany was having a ball. Everyone she invited to her shindig had shown up, live and in living color. Sean Paul was telling them to "Get Busy," and that's exactly what they did. Bodies were bumping, hips were gyrating, and fingers were snapping. There was barely elbowroom, but no one seemed to mind.

Alexis was sitting on the couch, so Tiffany carefully made her way over to her friend. "Scoot over!"

Alexis looked at the four other people who managed to squeeze onto the three-seater with her, then looked at Tiffany again. "Sit your drunk ass right there," she said, pointing to the arm of the sofa.

"You see your girl? I saw her in the kitchen a little bit ago," Tiffany asked as she rested beside Alexis.

"Who?"

"Dap! Don't act like you don't know who I'm talkin' about!" She laughed, overly amused by her joke.

Alexis gulped the remainder of her drink and cut her eyes at her intoxicated friend.

"Did she say something to you yet? You know she's been following your every move, waiting for the right moment to ask if y'all can be friends again. Remember those pencils with the half hearts on top with 'best' and 'friend' on 'em? She probably has one in her pocket for you. Did she give it to you?" She nudged Alexis. "It's in your pocket, huh? Which half you got? Let me see. I won't tell nobody."

With disbelief written all over her face, Alexis kept staring at Tiffany, who was now rolling her shoulders and bobbing her head to the music as if she hadn't said a word. It was best that she focused her attention on her rather than glance toward the other end of the couch to see Dap's reaction to Tiffany's words.

It didn't matter, though. Dap managed to hear almost everything, and charged over to her sister-in-law-of-sorts. "Did I hear my name?"

Startled, Tiffany almost fell off the arm of the couch, but regained her balance after leaning into the bookcase nearby. Oblivious to the tension in the air, she kept dancing to the music and casually slurred, "Hey girl," louder than she needed to.

"Don't let the alcohol get you in trouble," Dap continued. "Don't talk shit you can't back up."

"Yeah, okay," Tiffany said, waving her off.

Dap stepped closer and Alexis stood up. In the tight space, they were barely a couple inches apart.

"Bitch, I wish you would," Alexis said, glaring at Dap. "I dare you to touch her. Please give me another reason to fuck you up. If you even breeze by her too fast, watch how quick my fist helps you to the floor."

"I'm out. I don't need to be at this lame party wit' y'all lame asses anyway," Dap replied, while turning to leave.

Alexis pushed the back of her head, causing her to stumble forward. "Call me somethin' other than Alexis again," she urged.

Dap gritted her teeth and clenched her fists. She didn't want to go there with Alexis because of the situation with Tameka, but her combative spirit wanted so badly to grab Alexis' hand and break each of her fingers. For once in her life, though, she avoided confrontation and left peacefully.

It was a little after midnight, and Marlon had disappeared. Tiffany wanted to tell him why his sister was no longer welcomed in her home. She asked a few people if they'd seen him, then decided to text him after having no luck. When he responded, he told her that he was down the street somewhere with one of his boys. She hated that. He always left without telling her, especially at parties or other large gatherings. He didn't like to be around a lot of people for long periods of time, but she figured he could at least deal with it since it was *her* celebration. She sulked as she stood in the hallway watching everyone else have fun with their dates or newly found friends.

"Why you lookin' so sad? Ain't this your party?" Aaron asked as he leaned against the wall with a Michelob in his hand.

"I'm cool."

"Why ain't you dancin'? You too drunk?"

Before she could respond, he yanked her from the wall and pressed her pelvis against his. As they grinded to the Mad Cobra classic, Tiffany felt her hormones bursting with unadulterated lust. Their bodies moved in-sync in what seemed more like a simulated sex act than an innocent dance.

She cupped the top of his head, careful not to apply too much pressure to his freshly braided scalp, and put her lips to his ear. "Why do I want you?"

"'Cause you know how bad I want *you*," Aaron replied. Then, with his tongue barely touching, he signed his name on her neck, marking the territory he was willing to acquire by any means necessary.

It couldn't have been written any better. The setting was perfect...A party full of people who were too preoccupied with entertaining themselves to care about where she was; the song with clear instructions on what to do, *Flex...time to have sex*; a sexy man willing to follow those instructions; and a missing boyfriend. All of the aforementioned equaled trouble.

She looked up and saw Venni staring at them. "Umm...I'll be back," Tiffany said, pushing Aaron away. She rushed to the guestroom and into the bathroom. Her stomach was spinning and so was her head. She ran cold water in the sink and splashed it on her face. *Better.*

She laughed at her lack of control as she staggered to the bedroom and walked into the wall. *Okay...Maybe I'll lay down for five minutes.* She walked to the bed and dove onto the pile of coats. *Five minutes.*

A half hour later, Tiffany was still sprawled out on the bed in an alcohol-induced slumber. She could hear everything, though—the muffled music, beer bottles clanging, the constant chatter, her door opening.

Momentarily all the sounds became louder, but they were almost muted when the door closed again. She knew Marlon would return after he read her last text message.

***

Alexis chatted with an old high school classmate near the front door, when she felt someone's drink splash onto her arm.

"What the—?"

"My fault, sweetie," Aaron said, wiping her arm with the bottom of his shirt.

"You leavin' already?" Alexis asked.

"Yeah, I'll holla at you."

Alexis watched him leave in a hurry and wondered what his rush was. She scoped the party in search of Tiffany. Maybe he'd gotten a little too aggressive with his flirting and was told to leave. *Where is that girl?* she thought as she danced half-heartedly with the stranger who'd just approached her.

***

Marlon fumbled around the room for the longest, then crept over to Tiffany. She could feel him hovering over her, maybe to see if she was really asleep. She wasn't. Her eyes just wouldn't open. She lay there, waiting for him to pick her up and carry her into their bedroom.

That didn't happen. Instead, he lifted her shirt and kissed around her navel. His pecks were simple and sensuous, unlike any she'd ever felt from him. *Happy birthday to me,* she thought as he unzipped her jeans and tugged on them until they were just below her knees.

When he slid his finger under her panties, something didn't feel right. Marlon's hands were huge, so the slender fingers that massaged her insides couldn't have been his. She wanted to interrupt him, but lost her train of thought when he kissed her inner thighs. Her hand wandered to his head, and her eyes popped open.

Although the room was pitch black and she couldn't see a thing, she was sure the man between her legs wasn't her boyfriend. It was Aaron. His cornrows lay beneath her fingers as she moaned quietly. Her conscious couldn't override her curiosity. She'd been wondering for months why his tongue was the talk of every beauty shop in town, and the moment of truth was one lick away.

"We shouldn't do this," she finally said.

Aaron didn't say a word. He just attacked. His body language spoke volumes, and it told her that he'd been lusting after her more than words could express. By the time he was finished, she was curled in the fetal position, shaking from the aftershock of her multiple orgasms. As he opened the door to leave, he ran into someone.

Please don't be Marlon. Please don't be Marlon, Tiffany thought. She was too intoxicated to think of an excuse for being alone in a dark room with another man. Fortunately, it wasn't him. A female saying, "Oops! Sorry," was the last thing she heard before passing out.

Alexis found Tiffany lying on someone's leather jacket when she walked into the room. A few people told her that she was back there in bad shape after they retrieved their coats. Since Marlon hadn't returned, she asked the guy she'd been dancing with to help carry her friend to her bed. With the party having come to an end, she made sure everyone was out of the house, turned off the stereo, and looked around. There were plastic cups, beer bottles, and broken potato chips everywhere.

Damn that. I'm not the cleanup crew. She pulled out her key to Tiffany's house and locked up before she went home.

***

"You need to take them big-ass glasses off your face. Nobody asked you to come out the house flossin'," Alexis said as she and Tiffany neared Freddy's.

If anyone ever asked Alexis' opinion, Freddy's had the best Philly cheesesteaks in the South, and she was craving one today. She made Tiffany tag along to keep her company.

Though she had a headache from hell, Tiffany didn't mind. She was dying to tell Alexis about the previous night. She knew her friend would pass out once she heard the details of the most explosive orgasm she'd ever had.

She checked her lip gloss in the sun visor mirror, then adjusted her Chloe shades. "Don't hate. I'm always fabulous, honey. And my sister bought me these glasses for my birthday. As much as they cost, I need to be wearin' them every day."

"Sunglasses in December? You just wanna be seen."

"Oh, they see me regardless, sweetie pie. Don't ever forget it."

They laughed as Alexis waved her off. A minute later, they were standing in the restaurant's entrance, waiting to be seated. Alexis requested her favorite waitress' section, and within five minutes, they were sitting in a small booth by the window.

The cozy establishment wasn't the most exquisite, but it had character. The royal blue leather upholstery on most of the booths was either cracked or split, confirming that Mr. Freddy had been in business for seventeen years. The white linoleum floor was beyond worn, embedded with grease, dirt, and mustard stains that just wouldn't come up with a mop anymore. Instead of interesting paintings by known artists, the walls were adorned with autographed pictures of celebrities who had graced the place and tasted the delicious onion rings. Still, they kept a constant flow of patrons and the waitresses never had to worry about tips.

"Why are you looking at that?" Tiffany asked, as Alexis opened a menu. "You always get the same thing." She opened hers, then picked up a napkin. "These damn things are always so greasy! Do they poor Crisco on them for effect?"

Before Alexis could answer, Rasolyn hurried to the table with her white tablet in-hand. "I am so sorry, ladies. It's been crazy in here all day," she said, wiping her forehead with her sleeve. She looked at Alexis. "Hey! I haven't seen you in a while."

"I know, girl. There's been a lot goin' on," Alexis replied.

"Yeah…I heard about—you know. I'm sorry."

"Thanks."

"Y'all know what y'all want?"

"You know I'm havin' my usual. Give me extra cheese, though."

Tiffany ordered a chicken Philly and opted for a salad instead of fries. As they waited for their drinks, her phone beeped.

"Please don't tell me Marlon's already textin' you. We just left your house," Alexis said as she rolled her eyes.

Tiffany laughed. "No. It's a reminder. I have an interview tomorrow."

This was going to be her third interview. Numerous companies had been interested in her for months, but she wanted to get her degree out of the way. With a master's under her belt, she knew she was almost guaranteed the salary she deserved.

Safe Haven was the place where she wanted to work most, and she couldn't hide her excitement when she told Alexis about the position she was interviewing for. She would be working with teenage girls, counseling them on issues ranging from low self-esteem to sexual abuse. It was her dream job with an excellent benefits package and an on-site daycare center.

"Oh, Lord. A diva with a job as a professionaaaal. You gon' be walkin around wit' Gucci sweatbands on just 'cause you can afford 'em and you don't even work out," Alexis joked.

Tiffany laughed as Rasolyn handed her a glass of sweet tea.

"But for real…I'm proud of you, girl. You know all them folks are gon' offer you the jobs. There ain't nothin' like havin' choices. Do the damn thang."

Tiffany could hear the slight disappointment in her friend's voice. Instead of addressing Alexis' career woes, though, she changed the subject. "Enough about that stuff. I can't hold this in no more," she said.

"Hold what?"

"I kinda cheated on Marlon last night," Tiffany said softly.

Alexis almost spit her drink out. "Cheated with who?"

"*Kinda* cheated," Tiffany reemphasized. "He ate me out."

"Bitch, that ain't kinda cheatin'! What the hell is *kinda* cheatin'? If Marlon said some broad licked his balls, would you say he *kinda* cheated?"

"Shh!" Tiffany said, looking around to make sure no one heard her loud friend. "Since when did you become an advocate for any man?"

"I ain't nobody's advocate. Just don't give me that bullshit. Who the hell was lickin' on you anyway? And how did you pull that off with Marlon there?"

Tiffany reminded Alexis that Marlon left the party early and didn't return until 5 a.m. Without disclosing a name, she recounted her story of optimal satisfaction. She told of every detail: the gentle caresses, the mysterious silence, the magic fingers.

"I didn't know a tongue could do that! I thought Marlon was good, but…" She paused, staring into space. "Girl, I can't describe it! I damn near exploded. You know how some chicks squirt like dudes?"

Alexis held up her hand. "That is too much information. I don't wanna know how you bust a nut."

Just then, their food arrived at the table. Before Alexis took a bite, she paused and looked at Tiffany. "You still never told me who did all this amazing shit."

"Who would I tell Vicki's secrets to besides my Marly Bear?"

"Aaron?"

"You heard me say I was pullin' his braids, right?"

Alexis was confused. "What time did this happen?"

"I was drunk as hell. Do you really think I remember?"

"Ballpark."

"It was a little after I disappeared for a while. Everybody was still dancin'."

"And it was Aaron?"

Tiffany nodded as she chewed a mouthful of her sandwich. Alexis tried to recall the previous night, and she could've sworn Aaron left while Tiffany was in her room. She had talked to him before he went outside.

Maybe he came back and I missed it, she thought, taking into consideration that she was under the influence, too.

"So now what?" Alexis asked.

Tiffany shrugged. "He never said a word, and I couldn't say nothin' after he was finished with me. I think I told him I loved him when I came, though. I feel like an ass." She laughed.

"Yeah, that right there qualifies you as one," Alexis replied.

As the chicken, mayo, and cheese settled in her stomach, Tiffany started having regrets about the previous night. Not about just the physical effects of the alcohol she consumed, but more importantly its effects on her memory. After she spilled her guts to Alexis, she realized she couldn't even dig deep to give answers to the important questions she asked. Who, what, and where were covered, but when and why were foggy. Why would she allow things to go that far, and why didn't Aaron say anything to her? When did he leave the room, and when did Marlon enter? What if he planned to tell the whole town and destroy her family? What if more took place than him pleasing her? Did she return the favor?

After Rasolyn brought the check, they paid and then stood up to leave.

"Uh oh," Tiffany said as she put on her coat.

Alexis followed the direction of Tiffany's eyes that led to Jacqueline, who was standing among the crowd waiting to be seated. She rubbed her palms together. "Christmas done came early for me."

"I ain't workin' yet, so I don't have extra money to bail you out. Remember, we're in public, not a dark alley. Freddy won't hesitate to call the police."

Alexis ignored her and headed toward the door, while Tiffany followed closely behind. Within seconds, it was evident that Jacqueline saw them because she seemed fidgety and tried her best not to make eye contact. It was almost funny watching her attempts to trade places with her sons, which would've put them closest to the aisle. To her dismay, though, there were too many bodies in the small space and there was nowhere to go.

Tiffany tugged lightly on Alexis' coat as she stopped beside Jacqueline.

"How you doin'?" Alexis asked her new nemesis.

Nervously, Jacqueline replied, "I'm well."

"I bet you are." Jacqueline's dark skin lightened three shades as Alexis gave her a friendly pat on the arm and leaned in close. "Next time you see me, you better run. All that time you spent at the gym stalking my sister's fiancé should have you in perfect shape. Don't let me catch you."

Tiffany smiled and waved at Jacqueline as she followed Alexis outside. She loved to see Alexis in action because she was so unpredictable. Instead of knocking Jacqueline out first and asking questions later, she intimidated her with words. The mere thought of the conversation with Alexis was going to haunt her for at least a few months.

Alexis had fearlessness that Tiffany wished she possessed, but that personality trait only came from life experiences…ones that Tiffany had never encountered. Alexis didn't grow up in the 'hood or live in poverty, but she hung out in the streets as a teenager and was dealt a handful of hardships that scarred her. Still, it made her such a strong woman, and Tiffany lived vicariously through her at times, pretending that she, too, was just as strong.

***

It was Monday. Tiffany strolled slowly but confidently down the breezeway, headed to the parking deck. She smiled as she recalled Autumn's last words: *Ms. Price, you are the embodiment of our mission statement and there's no way I'm letting you get away from us.* That praise came after a highly impressive interview and $48,500 salary offer.

Everything about the today seemed perfect—almost too perfect. It was a beautiful afternoon with a sky so transparent she swore she could see clear to Austin. The sun emitted its brightest rays of the season, making it a satisfying seventy-four degrees, unusually warm for this December. Most of the days had been sixty at best, with winds that threatened to lift you off the ground if you weighed less than a hundred pounds. Today, there was nothing disturbing the calmness in the air.

Her phone vibrated in her briefcase. It was Marlon.

"Hey," she answered, effortlessly tucking the phone between her ear and shoulder so she could search the case for her car keys.

"How did it go?" Marlon asked.

"They want me!"

"That's Safe Haven, right?"

"Yep."

"That's cool, baby. You knew you had it on lock, though. How much they talkin'?"

"The hiring manager said—"

"Is that the party girl?" a familiar voice yelled from somewhere in the parking lot adjacent to the building.

Tiffany stopped and scanned the area in search of a familiar face to match the voice. It wasn't long before she saw Frenchie's dreads bouncing on top of her head as she ran in Tiffany's direction. The tangerine dashiki she wore commanded more attention than the blonde tips that were now decorating the ends of her freshly twisted locks.

"I'll call you right back, babe. I see one of my friends." She hung up as Frenchie approached her with a smile.

"What you doin' here?" Frenchie asked.

"I had an interview with Safe Haven a little bit ago."

"How did it go?"

"Well, you know. I try to do what I do best. How can they resist?" Tiffany joked as she curled her lips and dusted off her shoulders.

"You are way too much," Frenchie laughed. "Congrats. I'm assuming you got the job."

"Thanks. I haven't decided whether I'ma take it, though. Why are you here?" She narrowed her eyes. "Are you my competition?"

"If I was, it sounds like I already lost!" She held up a plastic bag with a styrofoam container inside. "I just came from lunch with Venni. She works in this building." Frenchie fell silent and stared as if she was waiting for a particular response.

Tiffany felt obligated to ask a follow-up question. "Does she work at Safe Haven?"

Tiffany learned that Venni worked on the tenth floor at Sheer Innovation, a top notch marketing firm that had been recognized in Black Enterprise a year before.

"What does she do?"

"Please don't make me lie to you," Frenchie said after a quick shrug. "I don't know her job title, but she does something with computers. She's responsible for their whole network and manages all the other computer whizzes there."

They continued their small talk for a while, then Tiffany changed the subject. "Did you enjoy yourself at the party?"

Frenchie raved about the fun-filled evening and the interesting people she met. She wanted to mention the secret of the evening, but wasn't sure if Tiffany would want to discuss it. After all, most of their friendly chats took place before and after lectures, during study groups at the student union, or at the Starbucks near campus where they often ran into each other. Details about their personal lives were rarely a topic unless one of Tiffany's children was sick or she casually griped about Marlon after a text messaging argument.

Tiffany was different from most black women Frenchie knew. She didn't pry into Frenchie's private matters, refuting the nosey, gossipy, two-faced spirit associated with most of the sistas she knew. Even though everyone in the psychology department knew of her sexual preference, her closest classmate had never even alluded to the topic. For two years, she never knew why, but after the birthday bash, it all became clear. Tiffany wasn't judgmental because they shared the same interest. The loving mother/girlfriend role was the Berlin Wall that hid the truth of her bisexuality. Too bad the wall crumbled to the ground when Venni busted through it.

As Tiffany recapped her favorite moments from that night, Frenchie couldn't help but feel invited into her circle. Since school was over, discussions about rational emotive therapy and cognitive dissonance were unnecessary. They had moved into a world outside of the classroom called "real life" and Frenchie happily accepted the invitation to go there.

Tiffany looked at her watch. "Girl, let me get outta here. I need to get home so Marlon can go to work. He's watching Tony. Give me a call sometime." She winked as she always did, then turned to walk away.

Frenchie waved and called out, "I'll make sure I tell Venni I saw you. She'll be sorry she missed you."

Tiffany stopped in her tracks. *Why does she keep talking about her?*

"Huh?" she asked, turning to face Frenchie again.

"Oh, I'm sorry," Frenchie replied sincerely. "Maybe I shouldn't have said that. I just thought—"

Tiffany still couldn't understand what her loud-mouthed classmate was talking about, and her face strongly conveyed her confusion.

"I know you have a family to worry about. I won't say another word," Frenchie continued.

"Another word about what?"

Tiffany could feel herself becoming angry, but she wasn't sure why. It was obvious, though, that her friend knew something she didn't about this Venni chick. She remembered speaking with her a couple times and making her a drink, but didn't recall any significant conversation.

At that moment, Frenchie realized Tiffany wasn't exaggerating when she joked about the majority of the night being a blur. She wished she would've kept her big mouth closed, but with Tiffany eagerly awaiting a response, there was no turning back. She had unknowingly committed to revealing a big part of Tiffany's night…and possibly her life.

"You don't remember talking to Venni?"

"Yeah, for a little bit. I don't know what we talked about, though."

Frenchie pulled Tiffany into the parking garage where they would have some form of privacy. "Listen. I don't know all the details, but you and Venni did something the night of your party."

Tiffany's eyebrows lowered as Frenchie continued with caution.

"Do you remember me walking in the room? You were lying on my coat. Well, I guess you wouldn't remember 'cause you looked like you were about to pass out when I moved you. Okay. All I know is when I walked in, me and Venni almost collided because she was coming out of the room. I thought she was getting her coat, too, but I remembered she left it in the car."

"So that's it?"

"I didn't get the impression that she was just using the bathroom. When I asked her later, she told me that the two of you were in there a while…"

Tiffany's skin crawled and her stomach turned. It couldn't be true. Aaron was the only person in the room…or was he? Did he set her up? Maybe he and Venni were dating and were into that freaky stuff—threesomes and such. She knew she got a weird vibe from them. So many times she wanted to interrupt Frenchie and adamantly deny the accusations, but as the story unfolded and each detail was revealed, she was surprised to hear more facts than fiction.

From the black and red lace thong she wore to the shaved area beneath it, Frenchie laid out all the proof Tiffany needed. There was something missing, though.

"So who did what? And what made them feel they could just come into the room with me?" she asked Frenchie, who looked like she wanted to cry for her.

Although it was a rhetorical question, Tiffany still wanted an answer, but received nothing.

"I was *not* that drunk. I've never been down with a ménage. And if I were, why would I do it without Marlon?"

Now Frenchie was puzzled. "Ménage?"

"Yeah…Venni and Aaron. Are they together or something? They were talking all night."

"Uh, no. They're cousins. There was nobody else in the room with you and Venni. She said she…"

60

...Made my body tingle in places that have no nerve endings. Introduced her tongue to my anatomy starting at the white tips of my manicured toes and ending at the third hole of my pierced ears. Gave me a stronger sense of sympathy for seizure sufferers after my body convulsed with pleasure from the playful flicks of her tongue. HER tongue!

I'm not a lesbian. I'm not bisexual. I'm not even curious! So why did it feel so good? How didn't I know? Did I know? Did the alcohol bury my inhibitions? Hell no. This can't be. She took advantage of me, that sneaky bitch. The mystery of the night isn't sexy anymore. It's disgusting.

Tiffany began to put it together. Aaron wasn't there. Venni was. She didn't say a word because it would've given her identity away. She knew what to do and how to do it because she's a woman. Tiffany thought "Aaron" didn't kiss her in the mouth because it was just a fling, but realized Venni didn't kiss her because she probably didn't want her hoop earrings to dangle onto her cheek.

"I didn't even touch anything but the person's head. Cornrows," Tiffany said. "The damn cornrows! It was supposed to be Aaron because he was the only man with cornrows."

Clenching the braids was the one thing she was absolutely sure of, and she recalled the beautiful long cornrows that the light-skinned woman sported when Frenchie introduced them.

Her body felt as cold as the cement wall she leaned against, drained of all its dignity. Her lifeless eyes stared at nothing behind their coating of angry tears. She was now fully convinced that Venni was the one with the magic tongue.

She made Frenchie swear not to tell anyone and made sure she got Venni's number so she could tell her the same. She was livid and couldn't wait to ask Venni why she would take advantage of her, knowing she wasn't down with that activity. If Marlon ever found out...

He couldn't find out, period. Nobody could.

5

Alexis:
Valuable Information

It was December 20th, just days away from Christmas. I was plagued with the spirit of Scrooge because I didn't have a thing to celebrate. Okay, you've got Jesus' birth, joy and love, goodwill toward men, etcetera, etcetera; but my grieving heart felt no joy, and if there was goodwill on earth, my sister wouldn't be dead.

Tielle invited me to her mom's to take part in their holiday tradition, but I was still debating on whether I would attend. I didn't rule out her invitation, though. It wasn't like Robert was going to be around if I wanted to spend time with him. He was leaving in two days to go visit his brother, Kaleb, in Atlanta and wouldn't be back for a week.

I did do a little shopping, only for Darius. Though he was just a baby, he knew his mommy wasn't with him anymore. His smile, though still radiant, wasn't as bright, and his eyes didn't open as wide with excitement for anything or anybody. The toys I bought with bright colors, flashing lights, and obnoxious sounds were sure to make him happy, though. It was a strategy that would work until he grew old enough to understand that those nice toys won't bring his mom back. Then how would Auntie Lexis make him smile?

Pastor Johnson told me to keep praying and the answers would come. I had my first grief counseling session with him the previous week, and it wasn't as corny as I thought it would be. We just talked. I was able to vent my frustrations and admit my fears without feeling like I was getting my head shrunk.

I was supposed to see him once a month for at least six months, but I wasn't sure if I would continue going. As far as I was concerned, I said all I needed to the first time. If praying would give me the guidance I needed, what was the point of telling the pastor the things I'd already talked to God about?

***

The night before Robert left, Tiffany, Marlon, Tielle, and Romeo came over. Tielle made her world-famous strawberry daiquiris for the ladies, while the guys drank their beer. After we'd had enough of playing cards, Tielle initiated a game of "Who Would You Rather?" something her and her sorority sisters played in her early college days. On most nights I would've ridiculed her idea, but we were bored and tipsy, so it sounded like fun.

"Who would you rather share a jail cell with? O.J. Simpson, Jeffrey Dahmer, Rick James, or Ike Turner?" she asked.

I went first. "Rick James, bitch!"

"Drug addict," she replied.

"O.J.," Robert answered. "He was the man on the field in his day. We could talk football the whole time."

Marlon agreed. "Yeah, I'm with that. O.J. for me, too."

"Crazy Ike!" Romeo said. "He'd probably have all kinds of stories to tell."

"You might wanna watch him," I warned Tielle. "Make sure you eat the cake at your wedding reception. He might be into beatin' women."

We laughed as Tiffany thought about her answer.

"I think I would go with Jeffrey Dahmer," she finally said. "Before y'all say I'm nuts, y'all have to remember I majored in the study of people like him. He would've been my dream case study."

"Oookay," Tielle replied. "I'ma go with Rick James—strictly for musical purposes," she said as she looked at me.

The questions kept rolling, and then there was a free answering session.

Tielle asked, "If there was only one sex left on the planet—your sex—what celebrity would you rather be with?"

"I'm out the game now!" Robert said quickly. "I don't even think like that."

"You act like it's real!" I said.

"Y'all women do that stuff. Men don't. We don't go around complimentin' our homeboys on their new kicks and sayin' how nice they look in their jeans," Marlon defended. "I'm with Rob. Y'all can answer that."

"I don't play that mess either, but it's just a hypothetical question. Y'all don't know how to play. I'd go with Janet," I replied. "She must be top-notch. Who else has an orgasm while they record a song? She ain't fakin' that shit. She does it too much. She's perfected the art of being sexy. Per-fect-ed!"

"Damn, baby," Robert said.

"I'm just sayin'…She turns herself on! Do you turn yourself on? If I was that sexy, I wouldn't need nobody else. I'd screw myself and be satisfied. That's some special shit. She's my hero."

Everybody lost it, and Romeo almost spit out his beer.

"Jada," Tielle said. "I don't have an elaborate speech explaining why, though."

Tiffany sat quietly.

"Well?" I asked after nudging her.

"I think I'm going with the guys," she said softly before returning to her drink.

"You always say how beautiful you think Trina is. Don't front now, baby!" Marlon said.

"I don't sit and admire her like that, so don't *you* front on me like I like females! If she looks nice in a video, yes, I'll say something, but that's it. Like I said, I don't wanna answer that question. Is that a problem?" Tiffany snapped.

"You don't wanna answer a lot of questions," Marlon mumbled.

"Alrighty then. We'll go with Trina and move on," Tielle said.

"Who pissed in your daiquiri?" I asked Tiffany.

"Nobody. Next question."

I rarely saw that side of her because it took a lot to ruffle Tiffany's feathers. I wondered if she and Marlon were having problems that I didn't hear about yet. Maybe he'd found out about Aaron.

The night came to an end shortly after that. Tiffany's little outburst ruined the fun mood we had going, and it was late anyway. After everyone left, I gave Robert some going-away sex for selfish reasons. Since he would be gone so long, I needed a little something to hold me over.

It had been a little more than a week since we'd gotten it in, so I pulled out all the stops—whipped cream, chocolate syrup, handcuffs, blindfold, feathers, and the incorporation of three new karma sutra positions I'd seen late-night while watching Cinemax. I had blown his mind and a portion of my own by the time we were finished. It was one hell of a goodbye.

The next day, our goodbyes were short and sweet—partially because he was running late as usual, but mostly because I was ready for him to go. I had work to do. As soon as I got back to the apartment, I logged in to the computer. Yari called as I was taking my coat off and entering Internet Explorer.

"How's your investigation going?" she asked, laughing quietly.

"I haven't found anything yet, but I'm lookin' as we speak. I'm still tryin' to guess the password for his email account," I replied. "Don't worry. You'll know when I find somethin' 'cause I'm wreckin' shop around here."

"Why even go through the hassle? If you don't trust him, what's the point of staying in the relationship? Y'all not even married."

I didn't have an answer for her. I think I just wanted the sick satisfaction of knowing I was right about his infidelity all along, but that would've sounded stupid if I said it out loud.

Yari knew I had nothing, so she moved on. "Have you talked to Isaac since the funeral?"

She loved him—was convinced he was the man for me. I couldn't justify leaving Robert when I met Isaac, but I was considering my possibilities after Robert began his questionable behavior. I told Yari that we'd only talked a couple times, but he usually texted me every day to check on me.

"I'm telling you, he's the one. Don't let him slip through your fingers!"

"I'm waitin' on you to start filming so you can hook me up with fine-ass Omar Woods. *He's* the one!" We laughed hysterically, though I was serious as a heart attack.

When she asked about Craig, I didn't have much to report. He barely answered his phone, so I didn't bother him. I knew he was still mourning over Tameka, so I tried to give him space.

"Everybody has a different recovery time," Yari said. "He'll come around."

I reminded her that Craig and I were never close, so I wasn't worried about seeing or speaking to him. I just missed my nephew. After she reprimanded me for sounding cold, I briefly searched my soul and made a grown-up decision—after work the next day, I would go see Darius… and Craig.

As Yari went on to tell me about her life, I made my third attempt to guess Robert's email password. No luck. She was in the middle of telling me about the Christmas program she'd planned for her church's youth group, when I screamed, "Woo! I'm a bad bitch!"

I apologized for cutting her off and cussing while we were discussing the nativity story. I felt like I'd won the lottery, though. After pretending "I" forgot "my" password, I answered the security questions and entered Robert's birthday into the email system. Ten seconds later, voila! I was able to create a new password and access his account.

"You are so crazy." Yari chuckled at my determination, while I entered the new code of my choice: dumbass03.

"I'm in!" I exclaimed before promising to call her back.

Fifty-eight messages. Three new. On the first page alone, all the messages were from the same person except one message from some spammer promising to make his manhood grow three more inches by summer. *Mo_BettaLuv_4u* filled the remaining spaces in the Sender column. I opened the most recent message.

December 21, 2003, 11:40 AM
Kaleb said you'd be in tomorrow at 1:20. Please come by to see me. We really should talk. Let me know what you think after you see the baby. I'm telling you, he looks just like Kaleb, only lighter.   -Monica

Good ol' Monica. I remember when I first found out who she was. In June, I found some pictures in Robert's drawer of a girl standing by the fountains in Atlanta's Centennial Park. I figured she was one of his exes, but when I dug deeper, there was a picture of her naked body covered partially by an oversized Puerto Rican flag and another picture of the two of them posing in front of an airbrushed backdrop at a club. He was wearing a shirt I bought him, so that ruled out my ex-girlfriend theory. There was only one thing to conclude…that fool was cheating on me.

She looked young—eighteen if I had to guess—and the flag must have represented her heritage. She was mixed with something, though. I assumed one of her parents was black. I couldn't front; she was pretty, but so am I.

When I confronted him, he quickly explained that we weren't together in January, when he and Kaleb met her at the club in Buckhead. She was a college girl who shook her ass in his face all night, got a few drinks out of him, and wanted to take a souvenir photo. He claimed he wasn't interested in her and that he was just having a good time, but he had to give up more information after I saw her number in his call log the following month. That's when part two of the story came.

He was so drunk, maybe he did give her his number, but he never thought she would call... He didn't know why she was calling all of a sudden, but he'd made sure to tell her he had a girl... No, there was nothing more to their acquaintance except the touching they did on the dance floor—no kissing, no sex, no remaining interest...

So why did he have pictures of the broad, and how did she send them to him? His lame excuse was that she was obsessed with him for some reason—had found his email and home addresses on the internet and sent them.

"She emails me almost every day. She don't even talk about nothin'. She sends me those stupid forwards and stuff. Baby, I don't even know this girl!" I remember him saying.

To prove it, he showed me the emails, and sure enough, she'd sent one in May saying she hoped he was pleasantly surprised by her care package.

"So why did you keep the pictures, Mr. Innocent Bystander?" I asked.

He couldn't help but laugh, which pissed me off. "I mean...I just...I'm still a man, baby. I ain't gon' lie. She looks nice in the pictures."

"Oh, so Puffy gets with J-Lo, and all y'all niggas wanna go get a Latina, huh? You need somebody to call you Papi?"

To keep me from quitting his ass right then and there, he ripped the pictures into tiny pieces and called Sprint immediately to change his number. Problem solved. No more Monica...or so I thought.

December 17, 2003, 9:13 PM
> *It would be nice if you'd return my calls. I just want to know if you're coming for sure. My mom's been asking. —Monica*

November 18, 2003, 1:26 PM
> *I'm just sending this to let you know I just got back from the doctor, and to cut out all the details, she says I'm dying. You don't have to care, but you need to know.*

November 11, 2003, 4:52 PM
> *I can't believe you! Now you have a girlfriend? Whatever. And you say I'm the one playing games. I was trying to put less stress on you, but Ricky's doctor ain't got a reason to lie. I was right there.*

September 16, 2003, 12:50 PM
> *When somebody leaves you a message and says it's important, you're supposed to return it.*

September 1, 2003, 12:31 PM
> *Can you answer your phone please? I'm assuming you got the pictures, but I have to tell you something.*

August 9, 2003
> *Did you get the pics? Make sure you don't lose these. I'll have to charge you to replace them next time!*

The messages seemed to coincide with Robert's explanation from way back, but a couple of them didn't sit right with me. Why would Kaleb tell her Robert was coming, and how did she know what Kaleb's son looked like? And what was up with him requesting a new set of pictures? Since I couldn't answer the questions, I called the person who could.

When Robert answered the phone, I asked where he was.

"Kaleb's," he replied. "He ran to the store. We're about to make dinner."

"Monica comin' over?"

I heard his heart stop. "Who?"

"Mo Betta Love For You. Don't play dumb now. That's who you been fuckin' whisperin' to after midnight." I proceeded to disclose the information I'd found.

After he yelled at me for checking his email without his permission, he explained. "Baby, I told you she's nuts. You see she was sayin' that she was dyin' and all that. She wants attention. Did you read the other ones where she complained about me ignoring her? What more do you need?"

"If she's nothing, why did Kaleb give her your damn itinerary?"

"Her older sister works in the same building with Kaleb and they hang out sometimes. He told her I'd be here and she must've told Mo."

"'Mo,' huh? Cute. Did she tell Mo to send you more pictures?"

"There weren't any more pictures. I never responded to that stuff."

I wasn't sure if I believed him, but his version of the story didn't seem so far-fetched after Kaleb returned home and corroborated the details.

I called Yari back and reported my findings. "February the first is all I have to say," she replied. "That's when we're moving in. The invitation is still open."

69

"So you think that's enough to go by?"

"Suspicion is all it takes. You shouldn't have to hack into that boy's email to get some answers. And you still don't know if he gave you the right answers."

Don't stay because you're comfortable. Leave when you're not, her words from our conversation after the funeral, echoed in my head.

***

The next day, I left work and headed straight to Craig's house, just as I'd planned. On the way there, Tielle called to offer me her extra ticket to WTIZ's New Year's Extravaganza. I quickly accepted. You can't dangle the opportunity meet the ballers of the music industry in my face and expect me not to go for it. I didn't know what Robert had planned, but I would be partying with the stars and drinking expensive champagne when the ball dropped.

When I told her I was on my way to Craig's, she warned me. "I'm worried about him. I think he's falling apart. I don't know what you'll see when you get there. I stopped by last Tuesday, and the house reeked of garbage. He hadn't taken it out because he refuses to go in the kitchen."

"Ugh. Why not?"

"Well, you know he'd have to go through the living room to get to it, and he's not with that. He won't even look toward the living room."

I hadn't thought of that. I guess it would be hard to walk through the room that was just drenched in your fiancé's blood. "But he could get to the kitchen through the back door," I remembered.

"Right where they found Smoke's body."

"Damn. Never mind." My level of discomfort rose. *What am I gonna walk in on?*

The pit of my stomach felt empty as I closed my phone, walked to the door, and rang the bell. As my finger touched the button, a chill ran through me. I recalled the evening I found Tameka. Strangely, almost everything was the same. Me on the doorstep wearing the same jacket, carrying the same purse, pushing that damn button. At least this time, Craig answered, interrupting my memory of seeing her unconscious body.

He invited me in, and I nervously followed behind him.

"How've you been?" he asked as he stuffed his hands into the pocket of his hoodie.

His question forced me to stop holding my breath. "I'm good. You know..." my voiced trailed on. My nostrils were pleasantly surprised to inhale the scent of lavender instead of the stench of month-old garbage. From what I could tell, the place was spotless. He had to have hired a maid.

"You alright?" I asked him.

"I'm makin' it."

Fruit baskets and wilted flower arrangements lined the floor of the foyer, and stacks of cards sat just inside the living room, reminding me of the scene at my apartment weeks before. I walked the perimeter slowly, reading the names on the tags.

"When you gettin' rid of this stuff? You gon' end up with fruit flies."

He shrugged.

I wasn't surprised that there was no trace of the Christmas holiday—not even a pine needle from someone else's house that got stuck on his jacket and fell off when he came home. The only saving grace for my place was the tabletop tree that Robert set up and decorated. It looked pitiful to me, though, because there wasn't anything else to complement it besides Darius' four wrapped packages.

"Where's my baby?"

"In his crib. It's about time for him to get up. Come on," Craig said, motioning for me to follow him upstairs.

I read the name "Jacqueline Randolph" on the largest basket with the fanciest decorations. "Why did that bitch send this? You been in contact with her?"

"Alexis, don't strum up old tension. Meka's gone. Their beef is over. I'm sure she sent it because she felt bad."

I remembered I hadn't told him about his ex's involvement with Tameka's shooting. Once I did, I could tell he was seeing red, even though his eyes narrowed so much that they looked closed.

"Smoke was her brother? She was following me? She sent him to my house?"

"Yes, but don't forget; she didn't mean for this to happen. He was just supposed to beat you up," I mocked.

I had evoked the emotion I wanted, so I didn't say another word about Jacqueline. If that bourgeois tramp thought she had a chance with my sister's man, she was definitely in for a surprise. Craig wasn't thrilled to hear she was a head case.

As I played with my nephew, Craig told me he'd received Darius' second HIV test results and he was still negative.

"How often does he have to get tested?"

"They really didn't want to test him now—said it was too soon— but I raised hell and they did it. It'll at least be another year. The one doctor said he'd rather wait two."

71

"Poor baby," I said, while stroking Darius' curly hair. "Not even a year old, and they keep pokin' you with needles."

Tameka was convinced that Darius was her miracle—that he won't have HIV. As I looked into his bright eyes, I silently prayed that she was right. He was innocent and defenseless, undeserving of a deadly, incurable disease.

"You look like a natural," Craig said with a subtle smile.

"Yeah, right. You know I don't do kids."

That was my auto reply, but my connection to Darius was natural. He had my heart from the day he was born, and I had a feeling my responsibility as Auntie Lexis was going to span beyond the normal duties since he didn't have a mom. I didn't know what was on Craig's mind, but I would be damned if another female came in and tried to play the mommy role.

An hour or so later, I said my goodbyes. It was time to call one of my boys and find out what everybody was doing for the night. With no work the next day, I was looking forward to smoking a little something to prepare my mind for the fucked up holiday I had in store.

"What y'all doin' on Christmas?" I asked Craig before stepping outside.

"Supposed to go to Aunt Rosie's with Tielle and all them. I don't know."

"Oh, that's right. I was gonna come get my baby. Well, I'll tell you what—I'll come get him tomorrow if that's alright. I have some stuff for him at the house."

"That'll work. Speaking of stuff," Craig said, stopping to clear his throat. "I have some more of Meka's stuff to give you. I just have to sort through it and box it up…you know."

"I know." I held my voice steady so I wouldn't share his melancholy tone.

We agreed that I'd pick Darius up at two o'clock, spend all of Christmas Eve with him, and take him home Christmas morning…

…And that's what I did. Although Craig tried to persuade me to go to Tielle's mom's, I refused without hesitation. As tempting as it was to see Dap and ruin her holiday, I wanted to be alone. I wanted to put my spiral ham in the oven, make a small pan of extra cheesy macaroni, and watch movies 'til I fell asleep.

After two plates of food, a few phone calls from friends, three movies, and a half hour nap, I was sitting on the couch, twiddling my thumbs. My mind wandered to the previous Christmas when Tameka bought me the interview suit I wore to the job I had grown to hate. *She would kill me if she was here right now,* I thought as I laughed to myself. My nonchalant attitude toward that hellhole would drive her nuts, something I was so good at doing. I reminisced about Christmases of the past, thinking of all the fun we used to have. I almost called my mom to ask her if she remembered which Christmas me and Tameka fought over a cassette tape and broke it, but I stopped after dialing one digit. I didn't need her. I had the journals! I picked up the one I had already been reading.

December 25, 1993

This Christmas was the bomb. I got most of what I asked for, and then some. Mom finally broke down and bought me the stuff she said was too boyish. I got the Chicago Bulls Starter jacket I've been drooling over. It's red, and nobody here has one. She had to get it from Chicago. Oh, and she got me and Lexis blue jean outfits with matching vests, and I got a Cowboys football jersey. I told Lexis she realized we weren't lying about that stuff being in style for girls when she watched Video Soul with us a few months ago. She should be glad we don't wanna wear the tight stuff. She didn't get us the Carhart jackets, though. She thought that was a little overboard because it's construction gear or something like that. I just think the tan coats are cute. I never knew they were made for a special purpose. It's cool. Daddy said he may get them for us if we both get at least a 3.5 on our report cards next time, so I'm gonna stay on Lexis to keep up with her homework. Other than that, I got five CDs, including the one from that new group Xscape, some church clothes, a Guess watch, and a VCR for my room. Grandma sent money, so I'll be able to buy even more stuff!

I held the book to my chest and laughed at the memory of that day. We were both so "hyped" (as we would've said then) about our gifts. That was the year Mom and Dad let me get color contacts. They said I had to be a teenager before I got them, and I was seven months into age thirteen. They surprised me that morning when I found the case on the bathroom sink. You couldn't tell me I wasn't fine when I popped in my hazel contacts and wore the Zana Di jeans that made my booty look big.

I loved the feeling I got when I read Tameka's accounts of life back then. Even though that was ten years prior and she was no longer with me, I felt like she was sitting right beside me, laughing just as hard. I flipped through random pages and spent more virtual time with my sister…

March 7, 1994

It's my birthday! Daddy took me to the license branch to take my test, and I passed!!! I wasn't even nervous. I'm not allowed to take the car anywhere until Friday, but I already know where I'm going. I'm going to the mall first, then to the movies. Daddy says no boys are allowed in the car, but...

May 7, 1994

I went to the movies with Rico today. We ran into Dap and some other girl at the concession stand. I still don't know why she doesn't like me. She stared me down, but I acted like I didn't see her. When Rico dropped me off, he kissed me, but it was sloppy. He wants to go out again tomorrow, but I told him I have too much studying to do.

May 8, 1994

Alexis got caught sneaking out the house. I told her not to leave out the front door, but she was too stupid to listen. She thought she was a pro since she didn't get caught before. She's about to be grounded for life! I didn't do anything today except talk on the phone...booooring!

June 19, 1994

We just dropped Alexis off at Leadership Camp. She didn't want to go, but Mom and Dad said if she didn't go, she'd be grounded all summer. I feel bad for her. Most of the kids there are geeks, and I don't think she's gonna fit in.

June 22, 1994

Something isn't right, and I don't have anybody to talk to about this. Mom and Dad were arguing—nothing new—and I thought I heard my name, so I stood in my doorway so I could hear better. They talked soft for a while, then I heard Daddy say that Alexis was getting out of control and that Mom needed to stop letting her get away with everything. She flipped!!! She said he couldn't tell her how to raise her child and that in the end, his opinion didn't matter. Daddy said something about it mattering before her big secret was out, then she really lost it. I've never heard her cuss so much. When I could finally make out what she was saying, I heard, "You're damn right she's mine. She doesn't need you around. You decided to maintain your role." There was more yelling, then Daddy left. Maybe I'm wrong, but I think me and Lexis have different daddies. My guess is that Darryl is hers if Daddy isn't because they argue about him too much. I guess this is an example of why they tell us to stay outta grown folks' business. It's too late now. I don't know what to do.

June 23, 1994

> *Man, I'm good! The first thing out Mom's mouth when I asked her about what I heard was, "Stay outta grown folks' business." She gets on my nerves. So, when she left for choir rehearsal, I asked Daddy. He apologized for me hearing their argument and then told me something like, "Believe half of what you see and none of what you hear." Maybe because I only heard part of what they were saying. Anyway, he made me promise not to tell Lexis because she would be upset over nothing. Then he said that we are both his girls and he still can't choose which one he loves more. He made me smile, but something tells me he's lying about Mom's words meaning nothing. I'm still gonna keep my promise, though. I'll never do anything to hurt my little sister, and telling her what I heard would kill her.*

> *Besides family drama, nothing's going on. Tyrone invited me to the movies, so I may go with him to see Speed.*

I stared at the page until the words became a blurry swirl of ink. I felt nothing and everything at the same time, wondering what I was supposed to do with that information.

6

Tiffany: Back to Normal?

Three drops of Visine lightened Tiffany's eyes from red to pink. At most, she'd been averaging two to three hours of sleep since the day she saw Frenchie. Her body desperately needed to rest, but her mind wouldn't permit it. Every time she closed her eyes for more than a blink's time, she thought about Venni's tongue tracing the oval of her womanhood, and the only way to block that image was to stay awake.

Her routine was polished now. Three pots of coffee, two twenty-ounce bottles of Mountain Dew, any chocolate bar, household chores, a *Fresh Prince of Bel-Air* marathon, and an infomercial about the latest exercise craze were sure to keep her awake until 3 a.m. By then, even her brain was exhausted, shutting down for a couple hours and allowing her to sleep relatively peacefully.

Besides the possibility of having a heart attack, avoiding sleep was turning out to be pretty productive. She could complete the day's laundry and housecleaning, prepare dinners using the latest Martha Stewart recipes she'd seen on TV, sing along to Barney's show with Tony, race Hot Wheels with Bryant, and let Bria examine her with every plastic instrument in her little doctor bag. All this, and she was still able to catch her daytime soaps and her favorite nighttime sitcoms.

Marlon was concerned about her new sleep pattern for the first few days, but quickly adapted to the nymphomania that accompanied her insomnia. His sex-crazed girl had returned with no stipulations of how long, how many times, how fast, nothing. Tiffany let him believe she was making up for their "lost" time while she was in grad school.

Subconsciously, she was hoping at least one of their sexual sessions would be memorable enough to erase the birthday experience she knew couldn't be topped.

It worked on Marlon. After a night of fun in the kitchen, her coochie had erased his memory. He hadn't asked any more questions about the panties that were already wet when he came home and tried to get some after her party, and that was a milestone. He had been grilling her about her overflow for about a week, but finally stopped the night she snapped at him at Alexis' apartment. After they left, Little Tiffany came through for her in a big way when Marlon initiated their make-up sex in the car. Her panties were saturated when he reached from the driver's side to explore, proving what Tiffany was hoping he would believe the week prior: at times, a woman's body has a mind of its own. Even though they were at odds, Little Tiff was still ready for action, and Tiffany gave Tielle and Bacardi all the credit.

Still, it was hard keeping such a huge secret to herself and the pressure was starting to show. She probably could've slept better if someone close to her listened to the story and empathized. Alexis was too close-minded, though, and Tiffany had reservations about telling Morgan who could be more judgmental than God-Almighty on the right day. So, she decided to weather the mental storm, knowing in time it would blow over and it wouldn't feel like someone was using her intestines for a double-dutch tournament. Her nerves were bad, though, and she was becoming more paranoid by the day. She overanalyzed everything people said to her, wondering if there was an underlying reason for every question they asked. "How are you?" was even suspect. Did that mean, "How are you holding up after your night with a lesbian?"

Venni's word was all she had to go by. She promised not to tell anybody about their night together. The more Tiffany thought about it, she wondered how loyal Venni would really be, considering the volume, tone, and language Tiffany used when she called. Nothing about her approach was civilized. Frenchie said Venni could be trusted, but how much did she really know about Frenchie? Be that as it may, her fate was in the hands of a loose-tongue lesbian and a former classmate who seemed harmless.

There was no more time to dwell on it. Christmas was two days away, and she had to finish wrapping Marlon's gifts and make sure she bought enough batteries for the kids' toys. She still hadn't found anything for Miss Tina, Marlon's mother. Well, she still hadn't *looked* for anything for her. It was crunch time like never before.

By Christmas Eve, Tiffany had found the perfect perfume for Miss Tina, stocked up on batteries, and wrapped Marlon's things. At six o'clock, Bria was helping her bake cookies for Santa as they sang "Jingle Bells" over and over. While they waited for the cookies to cool, Tiffany looked out the kitchen window and sighed. The gloomy sky and bare trees made it hard to be jolly.

"Mommy, why don't we get snow?" Bria asked.

"It doesn't get cold enough for it to snow here, Poochie."

"Where does it snow?"

"Lots of places, baby."

"Well, I want to move to Lotsofplaces. Santa brings more toys when it snows." Tiffany chuckled as she watched her little princess twirl around the kitchen. "Where's Daddy?"

"He's coming right now," Tiffany replied after hearing the garage door open.

Once Marlon entered with Bryant and Tony, the Christmas traditions continued. The entire family decorated the gingerbread house and then they popped popcorn to eat while they watched *A Charlie Brown Christmas*. Tiffany rested her head on Marlon's chest as she watched the flames in the fireplace dance. Five personalized stockings hung on the mantel just below the Christmas cards, all from her family. Their eight-foot tree stood majestically in the corner, dressed with gold and ivory decorations and multiple strings of pearls.

This is it, she thought. *It doesn't get any better.*

Marlon was thinking the same thing as he looked at his three children. Although Tiffany's traditions were sometimes corny and cliché, she was giving their kids something he never had growing up. True, he and his sisters made the most of buying each other gifts at Santa's Workshop at school, but they didn't share special moments at home. Some years, they were lucky to have a tree at all, let alone help decorate it.

He leaned down and kissed the top of Tiffany's head. She probably wouldn't want to cuddle the next day. He was almost sure of it. Why? Because he didn't have a ring. Another special occasion was here and the engagement ring wasn't. He could explain how he wanted to pay the ring off by her birthday, but his side hustle didn't bring in the money he had expected. However, since she didn't know about the side hustle, that wouldn't work. After all their years together, Tiffany still didn't understand the pressure she put on him to meet her rock star expectations. Marlon knew she expected the best of everything, and if she wanted the best diamond to floss around town, she would have to wait a little longer. Under any other circumstances, he would've been worried about her leaving, but their three kids gave him extra security and extra time. She wasn't going anywhere. He was her first, her last, and her everything, and in due time, he'd make it official.

By ten o'clock, the kids were asleep and Marlon and Tiffany were hard at work. One by one, they placed gifts under the tree—all but two. Each year, they surprised the kids or each other with something special. The year before, Tiffany bought the kids a swing set for the backyard and Marlon bought them a small pool.

When Tiffany rested her head on the pillow that night, she smiled. In the morning, she would get her surprise…finally.

***

All the gifts were open and wrapping paper was everywhere. The children couldn't decide which of their toys they wanted to play with first.

"Okay, guys. You know what's next." Tiffany's smile was bigger than the kids'. She turned to Marlon. "You wanna go first?"

"Naw, you can go 'head." His fingers typed hurriedly on his cell phone's keypad.

"Can you put your phone down while they get their surprises please?"

She had the kids put on their jackets and follow her to the backyard. Once there, she instructed them to stay near the patio as she ran to the garage.

"Beep, beep!" she yelled as she came out steering two Power Wheels Cadillac Escalades—one pink and one black. She didn't struggle with the bulky cars for long. Bryant and Bria darted to their respective vehicles and jumped in. "I didn't forget you, Tony." She reentered the garage and returned with a small motorized Jeep.

Marlon flared his nostrils and glared at Tiffany. They had discussed the Power Wheels back in September, but he didn't agree with spending over three hundred dollars on a toy car. For most people, that was a car payment. He tried to compromise, saying they would look for cheaper cars, but Tiffany pouted and didn't want to discuss it anymore. What was the point of getting the cars if they couldn't have one like Mommy, right?

Tiffany avoided looking at him, but couldn't continue to ignore him once he was in her face.

"I thought we agreed they didn't need these."

"No, you *told* me they couldn't have them. My daddy is in San Diego."

"They're too expensive! I'm not tryin' to be your daddy. I'm tryin' to be sensible. You've spent over seven hundred dollars on these cars. Plus, they have all those toys in the house."

"For your information, I didn't spend a dime. My parents bought them."

"Figures," Marlon said as he opened his phone. After reading a text message, he ran around to the front of the house.

While he was gone, a white Maltese puppy scampered into the yard. Tiffany quickly tried to gather the kids and shoo the dog away at the same time. Bria was tirelessly attempting to wiggle out of her mom's arms so she could pet the playful puppy.

"Y'all like him?" Marlon said with a smile. He placed a dog cage on the patio and leaned a bag of dog food against it.

That's it? Tiffany thought. *That's his surprise?* It wasn't a bad one. A dog was always a part of her big picture for their family.

As she watched the children play with the puppy they unanimously named "Billy," she wondered if she'd blown Marlon's proposal. Getting the cars for the kids may have pissed him off enough to delay such a beautiful moment.

Tiffany tried to sound cheerful. "Where did you get him from?"

Just then, Aaron rushed around the corner. "You forgot this, dawg." He handed Marlon a dog dish for food and water. "Merry Christmas, y'all," he said before leaving.

Tiffany was shocked. He barely even looked her way, and that was odd. After their slow grind at her party, she felt he should've had plenty to say. Maybe he was so reserved because Marlon was there. A part of her still wondered if he set her up by sending Venni into the room. Though that didn't make much sense, it would explain why he couldn't look her in the eye. She knew she wouldn't rest until she had a conversation with him, so she would have to make it her business to catch him at the gym to see if he'd act the same.

Portia A. Cosby

7

Alexis:
New Year, New Info, New Drama

I stared at the receiver and glanced back at the Yellow Pages...555-TURN. I wasn't sure why I was calling. Maybe because I wanted to hear Darryl's side of the story first. He had nothing to lose if he told the truth, but my mom did. My "dad" did. I guess I did, too.

Slowly, I pressed the black buttons. Each beep reminded me of a time bomb about to blow. *8...8...7...6.* There was a pause, then *BRRRRRING! BRRRRRING!* Two more times, and then a male voice.

"U-Turn, this is Darryl."

I hung up. After hearing the loud music and crowd chatter in the background, I realized it wasn't a good idea to call him on his job with questions about his sexual history, and especially when all I had to go by was a journal entry my dead sister wrote as a teenager. Was I really going to call him with that information and expect him to take me seriously? No, but I could stop avoiding the inevitable and call my mother.

She picked up after the second ring. "Well, a late Merry Christmas to you!" I didn't say anything. "Lexi?" I could hear her fumbling with her phone. "Lexi, can you hear me?"

"Yep."

"I called you yesterday, but I figured you and Robert were out and about."

"I was home."

"And you didn't answer?"

"Who's my daddy?" I refused to beat around the bush.

83

"Excuse me?"

I didn't hesitate to explain. Once I did, she developed a speech impediment. I hadn't heard that much stuttering since I sat beside Bobby Rush in fourth grade. When she finally got herself together, her tongue flapped with denial, and then came the anger.

"How dare you accuse me of being a two-dollar floozy? Who do you think you are? What kind of marijuana have you been smoking?" And then she asked the million dollar question. "Have you asked your father this ridiculous question?"

"He's next," I replied. "I see I'm gettin' nowhere with you."

"There's nothing to tell."

"Meka was right about you all along."

"Are you really going to hold Tameka's tenth grade journal writing against me? You know for a fact that she's hated my guts—"

"I know for a fact that you got me fucked up. She's had plenty of reasons to hate your fuckin' guts, and I think I have mine now. Why would she lie in her journal about what she heard you say to Daddy or whoever he is to me? I can't believe you'd even insult her memory like that. You figure you can say what you want since she can't speak for herself now?"

"Alexis Nichelle James, I am hanging up this phone because I will not tolerate this disrespect and foul language. I'm not one of your friends from the 'hood. You get yourself together and I'll talk to you tomorrow in a more civil manner."

"Naw, we won't talk tomorrow. I'm not givin' you time to come up with some crazy lie tryin' to get outta this one. I wanna talk to somebody who can give me the real. I feel like a fuckin' fool. I defended you tooth and nail to Meka, and we got in so many fights about your lyin' ass. I can't believe this shit!" I launched the receiver across the room and into the wall. Conversation over.

After I reassembled the phone, it rang. I dared the caller ID screen to display my mother's name, but "Tiffany Price" appeared instead. I wasn't relieved, because Tiffany's constant calls were getting on my nerves. I knew she didn't want nothing. It was just 7:30, the time we normally talk, so she called to shoot the shit. I turned off the ringer and slid the phone across the couch. *Maybe later.* I needed to talk to my dad first. I called a few minutes later, and he picked up the phone almost immediately. "I was just about to call you," he said.

"Oh, I guess she hurried up and called you, huh?"

"I assume you're talking about your mother. Yes, we just hung up."

"She's quick to call you now, but she wasn't callin' you when Darryl had her ankles to her earlobes," my voice trailed off.

84

"Listen, baby. What you read in Tameka's journal is much more complicated than you can imagine. She heard an argument. Your mom and I were angry. There were a lot of things said that shouldn't have been said."

"Daddy, please don't give me that BS. Mom was gettin' it from Darryl for years. I just don't understand how he could be my dad when we were living in Columbus when I was born."

"First off, I'm your dad. You understand? Now if you want to dig this grave, we'll dig it. I hope you got your boots on, baby girl."

"Bring it. I just want the truth."

...And he obliged. According to him, Mom met Darryl in Pittsburgh at a lawyers' convention. They kept in contact afterward and planned to meet at the next one in San Antonio a year later. I guess there was chemistry and fireworks, blah, blah, blah. Then I came along. Fast forward to us moving to Texas when I was eleven. We moved because Mom was offered a job paying eight thousand dollars more than she was making in Ohio. Daddy didn't know she would be working for the same company as Darryl—the guy he'd already checked for calling the house years before. That discovery ignited the flames of hell in the household that burned our strong family ties and eventually, my parents' marriage license. Tameka and I felt the tension, but never completely understood the root of their animosity...or at least I didn't.

I could hear the residual pain in my dad's voice as he recounted the story of my mom's fifteen-year affair with a man who offered a little more adventure and a lot more time. It was clear that he blamed himself partially for spending too much time at the office and not enough time at home, saying that Mom often accused him of having an affair with his secretary.

It was a lot to take in, mostly because I remembered the nights Mom would receive a page, make a phone call behind the closed door of the study, rush to her room to change into her tight jeans, and whisk past me and Tameka smelling like fresh perfume and Dove soap. She would double-check her makeup in the mirror by the door and leave twenty dollars on the end table. "Order pizza," she'd say. "I have to run to the store with Miss Nadine," Miss Coretta, or whichever other friend came to mind. I didn't think of how sketchy the scene looked. I was just happy we could order pizza and have the house to ourselves for a good three to four hours. Not once did it cross my mind that it didn't take three hours to pick up a loaf of bread and an eighteen pack of eggs.

After we hung up, I took a shower to clear my head. It didn't work. Instead, more memories flooded my brain, almost overwhelming me with disdain for the woman who gave birth to me. She pulled that shit off, right under our noses, but I think Tameka and I knew what was up after we heard about her affair with Darryl. We just didn't discuss it because her trips to the store with her friends worked to our benefit. Tameka would invite her boyfriend over, and as I got older, I did the same. Good times. Who cared what she was up to then? Ten years later, I cared.

Tiffany called again while I was drying off. It had to be important because she knew I would cuss her out if she was blowing up my phone for nothing.

"You busy? Please say you're not busy," she asked before I could finish saying hello.

I looked up at the ceiling tile and shook my head in preparation for her Marlon-doesn't-love-me story. Instead, she caught me by surprise, hyperventilating through her story of being mistaken for a lesbian. One of the ladies at the twins' preschool saw her at the gas station and asked her out. When she turned her down, the lady said, "She must have that on lock."

"What the hell did she mean by that?" Tiffany shrieked, almost in tears.

"How am I supposed to know?" She was always so dramatic, and I was all out of patience for the day.

"Somebody else insinuated I was bisexual the other day, too."

"I told you about hangin' out with Frenchie and company. If people see you around them too much, they think you do what they do. Birds of a feather…"

"Lexis, what am I gonna do?"

"Shake it off, I guess. You already know what I would do, but you ain't me."

I remembered somebody making a similar comment the night of Tiffany's party when I found her passed out on the guestroom bed. It was more general…along the lines of, "I didn't know she rolled like that." I didn't think about it then, but maybe they were talking about her and wondering if she disappeared with Frenchie during the night. She was the one who found Tiffany with unzipped jeans pulled halfway up her thighs. I explained that to her, hoping it would calm her down.

"You can't blame folks for thinkin' y'all had a little somethin' goin' on. You know that's not what happened. Be glad they don't know Aaron was the one in the room. If this version of the story gets back to

Marlon, he won't trip 'cause he knows you ain't gay, but if he gets the real version, there's gon' be some furniture movin'."

Listening to her problems gave me a much needed escape from my own. I didn't tell her about Tameka's revelation from the grave, and I still hadn't told her about the emails from Monica because I couldn't answer her follow-up questions. The only thing I was sure of was that neither one of the situations was over until I said so.

***

I waited until Robert came home the next day to tell him about my deceptive mother, but only after I questioned him about the baby he carried in the arm opposite the one that held his carry-on bag. My blood simmered as I thought of his possible responses, but only one response would cause it to boil: "Uh…Alexis, meet my son."

I leaned against the couch, digging my nails into its fabric and waiting for him to speak.

"We have a visitor, boo," he said with a wide grin.

"I see that."

He held the baby up to his face. "Do we look alike?" When my nostrils flared wide enough for him to count my nose hairs, he stopped the games. "This is Shemar, baby—my nephew. He's allowed to look like me." He laughed, but I was still thoroughly examining their similar noses.

Robert said he was watching Shemar for three days while Kaleb attended a conference in town. I knew Kaleb was coming back with Robert for a conference, but nobody had mentioned the kid tagging along.

"Why did Kaleb bring him if he can't watch him?"

"The meetings are just today and tomorrow. It's a weekend thing. And K's not in meetings all day. I'ma take lil' dude to the hotel after six so he can be with his pops."

"Hotel? Why ain't he stayin' here?"

"The conference is at the hotel, so it makes sense for him to stay there."

"Mr. Babysitter, huh? Don't get no ideas. Ain't a damn thing poppin' outta this," I said as I leaned closer and touched Shemar's tiny foot.

"Yeah, I know," he grumbled.

I ignored his comment and segued into my daddy dilemma. Robert had jokes when I first told him my mom had been giving it to Darryl.

"I knew Ms. Regina had it in her. You had to get your freakiness from somewhere!"

87

Portia A. Cosby

"He might be my dad, asshole," I replied. The smile lines on his face vanished. "Not so funny now, huh?"

He offered me his best advice: leave it alone. His parents divorced when he was five, but he didn't find out why until he was fourteen. His mom did some snooping and learned that his father had a son with their former neighbor in New York...and he was the same age as Robert. In his juvenile mind, he attributed his mother's nosiness to ending the marriage and hated his "new" brother for years.

"So you don't think that was information she should've known?" I asked.

"I just feel like some things are better left alone. I mean, me and Kaleb are straight now, but that kind of stuff changes your life, baby. I hated him for years. Mr. James has been everything a dad is to you. You gon' play him to the left if the DNA test says y'all don't have the same genes? Or are you doin' this to put your moms on blast?"

"Why does this have to be about them? This is for me. Is it such a problem that I wanna know who I can ask for a kidney if I need one?"

We went back and forth before he finally threw his hands in the air. "Do what you need to do. I'm here for you no matter what happens."

***

The weekend went smoothly until Sunday when Kaleb told Robert about an unexpected interview opportunity with one of the largest business law firms in town on Monday. Of course that meant somebody had to watch Shemar. Robert had to go to work, but I was on vacation through New Year's Day.

"What time will you be back?" I asked Robert as he nursed the heel I'd just stepped on.

"In a few hours, baby. I told you I'ma fake sick so I can leave by one."

I knew I should've lied and said I had something important to do, I thought as Robert kissed me goodbye on his way out. I called Tiffany to cancel our plans for the day. We were supposed to go to the mall at eleven to finish racking up on the after-Christmas bargains, and I still needed to find a dress for the WTIZ party. After a lot of coaxing, she convinced me to wrap Shemar up and bring him along for the trip with her three rugrats.

While we were in Baby Gap, we saw a stroller parked near the clearance rack with no adult in sight. I quickly approached it, noticing its familiar tan Eddie Bauer print.

"What you doin' in here?" I looked up and saw Craig holding Darius and about six outfits.

"Give him here," I said as Craig leaned over to see who was in the stroller I was pushing.

I wiped the tears from Darius' face. "What's the matter, D-Baby?" He whimpered a little as I held him up to my cheek. "I know. You miss Ti-Ti." I glanced at Craig. "Robert's nephew, dude. Ain't no surprises here."

He laughed and draped the unpaid merchandise over the stroller's handle.

"What the hell is that?" I asked. "Who are those for?" There was no way he was putting the mixed patterned, almost-cute-but-not-really clothes on my baby.

"What's wrong with 'em? Look. This one is on the mannequin over there. I think it looks good."

I searched Darius' section for replacement gear, as I schooled his pitiful daddy. "We can't wear everything white folks wear. That little white baby in the poster looks good in that, but D-Baby can't pull that off. How can you shop for yourself but not your son? I see I'ma have to handle this area of parenting, too." I handed him my selections. "Now hurry up and check out. We goin' to Urban World next."

"You 'bout to have my boy thugged out in Rocawear, Enyce and Eck□ like he's a little gangster."

"It's black folks like you who feed into the stereotypes. Wearing urban clothing does not make you a thug. Now, if he gets a toy gun and sags so his Huggies are showin', that's different."

Craig tagged along for a while, but left us after four other stores.

"That was interesting," Tiffany said as we proceeded to the next store. "I never thought I'd see the day you two would be able to shop together."

Hell, I didn't either, but it turned out that Craig was alright. I used to hate him with a passion, though, and he hated me more. Outside of his rude-ass comments a couple times while he and my sister were together, he wasn't a bad guy before. The good outweighed the bad. I just favored TJ because he was *always* good to Tameka. Their only issues revolved around him hustling.

While we were in one of the boutiques, I spotted the perfect dress for the party. It was tight and sexy but still classy, versatile. I could blend in with the groupies or the important folks with no problem.

Tiffany rushed over with a booger green halter dress. "How cute is this?"

"Not cute at all. You playin', right?"

Slowly, her expression changed. "Umm, no. Look at the back. That's sexy. I'm gettin' it."

"Don't wear that mess around me," I replied as we stood in line.

I paid for my dress and accessories and prepared to wait for Tiffany by the pretty smelling body lotions. When I looked up, she was out of the line, waiting for me.

"You were right. It wasn't all that."

"You were just gung-ho about that ugly thing, and now you don't want it? Go try it on at least."

She refused. Typical Tiffany. If I told her enough times that her kids were ugly, she'd start to believe it.

***

"Looks like I'll be hanging out with you tomorrow night," Tiffany said.

Since Marlon's oldest sister, Adrienne, was visiting from Seattle, he thought it would be cool for her to join them on New Year's Eve. Even though Tiffany didn't really like the idea of having a third wheel, she was willing to take one for the team. That was until he also included Dap and Carmen.

"So he's goin' without you?" I asked.

"Yep. So, you know what that means."

I spoke the words I'd rehearsed on every other holiday. "You weren't gon' get your ring anyway."

"Exactly. And I know he expects me to mope around this house, but I refuse. I already have a babysitter, so I might as well take advantage of it."

"I don't think you can go where I'm goin'," I answered slowly.

"I thought you weren't going anywhere."

I forgot that I hadn't told her about my plans with Tielle. When I did, she copped an attitude.

"Oh, okay. I'm starting to get the picture now. That's your new running buddy. You don't have time for me anymore."

"What?" I couldn't hide my irritation. She was reminding me of Ciara Sheffield, my best friend from seventh grade who was territorial over our friendship. If I sat with somebody else at lunch, she had her lip poked out. If she heard somebody else spent the night at my house, she wondered why she wasn't invited. And God forbid I rode the bus to the mall with somebody else—that definitely meant I hated her. Ciara was the reason I stopped having close female friends for a while.

"Give me a fuckin' break," I replied, inhaling my stress reliever. "Don't start that girly you-can't-be-friends-with-her shit. I've never run down my daily schedule to you, and I never will."

"It's not that. I just thought you would at least ask if I could go, too, but it's okay."

"I know it's okay because you can't go. She had one extra ticket—that's it. You know how that stuff works. What was she supposed to do? She's a local deejay, not Oprah. Go hang out with Frenchie and her homegirls. I'm sure they'll be somewhere lighting incense and looking deeply into each others' eyes when the clock strikes twelve."

"Bye, Lexis."

I was glad I pissed her clingy-ass off. I can't stand being smothered. She was guaranteed to be mad enough to not call while I was at the party trying to enjoy myself.

***

I caught Robert digging through my purse when I walked into the living room.

"I know they have metal detectors," I said, snatching the handbag and taking a quick inventory.

"I was looking for something else, but I found it." He held up a rubber.

"And look at the date on it. I haven't carried this purse in two years, nigga." Tielle knocked on the door. "You steady checkin' on me. Feelin' guilty?"

"Don't start."

"I'm already finished." I grabbed my coat and switched all the way to the door. "Happy New Year."

Tielle complimented me on my killer dress, while I posed shamelessly against the apartment building. I knew she was nervous as hell, thinking I was going to walk out the house in only a bra and miniskirt. We laughed all the way downtown as I told her how insecure Robert was about me being around people with real money.

"Little does he know, half the men there who would possibly be worth your time stay to themselves and just settle for some end-of-the-night booty that their entourages hook up. The ones who talk to you will be scrubs or just plain ugly," Tielle explained, almost crushing my hopes for the night. "Or they're just newbies looking for attention."

The lecture continued. "Don't leave the building with anybody, no matter how fine they are. Don't take egos personally. If Beyoncé shows up, don't attack her. And don't embarrass me or yourself," Tielle said as the valet drove away with her car.

"Dang! You act like I'm a kid or somethin'. I'm not gon' go in here humpin' on Lil' Breezy's leg or anything," I replied. "Give me some credit."

I slowed my stroll to admire the charcoal Rolls Royce Phantom with the coach doors and the tangerine Lamborghini that was parked in front of it.

"And don't ask them where the weed is, either." After I didn't say anything, she turned to me. "I know you heard me."

I laughed, but never agreed to that term. I had to get one last session in before I made my lifestyle changes for 2004.

We entered the palatial ballroom and my eyes widened to take in all the sights. A nerdy-looking Asian man sat in the lobby at a white baby grand piano, playing some kind of Beethoven-esque tune, while a group of men in tuxes waited in line at the small bar nearby. I playfully snapped my fingers and wobbled my head as Tielle and I proceeded to the main area where the real party was. When I heard Missy Elliott's voice over my favorite Monica track, I knew it was time to set it off. I grooved to the beat as I headed to the mega bar a few feet away.

Tielle joined me. "Good place to start." She scanned the room and waved to a few people. "This is network central, though, so go easy on the heavy stuff. Drink enough to relax—no more."

Maybe that would matter if I had a reason to network, I thought. The only folks I needed to talk to were the generous ones with green—paper and plant. I was at the gala to party, bullshit, and see if the celebs looked as good in person as they did on TV.

After we got our drinks, we moseyed to the table full of finger sandwiches, Club crackers, unrecognizable dips, and other fancy appetizers, eager to make a plate.

"Was haanin', shawty?" a voice called out as I loaded my plate with mozzarella sticks.

I looked up to see where the voice was coming from, then looked back down to continue my task. Dude was patient as hell because he was still waiting at the end of the table after my extra minute of stalling.

"So you my date tonight, right?" he asked. I watched my lip curl in the reflection of his platinum teeth. "Was ya name?"

"Anonymous." I used to like guys who had one or two gold teeth, but his mouthful of metal was ugly as hell and blinding me under the bright lights.

"You don't know who I am, do you?"

"Should I care?" I asked.

He told me the name of his song, and I realized he was a rapper out of Florida named B-Eazee. His music was on-point, but his face wasn't. That's why I'd never watched his whole video. He was hideous.

B-Eazee seemed turned on by the fact that I didn't care who he was. He kept inviting me to the V.I.P. area and tried to further entice me by pulling out the wad of money in his pocket as if it was really in the way of the Tic Tacs container he was digging for. If I was nineteen again, I would've robbed his ass in a heartbeat before the night was over.

Tielle came to rescue me and we walked around the gigantic room to see who we could see. "I tried to get Craig to come. My boss had an extra ticket," she said as we passed a couple San Antonio Spurs. "So many athletes attend this thing. He could've been networking, too."

"I'll network with him all night," I said, looking over all six feet, six inches of the one with braids. He smirked to acknowledge my stare and I did the same. Before I could go his way, though, Tielle yanked my arm and pulled me toward our original destination.

"Please don't mention you had an extra ticket when you're around Tiffany. Her high-strung ass will think I knew all along and didn't want her to come."

"I got you." She gasped like she suddenly remembered she left her curling iron on. "Hey, I meant to ask you...is she switching lanes now?"

"Damn, who told you?"

"So it's true?

"Naw, I'm just sayin'. Somebody is runnin' they mouth to a whole lotta people about some shit they don't know."

She revealed her source: her beautician, Wanda, who was notorious for spreading gossip. She was like the *Star Magazine* of the 'hood. A lot of her scoop was on-point, but this time, she had the story twisted.

"Well, when you go for your next appointment, tell Wanda my girl ain't no carpet licker. Somebody was in the room, but it wasn't—"

A short, bald man in a flashy suit stole Tielle's attention. I later learned he was an executive from Arista Records, but more importantly, he was my lifesaver. I'll be damned if I wasn't about to tell Tielle about Tiffany and Aaron like she ain't Marlon's first cousin.

I mingled with them for a little bit, but had no clue what he and Tielle were talking about. My eyes wandered, praying to see something or someone more interesting. Instead, some blonde haired, blue-eyed dude approached us. Tielle introduced him as Eli, her station manager. He seemed cool enough. The content of his conversation demonstrated his knowledge of urban music, but he wasn't that white boy trying to fit in with the black folk. You could just tell he was passionate about his job. As he ran down the list of celebrities he'd spoken to about visiting WTIZ, my eyes wandered again, and the rest of my body followed.

I didn't stray too far—just far enough to look for the basketball player I'd shared the brief stare with. I saw everybody but him. As I looked for the nearest bar to quench my thirst a little more, a waiter in a tight vest walked by with a tray full of champagne. I don't turn down free alcohol, so I took a glass and leaned against the nearest wall. Wrong move. On the other side of me were two chatty broads with nothing better to talk about other than how excited they were about MAC's new lipstick. After listening for a couple minutes, I glanced their way to see if they looked as superficial as they sounded. One of them looked familiar, but I didn't want to look too long because they'd think I was staring.

Eli danced over to me with Tielle following closely behind. I was impressed with how he moved, so I instinctively left the wall to join him. He was hanging until I turned around and did my signature gyration against his unsuspecting male part. When I noticed he wasn't dancing anymore, I turned around and laughed at his wide-open mouth and red face.

"I knew you wouldn't know what to do with this. You better tell him, LT. He don't want none."

"What if I do?" Eli replied.

"Isn't that Toni Valentine right there?" Tielle asked just as I was about to respond to Eli. She nodded toward the females I was just standing by.

Toni Valentine had the number one album of the summer and kept my ass wiggling every weekend in the club. She was supposed to be the female artist to contend with, some people even calling her the new Janet.

"I knew she looked familiar!" I said. "Yeah, that's her. Didn't she just get implants in her booty?"

"That's the rumor."

That's why she's trying to be low key. Without a second thought, I headed her way. "Hey, Toni," I said to the woman who was too engrossed in her two-way to look up right away. When she did, her face held the same "Who the hell are you?" expression as her stuck-up friend's. "I thought that was you when I was standing here, but I wasn't sure."

"Oh."

"You back in the studio yet? I need you to get on that third album 'cause I'ma need somethin' to break these dudes off with. I think there's still a nigga standing on the dance floor with his thumb in his mouth after what I did to him when 'Show Him Some' was playin'. And that was back in July."

She quickly stepped down from her high horse and laughed. "I'm glad you enjoy my music. I'll have a little somethin' new for you in March or April."

"Okay. Have a good evening," her flunky said, using her hand to shoo me away.

"Bitch, I ain't over here to sweat y'all. I just came over to give her props on her CD and let her know half the people approachin' her just wanna see if her ass is real. I shouldn't have said nothin' to y'all stuck-up asses."

Toni stepped in front of her friend, concerned about my interpretation of the extra attention she was getting. "Is that bullshit still circulating?" She went on to apologize for her overprotective assistant, then told me how her newly enlarged backside was the result of all the beans, cornbread, collard greens, and pig tails she'd been eating since she moved to Atlanta. "I'm a Cali girl. I ain't used to eatin' like that."

"Yeah, okay." No longer interested in what she had to say, I strolled over to Eli and Tielle. "I better not see that ho in the parking garage. She'll see how important she is when I tag her and Toni's bodyguards look the opposite way," I ranted.

Tielle shook her head. "Her assistant? Girl, they all think their job description spans beyond what it really is. Did you ask her about the implants?"

I explained. Eli cracked up. "I like your style."

"A lotta people do."

As the night went on, I kept drinking, kept socializing, and made my way to the V.I.P. area. I ran into Toni again, minus her personal ass-kisser. She was obviously drunk and full of conversation. Not only did she give me the details behind her own rumor, she randomly pointed out other celebs in the room and shared some MTV-News-Exclusive-type scoop. I almost threw up in my mouth when she told me that some of the hardest dudes in the rap game would be more interested in hollering at Robert than me and that if I looked more closely at some of the female stars in V.I.P., I'd see where they piled on cover-up to hide their herpes blisters.

She scored fifty bonus cool points when she introduced me to her homeboy from Long Beach who let me get a taste of Cali's finest before the stroke of midnight. With ten seconds left of 2003, I closed my eyes and reflected on the year—the drama, the fake bitches I removed from my life, Robert's photo collection of Monica, the secret I learned about my mom... how the next year wouldn't include my sister. If I could've held on to one moment, I'd pick any one that included Tameka. But when three seconds turned into one and everybody screamed "Happy New Year," I was reminded that time waits for no one. It was time to move on.

Tiffany:
New Year, New Outlook, New Beginnings

Tiffany stretched her arms high into the air and yawned. "Good riddance," she said softly as she turned off the TV. It was barely 12:01, but she'd met her goal. All she wanted to do was stay up long enough to say goodbye to a year that ended miserably. Though she'd completed her master's program and wooed the higher ups at Safe Haven, she was still unmarried, unengaged, and unsettled about her unexpected birthday gift.

This one will be better, she thought, while looking down at Bria, who was sprawled across her lap. Her poor eyelids were heavy as cement blocks well before eleven. Bryant begged to stay up as Marlon escorted him to his room with Tony in his arms. Tiffany laid Bria in the king-size bed she and Marlon shared, then poked around her closet. She retrieved her boxer pajama set from the bottom shelf and secured her satin scarf on her head. She wasn't just preparing for bed; she was sending Marlon a message.

He entered the room and changed into the clothes he'd laid out on the chair. The Girbaud jeans Tiffany bought him for Christmas looked as good as she knew they would, giving him breathing room without the sagging factor. *Jackass*, she thought. *He has the nerve to wear the outfit I bought him.* She gritted her teeth as she watched him from the bed. He brushed his hair meticulously in the bathroom mirror and soaked himself in cologne. Never one to be insecure, Tiffany drew her anger from being alone rather than from thoughts of Marlon getting new booty for the new year. He had chosen his sisters over her, and even though that was his family, she and the kids were, too. Was that a measure of his commitment to family? Maybe the ring she'd been wanting didn't come with the dedication she needed.

She faked sleep as Marlon exited the bathroom. He stood near the doorway by the dresser, gathering his watch and wallet. His phone vibrated in the chair. Quickly, he checked his appearance one last time, scooped his phone from the chair, and dashed out of the room. A moment later, he came right back and peeked into the room.

"I'll see you in the morning, boo. They waitin' for me."

No kiss, no apology, no consideration. When Tiffany heard the door close, her eyes opened.

***

"Happy New Year, chica!" Morgan exclaimed.

"Same to you, party animal," Tiffany replied, switching the phone's receiver to the other ear and nursing her newly aching eardrum. "Before you ask, I didn't do anything worth talking about last night. I had a babysitter, but my plans fell through. Me, Marlon, and the kids watched the ball drop, then they went to bed and he went out with his sisters."

"His sisters? He left you home? Don't tell me anything else about him. I can't even stomach it. Why didn't you and Alexis go out? I know she was into something." She paused briefly. "Oh, I forgot about her sister. She probably wasn't in the mood to party."

"No, she was in the mood. I just wasn't included in her plans. Her and Tielle hang out a lot now. She deejays at WTIZ, so she invited her to their big bash. Guess I wasn't important enough to attend."

"It's not always about you, princess. Stop being a hater. Anyway, guess where I am?"

"Are we talking international or what?"

Morgan laughed and assured her sister that she hadn't left the country.

Tiffany shrugged her shoulders and replied, "Vegas."

"Oh my God! You're good!" She went on to describe how Seth whisked her away on his family's private jet for their New Year's Eve date. "He paid for two separate rooms, too. I told him I don't play the roommate game. I've known him for a few months, but not well enough for that kind of action. He hasn't been farther than my living room, so I don't know why he thought we were bunking."

After Morgan finished her story, Tiffany updated her on the kids, being sure to highlight Tony's success with potty training.

"And what's the deal with the job? You make a decision yet?" Morgan asked.

"I'm going with Safe Haven."

"You don't sound excited. You sure?"

"Yeah. I'm just tired."

"You're full of it. What's wrong?"

After a long pause, Tiffany sighed. "Something happened, and I'll kill you if you tell anybody."

"Oh, boy," Morgan said. "Do I need to sit down?"

"You need to lie down."

Two minutes later, Morgan knew the whole story. "Tiff, how did you not know?" She wondered if she sounded as doubtful as she felt. Tiffany had always been curious about sex, dating back to the time she found their father's porn magazines under the bed at the age of ten. Morgan remembered how upset their mother was when she found one of the magazines under Tiffany's pillow. She thought it was Morgan's until Tiffany came home from school and casually admitted she'd taken it. In her eyes, their father did no wrong, so she didn't understand what the big deal was. That led to the show-me-yours-and-I'll-show-you-mine recess experiment with Becky Jean when they were living in Iowa. Tiffany still had scars on her behind from that whooping.

"I told you I was messed up. I thought I was dreaming until she—I can't even say it again."

"So, if you're sure of this, why haven't you gone to the police?"

"How embarrassing is that? I don't want to put this on record. It's water under the bridge now. Pressing charges on her won't change what happened."

"Rape is rape. She…" Her voice cracked. "You did not consent to what she did. That's your story, right?"

"Why would you ask me that?"

"Tiff, we grew up in the same house. Don't think I forgot." She exhaled slowly. "Curiosity killed the cat, baby sis. That's all I'm gonna say. And perhaps you should lay off the alcohol for a while since it incapacitates you so much." Her tone couldn't have been more condescending.

Tiffany was offended, so she hung up on her. She knew she shouldn't have shared the story with her, but her heart and mind were heavy, and at that moment, it seemed okay to vent to her sister. How dare she compare her pubescent curiosities to an adult happenstance? And it didn't take a genius to know that she needed to stop drinking. She'd made it her New Year's resolution after Venni told her she was telling her how horny she was all night. Still, she believed Venni couldn't be that stupid to think she was hinting for her to scratch that itch. She was engaging in general girl talk, but evidently, Venni and her girls didn't talk like that. And no, she shouldn't have been talking so freely to a stranger anyway, but...she was drunk...and looking all over for Marlon...thinking out loud.

"I guess I picked up the wrong vibes. That was my mistake," was Venni's simple response when Tiffany explained how she had misinterpreted their conversations all night. She didn't tell Tiffany that she recalled her telling her to touch her nipples to feel how hard they were on a couple occasions that night. She knew there was no reasoning with the panicked woman, so why bother? All she could do was assure her that her lips were sealed and stress that she never had to brag about her sex life. With men *and* women openly lusting for her already, boasting about a half hour with Tiffany was unnecessary. Tiffany was fine with that then, but today, her feelings were a little different. Somehow, people were finding out what went on in her guestroom. If Venni didn't tell, who did?

She couldn't sit around the house anymore, so she called Aunt Retha and asked her to watch the children.

"You were supposed to bring 'em over here last night, but you changed your mind. Now you want 'em over here? How you know I didn't make plans?"

"Because I know the Missionary luncheon is next weekend, Aunt Retha." Her aunt had no life outside of attending church functions. "Please?"

"You young mothers don't know how to manage. I used to take all five of your cousins to the shopping center with me. Y'all would rather go without than take your children to the market."

"You know that's not me, Aunt Retha."

"Bring 'em on over here."

Before she left Aunt Retha's doorstep, she had to agree to bring her back a pocketbook, one that didn't have "five hundred F's or G's on it." That was a deal. She could find a little no-name bag that was just her aunt's style.

When she stepped inside Macy's, she was in her glory. They were having their biggest sale of the year, and she was ready to take full advantage of the bargains. Although she justified her splurge with needing clothes for work, she later found herself in the activewear section, browsing through running shorts.

"They have some good deals in here," a voice called behind her.

"I know!" she replied, barely looking over her shoulder.

"I'm gonna rack up for the gym," the lady continued.

Why am I even here? Tiffany thought as she returned the navy and lavender shorts to the rack. *I don't work out.* Still, her fingers lingered on the hanger. The tiny shorts were cute—perfect for wearing around the house when she wanted to tease Marlon.

Her newfound shopping buddy joined her. "Get 'em. They're so comfortable," she said as she pulled a medium for herself. "You barely sweat because they're so breathable."

Tiffany tried not to laugh at the lady's excitement over workout gear as she turned to acknowledge her. "I would just be wearing them to—" She froze.

Venni continued to scan the rack until she realized Tiffany still hadn't completed her sentence. She looked over at her. "I'm sorry. I thought you knew it was me all along."

"Is that your favorite line? Get away from me!"

Venni lowered her voice. "There's no need to cause a scene."

"Oh, I'm more than justified to cause a scene. You've been going around telling people what happened!" She attempted to bring her volume down. "I can't believe I actually trusted you when you said that wasn't your style." Three nearby shoppers turned their attention to the two, but Tiffany paid no mind. "I should've gone to the cops like I first planned."

"Cops?" Venni pulled her to the side.

Tiffany snatched away. "Yes. That's who you talk to after you've been raped."

"You're blowing this way out of proportion. I haven't said a word to anybody and nobody has said anything to me. Somebody from the party must have picked up on something. If you wanna file charges, be my guest. But we both know if Aaron was in there instead of me, rape wouldn't have crossed your mind." She smiled at the older women who were following the action. "I'm about to grab lunch at the café past the movie theater. If you're hungry, I'll treat. We'll sit and talk about this without an audience. It'll be my peace offering."

"I don't think so."

Venni paid for her merchandise and waited for Tiffany to do the same. Tiffany glanced in her direction, wondering why she hadn't left. After she slid her credit card into her wallet, she attempted to walk past Venni who had her hand extended.

"No hard feelings?" she asked. Tiffany hesitated before shaking her hand. "Tiffany, I don't know what you think I'm about, but I'm a professional woman with a reputation. I don't want anything from you. We had a regrettable occurrence, I apologized, end of story. If anybody asks me about it, I'll deny it. No sweat. The last thing you need is to be pegged as a lesbian."

"I wouldn't care if it was *true*."

Venni leaned in close, speaking softly into Tiffany's ear. "If you really felt violated, the cops would've had me in custody by now."

Tiffany wondered if everyone could see the egg on her face as Venni walked away.

***

A couple days later, she found herself sitting at a table beside Venni's at Starbucks. It was the only one available in the crowded establishment. Engrossed in the two file folders full of paperwork and her laptop computer, Venni didn't even notice she was there. Tiffany tried her best to keep a low profile, but her plan was foiled when she knocked her cell phone onto the floor and it slid near Venni's foot. She jumped up to retrieve the device just as Venni reached down to pick it up.

In front of Venni's eyes were Tiffany's brown leather boots. Her eyes followed the boot-cut jeans from the tiny calves they covered to the small hips they rested on. Tiffany reached for the phone as Venni's face met her belt buckle.

"Thanks. I'm kinda clumsy."

Venni looked up at her face. "Hey, you! I didn't even know you were sitting over there." She returned to her seat and began to pack her things. "I had to knock out some work before I go in Monday."

"Oh," Tiffany said with an uncomfortable smile.

"Did you take the job at Safe Haven? I remember Frenchie saying they made you an offer."

"Yeah, I start Monday."

"I think you'll like it. Most of the people I know from that company are decent. Autumn is a sweetheart, and when you meet Janice, you'll see she's the mother hen there. Every week, she bakes cookies, pies, cakes…"

Tiffany laughed. "Are you from here? You don't really sound like it," Tiffany asked before sipping her latte.

"I've lived in a lot of cities, so my accent's a mixture of those. I'm from Gary, Indiana, but I lived in a Chicago suburb while I was a teenager."

"Gary? Where Michael Jackson's from?"

She laughed. "Yeah. We don't brag about him that much anymore, though."

"I know all about living everywhere. I was born in Alaska." Venni's facial expression asked the question. "My dad was in the Air Force," Tiffany answered. "What made you move here?"

"Nothing *made* me move here. I just wanted a change." It wasn't hard to sense the coldness of her answer.

"I just thought you moved because you have relatives here. Aaron's your cousin, right?"

"Yeah…You know he has it bad for you, don't you?" Venni replied.

"He lets me know every chance he gets."

"Well, if you and your boyfriend ever call it off, you know you have a substitute," she said with a shrug and a smile. "He's a good guy." She looked at her watch and stood up. "I don't mean to be rude, but I have to run. Good luck on Monday." Before she left, she turned back to Tiffany. "I still owe you lunch, so look me up in the building directory by eleven if you wanna go. I'm on the tenth floor."

***

Monday morning was chaotic. Tiffany stood at the stove wearing only a camisole and pantyhose, scrambling eggs. Marlon chased Tony around, while Bria and Bryant argued at the kitchen table.

"You gon' have to get him," Marlon said as he joined the twins and laid Tony's clothes on the table.

"Do you see what I have on? Do I look like I have time to get him dressed, too, and finish cooking breakfast? I don't see you picking up a spatula to take over," Tiffany replied.

"I don't have to be awake right now. I did you a favor gettin' them ready," he snapped back, pointing to the rowdy pair beside him.

"You did yourself a favor, honey. They're your children, too." She placed Bria and Bryant's plates in front of them.

"You need to kill your attitude."

"You need to kill yourself," she shot back before scampering into the bedroom to slip into her Donna Karan suit.

Although everyone she saw at the office had a more casual look the day she interviewed, she wanted to make sure she stood out as a professional. Her new coworkers would be clear that she wasn't there to play games and have no choice but to respect her.

She winked at herself in the mirror before coercing Tony into getting dressed. They were out of the house by 7:20 a.m., and twenty minutes later, she was introducing Tony to the women in the daycare center at Safe Haven. He took to them right away, which was a huge relief. All she needed on her first day was a distraught child screaming for her not to leave. Once he saw the Tonka trucks, it was like she was invisible.

Ursula, her immediate supervisor, met her at the front desk and they rode the elevator to the fourteenth floor. She escorted Tiffany to her office, a cozy space with a great view of a nearby park. Her large desk was bare except for a stack of manila folders, a company cell phone, business cards, her nameplate, and a shiny white and green "Welcome to Safe Haven" folder. In her mind, she'd already decided where the pictures of the children would be placed.

Once she removed her jacket and put her purse away, Ursula led her on a tour of the floor. Everyone seemed friendly except three women who gave her half-hearted welcomes. She watched their eyes scan her from head to toe faster than a copy machine, and though they wished the results would be the same as a copier, they could never be her. They were just mad because their "Sears special" outfits were the hottest thing in the office until she arrived.

I'm in the building now, bitches. Don't hate, Tiffany thought, as she and Ursula retreated to the conference room for a quick orientation.

There, she met Faith, the head supervisor, and Beck, a team facilitator who was familiar with the cases she would be handling. Beck looked like a Ken doll, handsome, with blonde hair that was styled with not a strand out of place. When he smiled, his perfectly straight teeth sparkled under the fluorescent lights. She knew all of his female clients had the biggest crushes on him. After they dispersed from the conference room, he walked her to her office and briefed her on the cases that awaited her attention.

Caitlyn's file was on top of the pile. She suffered from Body Dysmorphic Disorder. Beck explained that she was a normal looking sixteen-year-old, but she was convinced that her nose was too large for her face. She wouldn't take pictures, wouldn't go to school dances, and she wore a white mask over it when she went to the mall. Harley was fifteen and had Reactive Attachment Disorder. She thought everybody was her best friend, even all the boys in her neighborhood and in her class at school. This had become a problem because many of the girls avoided her and were rude to her, and some of the ornery boys took her kindness a step too far. Her mother left her at a supermarket when she was five, and she had lived in a foster home with a minister and his wife since age seven.

This was what Tiffany lived for. She couldn't wait to meet those girls and the six others so she could help them. One in particular touched her. Maleah, her only new client, was being abused by her twenty-year-old boyfriend. She was an intelligent, seventeen-year-old, star sprinter on her school's track team. Her mother convinced her to get help after Allen nearly broke her jaw a week prior. Though swollen and bruised, Tiffany could tell she was a beautiful girl, and she wanted badly to get her out of the destructive relationship. They had a great rapport, which eased Tiffany and Maleah's minds on both of their first days.

***

The next day at eleven o'clock, Tiffany thought about Venni's lunch offer. She was the closest thing she had to a lunch buddy since she was yet to be embraced by someone in her own company. She hated eating alone, so…

They ended up at the Treetop Bistro near the park. As they sat down, Tiffany began to have second thoughts. Venni seemed nice and all, but having lunch together was probably sending her the wrong signal…again.

"I was surprised when you called," Venni started. "I didn't know how comfortable you'd be with this after hearing all the rumors about yourself."

Tiffany shrugged. "You said it's a peace offering, right? Besides, what does it matter now? People have already made their assumptions."

Venni raised her eyebrows and twisted her lips in agreement. *What is so damn intriguing about this woman?* Tiffany thought as she caught herself staring at Venni's innocent eyes.

When the waiter arrived, she ordered the Smoked Salmon Salad, and Venni ordered the Roasted Eggplant Sandwich.

"I'm so glad I didn't have to go to the hot dog stand outside the main lobby," Tiffany said.

Venni's face wrinkled with disgust. "That's one thing you'll never see me eat."

"Let me guess. You're one of those people who have a problem with how they're processed."

"Not at all. Just a bad childhood memory."

"You have family here other than Aaron?"

She shook her head. "I have a sister in D.C. and my brother lives in California."

"What part? My parents are in San Diego."

"Burbank. He's a movie producer."

"Ooh, I've always wanted to be in a movie."

"What kind?" Venni smiled.

Is she flirting with me? "A romantic comedy," Tiffany answered.

105

As they talked, Tiffany noted Venni's style. "I need that watch, girl. What kind is it? Gucci?"

Venni was impressed. Tiffany knew fashion almost as well as she knew psychology. The fine yellow gold piece on her arm caught Tiffany's eye because it looked like something she would wear.

"I'm obsessed with watches," Venni said. "If you saw my dresser, you'd think I was crazy."

"I have to keep my obsessions under control now since I'm a mommy. You don't have any children, do you?"

Venni seemed to drift away for a moment. "I'm not cut out to be a mother," she eventually replied, while swirling the ice in her water with the straw.

"That's what I thought until I laid eyes on the twins right after they were born."

Venni shrugged. "I have a nephew. I'm satisfied with him."

"You sound like my girl, Alexis. Her nephew is her pride and joy, but she doesn't want kids."

"It's not always about what you don't want."

Venni's words hung in the air, begging for a conjunction to bridge the gap between awkwardness and understanding. The psychologist in Tiffany wanted to pry, invite elaboration, but her sensitivity recognized the pain behind the words. She remembered her mom's eyes holding that same emptiness when she learned she'd miscarried her and Morgan's younger brother, and wondered how long it had been since Venni's miscarriage or how many she had. Maybe she turned to women because she had a boyfriend who repeatedly blamed her for her inability to carry a child, verbally abusing her until she felt inadequate.

She probably feels safe with women because there's no pressure to consummate the relationship with a child, no reason to reveal that she feels less than a woman; just more reason to celebrate the femininity that her last male partner tried to destroy. The corners of Tiffany's lips curled slightly. She was pleased with her secret psychoanalysis and was willing to bet money that ninety percent of it was correct.

Their food arrived, but that didn't stop them from getting to know each other better. Outside of a few things, they had quite a bit in common. Venni had just moved into her new house, so they spent the rest of their lunch break talking about different contractors she should hire for special projects and the best art gallery to get paintings from.

When they returned to the building and went to their respective floors, Tiffany felt good. Venni was the professional, classy woman she claimed to be, and then some. She didn't make reference to their night together, stare at her breasts, or make offensive comments. If she was the predator Tiffany once thought she was, she would've taken advantage of one of the many opportunities she had to show her remaining interest. Without a doubt, she now believed Venni's version of the story wholeheartedly.

They met for lunch twice more that week. At times, Tiffany felt like they'd known each other forever. She was much more refined than Alexis, less judgmental than Morgan, and significantly more reserved than Frenchie. In three days, they knew a lot about each other, though Venni was markedly cautious not to reveal too many details. Some subjects were sore ones that she avoided like the plague. Their growing friendship allowed Tiffany to be herself without laughter or criticism. It was okay to like exquisite dishes and shop at high-end boutiques; and Venni didn't roll her eyes when she talked psychology.

When Friday rolled around, Tiffany was certain she made the right decision when she accepted the job at Safe Haven. Already she'd connected with her clients and made a new friend. What a great first week.

***

Friday evening, Alexis called from her car to see if Bria was ready. She had promised her goddaughter that she would take her to see "Sesame Street on Ice". Tiffany asked her to come in while she finished putting the barrettes in Bria's hair.

When Alexis walked in, she was surprised to see a stranger sitting at the dining room table playing with the boys. After a quick glance, she walked past Tiffany and Bria and went into the kitchen.

"You know you wrong for this one. I told you we gotta be at the arena before seven." She helped herself to a soda and looked again at the lady who suddenly didn't look so strange. Her eyes narrowed in an effort to jog her memory.

"Blame the princess here. She threw a fit when she saw her barrettes didn't match her outfit," Tiffany replied.

"I would, too," Venni agreed.

Tiffany looked at Alexis, whose eyes were still squinted. She was hoping to be done with Bria's hair in time to send her out the door with Alexis, but cleaning up Tony's vomit after dinner threw her off schedule. Now she had to introduce Alexis and Venni so she wouldn't seem rude, but just as she suspected, Alexis recognized her from the party.

"You look familiar. What's your name?" she asked.

"I'm Venni."

"You know Lawrence?"

Every muscle in Tiffany's body relaxed as Alexis associated her recognition of Venni with knowing her personal trainer, Lawrence.

"Like I know my social security number! He's my trainer."

"With his fine ass…I see y'all jogging every Saturday when I'm at the beauty shop. Y'all either dedicated or plain crazy, 'cause y'all don't miss a Saturday."

Venni laughed. "Yeah. We spend all Saturday together, from breakfast to dinner."

"Sounds like a good day to me." Alexis stopped there, not wanting to offend the woman she just met. If Lawrence was her man, she had already gone too far. "Did you just move here?"

"I've been in Texas for five years. I was in San Antonio until about nine months ago. I keep a pretty low profile. As you see, you recognize me from running, not dancing at the club."

"I'm Alexis, by the way. My fault."

Bria ran over to Alexis after Tiffany fastened the last barrette. "Look what I got!" She stepped inside a hot pink hula hoop.

Tiffany shook her head. "Girl, she begs me to do that with her every day." She pointed to a larger, turquoise one leaning against the wall.

"Aw shoot! Let me see you do it, girl," Alexis encouraged.

Bria poked her lip out. "I can't."

"Your mommy didn't teach you?"

"Hula hooping was not my thing. I can roller skate circles around anybody, though," Tiffany replied.

Alexis stood up and grabbed the larger hoop. "I'll show you, boo. Lexis was the hula hoop champ when she was little."

She swung the hoop to the left and her hips did the rest. Bria looked on in amazement, and after awhile, Alexis had to stop the hoop with her hand because it was still going.

"Freak," Tiffany said as Alexis and Bria prepared to leave.

"Maybe you need some lessons, too. If you up your hip game, you might get that ring you keep waitin' on." She smirked as Tiffany swatted, barely missing her arm.

"Nice meeting you," Venni said.

"You, too. I'll wave to you when y'all run by on Saturday."

When Alexis left, Venni looked at Tiffany. "Let me know if you need some help with your hip game. I know plenty of tricks." Tiffany frowned slightly. "With the hula hoop, nasty!" Venni finished.

Tiffany was still unsure of her angle, but fired back, "My hips move just fine, thank you."

"You right about that," Venni mumbled.

108

Tiffany had a taste for chocolate ice cream, so she offered Venni a bowl. "You like chocolate syrup on yours? I like chocolate on chocolate."

"There's no other way to go."

Tiffany kind of liked the word game they were playing, though she never meant to initiate it. After handing Venni the bowl, they changed topics, but her eyes stayed focused on Venni's lips as she took the ice cream slowly into her mouth and then licked the traces from her lips before she spoke. Those were the magic lips that kissed her precious pearl and sucked it until there was no more sensation left. If she wasn't a woman, Marlon could kiss their relationship goodbye.

She woke up from her daydream when he entered the house. She introduced him to Venni, who was now building Legos with Bryant.

"I've heard a lot about you," Venni said.

"Yeah, same here. I'm sure you've heard more than you needed to about me, though," Marlon joked.

"Your woman loves you. That's what it amounts to. And she's a *good* woman."

"That's what I've been trying to tell him!" Tiffany said.

"I knew that from day one," Marlon replied. "Y'all ain't tellin' me nothin'." He took off his hat and called the boys over to him. "Y'all gon' help me feed Billy or what?"

The boys jumped with glee, and the three guys were off to the backyard.

***

"Why am I the laughing stock of the whole gotdamn gym?" Marlon asked as he slammed his keys onto the kitchen counter.

"What? Don't come in here using that kind of language," Tiffany replied, nodding toward the living room where the kids were.

He walked within six inches of her and breathed heavily through his nose. "What happened the night of your party?"

Tiffany didn't flinch. She didn't even look up from the brownie mix she was stirring. "You were there. What do you mean?" She stopped stirring and held one finger in the air. "Oh, you wanna know what happened after you left to hang with your boys." She cut her eyes his way and placed her hand back on the spoon.

Marlon locked her wrist in place with his grip. "Don't play with me, Tiffany. For over a week now, people been whisperin' and gigglin' around me, but I didn't know what was goin' on. Finally today, my nigga, Aaron, came into my office and filled me in 'cause he didn't want me lookin' stupid no more."

"Filled you in on what?"

"You like girls?" She rolled her eyes and he tightened his grip. "Now ain't the time for that attitude shit. Did you mess around with that bitch from your job in our house? Was y'all up to somethin' when you had her in here the other day?"

"First of all, let me go." He did, and she pulled him further into the kitchen where the kids couldn't see. "Now, this is *my* house, and you ain't bought a damn thing in it. So, before you place your claim on it, pay the mortgage. If I had blowup dolls all around this place that I humped everyday at six o'clock, that's my business because this is all me right here."

Marlon used every bit of restraint in him to keep from grabbing the boastful arms that Tiffany used for emphasis. He usually excused the moments when she tried to act like Alexis, but she was pushing it today.

"You're asking about the night of my party. Did it ever occur to you that you wouldn't have to listen to hearsay if you would've stayed the whole time? I'm not entertaining this nonsense. If you were giving me more than three pumps and a bad attitude at night, maybe you wouldn't believe I'd look elsewhere. And since Aaron is so full of information, did he tell you that he asks if we can screw every time he sees me? I'll let you draw your own conclusion. If you believe that snake's story, leave. Call me and we'll work out the details of when you can see the kids."

As she studied Marlon's eyes, her heart river danced in her chest. He was fuming. She had pushed all of his buttons, challenging his role as a provider and pleasure-giver in their relationship. Though her complaints were valid, she wondered if she had taken it too far.

Without saying a word, Marlon turned on his heels and left, purposely knocking the bowl of brownie batter onto the kitchen floor on his way out.

"Why am I here?" he growled as he leaned against his Cutlass and looked at the house. The last time Tiffany tried to pull his card, he let her off with a warning. This time, he had to react. He would teach her a lesson. She may not have needed his money, but she needed him. Whether he was walking her home from school in their early days at Winfrey, changing her tire after she drove over a nail, checking the loud noise in the middle of the night, or taking care of the kids, she had always needed him.

It killed him to do it, but he got in his car, started the ignition, and backed out of the driveway. This would be the last time she'd test his manhood. He'd done too much for her and tolerated more than usual to keep their family intact; and she was pulling this? He didn't even want to think about the thousands of dollars he'd put into her ring—the ring that was about to be paid off. The jeweler could keep it, though, if he found out the rumors about Tiffany were true. His woman cheating on him with another female would be ultimate humiliation. Aaron had given him a lot to think about, but Tiffany did, too. Every time Tiffany came to the gym to see him, Aaron would stop her to say something. That didn't bother him until now. Was he trying to holler at his woman right under his nose? There were a few ways he could get his answers, and he would first start with his sisters.

Dap was the only one who could help him since she was at the party. She had no firsthand information because she left early, but she heard Tiffany danced with Aaron all night and was "getting freaky" with him on quite a few songs. Some people were saying they made out in the corner where they thought no one could see. She said she was waiting for more reliable sources before she blabbed to him, but since he asked…

She'd heard the lesbian rumor, but dismissed it without a second thought. She hadn't even heard of that Venni chick. "If you wanna worry about her doin' anybody, it'll be Aaron. I know a few girls who can't get enough of his ass. You really think your *good girl* would do that, though?" Dap asked.

Marlon shrugged. "Maybe she wanted to see what another man is like. I'm the only one she's been with." Dap frowned. "Don't look at me like that. I handle my business. I'm just sayin' she has some new people around her who could be putting somethin' in her ear."

"So what you gon' do?"

"Stay away from her 'til I figure this out. I'ma go get my clothes and stuff tonight."

Portia A. Cosby

9

Alexis:
Full of Surprises

"You got somethin' you need to tell me?" Robert asked as he hung his jacket in the hall closet.

I had just hung up with Tiffany after listening to another story about an exquisite lunch she had with Venni. She knew damn well I didn't care about some blackened tilapia with apricot sauce, topped with acorns or some dumb shit like that. I don't get my kicks from overpriced restaurants that serve food I can't even pronounce.

"What are you talkin' about?" I replied.

"That was your girl, Tiff, right?"

"Yeah. Why?"

He grunted, then chuckled just loud enough to piss me off. Before my patience ran out, he answered. "She hasn't tried to turn you out, has she?"

I was starting to get annoyed by the growing number of people asking me about my girl's sexuality. First, Tielle asked, and then a couple random chicks I know cornered me at the mall. Now Robert was running rampant with the rumor, believing it steadfastly.

"So what version have you heard?" I asked.

The story that circulated among the four o'clock barbershop patrons went like this: Tiffany had been experimenting with Frenchie since the beginning of October, but Frenchie got tired of teaching her the ropes and broke it off before Tiffany's birthday. Meanwhile, Venni was secretly lusting after Tiffany and took full advantage of the birthday girl's inebriation at the party.

113

That was the first time I'd ever heard a name associated with the bogus rumor. The red flags in my brain rose along with my eyebrows, as I linked the name that left Robert's lips with the one I'd been hearing from Tiffany's own mouth nonstop since she started working in her building. It finally made sense. Once people spotted Venni and Tiffany together on one occasion too many, she became the scapegoat. The gossip gatherers figured she had to be the one who "turned Tiffany out."

"Let me clear this up now before you go run your mouth to anybody else. Venni works in the same building as Tiff, and they hang out a lot now. That's all it is. They both like goin' to the ritzy places, so they're like long-lost sisters. Me and Tiff roll tight like that all the time, but nobody talks about us being gay because we've been close since high school."

Robert twisted his lips in disagreement.

"And the story probably got started by somebody who thinks like you. Me and Tiffany *been* lickin' on each other, let you tell it."

"You know I be playin' when I say stuff like that. And I ain't tryin' to keep no rumor goin'. I'm lookin' out for you. I don't like her anyway, so I won't hesitate to fight her like a man if she tries to take over my manly duties." He tried to keep a straight face, but couldn't hide the smirk that was fighting its way through.

I threw a pillow at him from my end of the couch, but I couldn't help but laugh, too. "I'ma start tellin' people that you and Romeo be pokin' each other."

"Nobody will believe that shit 'cause neither one of us is gay." His response implied much more than he verbalized, and he knew I had caught on. I must've looked as thrown-off as I felt. "You didn't know Venni is gay, baby?"

Hell naw, I didn't know! Venni looked like she should be judging Tyra Banks on whether *she* should be a top model. I'm not saying lesbians can't be pretty; it's just that Venni couldn't be a lesbian! There was no indication that she was into women. She was feminine in every way, almost like a Barbie doll with an edge. Her thin cornrows that fell about three inches past her shoulders were always flawless and accented with wooden beads, or she wore her hair in a simple ponytail that still complimented her beauty. According to Tiffany, she had a lifetime appointment slot with her manicurist at Pierre's Day Spa downtown and shopped at the upscale boutiques that most black folks don't even look twice at. And every time I saw her running, she always had fine-ass Lawrence by her side. I know those things don't really determine whether somebody is gay, but if I could come up with any argument to back up Venni's heterosexuality, it was him. There was no way she could be around that beautiful man and not cross the boundary between business and pleasure. Just thinking about his chiseled physique made me wanna go into debt paying him to work my ass out.

When I snapped out of my Lawrence daydream, I tuned back in to Robert's "I knew she was a freak when…" speech. As he named the people she normally hung out with and told stories he'd heard about her sexcapades, I cautiously watched two and two come together, and that shit was looking like four.

I would know if my girl is gay, wouldn't I? Tiffany couldn't be. She loved dick too much and dick loved her even more. Her three kids were proof of that! I caught myself thinking too long about it and was embarrassed. *If Tiffany knew I was entertaining this garbage, she'd snap.*

For the rest of the night, though, I couldn't shake the random flashbacks of my conversations with her. When I dragged her to Freddy's the day after her birthday, I remembered being confused when she said she cheated on Marlon with Aaron. I thought I was mistaken, but maybe I wasn't. I *did* see Aaron leave early, so there was no way he could've been in the room with her unless he returned through the back door. *Maybe that's why he was looking clueless when I mentioned Tiffany a while ago,* I thought. When I saw him at a bar and alluded to knowing their secret, I assumed he was trying to be discreet. But what if there was nothing to tell?

And she said he never said a word and didn't try to bone after he ate her out. EVERY man I know will at least make an attempt to get more than his tongue wet after giving a girl a few orgasms. What did he do? Jack-off in the bathroom and leave?

And why didn't he say anything? If he didn't talk before the act, he damn sure should've said something afterward. "That was good," "Give me a call," "Why'd you let me do that if you weren't gon' let me hit it?"…SOMETHING!

The lingering and most disturbing thought, though, was that no other guy at the party had cornrows or any other kind of braids. Tiffany was drunk as a skunk, but she remembered pulling on somebody's braids. I tossed and turned all night, wondering if it was Venni's braids she was yanking.

The next morning, I got dressed in record time and left the apartment without eating breakfast. I wasn't rushing because it was Friday and I wouldn't have to look at those two-faced bitches at work for two days; I just couldn't wait to get in my car so I could call Tiffany and get some answers. I didn't want Robert all in our conversation.

If Venni took advantage of my girl, knowing that Tiffany thought she was a dude, I was more than ready to meet her in their building's parking garage and whoop her ass. I had already counted the money in my emergency stash and had enough to cover my bail if she pressed charges instead of taking her beating like a real woman.

After three tries, I was pissed. Tiffany's voicemail played as soon as I finished dialing each time. I finally left a message. "Call me, tramp...ASAP."

It was 7:57 a.m., and Tiffany hadn't returned my call. I didn't want to be late for work again, so I gulped the last of my Tropicana fruit punch and entered hell. I waved at Marsha, the receptionist, as I hurried down the hall to the mailroom. As I stepped inside the wooden double doors, Charlene nearly ran into me. Instead of saying "Excuse me," she huffed and rolled her eyes. I took a deep breath and reminded myself that she was my boss. *Just don't say a word.*

Charlene looked at her watch. "Late again, huh?"

I looked at mine, then at the time clock across the room...7:59. "No, but I will be if you don't move so I can clock in."

She gasped quietly, removing all the air from her lungs, and rested her hand on her chest. Then once her foot grazed mine, she backed up, realizing she was in my personal space and obstructing my path to the time clock.

"You can stop clutchin' your pearls now," I said, while gliding by.

She understood my remark after she looked at her bare chest and heard Teesha snickering at her desk in the corner. I knew I should've kept my mouth shut, but I couldn't help it. She had been trying me since I started the job and expected me to deal with her menopausal mood swings and fifty-year-old hissy fits for ten dollars an hour.

As soon as I went to swipe my card, the green numbers changed...8:01. I glanced back at Charlene, who was wearing a smug smile. Practicing a self-control exercise I learned from Tiffany, I slid the card and silently walked to my desk.

3-2-1, 1-2-3. What in the world is bothering me? Five rounds of that surprisingly calmed me down, and I made a mental note to tell Tiffany that her stupid psychology stuff might really be legit.

I sorted through some paperwork and checked the two messages in my voicemail. Then it was time for my morning bullshit routine. It was my way of killing time before I actually had to start work. On mornings like that when Charlene tap danced on my nerves, I added on an extra two minutes just to cool down. I called it my "don't-fuck-her-up" tour.

The break room was my first stop. As usual, I stood in front of the vending machine, staring through the glass like something I actually

116

wanted would magically appear. Didn't work again. Next stop: the bathroom. I checked my hair, noticing that it was growing out a lot faster than I expected. *I gotta call Dee Dee so she can cut this shit,* I thought as I pulled at a few of the jet black strands.

When my phone vibrated on the counter and Tiffany's face flashed on the screen, I answered it right away. "What's wrong with your phone?"

"Nothin', girl. I turned it off last night and forgot it was off this morning. Marlon was the one who turned it on when he came to take the kids to school this morning. Do you know that fool went through my call log and text messages looking for another man's number?"

"What man?" I rushed down the hallway and stepped outside. "Did he find out about Aaron?" I tested.

"Naw, girl. Since he moved out, he's been paranoid. He thinks I'm screwing somebody else because I won't give him some. I'm like, 'Idiot, this is what people do when they're not together: nothing.' If I knew we would make love longer than a commercial break, he probably could've coaxed me into a little something last week. Oh! And now he calls himself being jealous of Venni. When he was in my call log, he saw that we talk a couple times a day and had a fit. He's pullin' a Robert. He swears I'm screwing her because we hang out now." She paused to sigh. "He hasn't been right since he heard that rumor."

I saw my opening and walked on through. "Speakin' of which, somebody else asked me about that."

When I thought about it, I noticed she was too nonchalant about such a serious rumor. From day one, she'd been shrugging it off like people were just saying she was pigeon-toed or had a big head.

"Are you absolutely positive that Aaron—"

I was interrupted when the glass door swung open and hit my back with deliberate force. As I turned around to see who had lost their mind, my phone slipped from my hand and landed on the concrete.

"Maybe that's a sign that you should be inside working instead of hiding out here talking on your phone," Charlene said as she stood in the doorway. "It is not break time, so I suggest you pray that your name is still on the payroll at the end of the day. I'm already writing you up for insubordination and being late again this morning. If I add this to the list, your career here is over."

I retrieved the plastic parts to my phone, thinking about how dumb I was for cancelling my insurance three weeks before. I thought five dollars was cutting into my budget, but the money for a replacement phone was going to *kill* my budget. In an instant, I grew angry from all the madness going on around me.

117

"I suggest *you* pray that I don't lay hands on you by the end of the day. Y'all bitches come out here every hour to smoke them cancer sticks and don't count those as breaks, but the non-smokers can't get a random five minutes outside? Fuck you. I'm on *my* smoke break."

I turned around and searched the grass for my battery cover, while Charlene continued her reprimand.

"Now you're threatening me?"

"No, I'm promising you. Don't think I didn't feel that metal door handle slammin' into my spine a second ago. You do shit passively. I don't. You can report me if you want, but I'll tell 'em you physically assaulted me and I responded verbally."

"You know, Alexis, I've tried to be understanding and sensitive to your emotions since Tameka passed, but you are impossible to deal with."

"This has nothin' to do with my sister. I'm sick of you actin' like I need this bullshit job or like this is a luxury career. I don't plan on doin' this for the rest of my life. Do you see me gettin' excited about the new postage machine or bein' territorial about my glue sticks and letter openers? This is your career. It's my pastime. So, I'll tell you what. Add this incident to whatever list you want, because I quit. I'ma mess around and kill you if I stay here another minute."

The silver battery cover glistened in the sunlight and caught my eye. I picked it up and put it in my pocket. "Write that shit down," I finished as I brushed past her and went to the mailroom to clean out my desk.

***

"Lexis, I can't believe you did that. Tell me this is April Fool's Day and you're just kidding," Tielle said as she rested her forehead in the palms of her hands.

When I didn't answer, she knew I was telling the truth. I knew I was wrong for acting out the way I did, but...Well, there was no good excuse. I still had bills, and I didn't know how I was going to pay them. My poor little résumé was full of jobs I had either quit or been fired from, so the chances of finding employment that didn't involve telemarketing or burgers and fries were slim.

The only reason I had the mailroom job was because Tameka pulled a couple strings and got me an interview. If she hadn't done that, I would've still been building displays, folding shirts, and cleaning out dressing rooms at JCPenney. Tielle's facial expression said exactly what I was thinking: *Meka would be so disappointed.*

I stared at the wall in front of me, which was a collage of singers and rappers from the past and present. To my right, autographs decorated a white wall-size poster with "WTIZ" printed boldly in gold. Each signature represented someone Tielle had interviewed or met randomly at the station.

A hint of envy swept over my spirit as I sat in the gray leather chair and observed my surroundings. Tielle's office was tight. The subtle hum of the bass line to Kanye West's "All Falls Down" penetrated the semi-soundproof walls, letting her hear just enough to recognize the song and sing along if she was having a bad day. Stacks of CDs sat unorganized in the far right corner, numerous piles of paperwork cluttered her desk, and the red light on her phone blinked repeatedly to alert her of the messages she had awaiting her attention. Hundreds of emails from listeners glowed on the computer screen and begged for a response from LT, the favorite female disc jockey on urban radio in our city.

"What's wrong?" Tielle asked.

"Just thinkin'." Tielle's raised eyebrows asked for more of an explanation. "This is your job," I said.

She looked at me like I was crazy.

"This is a cool-ass atmosphere, and it's your freakin' place of employment. You gettin' paid to do what you love to do."

"*Freakin'?*"

"Don't laugh at my self-improvement," I said as I trapped my own chuckle between my lips. "I'm tryin' to limit the cuss words to ten a day, and I know I went over that quota before nine o'clock. That's one of my substitute words."

Tielle made a poor attempt to straighten her face and look serious, nodding her head to be supportive. I gave her the finger.

"That's not improvement," she said.

"I'm starting with my words, not my gestures."

"Okay, but for real. What do you like to do? Once you figure out your passion and find a job you can apply it to, you'll feel like me."

It sounded easier than it actually was. I couldn't get past Point A. *What do I like to do that is job-worthy? Nothing.*

"You can burn in the kitchen. You ever think of doing something with that?" Tielle encouraged.

She knew that was a no-go from the way my eyes cut sharply in her direction. After we brainstormed for another five minutes, I stopped the torture.

"Tielle, don't worry about it. We can sit here all day and still come up with nothin'. I don't like to do nothin' besides run my mouth, and

I'm not about to do that in some call center, beggin' random people to buy a box set of *I Love Lucy* or *The Jeffersons* for $12.99 plus shipping and handling," I ranted.

"Okay. You're a people person, though. Let's run with that."

"Ain't nothin' to run with. My mouth works for me in everyday situations—not at a job. You see where it got me today. I'm your go-to person if you need to know a cute dude's name or who just moved into the empty apartment in the building. I ask people questions about the things everybody else is gossippin' about behind their backs. I'm bold and I'm honest. That's all I got. Now what the hell can I do with those qualities that'll keep Honda from repo'n my car?"

Tielle didn't know whether to laugh with the "outside me" or cry with the "inside me," but she definitely sympathized. She opened her mouth to respond.

"I might be able to come up with something." Eli's head fit comfortably between the door and its frame as he peeked into Tielle's office. He entered with authority but also with caution, being careful not to overstep his boundaries. "I'm sorry to interrupt, LT, but I couldn't help but hear your conversation when I was walkin' down the hall." He looked at me. "How you doin', Alexis?"

"You remember me?"

"Can't forget you, sweetheart."

You better stop flashing that Crest commercial smile at me, white boy, I thought, while taking notice of Eli's swagger that was very similar to the one almost all brothas have.

He sat on the corner of Tielle's desk closest to my chair. "You lookin' for a job?"

"What you got?" I asked.

"I can get you an internship here if you don't mind workin' in the radio industry."

"Doin' what? Is it paid?"

"Helpin' the deejays with various things, maybe answering some calls. Things like that. We might need you to help out with promotions from time to time. And we can pay you. The only catch is that you'll have the early morning shift."

"How much?"

"Nine."

"A minute or an hour?" I asked. He started to laugh until he saw I wasn't joking. I looked into his baby blue eyes. "Eli, I need a JOB. I got bills. I'm not a college student lookin' for a few extra dollars and class credit."

"You got experience?" he asked as he folded his arms.

Tielle spoke up. "She has plenty experience."

Question marks filled my wide eyes as I looked at her. She gave me a subtle wink and rolled with it.

"What kind of experience?" Eli inquired.

"She gets results...answers. For some reason, people talk to Lexis—even complete strangers."

"How does that benefit us?"

"You saw her at the New Year's party. Did you have nerve enough to approach Toni Valentine and ask her if she really had a butt implant like the tabloids reported?" She waited. "Nope. And I avoided her all night 'cause I didn't want to get caught examining her booty instead of making eye contact. But who walked right up to her, started a conversation, and got the scoop?"

I felt like patting myself on the back. I didn't think talking to Toni that night was anything special. I'd heard the rumors like everybody else, and since she was standing five feet away from me, I asked her if they were true.

"Who's the top urban station here?" Tielle asked Eli.

"We are."

"But who's closing in on us?"

He rolled his eyes. "WRDY."

"Why?"

"They're just the new thing right now. We have longevity."

"Wrong. They're hot because they have Tangie, who delivers the entertainment news. People love to tap into their favorite artists' personal lives."

"Nyce does our entertainment segment. We have that—"

"Nobody wants to hear a thirty-second synopsis about some stuff they already saw the previous night on *Extra*. You can't be serious right now, Eli. And Nyce isn't even into it. He's just doing it because he was assigned to it."

Forty-five minutes later, Tielle, Eli, and the Good Lord created a position for me. I was hired on a trial basis to cover entertainment news for WTIZ. I would have my own segment weekday mornings at 7:45 and 8:45. Eli said he'd give it a month to take off, but if it didn't, I'd have to settle for the intern position until I could work my way up.

I was determined not to mess up. Knowing I had the chance to have an office like Tielle's someday was enough motivation to make it to work on time, go beyond the call of duty, and blow Eli's mind.

Robert took me out to celebrate the next night. We ate at Ruth's Chris, then danced our food off at Club Dirty. It was nice to hang out like a real couple again, but I couldn't help watching him like a hawk after one o'clock. All it would take was one phone call to ruin our night. He was a smart man, because around closing time, I felt the phone vibrate on my booty when I was backing it up on him and he acted like he didn't feel a thing.

The night ended with a bang...literally. A good one, as usual. We tried to go to sleep after, but I couldn't tolerate the musty smell that was flowing from his armpit to my nose as we cuddled. I demanded that he take a shower and he insisted that I join him.

I hope he doesn't think we're goin' for round two, I thought as I threw back the covers and followed him to the bathroom.

I was just about to pull back the shower curtain, when I realized I didn't have a towel to dry off with. I ran through our room and into the hallway to get one from the linen closet. On my way back, I couldn't resist the opportunity that presented itself. Robert's phone was on the floor on top of his jeans, begging me to look through it. I peeked into the bathroom to make sure it was safe to snoop, and then I went for it. I had to see who called while we were at the club.

"I'ma be done by the time you get in here, baby," Robert yelled.

"You shouldn't be nowhere near being done—all that funk that was on you. I'm comin'."

I made it to his call log and saw the name "Davies" linked to the call received at 2:09 a.m. *Why does that name sound familiar?* I did the rest of my thinking in the shower, finally concluding that it must have been one of Robert's football buddies from college. They all called each other by their last names.

Around six o'clock, though, I sat straight up in bed. Davies was Monica's last name. It was on the envelope I found the pictures in months before. I could see it plain as day...the bubble-like cursive writing, the hearts in place of dots over her i's. *That shiesty bastard.*

I was too fired up to go back to sleep, so I walked laps around the living room. The biggest part of me wanted to call that bitch and cuss her out—tell her to leave my man alone. The other part of me was ready to pack my stuff and be out. Maybe Yari was right. *Why bother with the details? If I can't trust him, why the hell am I here? Because my hateful ass can't leave without making a scene.*

When Robert woke up, I acted like everything was fine. I didn't have to be around him long because he wanted to go work out before he left for Romeo's Super Bowl party. He had a semi-pro football tryout in a week, so he'd been dedicated to making sure his body is in its best shape by then. As he talked so enthusiastically about how he got his 40 time down to a 4.8, and how his broad jump was improving, it took everything in me not to ask if his Christmas workout with

Monica had anything to do with that. There was no need for questions, though—not directed at him. I wanted to talk to "Mo" to see if she had a different perspective of their relationship.

***

"Alright, boo, I'm out." Robert kissed me on the forehead and left. He wanted me to join him at Romeo's party, but I lied and said I didn't feel good.

In the hours that passed, I talked to Isaac and Tiffany, fried some chicken wings, and downloaded a few I'll-kill-you-if-you-cheat-on-me songs. I wondered why I was still sitting silently on the couch and not cussing the little bitch out in English *and* Spanish. I had the number and the opportunity, so what was the holdup? When I finally took off my mask, remembering I was at home alone where I didn't have to pretend, I was honest with myself. I was nervous. My daddy always told me and Tameka not to go looking for something we weren't ready to find, and I wasn't sure if I was ready for what I might hear on the other end of the receiver.

Fuck it. I gotta know, ready or not. I didn't block the number because it would look too shady. If she knew about me and didn't want confrontation, she wouldn't answer it. Every scared bitch avoids private calls.

"Hello?" a perky but desperate voice answered after one ring. She must've seen Robert's name on the caller ID.

I proceeded off the top of my head. "Yes, may I speak with Monica?" I asked, using my best fifty-something-year-old voice.

"Uhhhh…"

"I'm calling about Robert. This is his mother, Darlene."

"Oh. This is Monica."

Just what I thought…a scared bitch. "Sweetie, I'm just calling to see if you've heard from him. I've been trying to call him, but he hasn't been answering his phone. I'm in town visiting, and I need to ask him something about this high-tech dishwasher before I flood the place."

"Well…What made you call here? I don't know if you know, but I live in another state."

Think fast. "Oh, I'm sorry, honey." I chuckled like Ms. Darlene does when she makes a mistake. "Robert is on my cell phone plan and I noticed your number on there a lot. He told me who you were."

"He did? That's funny. He just started talking to me again about a month ago," Monica replied. "I've wanted to talk to you, but he won't give me your number."

"Oh?"

"Mrs. King, do you know you're a grandmother?"

"No, honey, you must be confused. His brother Kaleb has a son, but I'm not Kaleb's mother. I'm still waiting on one of mine to give me some grandbabies." I was playing the part so well, I was thinking of going to a casting call and joining Yari on the big screen.

"Kaleb has a son?"

"Yes…Shemar."

Monica said something in Spanish, her tongue moving a hundred flaps a second, then switched back to English. "So that's what he's telling people? Mrs. King, Shemar is my son—mine and Robert's."

The mama voice was gone. "WHAT?"

After I calmed her down and convinced her to stay on the phone, I got more details than I ever dreamed of. Monica was seventeen and lived in downtown Atlanta with her best friend. She confirmed Robert's story of how they met, but according to her, they had sex that night and kicked it the rest of the time he was there. Even though we weren't together then, it still bothered me that he had unprotected sex with a broad he didn't even know. Why? Because we got back together a week after he came home and were screwing…unprotected.

She claimed he never told her about me until she told him she was pregnant. I believed her. I believed the emails. I believed the voice that didn't want confrontation—just help. She was literally just a little girl who wanted help raising her son. Unfortunately, she got caught up with a lying jackass who only wanted to deal with his child from a distance so he could maintain his other relationship of three years.

"He kept telling me to stop calling because you were crazy and you already knew my address and phone number. All I wanted to know was when he was coming to see his son and how much money he could send each month," Monica explained.

"Well, lately, y'all have been havin' a whole lotta conversation about those issues…at two, three, and four in the morning."

"We weren't talking about that," Monica said quietly. "I've been in and out of the hospital, and Robert asked me to call to keep him in the loop. He told me to call between one and four."

Turns out, Monica was suffering from lupus and hadn't been able to take care of Shemar on her own since December, before Robert brought him to Texas. His way of helping out was to keep him for a week and then send him back to Monica's mother who was sixty, spoke minimal English, and had no transportation.

As we continued to share information, I dug through Robert's underwear drawer. I left the bedroom with a smile on my face, an agenda in my mind, and a platinum credit card in my hand. I plopped into the computer chair and interrupted Monica mid-sentence, asking what her schedule was the next day.

"I have class at eight, that's all."

I tapped away at the keyboard, plugging in dates on AirTran's website.

"You have your license, right?"

"To drive? Yeah."

"Can you get to the airport by eleven?" I asked.

"Huh?"

I briefed Monica on the plan. She was to leave class, go home to get Shemar, and board Flight 997 with nonstop service by 12:20 p.m. There would be a rental car reserved in her name that she could use to get to Robert's apartment. I told her not to worry about being underage because my buddy worked there and would handle that. Once she arrived at the apartment, she would find the key taped under the mat.

"He'll be at work, so make yourself comfortable. Just a couple things…Don't drink my Kool-Aid, don't eat my Cinnabons, and stay out of his bedroom. My stuff is still in there and I won't be able to get it all out tonight. Anything else around the house that looks like mine, stay away from it. You feel me?"

"That's fine. Wow. I like the way you think."

"Yeah, alright. Well…"

"What time will you be there tomorrow? Before he gets home?"

"I won't be there. We're not friends, sweetie. I will not be your welcoming committee. It's all good while we're talkin' on the phone right now, but I'm not ready to see you in person, baby girl. I'll make arrangements to get my stuff outta here. This right here is to get back at Robert, not create a fuck-him-girl sisterhood between us. Wrong is wrong. He should face his responsibilities like a man and stop pretending this shit didn't happen. Shemar is here. He's real, and you are, too. Maybe y'all can work somethin' out. It must've been love at first sight since y'all fucked the first—" A slow deep breath. "Just do what you need to do for you and yours, 'cause I'm done with him."

My voice quivered with that last statement. It was time to get off the phone because Monica was the last person I'd allow to hear me break down.

After we hung up, my emotions were all over the place. I wanted to cry, but I couldn't stop smiling as I looked at the computer screen. One confirmation for a one-way plane ticket that totaled $246.19 and another confirmation for a rental car reserved for a week at the cost of $163.60, all courtesy of Robert C. King, cardholder with Capitol One since 2001. Soon, my satisfaction was gone, and as uninvited tears rolled down my cheeks, I wanted revenge.

It was time to go shopping. By the time I got done, little Shemar had all the clothes, bottles, Diaper Genies, bedding, and furniture he'd need to set up shop at Daddy's house—next day delivery via American Parcel Express. The payback could only get sweeter if Robert had to deliver the items right off his truck!

I drove around for a half hour, riding past Romeo's place twice. I had the spray paint and brick ready, but it wasn't enough. Damaging Robert's car wasn't enough. I wanted to damage him, and the online spending spree was a damn good start. His football career was next on my list. I envisioned myself busting him in the knees with a baseball bat in a Tonya Harding-like attack...the sweetest revenge.

I found myself standing on Tiffany's porch with my overnight bag. I could hear her screaming, so I wondered if the Patriots scored another touchdown. *I'm not trying to ruin her night*, I thought as I contemplated where else I could go.

My cell phone rang, almost scaring me to death. I dug it out of my purse and looked at the screen. "What's up?" I answered.

"You watchin' the game, girl?" Tiffany asked.

"Naw. What's happenin'?"

"It's halftime right now. Janet and Justin are performing."

"I'm at your door."

"What?" She peeked through the blinds for confirmation.

After I stepped inside, Tiffany bopped over to the living room and danced like she knew the routine. As funny as her performance was, though, my anger wouldn't let me crack a smile. I put my bag down and tried to look like nothing was wrong. She was engrossed in the TV, so I had plenty of time to get it together.

"Oh my goodness!" she yelled all of a sudden. She stood in the middle of the floor with her hand over her mouth. "Lexis, did you see that?"

I walked to where she was. "Un unh."

"He just ripped her shirt and her tittie was waving to the camera!"

Now that made me laugh. Tiffany explained it to me in detail, then replayed it on TiVo. Once she got over the halftime hoopla, she looked at my face and then at my bag.

"Aw hell! You hiding from the cops? You got your getaway bag; your face is all twisted up. Did you run into Jacqueline?" I shook my head. "Dap?"

I told her everything.

126

"You wanna go get your stuff now? I told you he wasn't right. I knew *somethin'* was goin' on. You ain't gotta take that mess from his sorry ass. What do you need him for? We're independent women, honey. You can do bad by yourself!" Tiffany fussed, while putting on her sneakers and searching the living room for her keys.

I sunk into the thick cushion of her loveseat and had the deepest revelation of my life. "I'm not independent. I don't have shit. Where am I supposed to sleep tonight?"

I laid on my side, face buried in my hands, and cried like Tameka died all over again. *Tameka,* I thought. My dependency on others was her pet peeve, but she was always there to pick up the pieces when I messed up. I should've been sitting on her couch, listening to her scolding about my immaturity or something. More tears. It sunk in. My lifeline was gone, and the man who was supposed to be my backbone had scoliosis like a motherfucker.

Tiffany froze. What could she say? I was right. I had absolutely nothing to my name. No apartment, no job, no family in town. My cell phone was even on Robert's account. Finally, she spoke.

"You know you can stay here. Don't say you don't have anywhere to go. Are you actually thinking about staying with him because he has an apartment?"

"Hell no," I assured her. "I'll sleep in my car if it comes down to it. It's the only thing that's mine." We sat in silence, the Super Bowl commercials making the only noise for a while. "I want my sister."

I pulled out my cell phone, went to my phonebook, and stared at the entry I never deleted—MEKA. "I want my fuckin' sister!" I said louder.

All the emotion I had suppressed since 1:54 a.m. Thanksgiving morning spilled onto Tiffany's shoulder as she sat beside me, searching for something to say. I was weak—a feeling I'd never felt before—and I didn't like it. I'd won the game, caught Robert in his lies. So why didn't I feel like the champion of the world?

10

Tiffany:
Here For You

It wasn't long before Tiffany's shirt was soaked. She didn't know what to do. Alexis was the strongest person she knew, and seeing her vulnerable was shocking. Since Alexis didn't have that strong of a reaction when her sister died, Tiffany concluded that her breakdown was over much more than Robert. Her friend was realizing that her tough-girl image was just that—an image—and she was now a part of the human experience that included emotions and situations you can't always control. A good fist-fight or cursing-out had solved everything and protected Alexis from life up until now.

This was the first time Alexis felt defenseless enough to think of needing Tameka, and she broke when she remembered she wasn't around. She was finally feeling everything she should've felt at the hospital, the wake, the funeral. Tiffany should've seen it coming, Alexis spent so much time pretending to be strong and hadn't mourned her sister's death. Robert's infidelity was just the straw that broke the camel's back.

Tiffany let Alexis vent—blame Robert for everything that had gone wrong in her life since they met. She even went as far as blaming him for Tameka's death. True, their argument made her ten minutes late getting to the condo, but who's to say she would've rescued her sister with bullets blazing from her gun? What if she would've arrived just in time to join her sister in the cemetery?

That's the last thing she wants to hear, Tiffany thought.

"Listen to me," she started. Alexis maintained her position, tucked safely between Tiffany's cheek and shoulder. "You knew about Robert. Deep down, you knew. Today you got your confirmation. He didn't play you. He thought he did, but you found out. He played himself. Kids ain't no joke. Now he has to take care of a child when he acts like a little boy himself. They gon' be fighting over the Playstation! Can you picture that?"

Alexis chuckled a little, relieving Tiffany as she continued. "I told you he was up to something. I've known it all along. That's why he doesn't like me. But see, he did this to himself. It was only a matter of time. While he was so annoyed with me calling you, he should've been focusing on his own call record with Miss Thing. I hope I run into him somewhere. I can't wait."

She sat her friend upright. "Can we please go get your stuff now? This chapter of your life is done. You're putting ellipses where you need to slap three exclamation points. Don't drag out the inevitable."

"I told you not tonight. He's not gon' see me like this. I just wanna go to sleep. I need to end this day."

"Do you hesitate to flush your shit down the toilet?" Tiffany asked as Alexis raised her right eyebrow. "Then don't hesitate to get rid of that piece of shit either. I'll give you tonight because I know you're hurting, but tomorrow, you need to grab your nuts and make this ending official. Ain't that what you tell me? Grab 'em. My offer still stands to go get your stuff now. I'll go by myself. I wish he would say something crazy to me."

Alexis toppled over, her head landing in Tiffany's lap this time. "I hate him!"

A loud shriek followed her words—the exact noise Tiffany wanted to release when her nervous system reacted to Alexis' face touching her thigh. The tingles tickling her fancy were too much like the ones she felt when Marlon touched the butterfly tattoo on her pelvis. She rested her hand on Alexis' back and stroked from her shoulder blades to her lower back…slowly…deliberately.

"I'm gonna go to bed," Alexis said, easing off of her friend's leg. "I feel like one of your damn kids," she joked. "I got you pattin' my back like I just got cut from the cheerleading squad or somethin'."

They shared a laugh as Tiffany led her to the guestroom. "It's all yours." She flipped the light switch and started to close the door, but peeked in one last time. "And you're sure you don't want me to go to the apartment, right?"

Alexis opened the door wider and smiled. "If you don't take your crazy ass to bed…"

She reached out and hugged her friend—her homegirl who always had her back. She couldn't help but tear up just a little as Tiffany squeezed with sincerity. Tiffany melted into their embrace, absorbing her friend's distress and anger.

"Alright, Tiff! I'm not about to commit suicide or nothin'. You can let me go." Tiffany quickly released her and tried not to look as awkward as she felt. "I'm not tryin' to hurt your feelings. I'm just sayin'—you hugged me like it's the last time you'll ever see me. I'm goin' to sleep—not to the Promise Land."

Well, I'm glad that's how you took it, Tiffany thought as Alexis turned back with her fist extended.

"Thanks," Alexis said. Short, sweet, and sincere, her word of gratitude was accompanied by a slight smile and a bump to Tiffany's knuckles with her own.

As she retreated to the living room, Tiffany took a deep breath. That was close. She didn't mean to hold her like that. She would never make a move on her best friend. She would never make a move on a female.

***

The elevator bell rang loudly in Tiffany's ear and reverberated in her brain just enough to enhance the headache she suffered through all day. It was only Thursday, and the thought of one more day dealing with everyone else's problems was enough to make her want to scream. Two of her clients were pregnant—one by her stepfather and the other by her boyfriend who'd just been awarded a life sentence for the grand act of murdering a teacher at their school. Then there was Ashley, a sixteen-year-old who would be gorgeous if she gained some weight and stopped thinking eighty-six pounds was sexy on her 5'8" frame.

As the doors opened, she stepped into the empty box and leaned against the back corner. There was no relief. No way to simply go to the bottom floor and leave her cares on the fourteenth.

Though she really didn't mind, she knew she'd go home and listen to the latest development in the Robert and Alexis drama. She wondered which way it would go today. Did he leave four new messages cussing Alexis out because he was stuck with Monica and Shemar? Five messages threatening to report her to the police for credit card fraud? Or six messages begging her to talk to him so they could work it out? Alexis' recap of their conversation would almost be funny, but Tiffany could read through Alexis' sarcastic humor and see how much she was hurting.

131

Tiffany had problems of her own, though. For some reason, she was looking at Alexis differently, noticing the round backside that one wouldn't expect on her petite frame and the hips that stuck out just enough to support it; the tattoo of the dime etched just above her crack, suggesting that she was a "10"; the way she walked with more of a switch when she was mad; her almond-shaped eyes that threatened anybody who tried to stare into her soul; the tapered lining of her haircut that exposed her slim neck and invited an interested party to gently kiss it until she begged for mercy.

I've got to stop hanging around Venni so much, Tiffany thought. Their playful banter was clearly messing with her mind. She couldn't be gay. People are born gay. That's what she learned in class. There had been hundreds of studies about it. Frenchie even did her thesis on it! She said she knew since kindergarten that she liked girls. But if left up to Tiffany's family, church members, or close friends to decide, they would declare the opposite—that it was a decision. If that was true, she could be ruled out without question. Why would she decide to be gay? She hadn't met a penis she didn't like, although she'd only had sex with one man other than Marlon.

The analyst in her couldn't simply chalk her feelings up to being confused. It had to be more complicated than that. Venni made her feel like no man ever had, and now she was questioning her sexuality. Could one night make her gay, or was she like a fiend, looking for that same high, associating it only with women now? After all, receiving oral sex was her favorite pastime and the sure-fire way for Marlon to get back in her good graces whenever he messed up. And was her growing friendship with Venni adding to the problem? She enjoyed their time together, even the subtle flirting on Venni's end. It was the ultimate boost to her ego to know she was attractive to both sexes. So that would just mean she was starving for attention. Marlon sure wasn't giving it to her anymore, right? No…that didn't explain her new appreciation for the female physique.

Soon, she had it. With the growing acceptance of lesbianism in the U.S., only one thing could be true: every woman had the potential to be gay. Women open up to each other with ease, are comfortable showing affection toward each other, and have no qualms about complimenting each other on their looks. Just a week ago, she recalled telling Alexis that her new shirt made her breasts look bigger. She wasn't hitting on her, but she noticed.

Every woman notices. That means we're all one experience away from being attracted to each other, she thought.

For some women, it was sexual abuse or physical abuse that sent them into the arms of another woman. Others were just fed up with the Mars/Venus deal, feeling that no one would understand their feelings better than someone like themselves. Then there were women like her—unexpectedly given a sample of life on the "other" side—confused out of their wits. And even after deducing her theoretical interpretation, she was confused as ever.

BOONG! The elevator stopped abruptly at the tenth floor, interrupting Tiffany's thought pattern. Venni stood at the open doors with a smile. "Hey, you." She joined Tiffany at the back as she arranged the papers that were sticking out of her laptop bag. "What are you doing here so late?"

Keep it short and sweet, Tiffany thought. "Got stuck finishing paperwork. It's been a long day."

"Oh, I can definitely relate. I should've been gone two hours ago, but one of our databases had a glitch. Then, the new guy's computer crashed and I had to bring it back to life. If his perverted ass wasn't looking at porn all day, it probably wouldn't have shut down. You should've seen his face when the system recovered and all those freaky websites showed up in his log. Animal Love, Hot Teen Farmer Boys…"

Tiffany couldn't help laughing. "What did you say when you saw them?"

"I didn't say anything. I just looked at him and shook my head."

"He'll probably resign tomorrow!"

"Yeah, and go hump a cow or something."

They shared another laugh and Tiffany realized it was the first time she'd laughed all day.

"You wanna grab some dinner? I'm going to Flamingo Rose," Venni asked as they exited the building.

Tiffany hesitated to answer at first, but then remembered that Marlon and the kids were at his mom's for dinner. Although she was supposed to join them, she decided to dine with Venni. She didn't want to be bothered with Miss Tina's ridiculous stories and useless chatter about the latest plot twists in her favorite soap operas anyway—not today. And even though Marlon had calmed down and moved back in, their interaction was still a little constrained. Dinner with Venni would definitely provide a more relaxed atmosphere. To avoid conflict, she stepped back into the lobby where it was quiet and called Marlon, telling him she was still working and would get some food on her way home.

Flamingo Rose was a new restaurant designed only for the elite.

Located just a few blocks from their building, it sat in downtown's busiest area and fed many local celebrities, millionaire businessmen, and people like Venni and Tiffany who had the money to blow every once in a while.

"I've always wanted to come here, but Marlon is so tight with money. He ignores me every time I mention this place," Tiffany said as they sat at a circular table for four.

"This is only my second time eating here," Venni replied. "Those broke girls at my job look at me like I asked them to donate an organ whenever I invite them here for lunch. If they had any class, they'd know I was paying since I asked them to join me." She shrugged. "I knew you'd be down, though."

"I'm always down to eat."

"Oh yeah?" Venni asked with a subtle smile that contradicted the sexual connotation of her remark.

Tiffany didn't know how to react, so she didn't. "Do you know if their salmon is any good?" she asked, staring at the menu.

"I hear it is," Venni answered, noting Tiffany's discomfort.

They ordered their entrees and made small talk while they waited. Venni asked Tiffany what her and Marlon's Valentine's Day plans were. After her eyes did a 360, Tiffany waved her hand.

"He claims he has a big night planned, but I'll believe it when I see it. He's never made a fuss over it any other year. He just buys me flowers and candy so he doesn't have to hear me whine."

"Maybe you'll get that ring you've been waiting for."

"That's what I'm hoping. I'm long overdue after six years, three babies…"

"If you don't mind me asking, what happens if you don't get a ring?" Tiffany looked into Venni's always attentive eyes, unable to give her an answer. Venni sympathetically shook her head. "Wow."

"What?"

"Judging by the look on your face, you would've thought I asked you what you would do if one of your kids died. That amazes me how women let men control their destiny." Tiffany tried to interject, but Venni continued. "You won't *really* be happy until he makes you his wife. It just bothers me how men think sometimes. Why do you have to wait for each holiday to come around to see if he'll man-up? He didn't wait to put all those babies in you, did he? Did he hold off until Veteran's Day or Cinco de Mayo?"

As Tiffany's eyes diverted their focal point to the linen napkin resting on the table, Venni backed off. "You know, I'm sorry. I've overstepped my boundaries. I'm in no position to judge your

134

relationship. You two have history, and sometimes that's stronger than anything else."

"Is it really, or is that what we're conditioned to believe? You're right. I have been depending on his proposal to complete me, and…"

As Tiffany continued, Venni became distracted. She directed her full attention to two women walking toward them who were being escorted to a table nearby. It wasn't the short sista's fierce haircut and gorgeous face that made her stare; and although the taller Puerto Rican beauty was absolutely stunning, she wasn't interested in getting to know her. She already knew her. She knew both of them…she thought.

Tiffany stopped talking once she realized Venni wasn't listening. She looked at the females, wondering why Venni was so engrossed. *Does she think they look better than me?* she questioned. *Why do I care?* she questioned again.

The women sat three tables away and seemed to be having a business meeting of sorts. The Latina was busy maneuvering her stylus around her Palm Pilot, while her counterpart flipped through a weekly planner and penciled in information from time to time. Venni's eyes still held their position, but almost stared through them, a sign that her mind was a million miles away.

If she had longer hair, a fuller face, and was ten years younger…And if G was four inches shorter…Damn, she grew! Venni thought.

Suddenly, the waiter rushed to the table, blocking her view. "Sorry, ladies. Would you like more wine while you wait for your meals?"

After he poured, Venni asked a favor of him. "Can you ask those ladies if they know anyone named Holly or G?"

He obliged.

"Do you know them?" Tiffany asked as the waiter went in the opposite direction.

"I think." She looked nervous, almost uncomfortable, and Tiffany wondered if she should feel the same.

Even in the dim light, it was apparent that the ladies were horrified when the waiter relayed Venni's question. He pointed to their table, but the black lady refused to look their way and seemed to chastise her more curious friend for trying to do so. It wasn't long before the anxious Latina stood before Venni and Tiffany.

"So who wants to know if we know—"

"G, it's me," Venni said, looking deep into the woman's eyes.

The woman returned the gaze. "Naomi?"

It was one of the weirdest things Tiffany had ever witnessed. Was "Naomi" Venni's middle name or her real name for that matter? She listened carefully to their conversation and wondered if she was witnessing the reunion of three women who hid a body and ran off to separate parts of the country. Everything fit. It had been years since they'd seen each other, they had aliases, and they were discussing a man named Cole who sounded like he was their boss at one time. No! Tiffany had it! Cole was the ex-boyfriend Venni had all the miscarriages with. He was probably abusive, and one day, Venni accidentally killed him. The women were her childhood friends who helped her hide his body.

G summoned Holly to the table. She recognized Venni, but didn't seem too excited to see her. Nevertheless, the waiter made accommodations to seat the four women together. Venni briefly introduced Tiffany as her friend, and the catch-up session began. Who was married or single; who had children; who had sworn off men; who went to college, etc.

After all the niceties were finished, an awkward silence haunted the table before Venni spoke up. "So you haven't heard *anything* from him?" Her question was directed at Holly, who still seemed guarded.

Holly glanced at Tiffany before answering. "No. That was the whole point of leaving, right?"

"You never did, did you?" G asked.

"Hell no. He wasn't gonna find me out in the sticks of Louisiana," Venni replied, as they laughed. "Where did y'all go?"

"Orlando," G answered. "Even if he did find us there, my cousin Julio had something for him. We still live there now and so does Julio!"

Holly kicked her under the table—a grandiose move everyone was aware of.

"H, we were in that mess together. Do you think I would tell somebody where you are if they asked me?" Venni said with sincerity. She turned to Tiffany. "Sorry we're talking around you. We just know a mutual asshole from way back."

"I know plenty of them!" Tiffany replied. As more of the pieces fit into her fabricated story, she was convincing herself that her new calling was to work behind the scenes of *Unsolved Mysteries*. "So you two are from Florida, huh? What brings you here?"

"We're here on business," Holly answered quickly. Venni's eyebrows rose. "Y'all work for the same company?"

"Pretty much."

Tiffany's business cell phone rang loudly in her tote bag. "Excuse me, ladies," she said, while frantically rummaging through the sack full of junk...Bria's long-lost hair bow, Tony's bouncy ball, an old electric bill, the book she was supposed to read for her book club a month ago.

She managed to balance everything in her lap while she checked her voicemail.

G pointed to the book when she was done. "Is that good?"

"Girl, yes! I didn't have much time to read it while I was finishing school, but I've been able to jump back into it the past few days. I'll be done soon, so I hope she has another one coming. It's one that has to have a sequel, you know?"

Venni's two acquaintances exchanged a weird look. "Can I?" the sassy señorita asked. Holly shook her head no. "What will it hurt? Stop being so paranoid," she said to Holly, before turning to Tiffany. "This is the author of that book, KeKe Red."

Holly looked at G, and there was no question how she was feeling. "Why would you do that? The whole point of the penname is to remain low key, and you can't keep your mouth closed after only two months?"

"If it means anything, I won't tell anybody I met you," Tiffany said cautiously.

"Thank you, Tiffany. I'm glad you're enjoying the book. There's just a reason why I write under a pseudonym, and I feel very strongly about my privacy," Holly replied as she glared at G. "Excuse me." She left the table and headed toward the powder room in the lobby.

"She really doesn't think it's over, does she?" Venni asked.

"Keyonna—I mean, Holly—is just afraid that he'll pop up and ruin everything she has going. If her husband or daughters find out...I don't know. She has more at stake than we do. You left before she got—" The chatty woman caught herself.

Tiffany stood up. "I'll let you ladies finish. I have to return this call."

Jenny did sound frantic. All Tiffany could make out in her message was that her father was getting out of prison in two weeks and he called to let her know. This was the same father who molested Jenny and her little sister up until he was convicted of armed robbery three years prior.

Tiffany stood in a corner by the entrance, hoping Jenny picked up. She had been suicidal before, and the news of her father's early parole was more than enough reason for her to try one more time.

**

Holly exited the bathroom. As she placed her lipstick in her purse and rounded the corner, she ran into the back of a man. They both apologized.

"I'm probably in a bad spot anyway," he said.

137

Their brief glance turned into a gaze of familiarity. Holly dismissed her own thoughts as she walked toward the dining area.

"Noel!"

She instinctively turned around. It *was* him. Craig Thomas was her teenage love—her long-lost love—and he was standing three feet away from her. He approached with caution.

"Sorry for yelling. I don't know if you remember me, but—"

"Do you really believe I'd forget you, Craig?"

He smiled the smile that captured her when they first met in Chicago. He had so many questions…Did she live there? What was she doing now? Was she still in touch with Gabi? How old was her daughter now? She wanted to ask if he had any children, but the sensitivity of the subject stopped her.

"You still look good," he said, admiring the body that was much different than her sixteen-year-old frame.

"You, too."

He pointed to her wedding ring. "You didn't…"

"No. *Hell* no, I didn't marry him."

Craig reached into his back pocket and handed her a business card. "We should catch up. Will you give me a call?"

"I probably won't," Holly replied as Jacqueline joined Craig.

"I'm ready, Hon." Jacqueline linked her arm with Craig's.

Tiffany watched their introductions from the corner, wondering how Craig knew Venni's friend; but the most important question was: Why was Craig having dinner with Jacqueline?

She made her way over to the trio. "Hey, Craig! What are you doing here? Who's your friend?" *You need to know that I see you, negro, and I will be briefing Alexis when I get home*, she thought.

"I'm Jacqueline," Miss Priss said, showing all her teeth.

"Oh! I thought you looked familiar."

"Yeah, you do—"

"You were the one stalking my best friend's sister!" Tiffany was still smiling, but Jacqueline wasn't, as her head jerked in every direction. "She's not here. Don't worry."

Craig was visibly embarrassed. Tiffany patted his arm on her way back to the dining area. "Have fun with that."

Holly slipped away with Tiffany, only to find Craig's business card sticking out of the unzipped portion of her purse. Did she really want to reopen that can of worms?

The evening ended with the ladies dispersing in the parking lot and Venni walking Tiffany to her car. "Guess going out for drinks is out of the question, huh?"

Tiffany nodded. "I already missed tucking my babies in."

"Note to self. Find somebody to tuck me in," Venni replied. "See you tomorrow?"

"Yeah, if you can find me under the stack of work I have waiting on me."

"I can find you anywhere." She winked and walked to her silver BMW convertible, two cars away. "Drive safely!"

11

Alexis:
Absolut, Take Me Away

It was Friday, and I made it through my first week of work with no problems. "What's the Word?" debuted Monday with me sitting nervously behind the mic, knowing that my job depended on listeners liking my approach to entertainment news. Tielle gave me a pep talk beforehand, encouraging me to relax and be myself. She made sure to stress that I had to watch my mouth, though. I had no problems with doing so, and that stipulation was proof that the job was perfect for me and my self-improvement campaign.

If I wanted to keep my car, I had to keep my job. If I wanted to keep my job, I had to be mindful of the FCC. According to Tielle, they were fairly lenient until Justin showed Janet's tittie to the world. I was cleaning up my foul mouth until the Robert ordeal took place, but even when I was doing good, I had a few slips. With the pressure on, I thought I was going to throw up, but once I read my first sentence, I relaxed and felt right at home. After my first day, I was convinced I'd found the perfect career.

The job had been a wonderful distraction from thinking about Robert's new family and his numerous phone calls. I guess he wasn't pleasantly surprised when he found Monica and Shemar sitting in his living room Monday evening after he got off work, because he'd been blowing my phone up. I had only talked to him once, and that was only because he kept calling the radio station, and I didn't want to be fired over his nonsense.

141

He was stunned to hear that I hadn't listened to the majority of the voice messages he'd left. After the first five, the ones that followed were repetitive and pointless, so I didn't listen to any more. As far as I was concerned, there was nothing he could say that would make me want to forgive him, move back in, or even talk to him...or at least that's what I thought.

Don't ask me how, but he convinced me to go to his apartment so he could explain the whole story. Part of me wanted to hear what he had to say, but really, I wanted to get the rest of my things and some of the things I'd bought him throughout the course of our relationship. There wasn't a damn thing I could do with his big-ass pants, manly watch, and size 12 shoes, but I'm vindictive like that.

The next day, I banged on his door, wondering if Monica was going to answer. I still wasn't sure if I could see her without instinctively slamming her head into the doorframe one good time or kicking her in the coochie she so easily let my man slide up in. Luckily, she wasn't there. Robert said she had gotten sick three days before and had been in the hospital since. I could tell he wasn't lying because he looked stressed. I could only imagine how many times he'd been getting up with Shemar in the middle of the night, not knowing what the hell to do to get him back to sleep.

The vibe between us was awkward. He didn't know whether he wanted to strangle me or hug me, so he did neither.

"Well," he said.

I waited a while, but he said nothing else. "Well...you gon' talk or what? If not, I'll just grab the rest of my stuff and go."

"I was lookin' for an apology, but—"

My icy glare froze his tongue. He found it best to shut up and be thankful his credit card was the only thing that felt my wrath. With my baseball bat still leaning in the back corner of his closet, one wrong word could've had him picking fragments of his kneecaps out of the carpet.

His tone changed. "I didn't mean for you to find out like this."

"No, let's rephrase that. You didn't mean for me to find out— period."

"We weren't together when it happened, Lexis."

"Right. But we were together when you lied about those pictures she sent you. We were together when she told you she was pregnant. We were together when you were gettin' late-night updates on how your boo was feeling and texting like you were a data entry specialist. You lied right to my face when I asked you what was up. It's not so much that you lied, either. Everybody lies. It's how far you took the lie. Kaleb's baby? You had me watchin' your son like a fuckin' idiot."

"I was afraid of losing you."

"I swear all y'all niggas read the same cheating man handbook with the age-old, tired-ass comebacks. The problem is y'all too stupid to realize they don't work," I said, while heading to what used to be our bedroom. "And you know what's really crazy? Her mom could get you for statutory rape if she wanted to. What kind of man are you, bonin' a seventeen-year-old? That's nasty as hell."

"She's in college. She's not seventeen, so talk what you know."

"Oh, I know. You and your dick just assumed she was eighteen when she said she was a freshman in college. I got the scoop. You just hooked up with a child prodigy. Baby girl—pun intended—just turned eighteen last month. I should've bought a crib for her little ass, too."

"Okay. You wanna act like the innocent party here? Don't think I don't know how much you and Isaac talk and text."

"Apples and oranges."

"Why, 'cause it's not late at night?"

"I have plenty reasons. Because you never told me it bothered you; because we don't whisper sweet nothings to each other; because we haven't had sex; and because we don't have a kid that I have to justify to you. Try again."

Robert tried a little bit of everything. More blaming, then begging, pleading, yelling, crying. Nothing affected me, even though I had never seen him cry.

His final question was, "What can I do to fix this?"

"Go to hell," I answered without blinking.

His phone rang, but he didn't take his eyes off me.

"Answer it. We're done. And like I told you over the phone, this was a waste of my time."

He glanced at his screen, while I gathered my purse and two trash bags. "Lexis, wait. I have to answer this."

I stopped, but didn't turn to face him.

"Hello?" A pause. "Yeah, speaking." A longer pause. "What?" A hint of panic. "She's what? No, I just talked to her an hour ago."

I turned around. Robert had his hand on his head, and his face looked like it did in his four-year-old Easter Sunday picture when he cried because he didn't want to say his speech.

"What am I supposed to do?" he asked, sounding like a four-year-old, too. He lowered himself onto the couch and rested his head in his lap.

Did Mrs. King die or something? I thought, as my mind flashed back to the doctor pronouncing Tameka dead.

"Who's gonna take care of this baby?" he asked the person on the other end.

At that point it was apparent that Monica had lost her battle with lupus. I stayed until Robert hung up the phone, but had no clue what to say. Instinct: "That's what you get." Decorum: "I'm sorry to hear that."

I went with the latter. As he looked up at me, I saw myself. I saw the shock of hearing someone close to you died. I saw the need for comforting words or a hug—the need for someone to snap their fingers and reverse the situation. I couldn't offer him any of those things, so I turned back around and left.

I was almost home when I remembered I had a meeting with Pastor Johnson. It was session three of my grief counseling, which I still didn't think I needed. I wasn't grieving any more. I was just pissed that Tameka was gone. Wouldn't that qualify me for anger management? Pastor Johnson was a cool guy, though, so I didn't mind stopping in to talk to him once a month.

He'd been on me about joining one of the ministries at church, but I told him we had to take baby steps. When I reminded him that my language still fell short of the kingdom at times, I imagine he pictured me cussing somebody out for ignoring me at my ushering post and agreed wholeheartedly. Getting to the sanctuary on time every Sunday was new for me. He needed to take that as progress and accept anything else as a bonus.

One of Robert's favorite songs played on the radio as I sat at the red light. *Maybe I shouldn't have left him like that,* I thought. If I hadn't already experienced death, I probably wouldn't have had any sympathy for his cheating ass. But since I did, my conscious was tugging at my heartstrings, telling me to call him. I reached for my phone in the cup holder, but it was already ringing. The alert said I had ten text messages. When I retrieved them, I saw it was really just one very long message that was broken up by the phone company.

I knew u wouldn't answer ur phone, and that's cool. I figure u won't ignore a txt msg cuz it's 2 tempting 2 read. All I have to say is FUCK U. U just walked out on me after I found out Shemar don't have a mom no more & that proves u don't have a heart, u selfish bitch. It's all about u all the time. U told me I nvr luv'd u. U nvr luv'd me if u can hold on to some stupid shit during a time like this. I got u Lexis. U ain't gotta ignore my calls no more either. I'm done wit ur ass. I wanna see u try to find a better man than me. Yeah I messed up, but I'm human. U just mad cause u thought I was a cake ass nigga who

144

would nor play u. U had ur fun, I had mine. I just got caught up. Ain't nobody gon take care of u like I did. Tiff gon get tired of u stayin wit her then where u goin? Meka ain't here to rescue u no more. LT don't wanna b bothered wit u. Ur credit is messed up so nobody gon lease u a damn thing. Good luck wit that, Miss Lexis. Have fun n the real world.

The car behind me honked its horn. When I saw the light was green, I proceeded to the church parking lot and parked. I needed to think…rationally. I thought about Robert's message. *Bitch?* He never had the balls to call me a bitch before.

I laughed, though nothing was funny, and started to call him but stopped myself before I pressed any numbers. *I'll just go back to his house so he can talk his shit to my face.* I glanced at my purse and tapped my fingernails on the steering wheel. I was becoming more infuriated by the millisecond.

As I pressed down on the brake and reached for the gear shift, Pastor Johnson pulled into the space beside me. He hurried out the car and tapped on my passenger window. I tried to mask my disappointment as I rolled down the window.

"Don't leave me, Sister Alexis. Sorry I'm running late. I had to drop the Mrs. off at the beauty salon. Come on in."

I guess it was a sign, an act of protection. There was no doubt that I wouldn't have hesitated to put a couple hot ones in Robert if he would've called me a bitch to my face. Sitting in Pastor's cozy office was more comfortable than being in a cold holding cell, though.

***

It was 8:30 Friday morning, and I was checking my email in Tielle's office. Lately, I'd been receiving messages from listeners—some who told me they loved my segment and others who called themselves leaking juicy gossip based on what their best friend in New York heard from a coworker.

As I logged out and took the last bite of my doughnut, my phone vibrated. It was my mother. We hadn't talked since I cussed her out after Christmas, so I answered to see if she was ready to tell the truth. "Yes?"

"Oh, so you're answering your phone now I see. To what do I owe this pleasure?"

"It won't be a pleasure if you called to feed me more BS."

"I was about to fly there if you didn't answer today."

145

"Yeah, okay. But Meka got raped and it took you how long to come see her? Whatever, Ma. Can you tell me what you called for? I'm at work."

"Alexis, I know you were fired from your job. I called there a week ago. Now if you agree to do away with this unruly attitude and stop all this commotion about your father, I'll be more than willing to put a check in the mail today. I know your bills aren't paid, because I talked to Robert last night and he made it clear that you two aren't together anymore. Don't push me away. I'm all you have."

"I don't have to lie to you about working. I'm at work! I'm capable of gettin' a job despite what you may think. So keep your damn check. I've got plenty money coming in—enough to get a DNA test as a matter of fact. Guess your money can't bail you out this time."

I started to hang up, but placed the phone against my ear again to make one last statement. "And by the way, I'm doin' fine after the breakup. Thanks for asking. Findin' out Robert has a kid wasn't nothin'."

I wiped my sweaty palms on my jeans and grabbed my things so I could leave. When I looked up, Tielle was standing in the doorway. She'd heard what no one besides the parties involved knew. She didn't say much, but offered a listening ear to use at my disposal. While I was at it, I told her the details about my breakup with Robert. I didn't want to discuss it before because I couldn't talk about it without feeling the disturbing urge to go "f" him up. With almost a week under my belt to calm down, I was okay with sharing. Still pissed, but ultimately okay.

"I'm so proud of you," she said. "You're starting to get it."

"Get what?"

"Adulthood."

I rolled my eyes. "Okay, Tameka Jr."

"You know if this happened a year ago—no, six months ago—you'd be telling me this story wearing an orange jumpsuit."

"I think they're blue here." We laughed.

"You'll be alright," Tielle said, giving me a look I didn't quite understand. "Just keep your distance from him."

The next day, Dad called to wish me a Happy Valentine's Day and ask me to reconsider the DNA test. As I expected, Mom called him and begged him to intervene after I told her there was no changing my mind. I guess he didn't realize I was serious when I told him the same thing a month before.

"Do you really need to take it this far, Pooh?" he asked.

"Do you really have to ask me that? How would you feel if you found out there's a toss-up over who your dad is? I need to know. You should wanna know, too," I replied.

He had to have looked at me over the years and question our biological ties. My only resemblances to him were my complexion and long eyelashes…Whoop-dee-doo! He was quiet for a long time.

"Hello?" I checked.

"You've always been my baby girl. I don't wanna lose that," he replied. Although he tried to hide it, he was on the verge of crying.

"You were the one who said nothing would change."

"For *me*. What happens if Darryl is your father? What's the next move? You're gonna want to get to know him, right?"

"I don't know. I guess it depends on him. I don't know details, Daddy. I just want to start at point A and go from there. Do you think I'm not gonna talk to you anymore? Regardless, you're the man who raised me."

"You're all I've got," he replied. This time, he couldn't conceal his emotion. "Somebody already took Tameka from me. I didn't stop him. I couldn't stop him, but I can stop this. I'm not losing my other little girl!"

I took a deep breath to maintain my composure. I understood where he was coming from. He lived for me and Tameka. We were his princesses no matter what. I mean, Tameka stripped for four or five years and he never thought differently of her. Darnell James was the polar opposite of everything the black father is stereotyped to be. He was always there for us—not just as a physical presence—and it was a true measure of his character that he was still my "daddy" after he learned he wasn't the only contender for that position.

"You're not gonna lose me, Daddy. I promise. Can you just do this for me? I'd hate to drag you onto Maury Povich's stage."

That made him laugh, and I was relieved. He didn't know I'd already warned my mom that I'd really do it if she refused to cooperate. After I painted the picture of her girlfriends watching us on national TV and her good-as-gold image tarnishing before her eyes, she reluctantly agreed to the test. Once Daddy agreed, I had two consenting DNA contributors, and there was only one person left…

***

-*Happy V-Day, Pretty Lady* appeared on my phone's screen a little after eight.

I put my drink down and replied to Isaac:

-*Fuck love. But thank u.*

Seconds later, he replied:
- *If I was there, u wouldn't say that. Ur boy isn't taking u out?*

- *No, he's probably babysitting his kid. Long story. We ain't together. Drinking my cares away for the night.*

-*Kid? When u sober up, I'm here if u want to talk.*

I gulped the rest of my Absolut Mandarin concoction and went to Tiffany's kitchen to make another one. When I returned to the den, I had another text from Isaac. It was a picture of him with his lips puckered, and it read:
-*I can make it better if you let me.*

Even though the picture was meant to be goofy, he still looked good.
- *Don't send me pictures of kisses I can't have.*

-*U can have whatever you want. Ur single now.*

-*Well, I want to see u. And I want a picture of something else.*

Just then, the front door slammed and Tiffany stomped in. "I am so done!" she said after throwing her purse next to me.
"What happened?" She and Marlon had plans, but since she was home so soon, I knew something went wrong.
"Where do I begin?" she asked. She held up her left hand. "With my naked finger or Marlon standing me up for dinner?"
"Marly Bear didn't come through, huh?" I said in a high-pitched tone.
"It's not funny, Lexis!"
I laughed anyway.
"Are you drunk?" she asked.
"Yep, and I suggest you get like me. I'm havin' a great Valentine's celebration by my damn self."
Tiffany couldn't be mad after she saw how good I was feeling. "What are you drinking?" she asked. "I might as well join you. His mom has the kids all night anyway."
"Absolut…and a variety of juices and berries!" I laughed as another message came through on my phone. When I flipped it open, I laughed harder. "Cornball."
He sent me a picture of his index finger with the message: *You have*

148

to wait for that…but it's bigger than this. LOL

"What kinda crazy text did you get?"

I waved her off.

"What are you in here doing? Having phone sex as a Valentine's Day date?"

"Tryin' to. Isaac's a good boy, though. I like the mystery."

"Oh, boy. Poor Isaac doesn't know he's dealing with a certified freak."

"Certified, baby!" I said as I texted him back and told him I should've left Robert for him a long time ago. There was something magnetic about him, and with every conversation we'd had since the funeral, I had been drawn in more and more.

"I'm about to make a drink so I can be on your level. Please don't let me come back and find you masturbating with your phone in front of you."

As the night went on, Isaac and I kept texting, while Tiffany and I kept drinking. She found a bottle of champagne from New Year's, so we popped the cork and pulled out the flutes. After she poured our first glass, we held the flutes high. "To us…"

"…And not them," I finished.

"To real love and happiness…whatever that may be."

"And new beginnings with a man who has his shit together and no kids! And he probably has a bigger dick!"

"And…" Tiffany started, and then busted out laughing. "Did you just—? Girl, drink the champagne and shut up. You are so nasty."

"Don't call me nasty, trick. I remember some of your stories about you and Marlon. A little back door action? Remember that?" Tiffany threw a nearby magazine at me. I laughed as I dodged it. "And you liked it, you triflin' ho!"

"I can't believe the oral queen is criticizing me," Tiffany replied.

"I'll be that. I'm good at what I do, so you called it correctly. The queen, bitch. These lips will make any man cry for his mama, and I'm not exaggeratin'."

She cracked up. "I can't picture Robert callin' out for Mommy."

"Picture it. Nobody can touch me in the bedroom, and that's why his dumb ass was still callin' me. I put that broad right in his lap, and he was beggin' me to come home in front of her face. I thought she was so great, though. What happened to the undeniable chemistry that led to their lovely rendezvous in Atlanta? Where is that now?

"And how can he text me and say fuck me when he's in the wrong? Did he think I was supposed to go back to him just because ol' girl is dead? Fuck me? Fuck *me*?"

"He's just trying to get to you however he can. If he can't have your affection, he'd rather get you worked up. Either way, you're still focusing on him. That's how they are, girl."

"Do you know how much I held my tongue when I went to see him? I coulda murdered his pride and left with his balls in my pocket. I took the high road and that dude came at me on some gutter shit!"

I was slowly leaving the comfort zone the alcohol had taken me to and reentering reality. At a much faster pace, my anger was transforming into pain, and before I knew it, I was crying. It was a different feeling from the one I felt when I first talked to Monica. I was devastated. Robert had hurt *me*—not just my pride.

"I'm tired of fuckin' cryin'!" I yelled, punching the seat cushion.

Tiffany kneeled in front of me so we were face to face. "Then stop! Forget him! Do you think he's crying over you right now?"

As harsh as her words sounded, she was right. I tried to sniff my tears dry.

"Get it all out now, because after today, the crying stops. You don't need him anymore, Lexis. You know I've got your back."

I nodded in agreement. Next thing I knew, her hand was caressing its way up my thigh and her lips were on mine. A few seconds passed before I comprehended what was happening. I pulled away and swung, hitting her square in the mouth.

12

Tiffany: Oops is Too Late

"I'm sorry!" Tiffany exclaimed as she held her jaw and checked her lip for blood.

"What the fuck is wrong with you?" Alexis asked, wiping her mouth with her forearm.

"I just—I got—I—" Tiffany struggled.

Alexis glared at her friend. "That bitch *did* turn you out! She turned you out and now you tryin' that shit with me?"

"Alexis, I said I'm sorry."

"Sorry? So now I'm supposed to be over it? You put your lips on me and say 'Sorry' like you accidentally stepped on my toe? You are outside of your mind. You ain't sorry."

Tiffany bit her bottom lip and silently scolded herself for breaking her New Year's resolution. Drinking too much had gotten her into trouble again. She couldn't believe her suppressed crush on her best friend had revealed itself like this. She tried her best to explain to Alexis that she wasn't lying about who she thought was in the room when she first told her about the infamous night.

"But you never said a word when you found out the truth. I should've known somethin' wasn't right. The whole story seemed shady. Now, your weak-minded ass done started likin' girls because that broad licked you low and made you cum." She searched the couch cushions for her phone.

"It's not that simple," Tiffany said softly. "I feel different around her."

"An electronic gadget can give you an orgasm! Hell, your finger can! It *is* that simple. All of a sudden, a chick sucks your toes and you bust a *different* nut? Yeah, you feel different alright. You feel gay."

"It's not just sexual, Alexis," Tiffany replied, standing to defend her honor.

"Kill that noise, Tiffany. You just kissed me." She found the phone, put it in her pocket, and headed toward the hallway.

"Well, you don't have to be so hurtful. I apologize for getting caught up in the moment. I didn't mean to kiss you. Now you know my secret. That doesn't make me less of your friend. I'm still the same person whether I'm bisexual or not."

Alexis stopped. "Save that gay advocate shit. This ain't about you bein' gay or 'bisexual' as you put it. Your lips touched *mine*. I don't play that game. You can be gay without bringing me into it. I'm out." She stormed down the hall and reached the guestroom in six long strides. Once there, she pulled a suitcase from under the bed and then paused to make a phone call. "Hey, I need a favor."

Tiffany had only heard Alexis' voice carry that furious quiver two times before. Once when they found Tameka after she'd been shot, and again when she told her about Robert and Monica's connection.

"Can I stay there tonight?" There was a beat, then she cut her eyes in Tiffany's direction. "You don't wanna know...Alright. Thanks. I'll be there in fifteen minutes."

Tiffany's heart sank as she watched her best friend toss her belongings into her luggage, garbage bags, Wal-Mart bags, whatever. She tried to convince her to stay, but Alexis wouldn't stop packing and wouldn't say a word except when she angrily mumbled about her high being blown and Tiffany ruining her already depressing evening.

After making three trips to her car, Alexis returned to make one last check. She examined the room from the doorway while Tiffany made her last plea.

"You don't have to leave, Lexis."

"You wouldn't say that if I told you what I want to do to you right now."

Tiffany had no response. All she could do was watch her best friend turn her cold shoulders and walk out.

Alexis ran into Marlon once she reached the porch.

"What's happenin'?" he asked, stopping to chat.

"Hey," Alexis replied, her voice lacking the same enthusiasm.

"Don't tell me you got an attitude with me, too. Tiff told you what happened, huh?"

"I couldn't care less about y'alls relationship."

"She's shitty, ain't she?" No answer. "Good. She's right where I want her."

"That's nice." She walked to her car. Marlon followed.

"Hold up! Damn! You got a late-night creep or somethin'?" When she opened her door, he could see her luggage. "You movin' out? Rob romanced you into goin' home, huh?"

Alexis' facial expression answered his question.

"My bad." He reached into his coat pocket. "I ain't gon' hold you up. I just want your opinion real quick."

He pulled out a ring box and handed it to Alexis. If anyone could tell him whether it met Tiffany's outrageous standards, she could. When she opened the box, her jaw dropped. He'd picked the perfect ring for the self-proclaimed "Diamond Princess." The antique style platinum band was covered with round diamonds, and the center marquise diamond was a rare green, her favorite color. The colored stone gave the ring the uniqueness Tiffany required, and the tiny diamonds encircling the band added an extra sexy flashiness.

"Damn," was all Alexis could mutter.

"That's what I thought," Marlon agreed. "The perfect ring for my perfect lady."

Alexis grunted, a response that invited questions, demanded more of an explanation. She wouldn't give details, just advice. "Make sure you know your perfect lady before you ask her a damn thing."

What does she mean? I've known Tiff six years, and I know her better than she knows herself. He knew if he pissed her off on Valentine's Day by doing everything wrong and acting like he didn't want to be bothered, his proposal would totally catch her off-guard.

He tried to read between the lines and wondered if Alexis was referring to the night of Tiffany's party. Too many rumors had circulated, and though he wished he could forget about them, a part of him still had a feeling that something went down. Did he want to know? Even if he asked, he knew Alexis would never tell. Like men, women have an unspoken creed: "Don't tell his ass shit!"

He asked anyway. "This got anything to do with the party?" He smelled the alcohol on Alexis' breath, and if she was drunk enough, maybe she'd tell him.

"You can't always ignore what you hear," she answered before plopping into her seat and shutting the door. Marlon stepped back as she started the car and rolled down the window. "Before you ask her to be your wife, ask her why I'm leavin'."

Marlon struggled to make sense of her clues as she backed out of the driveway and sped off. Tiffany watched nervously from the dining room window. She couldn't imagine what Alexis handed Marlon before she got in her car. As Marlon neared the porch, she ran into the den and pretended to read a magazine.

He took longer than usual to come back to where she was, which led her to believe Alexis told him about the kiss. On a night like this, he should've been running to find her and apologize for standing her up. When she thought about it, he didn't even have flowers with him! Her emotions were all over the place. She was disappointed and angry, but somewhat relieved. She was a firm believer in signs, and this could have been a sign that he wasn't the one.

Marlon looked at the ring once more before closing the box and returning it to his pocket. Would he let Alexis' vague statement stop him from making the proposal he'd planned for so long? His vacillant footsteps led him to the den, where Tiffany was lounging on the couch holding the *People* magazine she had already read. Two empty glasses and two champagne flutes, one half empty, sat on the coffee table next to a pink envelope that was torn in half. On the floor in front of her, a bag of frozen corn lay next to a paper towel.

He cleared his throat to get her attention.

"Surely you're here to retrieve your belongings again and move back with your mother for good. Please tell me your phone charger's in here, because you can't possibly think you can enter this room and speak to me without some hospital discharge papers in your hand."

As Tiffany looked him over, he reached into his pocket.

"You look like a picture of health to me. Don't waste your time, Marlon. You and I both know you stood me up, and it wasn't because you were rushed to the hospital for an emergency. Let's just end it now. I can't let you hurt me anymore."

"Alright then. I'll just leave this here and I'm out." He set the ring box in front of the half empty champagne flute and walked to the bedroom.

When Tiffany finally looked to see what he'd left, she stopped breathing momentarily. Was this a joke? After she opened the box, she was sure Marlon was serious. The five-carat beauty sparkling before her eyes showed his earnest attempt at sealing their deal.

She ran to the bedroom where Marlon was anxiously waiting. "You still kickin' me out?" he asked.

Of course not. Instead, she allowed him to get on bended knee and affirm his love for her. His words were well thought out and sweet, but the only four that stuck in her head were, "Will you marry me?"

She had to explain her swollen bottom lip when she flinched during their kiss.

"Did Lexis do that?" Marlon asked.

"Yeah. It's fine, though. I put that bag of corn on it." Tiffany's story was simple. "She hit me because I told her she would be stupid if she got back with Robert. I told her she couldn't stay here anymore. I've done too much for her, for her to treat me like that. I don't care how drunk she was."

They redirected their focus to the wonderful remainder of the night they had ahead. It was celebration time…no clothes allowed.

***

Tiffany stretched her neck on each side in an attempt to relieve some of the tension. She reclined in her chair and studied the dazzling rock on her finger. *What's missing?* she thought. After a while, she had it. The truth was missing—the truth that if spoken, would change her and Marlon's relationship for good. It was a truth that she still didn't understand and one she couldn't rationalize. Somehow she had developed feelings for Venni, and those feelings were interrupting her and Marlon's journey to living happily ever after.

Her 2:30 appointment cancelled, so she had an hour to burn. She called Alexis for the tenth time, hoping she would finally pick up and talk to her. She wanted her friend back. Alexis still didn't know that Marlon proposed. Five rings, no luck. There was no point in leaving another message.

That was it. Her relationship with Venni was causing too many problems in her life and threatened to do more harm if she continued to associate with her. Though they had only formed a platonic bond, the shadow of their one experience hovered over Tiffany like bad karma. She reached for the phone again, but quickly retracted her hand. This conversation had to be face to face.

She rode the elevator to the tenth floor and rushed to Venni's wing. As she got closer to her office, she was happy to see the open door, which meant she wasn't busy.

"We need to tal…" Her words fell dead as she entered Venni's office and saw Aaron sitting to her right.

He chuckled. "She'll be back in a few minutes."

"Oh, you're talking to me now? The last time I saw you at Fit Club, you looked right at me and turned the other way."

"Why do you care?"

"I don't. It's just—"

"You get all the attention you need from my cousin."

"That is so old. Do you know how many times I've heard that rumor? And you are such a hater. How dare you go to Marlon and tell him something like that? He almost believed you."

He leaned forward and looked into her eyes. "You can't run game on me. I was there." His tone made her uncomfortable.

"I'm not gonna argue with you. It's obvious that you're jealous. You couldn't break me down and have your way with me, so you ran to Marlon with the fictitious story everyone else was circulating. Guess what?" She held her left hand near his face. "It didn't work."

The green diamond was indicative of the envy that inspired him to do such a heinous act. His ill feelings were deeply rooted, although Tiffany had nothing to do with them…at first. She was just at the right place at the wrong time.

From the time Venni moved in with Aaron and his mother when they were teenagers, they were close—like brother and sister. They hung out together, went on double dates, everything. When she started dating women after college, she became his competition. Unbeknownst to her, he felt threatened when she was around, wondering if one of his freaky bi-curious girls would find her attractive and gravitate her way. Lo and behold, it happened. While Aaron was out with his main girl at the movies, he saw Venni and one of his other girls flirting and sharing popcorn. Venni would have never done that on purpose. She had never heard Aaron mention the girl, nor had she seen them together.

That was believable then, but at the party when Aaron told Venni that Tiffany was the girl he lusted after now, she should've known she was off limits. He saw them talking quite a bit as the hours went by, but whenever Tiffany wanted to dip it low, she found him and they heated the whole place with their dancing. The mixed drinks heightened her sensuality toward him, but she was still aware of her commitment to Marlon. After she made him rock hard dancing to Mad Cobra, there was no way he was leaving without emptying himself…in her.

As Tiffany stood before him in Venni's office, he weighed his options. Should he bust her bubble and tell her what he did? He'd run the risk of her going to the cops, but it would almost be worth it to see the haughty expression leave her face. Besides, she couldn't prove a thing because the drug was long gone from her system.

"Close the door," he commanded. "Let's get it all out right now." Once they had complete privacy, he smirked. "I saw everything. She had your legs pointin' to the sky and you were enjoyin' every second." His play-by-play was as accurate as it gets since he was watching through the guestroom window.

"So y'all did set me up!" She scanned Venni's plush office, looking for the first item she was going to destroy.

"V didn't know." He went into further detail, explaining how he used one of the Rohypnol pills in his pocket to weaken her judgment shortly after Marlon left. He was supposed to deliver the drugs to someone after the party, but couldn't resist using one to see if they really worked. When Tiffany excused herself and went in the room, he figured he'd pretend to leave in case anybody found her and suspected foul play. There were plenty witnesses to say he left, but nobody could say they saw him return through the guest bedroom window.

He didn't get that far, though. As he proceeded to crack the window, he saw his cousin enter the room. The pill was obviously working, but Tiffany wasn't completely unconscious. Judging by the fixed arch in her back, there was no question she was relishing Venni's tongue tricks.

Tiffany cringed after hearing she was drugged. Aaron didn't seem like the type. "You asshole! Conscious my ass! I was out of it. I thought *you* were Venni that night."

He felt bad, briefly. Ever since he'd seen her with Venni, he thought she had been turning him down because she was into women. Tiffany let him have it, belittling him so brutally that he hit her with his hardest blow.

"I'm not a drug dealer and I'm not desperate. I told you I was holdin' the pills for somebody. You can go to the cops, but make sure you tell 'em your dude gave 'em to me."

She rolled her eyes.

"You think I'm lyin'? Where do you think he went when he left your party? He had to go make some paper. How do you think he paid for that ring you're so proud of? Do you see colored diamonds like that in the jewelry store in the mall?"

With nothing left to say, Tiffany tore out of Venni's office, nearly running her over in the hallway. Venni managed to stop her.

"Hey, you! Where you runnin' off to? Were you in my office?"

"Yeah, to tell you I'm no longer associating with you." She continued on her hasty path, lying to the Safe Haven receptionist about a family emergency and leaving the office.

She whipped her car into the handicap space closest to the Fit Club doors. Her tires screeched and her head jerked as she recklessly put her SUV in Park. She didn't take the time to wipe off the streaks of mascara painted on her cheeks or blow her nose that was full of misdirected tears.

Her palm pushed the metal office door with such force that the handle collided with the wall behind it. Marlon flinched slightly, taken aback by her grand entrance.

"Six days. Six damn days of completeness, of bliss, and now it's over." Marlon wanted to crawl into a black hole as she vocalized her pain, her disgust, her disappointment. "I don't even recognize you. I've loved you through a lot of things, but…" She shook her head, unable to continue.

"Baby, I'm not doin' that no more. I just had to get enough money to pay off your ring."

"And get the new paint job on your car. What else are you selling? Scratch that. I don't wanna know."

"Okay, I'm sorry I lied. It's over now."

"It's not over! Do you know why he told me? Because he put one of *your* pills in my drink during my party."

"He *what?*"

"Your 'hustle' landed me in the bed with Venni!" She suddenly realized her emotions had gotten the best of her when she glanced over her shoulder and saw Marlon's open door and his clientele's open mouths. "So much for your side gig not affecting me, right?"

She pulled the ring off and looked at it one last time. Her dream had come to an abrupt end. She threw the piece at Marlon, hitting him in the chest, and then stormed out as quickly as she had blown in.

Their exchange was more intense once Marlon arrived at the house. His clothes were neatly folded, waiting for him on the couch, his shoes were lined by the door, and Tiffany was in the basement washing the remainder of his things. He wanted to laugh. She couldn't even put him out the right way. He'd never heard of a scorned woman being so kind.

There were too many other things that weren't laughing matters, though, starting with Tiffany lying about being with Venni.

"Why didn't you just tell me the truth? You didn't think I would understand that?"

"I don't understand it, so how could you? Up until today I didn't know I was drugged, so I thought I got drunk and experimented."

"Well, you didn't know she was a chick, right? You didn't know what happened."

"I was out of it, but I knew what was going on. I felt everything…"

"You sound like there's more to it."

"I liked it. I had the best oral sex possible and it was performed by a female." She laughed. "I can't believe I just said that, but I'm okay with saying it. You want the truth, Marlon? Venni made me feel good."

He tried not to show his weakening spirit. "So you wanna be gay now?"

"I want to be happy. My eyes were opened today. Really, they've been open, but I've been squinting to overlook the obvious. I love you, but lately, you haven't been making me happy. I thought the ring would do it and it did, but only for a few days. Maybe we're just too different."

Marlon couldn't speak.

"I don't want a little boy who takes the easy way out. Selling drugs isn't the only way to make money. It's the quick fix. I needed to see that way of thinking in you. This all happened for a reason."

"This all happened because your spoiled ass had to have a millionaire's wife's ring using a middleclass man's budget. I had to do what I had to do because I didn't wanna keep disappointing you. Yeah, I got money the quick way, but don't act like you would've waited patiently for me to get it honestly. I busted my ass tryin' to get that thing to you so you could stop pouting every holiday. Now 'cause you found out how I got it, you wanna have all these feelings against our relationship and blame me for what Aaron's dumb ass did."

"Are we calling each other on the carpet? You do a lot of things the fast way, and I have been nothing but patient and understanding about them—namely your three-minute hump and run that used to only happen when we didn't want the kids to catch us. You have *not* been coming with it in the bedroom and you know that's a key issue. Don't be mad at me because a woman outdid you."

He walked toward her, cornering her by the dryer. "You not happy with me? Go 'head and run to Venni. You don't know what you want. You're a fuckin' follower. You have a couple gay friends and you wanna be like them now. So just like you don't want a 'little boy,' I don't want a chick who doesn't know who she is. Fuck you!" he said, staring rabidly into her eyes. His words felt like they slit her throat. As he walked away, their eyes remained fixed on each other. *He's actually leaving,* Tiffany thought. *And I'm letting him.* Her body shook like a leaf from the aftershock of his explosion, and the tremors only became worse as she listened to him throw things around upstairs.

The doorbell rang and she had to get herself together. *Please don't let this be Venni.* She jogged up the stairs and looked at the microwave display...5:30. Whoever had stopped by would have to come back later because she had forgotten to pick up the kids. She backtracked to get her purse and then answered the door, nearly running into Marlon on her way.

She better not have called the cops, he thought as he stood with his hands in his pockets.

On the other side of the door, a visibly annoyed Alexis stood with Tony, Bryant, and Bria. Tiffany greeted them with hugs and kisses before they ran to Marlon.

"How did you…"

Alexis told her about her phone calls from Safe Haven Daycare Center and the aftercare program the twins attended. "Y'all didn't answer none of the numbers y'all gave them, so they called me. The lady at Safe Haven said you had a family emergency."

Tiffany thanked her and said she was just about to leave to get them. "I have until 6:30. I don't know why they would panic like that."

Alexis could see that something wasn't right, starting with the bookshelf that was turned over and the dining room chairs that lay on their sides. "Okay, well it looks like y'all fine. When you drop them off tomorrow, have them take my name off the contact list."

As she turned to leave, Marlon emerged from the den. "Hey, Lexis! Why did you hit her in the mouth the other night?"

Tiffany's eyes widened.

"Did you ask her?" Alexis replied.

"And why did you move out?"

"He knows," mouthed Tiffany.

"You told me not to ask her nothin' until I found out why you left, and I didn't listen," he continued.

"From the looks of things, now you know."

Tiffany followed Alexis to her car. "Thanks again, Lexis." Silence. "Can you tell me when you'll be ready to talk to me again?" Nothing. "I'm *sorry!* Goodness! I was wrong, but you can't blame me for feeling you out. Remember the Janet Jackson thing when we played the game with Tielle?"

"Bitch, that was hypothetical and it was for fun. It was a game. You know good and damn well I'm not with that shit. It's a wrap, Tiff. You said 'sorry,' now keep it pushin'. I just ain't pushin' with you."

***

After she fed and bathed the children, Tiffany attempted to unwind in the den. She turned on *Who Wants to be a Millionaire,* but couldn't get her mind off of the day's events—especially when her phone continuously played Venni's ringtone from the kitchen counter. She had been calling all evening, so Tiffany finally checked her voicemail to see what she had to say.

This outta be good, she thought, holding the phone to her ear.

FIRST UNHEARD MESSAGE
"Tiffany, please call me back. Aaron just told me what he did. We have to talk."
NEXT UNHEARD MESSAGE
"Tiff, call me. I want to make sure you're alright."
NEXT UNHEARD MESSAGE
"Hey, Tiffany, the receptionist said you left in a frenzy, and I still see Tony downstairs…Uhh…Call me."

The messages went on and on. Venni felt terrible about her cousin's misconduct and felt partly responsible for it. He did tell her about his crush on Tiffany, but when Tiffany expressed her sexual needs to her, Venni conveniently forgot about Aaron. Tiffany was one of the finest women she'd met since she'd moved to Texas, and if memory served her right, she hadn't responded to Aaron's advances. Really, he should've felt like less of a man, using a pill to help him get some. Was his game that weak? The more Venni thought about it, though, she wondered how much of a factor the roofie was in their experience. Did Tiffany really enjoy herself, or could a cat have given her the same satisfaction?

Tiffany wondered the same thing while glancing at another incoming call from Venni. *I'll deal with her later*, she thought as she turned the dining chairs upright and pushed them under the table. Her tired eyes scanned the open space, surveying the remaining damage in the living and dining areas. Marlon had never been so destructive.

Bryant marched through the pile of books that were once housed on the mahogany bookshelf, singing Barney's cleanup song. "You made a mess, Mommy."

"Aren't you supposed to be sleep? What are your brother and sister doing?"

"Sleeping. I'm not sleepy, though. What you doing? Cleaning up your mess?"

"This is Daddy's mess, stink."

"Where is he? He has to come clean it up."

She couldn't answer him. Explaining Marlon's whereabouts to their children was going to be the toughest part of their breakup. "Do you think you can help Mommy?" she asked, working to keep her voice steady.

He nodded, and twenty minutes later, the place was almost back to normal.

The doorbell rang a little before nine o'clock. Tiffany's lips smiled slightly as she prepared to hear Marlon's apology. She didn't expect to see Venni instead.

"Sorry for just dropping by, but I was getting worried."

"I didn't jump off a bridge," Tiffany replied.

Venni nodded toward the door. "Do you mind?" Tiffany stepped to the right, allowing her to enter. "I know you said you don't want to associate with me anymore. I just want to apologize face to face for what happened that night. If I had known what Aaron did…"

"So he told you. Look. There's no need to revisit it. It happened and we can't change it. Lord knows I would if I could."

Venni winced slightly from the blow of the comment. "I understand, but I can't say the same. I thought we were a good match—as friends," she emphasized. "I don't befriend females often."

"I guess I don't mean 'change' as in 'erase,' but I would edit a lot of things. That one night isn't just altering *my* life. My children don't have their father in the household with them anymore. That's something that's always been important to me."

"Well, I guess I'll get out of here," Venni said. "Have they set bail yet?"

"Bail for who?"

"Marlon. That's why I came unannounced. I knew he wasn't here yet." She explained how Marlon went to Aaron's house and beat him until his knuckles were raw. "I think he assaulted an officer, too."

Frantic, Tiffany called the county jail to get information on Marlon's charges. Without a second thought, she loaded the kids in the car, stopped at the ATM, and drove to the jail. As she exited the vehicle, she saw Dap and Carmen, Marlon's other sister, walking by.

"Are you coming to bail him out?" Tiffany asked, still standing next to the truck.

"Why are you here?" Dap asked.

"Feelin' guilty? Why don't you go to your girlfriend's house or somethin'?" Carmen quipped as she walked toward Tiffany.

Tiffany opened the car door and stood behind it. She wasn't looking for a fight, and that's all she would get with the two hoodrats. When she put it in perspective, it was a godsend to see them because she didn't want her children to ever see the inside of a jail. Shoot, she could use her money on something more worthwhile anyway.

"Well, if you have it handled, I'll leave." She slid into her leather seat and closed the door. Since the women were still standing in place, she rolled down her window. "And Carmen, I don't have a girlfriend."

13

Alexis:
Familiar

"If you don't want me to come, just say so." Isaac's tone was demanding compared to the laid back drawl I was used to hearing.

We'd been going back and forth about him coming to see me after my drunken-text-message confessions about Robert and Tiffany on Valentine's night. I was serious when I told him I wanted to see him then; but when he called with dates in mind, I wondered if I really wanted to be bothered.

"You want to be my rebound man?"

"Sweetie, I just want to come cheer you up—even if it's only for a weekend. We're friends, right? I told you I could make you feel better and I was serious. You were all about it while we were texting, now you're singing a different song. Be straight up with me."

"I don't know what I want. Between investigating who my dad is, wiping a broad's spit off my lips, and being homeless, I don't know which end is up."

"Well, I'll stay put. I can care from afar."

Isaac was such a genuine guy. Everything about him intrigued the hell out of me, and no man had held my attention as long unless I was screwing him. He had done nothing but kiss me on the cheek and talk to me on the phone, and I was open. I had *been* open, but I was holding Robert down as my man. Since he was history, I was free to explore Isaac in every way. The problem was he lived over 900 miles away.

I pulled into a parking spot near the leasing office of Summit Apartments. I had been to four other places, and the leasing agents at two of them said I would have to pay a ridiculous amount of money before I could move in. I hated to admit it, but Robert was right. I was fighting an uphill battle.

Isaac wished me luck before we said goodbye. Thinking things were about to start looking up, I walked into Summit's leasing office and got shot down once again. I didn't even fill out an application once the lady told me the rent was $950 a month.

I pulled into Craig's garage around six. I had been staying with him since Valentine's Day. He was the only person I felt comfortable calling on a night like that. Tielle was entertaining Romeo, I didn't deal with Dap anymore, and I knew Craig wasn't celebrating the special evening with anybody. If he hadn't taken me in, I don't know where I would've ended up. Tielle offered to let me stay with her after I told her what happened the following Monday while we were at work, but if it wasn't broke, why fix it?

Our living arrangement worked well. I was able to spend more time with Darius, and I think my presence helped Craig think of something other than Tameka's death. I forced him to go places with me so he would stop moping (and to keep me from moping, too). I even had him watching *American Idol*. He acted like he wasn't into it, but I can almost guarantee he went to his room every Tuesday night after the show and voted for Fantasia. Most importantly, he had finally migrated downstairs and would spend a couple hours in the kitchen and living room.

When I walked in, Craig was in the kitchen. Following my usual deliberate path around the area that was once drenched with Tameka's blood, I strolled through the living room to join him. Darius was in his highchair, waiting for my kiss.

"How did it go?" Craig asked. I dismissively waved my hand. "I told you don't rush to get out of here. Me and Darius like the company."

"What are you about to ruin over there?" I asked as he added paprika to the pot. I put my purse down and joined him at the stove. "Move. I got this."

A half hour later, we were eating dinner. I caught him staring at me as I sipped my sweet tea.

"What?"

"Do you know how proud Meka would be of you? Look at you. You have a job you enjoy, you've stepped in to help me out with lil' man..."

"You sound like my da—" I caught myself.

"Mr. James?" He laughed. "Don't let him hear you say that. You know your pops still doesn't like me."

"I don't either," I joked.

Darius laughed like he knew what was going on. In his excitement, he knocked over a travel coffee mug that was on the counter. Craig and I hopped up, thinking the same thing: coffee, hot, burns, Child Protective Services. Luckily, the mug was empty. When I picked it up, I noticed a lipstick print.

I held the cup near his eyes. "Whose cup is this?"

He snatched it before he realized it, then apologized. "Aunt Rosie stopped by earlier. I gotta get this back to her. You know how she is about her coffee," he said, putting the cup in the sink.

"Snatch something from me again and see if you don't have some missing fingers," I warned with a smirk. "We ain't that cool."

"You love me."

"Somebody told you wrong!" I popped him in the head with Darius' empty bottle. "Now fill this up while I give him a bath."

Later that night, I was in a deep sleep when I heard Darius crying. He usually slept through the night, so I jumped up to see what was wrong. With my eyes barely open, I navigated down the dark hall and stopped when I felt the door frame. I could immediately see what was pissing D-Baby off. I laughed as I gently released his right foot that was stuck between the bars of his crib. His eyelids fluttered as I played in his curly hair, then he drifted back to sleep.

When I turned around, Craig was standing just inside the doorway wearing nothing but a towel around his waist. I could tell he'd just gotten out of the shower because beads of water were still rolling down his chest.

"I thought I heard him," he whispered. "My bad. I was just finishing up."

Late-night bathing had become one of his commonplace rituals. When he couldn't sleep at night, which was most nights, he jogged around his neighborhood and showered once he returned.

I shooed him away. "I got him back to sleep now. We don't need your assistance."

Instead of leaving, he joined me at the crib and leaned over to look at Darius. "Well, I need your assistance. You know how they say everything happens for a reason? You've helped me so much since you've been here." His eyes were fixated on mine. "Who would've thought?"

Like it was natural, he leaned toward me…and I didn't back up. Our lips joined in a passionate but desperate kiss that triggered our violent exchange of emotions. He gripped the back of my neck, almost as if he was choking me, while I dug my nails into his back. Our interaction was one of love and hate. The closeness felt good, but the vibe was bad. We were reaching out to each other for the wrong thing, for the wrong reasons.

As Craig reached for his towel, I pushed him away. My widened eyes took in his startled expression as he, too, realized what we'd just done. The shame of the situation left me speechless as I exited the room and returned to my own.

What did I just do? I thought as I fell backward onto the bed. I had betrayed my sister in the most cowardly way…by accident. Craig was alright and all, but I never looked at him like that.

I almost drove myself crazy trying to figure out why he went for the kiss in the first place. Was it because I had been playing Tameka's role in every other way? Was it just a case of him giving in to the raging hormones that hadn't been calmed in a while?

I adjusted my pajama top, then froze. That was it. I had on a pair of Tameka's pajamas. I felt close to her when I wore them, so he had to feel something seeing me in them. The picture painted itself as I recalled him commenting on me wearing her perfume a couple days prior and effortlessly noticing the lip gloss I'd taken from her cosmetic bag. In his mind, I was Tameka. By no means did he want to kiss me. He wanted me to be her.

The next morning was awkward as hell. I whisked by him in the hallway, barely mumbling 'Hey' on my way to work. All day, I felt…wrong. I needed feedback from somebody, but there was no one I could talk to who wouldn't think I was the most selfish, inconsiderate, disrespectful bitch they'd ever met. Tiffany would've been a possibility if we were still cool. She would've seen it for what it was—a slip-up that was part of our grieving process. I knew that, but the question was: Were we going to act like it didn't happen and go back to our "normal" relationship?

There was nothing left to do except what I thought was best. I rushed to the condo after work, packed my things, and left Craig a note. I was taking Tielle up on her offer and moving with her until I could find an apartment of my own.

***

"Girl, I would've been the top story on Nancy Grace if she would've done that to me! 'Friend kills best friend-turned lesbian. Chops off the lips that kissed her'," Dee Dee said as she finished lining my neck.

She had been my beautician since I was seventeen, so she was more like a cool auntie than an impersonal stylist. We talked about any and everything. She knew who Tiffany was because Ava, another stylist in the shop, did her hair. They asked me where she was, and I told them I didn't care and why.

"Yeah, so I don't know where she is. She's a smart girl, so she probably changed her appointment. Running into me ain't a good idea," I told Ava.

"So you haven't talked to her since?" Dee Dee asked.

"Hell naw. And she calls every two hours."

"How do you come back from that?" Ava questioned.

"You don't. If she's into chicks now, that wasn't my business until she came at me. Me and Tiff been cool since she moved here."

Ava shook her head. "I never would've guessed."

As Dee Dee spun my chair around, I saw Venni and Lawrence run by. Venni smiled and waved.

"You know her?" Dee Dee asked when I waved back.

"Tiffany knows her."

"She looks cocky, like she knows she's the shit. She jogs past here all the time with her pretty boyfriend, smiling like 'Look at us.'" The scowl on Dee Dee's face was hilarious.

"He's not her boyfriend. She'd be more interested in you than him." Ava's jaw dropped after she processed my statement. I retrieved my purse from Dee Dee's counter and handed her my money. "That's who got your girl sprung, Ava. I'll see y'all next week."

I strutted out of the shop, leaving the ladies to fill in the blanks.

It was 2:30 p.m., and I was supposed to meet Tielle at the bridal shop at three o'clock. She and Romeo had set a June date for their wedding, and I had to get fitted for my bridesmaid dress. As I pulled away from the curb, she called my cell phone.

"I just got done, LT. Chill. I'm on my way," I answered.

She laughed. "I need a favor. Can you pick my mom up? She's at the church."

As I approached the light, I made a quick u-turn and headed two blocks down. Miss Rosie was outside waiting.

"Hey, honey," she said as she plopped into the passenger seat, the scent of her Beautiful perfume filling the car.

We talked about the wedding and how excited she was. Though she spoke of how much work and money she'd put into the ceremony, I knew she wouldn't have spent her time doing anything else if somebody paid her.

"I told Tielle she better figure out what centerpieces she wants for the tables so I can start on 'em now. I need a head start!"

"Four months early?"

"Child, yes! I'm not like you young girls. I can't stay up all night the night before the wedding, doing last minute things."

"You gotta pull out your coffee!" I said, remembering that I still had her mug on the backseat. I pointed to it and told her to remember to grab it when I took her home.

"That ain't mine, honey. I don't drink coffee. Never did. What made you think that was my cup?"

"Craig said..." I glanced at Miss Rosie's lips and was reminded that she didn't even wear lipstick. *Lying motherfucker.* "Never mind. I got confused. I know whose it is." Though I didn't, I planned to ask Craig when I saw him again.

***

We met at our new exchange spot, a McDonald's parking lot near Tielle's house. Picking D-Baby up at Craig's had proven to be extra awkward the first two times after the kiss, so I told Craig we'd meet on neutral turf. When I saw him get out of the car, I changed my mind about confronting him. Why would I want to hear another lie?

"You should've seen him earlier," Craig said as he handed Darius to me. "I think he was pointing at Meka's picture."

"I hope he wasn't pointin' at anybody else's."

"Huh?"

I fastened Darius' car seat. "What you got goin' on tonight?"

He shrugged. "You know me. I'll probably just go to the gym and work out a little bit; hang out with Marlon. We should take Darius somewhere tomorrow. I'm free all day."

"I'm not." I walked around to my side of the car.

"What about Tuesday or Wednesday after work?"

"Nope."

"Lexis, we made a mistake. We discussed this already. Avoiding me doesn't change anything."

"This is about Darius. Not us. I'll call you when I get out of church tomorrow so you can pick him up."

I could barely stand being in his presence. I wanted to believe there was some other explanation for him lying about the coffee mug, but I couldn't convince myself that he was secretly cross-dressing in his spare time. As I watched him pull away, I wondered if Tameka was watching him and if she approved of him moving on so quickly.

***

Another long morning of apartment hunting landed me on the south side of town. I was in an area I'd once claimed as my stomping grounds, populated with liquor stores, corner stores, nightclubs, and late-night fast-food joints. It was where I met my boys Will, Jeff, Green, and Tank; where I met marijuana and vodka. Their grime was the perfect match for my grit, and I felt more at home chilling with them on the block than in our boring cul-de-sac on the west side. I knew nothing about that neighborhood until Tameka started working there the summer before she started college, but after I snuck out once to follow her, there was no keeping me away.

I rode up and down Menzie Boulevard, contemplating whether I should stop. *Why should I? What am I going to say?* As I passed the building again, I thought of a strategy. "Just walk in and act like you need directions," I said aloud. "You're right here. Stop trippin'."

When I pulled into the parking lot, my heart started racing. I stared at the unlit neon sign that read "U-Turn". *It's now or never.*

I left my original plan in the car along with my nerves, and acted on sheer impulse—what I do best. As I approached the door, I read the sign posted to the left. Just like I thought, the place was closed and the door was locked. The bar didn't open until three, and the "Exotic Theater" (as Darryl called it) didn't start until five. Even though it was a quarter after one, I knew he was inside because his plum Lexus with the "U Turn" license plate was parked in its usual spot next to a Jaguar. I laughed at the Jag's corny plate that read, "ECON QN."

After three attempts at banging on the door and getting no answer, I turned to leave. *Maybe now isn't the time.* Before I made it to my car, though, I saw a delivery truck driving toward the back of the building. *That's it! That's my way in.*

I did a smooth walk-run to the back door, arriving just as the heavyset driver exited his truck. He was fumbling with his clipboard and finishing his Coke, so I rang the buzzer first like I had something to deliver. Almost immediately, the door swung open and a winded man appeared.

Without looking at me, he said, "Sorry about that. Somebody was at the front door, too. Guess I missed 'em." He picked at his pants, overly concerned about what looked like a mustard stain.

"It was me," I replied.

He looked up. After noticing that I wasn't dressed like a delivery person and didn't have an invoice in my hand, he made an assumption. "We don't do walk-ins, Sweet Pea. Call for an interview." His eyes traced my curves. "We're not really hiring, but I think I can make an exception. What's your name?"

My words were stuck in my mouth. Otherwise, I would've cussed him out for thinking I was an unemployed stripper. I wasn't positive that he was Darryl, but everything about him told me it was him. His eyes were so dark that they looked black, and his eyelashes were unusually long for a man. His cheekbones were pronounced, but not overly, and a small dimple indented his right cheek just across from his salt-and-pepper goatee. Maybe I was paranoid, but those features matched mine, and I wasn't sure how to feel about that.

"Should I just call you 'Pretty Lady'?" the man asked.

"No. I'm Nichelle." I always used my middle name when I didn't wanna give out my real one.

He offered his hand. "I'm Darryl. I own the place."

"Nice to meet you," I said, forcing a smile.

"Alright, I'm gone. Call me later," a female voice called from inside.

He turned and waved his hand. "Okay, baby."

Still playin', I thought. He was probably winded from having some lunchtime fun, not from trying to answer the other door.

"Listen, Darryl. I'm not here for a job. I just want to give you this." I handed him a yellow Post-It note with my mom's name and number written on it. "Y'all need to talk."

He pulled the paper from my finger, looked at the name, then into my eyes. "What's this about?"

"Ask her." I walked away with my fists and teeth clenched, angry that I didn't tell him everything right then, angry that we looked like father and daughter.

Isaac called as I was leaving. He wanted to see if I'd actually gone through with what I'd been planning for days. I told him how I choked.

"Don't be so hard on yourself. At least you gave him her number. He'll call. Trust me," he assured.

"Yeah, to set up a booty call for old time's sake if nothin' else. He probably already has her number."

"You are so much like your sister, laughing stuff off that's bothering the hell outta you."

"We must get that from our mother, 'cause I can tell you now that we don't have the same father." Deep breath. "Can we change the subject?"

My mother beeped in, so I told Isaac I'd call him back. "Why on earth did you go to Darryl? I told you I would handle it," she snapped.

"Well, you weren't movin' fast enough and I wanted to see what he looks like."

"Are you happy now?"

"Hell no! We look alike."

"Oh, Lexi, stop it. You do not."

"He must think so, too, if he called you so quick."

"Yeah, because you planted it in his mind."

"I didn't tell him anything. I just gave him your number."

Apparently, Darryl had an inkling that I was there to tell him I was his long-lost daughter…and not just because he had been banging my mother for years, but probably because when we looked at each other, it was like looking in a mirror.

"I have half the mind not to participate in your little test now. This is becoming a circus."

"And you're the only one wearing the red nose and curly wig. Since half of your mind doesn't want to participate, that's fine. Let the other half know that the test can be done without you. Your DNA would just provide stronger results."

She threatened to call Darryl and tell him not to participate either. When I reminded her that it would only take me and Daddy's results to know whether I was a love child, she released an exasperated sigh. "This is absurd."

"I want this done ASAP, so clear your schedule for next month. I'll let you know the date after I talk to the lab."

I walked into Tielle's house, all worked up about my mother's who-gives-a-damn attitude. I was so ready to join her on the couch and talk about it, but instead, I found Romeo sketching something in his pad. He jumped when he saw me.

"I thought you were Tielle," he said as he relaxed and set the pad on the coffee table.

"Same here."

He told me a secret. He was sketching a portrait of Tielle that he was going to transfer onto a huge canvas and paint as part of his wedding gift to her.

I commended him, thinking how if Robert could draw, he would probably think to do the same thing. He was a thoughtful guy to be such a tough athlete. Then, I remembered how he wasn't thinking of me when he was trying to find a comfortable position with Monica on the little twin bed in her dorm room.

"My bad," Romeo said. "I'm talking about all this stuff when…Have you heard from Rob?"

"We don't have nothin' to say to each other if you take away the expletives."

"He'll come around. He misses you. He knows he messed up."

"Fuck that. I don't want a man that only has hindsight. We all learned the same thing in health class. You put it in; you squirt; you have a kid. He's lucky I ain't burnin' or itchin' 'cause Shemar would be an orphan."

Romeo couldn't help chuckling a little. "Damn, you ruthless."

Isaac texted me, saying he didn't want to bother me but that it was kind of urgent I get back to him before five o'clock. I forgot I was supposed to call him back a couple hours prior, so I excused myself and called him right away.

"I have good news," he said. "I've had something in the works since we talked the other week, but I didn't want to say anything until I had some definite information. I'm good friends with the owner of Smoothies, and his wife is the property manager at Rockville Landing. I won't bore you with the minor details, but if you have $500 to give her by the end of the week and $639 for the first month's rent on move-in day, she can have your apartment ready by the first. Somebody just broke their lease and she has conveniently misplaced the waiting list until Friday."

"What about my credit?"

"Didn't I just tell you she manages the place? Can you swing $639 or what?"

Without hesitation, I said yes. Rockville Landing Apartments were beautiful, ivory, three-story buildings located about a mile and a half down the street from Smoothies, just minutes from a premier shopping area. I had never been inside one of the units, but the keycard-activated gate led me to believe they were pretty damn nice.

"Wow. I'm about to have my own place thanks to you. How— Why did you do this?"

"It's what I was gonna do when I came down there. After you said not to, I called my guy and told him to get things rolling without me."

"To make me feel better…" I said under my breath. Suddenly I felt like the shallowest chick on Earth.

***

The first came quick. I finished my second segment of "What's the Word?" and hauled ass from the station to Tielle's so I could finish packing my last few boxes. The day marked the beginning of a few things: the week, the month, and my lease! Before leaving work, I had called my boys Will and Tank to see if they were still going to help me

172

move and was happy to hear they were on their way to the U-Haul location on my side of town.

After I heaved the boxes into the car, I looked at my cell phone…12:09 p.m. Tielle was supposed to call me when she was leaving the station, and she said she was leaving right after the morning show. When 12:27 p.m. rolled around, I didn't know what to do. The reservation was for 12:30 p.m., the guys were probably at the place waiting for me, and I was counting on Tielle to use her credit card to reserve the truck. I opened my phone to call her, but her house phone rang and threw me off. Instead of dealing with either phone, I decided to get in the car and make it to the spot before U-Haul gave my truck to somebody else. Five minutes later, I pulled into the parking lot looking like an idiot. Everybody was there waiting for me.

"Did you forget to tell me you were cutting off your phone today?" Tielle asked. "I called when I left work to tell you to meet me here."

"My phone ain't off. I just used—"

No, I hadn't used it all day…and I didn't have fifty missed calls from Tiffany. As we listened to the U-Haul man give us the details of the rental, I clenched my fists, wishing Robert was there to feel their impact. He got me good. I knew the day was the beginning of a lot of things, but I didn't expect it to be the beginning of war.

All afternoon while we moved, I had the voices of an angel and two devils giving me advice on how to handle Robert's underhanded move. My boys were ready to get at him. One word, and they would be outside his apartment door waiting for him to get home from work. "Miss High Road" Tielle kept telling me to wait until after we were done moving to make my final decision. Again, she told me to trust her. I didn't trip because Will and Tank would still be on "ready-set," eager to whoop Robert's bitch ass on cue.

We finished around 4:30 p.m. It was an easy move because I really didn't have a lot of stuff. The fellas wouldn't take money, so I bought pizza and beer, and we sat around for a couple hours. When they left, I looked around my place and exhaled.

"Feels good, doesn't it?" Tielle asked.

I nodded. "Just gotta get some furniture. Maybe I'll see about renting some 'til I save up."

I had Tameka's living room set in my storage space, but when Will went to move the loveseat, I told him to leave it. Though it was only a few years old, I knew I wouldn't be able to enjoy watching TV on it, take a nap on it, or entertain company on it.

"Oh yeah!" Tielle said, removing an envelope from her purse. "Here." She handed it to me and waited while I opened it.

It looked like another piece of junk mail from an insurance company. When I read the paper inside, my fingers lost all feeling and the check hit the floor. Yes, it was a check…for twenty thousand dollars. Tielle explained that Tameka had taken out a separate life insurance policy after she found out she had HIV, and I was the sole beneficiary. Darius wasn't around then, so I guess that would make sense, but she kept it like that even after he was born. Of course, he was the beneficiary on her other policy from her job, though. I picked up the check and stared at the figure, remembering all the times she bailed me out of bad situations.

"Only Nicole and I had control over when you got the money. Meka talked to us at the hospital in Columbus and said you could only have the money once you matured, because she didn't want you blowing it on stupid stuff. I think you're ready. Don't let your sister down."

I leaned against the kitchen counter, holding the check to my heart. With my other hand, I pointed to the sky, acknowledging Tameka's thoughtfulness. I could feel her smiling proudly. She always knew I would never be her, but for what it was worth, I was damn close and she knew it. I kissed the "TJJ" tattoo on the inside of my wrist, hoping somehow she could feel it. Tameka Janese James had come to my rescue again…from the grave.

"Let me know if you need help furniture shopping," Tielle said with a smile.

After she left, I stretched out on my living room floor and closed my eyes. There was something poetic about the day. Robert hit me with his hardest and lowest blow, but I wasn't affected. I could use the money from Tameka to get a phone in my own name. During my first grief counseling session with Pastor Johnson, he told me everything was in divine order and that God allowed things to happen when He saw fit. After the day's experience, I believed him.

I still wasn't finished with Robert, though. From the nasty text message to the phone disconnection, he was getting away with too much for my taste. Before I went to sleep, I called the station to see if I could pre-record my segments at 5 a.m. instead of being live in-studio because I didn't realize how much business I had to handle regarding my new place. They contacted Eli, who said it was cool. Then, I called Tank and asked him to meet me at American Parcel Express in the morning. I had to remind Robert's stupid ass that he should never test my gangster.

***

174

Tank and I watched Robert's delivery truck leave the dock at 8 a.m. the next day. At 8:04, I was using my key to get into his Expedition. When I saw Shemar's car seat in the back, my level of pissosity rose five points. It was a reminder that his wandering dick started our war.

For kicks, I used Tank's phone to call him.

"Yeah," he answered.

"Why couldn't you tell me you were cuttin' my phone off?"

He laughed. "Whose phone are you using?"

"Ya mama's."

"Why don't you use your dad's phone? Oh, that's right. You don't know who that is."

If ever I needed more fuel to add to my fire, his last comment gave me plenty. *Laugh it up, bitch,* I thought, as I hung up.

We arrived at Will's auto shop a few minutes later. When we left, the 22's I had him put on the truck a year before were leaning against the wall in the shop and replaced with some old, balding tires. Seems Robert had forgotten about those while he was chatting with the Sprint agent about disconnecting my phone. He thought he was the shit, rolling around with the wheels gleaming. Now he had some dusty tires with no hubcaps. He had made his best move, and in turn, I made mine. Checkmate.

By 11:30 a.m., we were back in Robert's parking space, but I still wasn't satisfied. Before we exited the truck, I reverted to being the no-holds-barred bitch I'd been trying not to be. I turned the ignition off and pounded on the key until it bent. Tank moved my hand out of the way and broke the key off with two simple moves.

"Is that what you were trying to do?" he asked, placing the broken piece in my hand.

It sure was. Since Robert thought my paternity dispute was so funny, I figured I'd give him something else to laugh about. *You ain't drive your truck home now, asshole. How funny is that?* I made myself laugh as I carved "Ha" in the driver and passenger seats with my knife.

Tank shook his head. "Y'all women are coldblooded. I feel like I'm breakin' the code."

"What code?"

"The manhood code. This is crazy watchin' you do this shit."

"Women are only like this when you fuck us over. And damn y'all's code. You're here 'cause I'm your homegirl."

"No doubt."

For my grand finale, I used my knife and my eleventh grade art class skills to draw a hand with the middle finger sticking up. "Now let's go."

On the way to my car, I saw one of Robert's coworkers. I could tell he recognized me, so I waved. Although he waved back, his eyes questioned the validity of my presence. Just to show him I wasn't nervous, I beeped when I rode past him and yelled, "Good seeing you again!"

***

Later that evening, Tielle knocked on my door.

"Why you knockin' like you're the police?" I asked when I opened it.

"Because the police were just at my house looking for you."

I peeked through the blinds. "They didn't follow you, did they?"

"No. I told them you moved out and I wasn't sure where you went. What did you do?"

"Nothin'."

She twisted her lips.

"You don't wanna know, LT."

"Does this involve Robert?"

"I guess, unless I killed Jacqueline while I was sleepwalking."

"Alexis…"

"Romeo didn't tell you? I'm sure he knows by now."

"He's out of town."

I wouldn't tell her because she wouldn't be able to lie to the cops if they went back to her house with more questions. "I couldn't let it go. He came at me on some bitch shit, so I showed him how a real bitch does it. I should've known he'd call the police."

"Whatever you did isn't satisfying enough to go to jail, is it?"

"Naw, but if I still had that brick and the can of spray paint in my car, maybe it would be."

Tielle looked to the sky for assistance, but if she knew like I knew, God was not pleased with me for the day.

"Lexis, you've got too much going for you now. Why are you putting so much energy—negative energy—into that fool? If you turn all that into positive energy and use it to better yourself, do you know what could lie ahead? Come up with a scheme to take your job to another level. Plan to get your credit straight instead of planning his downfall. That'll happen on its own. I know he pissed you off, but you have twenty thousand dollars now. Don't you think you can get your own phone with that no matter what the security deposit is? You need to be smart. That money wasn't meant to be used for your bail bond."

With no more words left, she walked out, leaving me plenty to think about.

After I ate dinner, I called Yari to give her my house number. We hadn't talked in over a month, since she first moved to Atlanta. She was happy to hear I had my own place, but she wasn't happy to hear about my retaliation to Robert's action.

"…And where is all this language coming from? He's taking you out of your game, Lexis. You sound like a sailor again."

"That's because I'm still heated, but I've already thought this out. There's too much goin' on with me right now to think I can stop cussing cold-turkey. I gave up on that a long time ago. I'ma be me before anything, so I had to set realistic rules. 'Ass,' 'Damn,' and 'Hell' are okay for me to say."

"You are not serious."

"All those words are in the Bible. Tell me they aren't. 'Shit' is okay from time to time if somethin' pisses me off, but I'ma try to stay away from the 'F' Bomb and 'MF.' If I use them when I'm talking to Robert, though, they don't count."

She was almost in tears, laughing at me. "Let's change the subject. What's Isaac up to?" I told her how he arranged for me to get the apartment and that he wanted to visit. "Go 'head, Isaac! That's your man, Lexis. I'm gonna keep telling you until you believe it."

When I told her I told him not to come, she flipped. "You're using the distance as an excuse, and your hesitation will only allow Robert the chance to move back into your heart."

"There's no chance of that. I gave him my heart and he gave somebody else a baby."

"So what's the big deal? Let Isaac come. It's not like he asked you to marry him. And if y'all are meant to be, you'll end up in the same city. Baby steps, girl. He just wants to see you. You know you like him. You didn't keep in touch so long for nothing."

"He would be my rebound if I get with him now."

"Stop! How many times did you move on to the next guy when you and Robert broke up before? That man got you an apartment because he saw you were down. Has that not hit you yet? Don't be afraid of real love. I think you know it's possible with Isaac and you're not sure if you're ready. It's no coincidence that you're feeling him and he's not even your type. It was no mistake how you met. Call that man back and stop playin'."

I didn't have a rebuttal.

"And last time I checked, if you get a rebound, you have another chance to score," Yari continued.

"You are so corny."

"And you are so stupid. Most men arrange to get you flowers, not somewhere to live."

I finally got her to move on and tell me how she liked life in Atlanta so far. She described the entertainment scene, saying there was always a convention, party, concert, stage play, or after-party going on. Just as I had heard, she said it was common to see a celebrity walking around like a "regular" person. She had already seen Keith Sweat at the mall, Michael Vick at the gas station, and Whitney Houston at The Cheesecake Factory.

"You know I'm not used to this. Who did we ever see rolling around Columbus?" We laughed. "When your lease is up, you should really consider moving here. I've already done some research on the two hottest radio stations here. If they heard your delivery, I know they would want you on their team."

She had given me something else to think about. Relocating to Atlanta was something I'd talked about since I fell in love with Another Bad Creation and Kris Kross in 1991. With Yari living there, it had become more than a childhood dream; it was a strong possibility.

I felt overwhelmed as I sat against the living room wall. Tielle was right. Yari was right. Robert was still winning because I wasn't focusing on me and my happiness. I tapped my fingers on my chin as part of my contemplation, then picked up the phone to call Isaac.

14

Tiffany:
She Loves Me...She Loves Me Not

At 2:23 a.m., Tiffany awoke to the sound of *Phone Booth*'s main menu music. After glancing at the clock, she realized she had fallen asleep, only making it through two and a half of the four DVDs she'd rented. Instead of retreating to her bedroom, she pulled the large fleece blanket from the basket beside the couch and returned to the chaise. The rain tapped on the window near her, creating the perfect ambience for her somber disposition. The night looked cold and uninviting, a representation of the world as she would know it from now on. Society didn't accept the color gray. Everything was supposed to be either black or white, and her life events were neither.

Maybe if I stick to my original plan and end my friendship with Venni, I can avoid a bunch of confusion, she thought. But that wasn't what she wanted to do. Venni was a genuine person who was turning into a close friend. She couldn't explain what she was feeling for her, but she was sure it felt good. She always had a good time when they hung out, often feeling they had more in common than she and her blood sister. And since she indulged in making herself happy...

Tiffany reached out to Venni the next day at work between her 9:15 and 11:00 appointments. Keeping the conversation informal, she asked what Venni was doing for lunch and joked about the Hot Pockets she'd rather not eat. They decided on Marty's Italian Restaurant at 12:15. Like usual, the ladies caught up on current events, but each purposely shied away from talking about Tiffany's personal drama with Marlon.

"What are you doing this weekend?" Venni asked before biting into her breadstick.

"Nothing exciting. Marlon has the kids, so I may go lose my mind at the mall."

"Do you want to go to the NAACP gala on Saturday? Lawrence was gonna go but he has pneumonia. No sense in wasting the ticket."

Tiffany hadn't been to a black-tie event in over a year. That wasn't Marlon's thing. If they went out, it was to dinner and a movie. It was like pulling teeth just trying to convince him to go to a concert when one of her favorite artists was in town. Now she was presented with the opportunity to rub elbows with the elite, and saying no was not an option.

On Friday, Marlon came by to pick up the kids and the remainder of his belongings. Tiffany had just stepped out of the shower, and was drying off when he walked into her bedroom. She screamed at the top of her lungs. "What are you doing here?"

"I'm supposed to be here."

"Yeah, at seven."

"Well, I had to come now. I called, but I see you were in the shower." Try as he might, he couldn't stop his eyes from looking at Tiffany's petite frame.

Observing this, she propped her leg on the bed for support and dried her lower body as if he weren't there. "That reminds me. I need my key back."

"What if there's an emergency?" he asked.

"The proper authorities will be alerted and they can break the door down if necessary. My key," she repeated, waving her finger between the key ring in his hand and her dresser, and then brushing by him to get some panties.

He nodded at the Nordstrom dress bag that lay on her bed. "I see you've been shopping again."

"Is there something you need in my room?"

He wanted to scream, "You!" but instead, he said, "Yeah. I left a couple of my shirts and my blue Timbs." As he gathered his things, he asked, "You goin' somewhere special?"

"Everywhere I go is special," she answered with her hand on her hip.

"Is Venni going with you?"

"Do you hear me asking what your weekend plans are?"

"You already know I'm not goin' nowhere."

She wiggled into her jeans. "Well, it sucks to be you."

"Tiffany…"

She gave him little attention as she finished dressing. "Are you gonna finish your sentence?" she finally asked.

He grabbed his boots and headed for the bedroom door. "Nah." He placed the key on her dresser. "I'll have 'em back here at the same time Sunday."

He'd thought of reconciling but was glad he'd caught himself. Tiffany's self-absorbed ass didn't even ask how he was doing after being arrested. Since life was always about her anyway, he would help her stay focused on number one and leave her alone.

***

When Saturday evening came, Tiffany glowed with exuberance. The night could only have great things in store. She thought of the environment she would be in, the people she would meet, and the moving speeches she would hear. No one would be shaking a tail feather to Nelly or moving their body like a snake. They would grace the dance floor with a waltz and at most do some Chi-town stepping to the appropriate music. It would be a scene from the "stuffy" life that suffocated Marlon, the life she was comfortable with. After she put her last diamond stud in her ear, she looked in the mirror. The woman before her was free to be herself, and there was no feeling like being free.

Tiffany arrived at Venni's just before six o'clock. Venni opened the door shortly after the last chime sounded wearing a black hooded robe. "Watch out now! Look at you, lady! Come on in."

"I try to do what I can," Tiffany said with a joking confidence that wasn't too far from her truth. She looked immaculate in her ivory evening gown.

Venni was also striking. It was Tiffany's first time seeing her with her hair down, and her silky mane took her to another level of sexiness.

"Sorry I'm not dressed yet. It won't take me long to get ready. My sister called to tell me my nephew was in the hospital and I lost track of time," Venni said, leading Tiffany inside.

"Is he okay?"

"Yeah. His appendix busted. He had surgery this afternoon."

Tiffany could see the lingering concern on Venni's face. "You're close to him, huh?"

"That's my little man. You want something to drink?"

Tiffany declined, not wanting to mess up her lip gloss. Instead, she asked for a quick tour of Venni's grand digs.

181

"What do you do for Innovation again?" she asked, stretching her neck to admire the high ceilings.

Venni laughed. "I'm a computer and information systems manager."

"Can I be trained in that? I feel like I've chosen the wrong profession." She ran her hands across the russet brown leather couch in the living room and noted the 50-inch flat panel TV mounted on the wall.

Every room had a unique color scheme, modern but classy. Even the laundry room was decked out with a blue washer and dryer. This woman had to be her soul mate.

The tour ended upstairs in Venni's bedroom. Tiffany wandered into the bathroom and lost her breath. From the burgundy marble floor to the steps leading up to the oval whirlpool bathtub, it was her favorite room.

"Now this is living," she said. "You make me wanna call my sister right now and tell her to find me something like this."

"Oh, that's right. You said she's in real estate."

Tiffany nodded as she rubbed her hand across the matching marble countertop. She would be late to work every day if she had a bathroom like Venni's. It was like a spa.

"Let me get dressed. If you wanna look around some more, feel free," Venni said, then walked across the spacious room to her closet.

Looking in the mirror, Tiffany picked at her hair and adjusted her breasts so they settled into her strapless bra correctly. As she and Venni joked about the pains of being a woman, she glanced her way and then jerked her head back in amazement. Venni's body looked like the work of an artist—like someone took their time to make sure she was perfect. Every muscle was toned on her athletic frame, but her skin still had its womanly softness. Her C cups only needed the bra for decoration, as they sat with perkiness worthy of envy, and her well-rounded backside looked like it was shaped by her past experiences with a man.

"Can I ask you something personal?" Tiffany asked.

"Shoot."

"Have you ever been with a man?"

Venni stopped shuffling around but didn't turn to face Tiffany. "Sexually?"

"Yeah."

"Yeah. Can you come zip me up?" Venni asked. Tiffany joined her in the walk-in closet that looked more like an extra bedroom. "What made you ask that?"

"Just wondering, I guess," Tiffany replied with a shrug.

As she reached for Venni's zipper, she observed eight dark circles spaced strategically down her spine. They looked like scars from a cigar burn or the result of some weird voodoo ritual. Tiffany didn't think that was too far-fetched since Venni lived in New Orleans for some time.

"What happened here?" she asked, pointing to one of the scars.

"A man," Venni replied. Her chuckle made Tiffany think there was a comical anecdote about the marks.

"Was he into kinky sex?" she asked, chuckling also.

"Not that one. He was into being a dickhead."

As the zipper closed Venni's dress, Venni's statement closed that conversation.

"Let me spray my hair. Then I'll be ready," she continued.

While in the car, the ladies engaged in lighthearted conversation. Tiffany spent much of the time asking Venni about the features in her BMW and singing along to the songs on the radio. When they arrived at the Hyatt, butterflies filled Tiffany's stomach as she waited for the valet to open her door.

"Let's do it," Venni said before the two sashayed in.

Inspiration was in the air. As Tiffany listened to two black men who were a part of the civil rights movement tell of their fight to gain respect in a courthouse where they were the only faces of color, she delighted in their strength. It was hard to fathom a time when social status didn't override the color of one's skin. Even though one was an attorney and the other a judge, they were still mistreated and disrespected. Their speeches were reason enough to have enjoyed the event, filling her heart with a new sense of pride and appreciation for those who came before her. It didn't hurt to hear words from public figures like Tavis Smiley, Judge Glenda Hatchett, and music from Musiq Soulchild, though.

She could say her elbows were adequately rubbed after meeting some affluential locals. When she went to grad school, her key objective was to someday own a private practice, and she wasn't shy about letting anyone know throughout the evening. In the end, she walked away with the business cards of a hospital president, a police chief, and a senator among others.

After saying goodbye to Venni in the driveway, she got in her SUV and headed home. The digital display read 12:38.

"She should be up," she said, while dialing Alexis' phone. Her report wouldn't be as juicy as Alexis' New Year's Eve one, but she had to tell her that she met her favorite TV judge.

The phone rang twice and went to voicemail. When she tried again, it rang four times before it went to voicemail. *Why did I think tonight would be different?* she thought, as she threw the phone on the passenger seat and turned up the radio.

***

Tiffany pulled into Aunt Retha's driveway at 10 p.m. The kids had been visiting with her aunt's grandchildren for three days, and it was time for her to be relieved. Once again, Craig's Chrysler 300 was parked in Jacqueline's driveway next door. He seemed to be a regular there for the past few weeks, sometimes even leaving with Darius in tow. She tried to let Alexis know numerous times, but since she still wasn't accepting her calls, she figured she'd let it be. It wasn't her business anyway.

Venni reminded her of that every time she reported another sighting during their conversations. Though that was true, Craig was still wrong. And even though Tameka was the one Tiffany felt was being disrespected, Alexis was her representative and she deserved the opportunity to cuss Craig out in honor of her sister.

Jacqueline was eating it up, too. Tiffany would watch their goodbyes from her aunt's window—Jacqueline locking her arms around Craig's neck and planting pecks around his face. If Darius was there, she'd squeeze him tightly and tickle his neck like she was family.

"You know you too late," Aunt Retha said when she opened the door. Her housecoat was pulled tight and her hair was set in rollers. "Them kids is sleep. You know I don't believe in no children blinking past eight o'clock, and you ain't wakin' them up."

Tiffany dropped her head and smiled. "I'll just stay the night."

Like clockwork, she peeked out of the kitchen window, and every time, she saw Craig's car. Surely he wasn't staying the night. When morning came, his car was still there, and she could no longer mind her business. Alexis' matters used to be her business, and even though their friendship was strained at the moment, she had to reach out one more time. This time, she decided, she would leave a detailed message. Only this time, the pre-recorded operator informed her that Alexis' number had been disconnected.

As planned, she got the kids ready and took them to Chuck E Cheese. One of the little girls from their church youth group was having a birthday party. As the children romped around the play area, Tiffany's mind stayed on Craig and Jacqueline. Something was telling her that Alexis should know.

184

After whispering to Sister Chambers, she rushed out of the building and headed to the beauty salon. If Alexis kept her usual appointment, she still had time to catch her and tell her. When she pulled up, she took a moment to play out every scenario that could take place. All but one involved Alexis being unreceptive, but even if she didn't say a word to Tiffany, she would at least hear what she had to say.

Guardedly, she entered the shop. The door chime announced her entrance as a few heads turned her way.

"What are you doing here, Miss Thing? I thought you were scheduled for next Thursday," Ava asked as she worked a relaxer in her client's hair. Her widened eyes glanced at Dee Dee, who had Alexis in her chair.

"Yeah, I am. I have to tell her something." She pointed at Alexis, but still stood at a distance.

Dee Dee tapped Alexis on the shoulder with her rattail comb, then used it to direct her attention toward Tiffany. Once she saw her former friend, she turned back around.

Tiffany slid her hands into the pockets of her leather jacket and moved closer to Alexis' chair. "Hey," she said softly.

Alexis ignored her, while Dee Dee and Ava looked on.

"Lexis, I need to talk to you. It's kind of important."

"How many times are you gonna try to apologize? I got all the messages you left. I didn't call back on purpose. Why are you here? Are you stalking me now?"

The other stylists stopped what they were doing and tuned in, while the women under the dryers slowly lifted the hoods so they could hear.

Tiffany inhaled and exhaled slowly as she secured her bottom lip between her teeth. "No, I'm not stalking you. I tried to call your cell but it's disconnected. I knew you'd be here. There's something you need to know about—"

"You knew I'd be here, so you came. That's stalking. Get outta here while you still have a little pride left. You don't know nothin' that I need to know. You just want an excuse to talk to me. I'm sorry you don't have nobody else, Tiff. I really am. But you did this.

"Don't you teach those girls you counsel about that 'good touch, bad touch' stuff? Short, friendly hugs are okay. Two seconds. That's a good touch. You're not supposed to wrap your arms around me and hold me while you rub my back and imagine what I taste like. This cat only likes dogs," Alexis ranted. "And not bitches either!"

Although they tried not to, everyone in the salon laughed in sync. Some even high-fived each other in agreement. The chorus of giggles and chuckles pierced Tiffany's ears as she struggled to maintain her composure; but nothing cut deeper than the hateful words spoken by the woman she once regarded as her sister. Alexis was humiliating her in front of people who knew and respected her. The troubling part was that she wasn't sure if she was more embarrassed because Alexis was cussing her out or because she had announced her personal business to the gossipy bunch. There was plenty she could have said in response, but a war of words with Alexis could quickly turn into a battle with fists—especially if Tiffany said the vile words that were on the tip of her tongue.

She placed her Chloe shades on her face. "I guess some things never change. Don't say I never tried to look out for you." She pranced out of the salon as if she weren't phased, using the glasses to hide the hurt in her eyes. It was okay. Alexis would have to find out about Craig and Jacqueline from a different source.

The following week was filled with the same monotony and the same hint of relationship confusion. Two things were clear, though: she and Venni had grown closer, and she and Alexis were further apart than ever. Another weekend of freedom landed her at Venni's house, lounging on the sofa.

The night before, she and Venni had another intimate experience. What started as quick-witted flirting led to slow, sensual touching and kissing, and ended with Venni trickling Moet down Tiffany's stomach, licking it from her body just before it reached her opening. With the addition of a few grapes coated with Tiffany's natural flavoring, Venni proved herself to be a connoisseur of pleasure, sending Tiffany to the moon again.

Venni came in from her afternoon run. "Your girl is crazy," she said, taking out the earbuds to her MP3 player.

"Huh?"

"Alexis. They just played a clip from yesterday's "What's the Word" when she was talking about how R. Kelly still hasn't gone to trial. Next time you talk to her, tell her that was some funny stuff."

Tiffany looked away.

"She still isn't talking to you?" Tiffany shook her head. "And this is because of us?"

It was easier to say yes than to explain the kiss.

Venni sucked her teeth. "I can't stand ignorance. I'll be back. I'ma take a shower."

When she returned, she found Tiffany standing by the patio door with her hands stuffed in her pockets, staring at the landscape. "What's up, Tiff? You've been quiet all day."

Tiffany exhaled. "Can we talk?"

Venni sat down and prepared to listen. She knew she shouldn't have done that again. She could tell Tiffany was uneasy just after she climaxed the previous night. Tiffany was too much of a thinker and had been overanalyzing their dealings from day one. She was probably feeling guilty for being with a woman again and delighting in every second of it.

Early in her sexual career, she learned not to lay with virgins because they became nuisances; but she didn't think that applied to Tiffany, the woman whose body emitted sexuality the night they met.

"It's about last night," Tiffany began. "I feel like I need to apologize."

"For what?"

"For not…returning the favor. I don't know what to do."

Venni laughed. "For me? You don't have to do anything. Satisfying you satisfies me."

"I find that hard to believe."

"You find it hard to understand. Our relationship isn't about having an orgasm as far as I'm concerned. I can cross my legs and get that."

"That sounds a little creepy."

"What? Crossing my legs or satisfying you?"

"Both."

"Tiffany, I've had enough sex to last me a few more lifetimes. If no one ever touches me again, I'll be just fine." She pulled the front of her basketball shorts down and revealed a shiny barbell pierced through the skin covering her clitoris. "That's my orgasm waiting to happen. And as for the satisfying part, that's all I know. It's what I've been good at since I started having sex, so I mastered it. I aim to please…and I like to make people squirm."

Tiffany's eyebrows rose. Venni was a freak. As her hormones danced with glee, she recognized her attraction to this person: Venni was down for whatever—what she'd always wanted to be. Marlon had limits, so she hadn't been able to fully explore her sexual self. He was far from traditional, but didn't "believe in" doing adventurous, kinky, and downright nasty things with the woman he loved.

She noticed something else while Venni had her pants down…a tattoo on her lower abdomen, just above her pubic area. "What does that say?"

Venni hooked her thumb under the elastic of her shorts again and pulled them down just enough for Tiffany to read. "Father, Forgive Me" was written beautifully in script.

"Look at your face," Venni said with a smirk. "You don't know what to think about me, huh?"

No, she didn't. With her mysterious half-answers and jaded attitude toward sex, Venni was a personified riddle.

"Let me guess. That's your way of saying you can't help how good it is."

"That's what I used to tell people," Venni replied.

"What do you say now?"

"Nothing. I've been through a lot, and that's what it means."

"O…kay. So what is this? What are we doing? Are we friends? Are we friends with benefits?"

"It is what it is. We're having fun."

***

Sunday was a great day. Blue skies, budding leaves, and the warm sun hinted that spring was not far away. Tiffany stood on the church steps with Aunt Retha.

"He's coming back soon," Aunt Retha said.

Tiffany rolled her eyes. The one thing she hated discussing was the end of the world, a topic her aunt always discussed.

"I ain't never seen a sky like this in March. Where's the rain? Where are the clouds?"

"I'm sure it was like this last year, Auntie." Her mind wandered to the previous year as she tried to remember what she was doing then. Though she couldn't recall specifics, she knew she was spending time with Marlon and their children. Times had changed.

"No, it wasn't. I was at revival this time last year. It was a Friday because it was youth night and Reverend Rogers preached. It was chilly."

"How do you remember this stuff?"

"Because I ain't got nothin' better to do!" Aunt Retha laughed at herself. "You probably don't remember nothin' about the whole month of March 'cause you was out partying all the time. Matter of fact, you were at a party while I was here 'cause the babies were with me."

As her aunt took a moment to chat with a fellow member of the usher board, Tiffany's mind flashed to the birthday party she attended.

"I have to go," she said, interrupting Aunt Retha by tapping her on the arm. "I have something to do before Marlon brings the kids home."

She scuttled to her car, careful not to scuff her new Michael Kors pumps.

"Y'all still havin' problems?" Aunt Retha called out after her, But Tiffany was long gone. Curious about her abrupt departure, she looked on as her niece fussed with her cell phone. "Lord Jesus, please protect that child. Don't let her run off and do something crazy."

15

Alexis: Regrets

March 7th...a beautiful and gloomy day. The weather made it beautiful. The day's significance made it gloomy. It was Tameka's birthday. I stood in front of her headstone and stared. Just a year before, we were picking out clothes to wear to her party.

As I set the flowers on the grass, I noticed another bouquet. "Craig," I said aloud, before reading the card attached.

I don't consider you a victim of circumstance; rather a fighter of all odds. Happy Birthday. Your journey was not in vain and you live on in more hearts than you know – Tiffany

I placed the card back into its plastic holder. *Wow! She remembered.* Real friends remember stuff like that. Still, I would've felt stupid calling to thank her after I went off on her at the salon. I'd figure that out later. I hadn't visited Tameka's grave since they buried her, so for the short time I was there, I was going to devote all my attention to her.

I wrung my hands. "Umm, I don't know what to say. I see people on TV talking to headstones all the time, so I guess it's okay. So much has been—"

I was interrupted by footsteps that seemed to be heading my way. Before I turned around, I heard Darius' jibber jabber.

Without any words, Craig handed him to me and walked closer to the headstone. He placed his flowers, then bent over and kissed the stone. Darius playfully waved a piece of paper in the air, hitting me in the eye with it. When I looked, it was a picture of Tameka. That's all he would know his mother as: a picture, a tombstone.

191

I leaned my forehead against his. "It's your mommy's birthday, D-Baby."

He moved his head rhythmically from side to side. "Ma ma ma ma ma ma." I held him tighter, then squatted so he could touch the stone. He laughed as he rubbed the rough surface.

Craig was in his own world. Tears streamed down his face as he whispered to the headstone. I felt like I was invading their privacy, even though I couldn't hear a word he was saying.

"I'm gonna take him to the car with me," I finally said. When he didn't respond, I changed my mind. "Well, I'll just take him home with me. I'll call you when we're done hangin' out." Truth is I didn't feel comfortable leaving him with his dad, who was looking pretty bad.

***

The next day, I went to court to pay my fine. The cops caught up with me as I was leaving work the day after they went to Tielle's. The arresting officer immediately recognized me because he was one of the men who guarded our house while crazy-ass Smoke was threatening Tameka. I told him Robert knew I was taking the rims and that's why he hadn't taken his key back. I admitted to breaking his key and slashing his seats, but said he destroyed his own paint because he planned to get a new paint job in the summer anyway. He cut me a little slack on the charges, though I don't think he fell for my story. When I went to court the first time, the judge hit me with a fine, and that was that. Thanks to Tameka, I was able to pay the balance in full, and I no longer owed society or Robert a penny.

The clock in my car read 12:12. In eighteen minutes, I would be sitting with the infamous Darryl, having lunch. We had talked once since my mother gave him my number, but he said he'd rather discuss the deep stuff in person. Curious to learn more about him, I agreed.

I was ten minutes late, but only because I sat in the car for fifteen minutes staring at Darryl's name in my contact list. I was so close to calling and cancelling, but since he agreed to the DNA test, the least I could do was eat with him.

When I entered the restaurant, he spotted me and waved me over. As I approached, he stood and pulled out my chair. "So we meet again, *Alexis* Nichelle," he said coyly.

I settled in my seat, wondering how such a gentleman could screw another man's wife.

"You having a good day so far?"

"Something like that." I barely made eye contact with him.

192

"How strange is this, huh? One day, we're just a name to each other. The next day, we think we're related," he said, studying my face.

The waitress came to our table and focused all her attention on Darryl. "You ready for drinks now?"

He nodded my way for me to order first. "Let me get a Crown and Coke and a water with lemon," I replied, knowing that Sprite was not going to be enough to calm my nerves.

"Gin and tonic," he said to the smitten woman before she switched her way to the bar. His face was solemn when he turned back to me. "Hey, I was telling your mother how sorry I was to hear about Tameka."

I had purposely stayed up the night before reading the journals Tameka wrote in while she worked at U-Turn. She had nothing negative to say about Darryl. To my surprise, she often spoke of his protectiveness being one of the main reasons she stayed there so long.

"I think about her everyday. Her birthday was yesterday," I said.

"She was a special girl. I always knew it. Everybody knew it. That's why I had to check quite a few knuckleheads that used to wait around after hours to holler at her. I told her not to fool with that TJ cat. That boy stayed in so much trouble. I bet every cop in town knows him."

"Well, he loved my sister."

"Love don't make him a real man. I bet that joker still doesn't have a job."

"Naw, he's dead, too. The same guy killed him a few weeks before he killed Meka."

The waitress placed our drinks on the table. My glass barely left her hand before it was up to my lips.

"Regina didn't mention that. I hate hearing that we lost another young brother to the streets."

"You sure about that?"

"I don't wish death on anybody. He's not the father of her son, is he?"

"No." It was time to get the focus off of Tameka and TJ and back on him. "Do you have kids?" I asked, after taking another swig of my drink.

"Six. Four boys and two girls."

He had been married twice, but said the women couldn't handle the nature of his business. His first wife liked the money he made from his law practice, but hated the time he put in. His second wasn't comfortable with him looking at naked asses all night. He prided himself on being a good father, claiming that he was in touch with five of his six children. The daughter who didn't talk to him was a hardcore

Christian who was sickened by his occupation. She moved out of state once she was of age, just so no one would associate her with him.

"All your other kids live here?"

He nodded. "Two of my sons are lawyers like me."

"What made you stop practicing law and open a strip club?"

"Guilty pleasure, a booming market, and a terrible quarter at the firm." He paused to take a sip from his glass. "I'm not a bad guy, Alexis. I won't say I haven't done bad things…"

"Yeah. Adultery *is* pretty bad."

"So is fornication. I'm sure you're not a virgin."

On TV, the actress portraying me would say, "Touché," but in reality, "You don't know nothin' about me," came out.

"Alexis, I'm just saying don't judge me. There's more to a story than the title."

"Well, let's skip to the chapter that brought us here."

"If you're my daughter, I want to get to know you. It's as simple as that."

"They don't sell Cliffs Notes about Alexis James on Amazon.com. It's not simple. I can't paraphrase twenty-three years of my life for you."

He rubbed his goatee with his thumb and smiled slyly.

"Something funny?" I asked.

He kept smiling, looking like the proud parent of a high school musical star. As I became more perturbed, he shook his head. "You just remind me of somebody."

I looked at my watch and downed the rest of my drink. "I'ma pass on lunch. Does any day work for you?"

"For the test?" he asked. "Just schedule it. I'll be there."

"I'll call you." I hesitated before standing. In essence, he had done nothing wrong. He was nothing less than a gentleman and had handled my smart-ass mouth very well. That was the frightening part, though.

"Okay." He stood and held my hand. "Next week, lunch at U-Turn. I've got the best wings in town. No heavy conversation. We'll just turn on the big screens and hang out. Cool?"

"I'll call you."

***

"Today's the day, right?" Yari exclaimed on the other end of my cell.

"What did you do? Set a reminder in your phone?"

"No. I just remember special occasions."

"Yes, he comes in today. I'm on my way to the airport now."

Isaac's plane was scheduled to arrive at 5:40 p.m., and I didn't want to be late. I was lucky he still wanted to come after I played him to the left when he first offered.

"Enjoy yourself, Lexis."

"I will."

"Let him do what he came to do."

"Did you talk to him or something? Just what do you think he's coming to do?" I asked.

"Sweep you off your feet."

"Have you ever thought about writing a movie when you're done acting in this one? You're talking like this is a fairytale."

"Every fictional story has a touch of reality. Remember that. Okay, I gotta go. My break is almost over. I'll call you in a couple days," she said in one breath.

Right after we hung up, Isaac called and said he had just left baggage claim and would meet me outside. My timing was perfect; I'd just exited the freeway. I spotted him with no problem because he was the only sexy man in sight. He stood at the curb holding two bouquets of flowers and a rolling suitcase.

He is doing too much, I thought. *Two?*

After he situated the luggage in my trunk, he hopped in. "What's up, sexy? You're looking good." His hand grazed my thigh.

"You, too. Don't you start touching on me. You know I'm vulnerable right now." I laughed and so did he.

"Hope you like lilies," he said, handing me the red and orange bouquet. He placed the white roses in the back seat.

"Thanks," I replied.

Hell, I'd like any flowers that didn't come with a damn apology. All the ones from Robert carried a "My bad" sentiment.

"They reminded me of you 'cause they look fiery."

I smiled and shook my head. He would be the type to get me flowers that symbolize something.

When we got on the highway, he asked if we could stop by the cemetery before we went to my apartment. He wanted to put the other flowers at Tameka's headstone. Once again, I had underestimated the kind of man he was. He wasn't trying to woo me with an overabundance of flowers. He wanted to pay his respects to the woman who'd inadvertently brought us together.

When we got to my apartment, we relaxed for an hour and then got dressed. He was taking me to Smoothies. I kind of figured that would be on his agenda, so I already had an outfit in mind. I had just applied my lip gloss when somebody knocked on my door.

I exited the bathroom and looked at my watch. I had put in a work order for maintenance to fix my ceiling fan, but since it was after hours, it couldn't have been them. I could only see the back of a man's head when I looked through the peephole, and I'll be damned if it didn't look familiar.

"How did you find out where I live?" I asked as I violently flung the door open.

Robert waved a white handkerchief in the air. "Truce."

"You need to answer my question."

"Romeo mentioned it in conversation the other day when I asked him where Tielle was."

"Yeah, and I'm sure he mentioned my apartment number. What do you want?"

"To talk. I miss you. I know things have been crazy, baby, but we gotta stop lashing out at each other. We need to talk."

"You talk on the phone and visit when you're invited."

He cleared his throat. "I couldn't call."

"Oh yeah! Because you cut my phone off, dumb ass!"

He reached in his jeans pocket and pulled out a pink Baby Phat RAZR phone. I think that was my cue to run across the parking lot to my storage space and roll out his 22's.

"I was wrong for that. It was the only way I could hurt you. I didn't mean for it to go this far." He peeked into the apartment. "The security deposit for this place was bananas, huh?" I shifted quickly to block his view. "It's the same number," he said as he offered me the phone.

I wiped his chest with my hand. "Why you do that?" he asked, checking his shirt for stains.

"You can take the 'S' off your chest now. I don't need you to rescue me no more."

"I see. You got your new job and a little more paper, so you playin' the independent role."

"And you got a kid and a new set of problems playin' the daddy role. You can keep that shit to yourself."

"You know, Lexis, you ain't squeaky clean. I should've had a child already. You're quick to forget about that, though."

He was trying so hard to get to me. I wouldn't break, though. "That's real classy. Do me a favor. Get out of my doorway and leave me the hell alone."

"How many times do I have to say I'm sorry?" His foot stopped the door from closing. He sounded enraged, but his face was damp with tears.

"None. You're only sorry 'cause you got caught anyway. If I wasn't playin' detective, you wouldn't have told me that Shemar was yours."

"I was gonna tell you. I just had to find the words."

"When? When he turned eighteen?"

The tears kept running. "I need you. You're my rock, baby. This football stuff is about to go through and I want you to enjoy that life with me."

With a stone face, I clapped. "Love the theatrics, but Robert, you look soft. Stop weepin' on my doorstep and go take care of your kid. Enjoy that life with him. We're not taking a break. We're through."

Isaac entered the living room wearing a striped button-down shirt, a chocolate brown blazer, and some jeans. He glanced my way. "Everything alright?"

"Yeah. He was just leaving. You ready?"

"It's like that?" Robert asked before launching my phone across the parking lot. I shrugged. "I knew it," he continued. "You were cheatin' on me with him all along."

"If that'll make you sleep better at night..." I closed the door.

"You straight?" Isaac asked.

"Always," I replied, flinging my purse onto my shoulder. When I realized how empty it felt, I asked Isaac to wait a few seconds while I retrieved Blaze from my bedroom. Once he was in tow, I was ready to roll.

Before we got out of my car, Isaac asked that I leave my gun behind. "...When you're with me, I'm all the protection you need."

When I frowned, he questioned my expression, asking if I thought he wasn't capable of protecting me. Though I didn't think he was soft, I couldn't picture him getting into a fistfight. When we spent time together in Columbus a while back, I'd wondered if carrying my weapon made him uncomfortable, but this was the first time he had indicated it. Instead of answering his question, I took Blaze out of my purse and placed him in the glove compartment. Through my self-administered anger management, I'd learned to choose my battles wisely. We were going to Smoothies, a laid back environment. Why make a big deal over that?

Tielle and Romeo were sitting near the stage when we walked in. She waved us over and invited us to join them.

"I don't wanna be rude, but I've been waiting for months to have this lady to myself," Isaac replied. "We'll check y'all out afterwards."

Tielle grinned as he led me to a table behind them. We ate, drank, and listened to the mellow sounds of the band. Occasionally, someone would step to the mic and perform spoken word. Isaac's friend, the owner, came over and said something to him, but because of the noise, I couldn't hear what they were talking about.

After some lady finished her angry poem about the destruction of the environment, Isaac excused himself from the table, saying he'd be back. He followed the owner onto the stage and sat at the keyboard to accompany the man's vocals. Here and there, I even heard him harmonizing along. I had never kicked it with a guy who could sing or play an instrument, and found myself impressed and a little aroused. The thought of him singing in my ear before sexing me gave him extra points.

When he returned to the table, he told me he also plays the drums and the guitar. We talked a lot about his life—the years that molded who he was. He was highly influenced by his grandfather who'd taught him to play the guitar and passed away when he was seventeen. I enjoyed learning more about him. Almost everything we discussed explained his maturity level and why he seemed like such a good man— too good for me.

By ten o'clock, we'd had enough. I tapped Tielle on the shoulder to tell her we were leaving, and she asked us to wait for them to get their bill. I told her we'd be outside.

Isaac's hand rested lightly on my lower back as he led me out the door. Immediately to our left, three men stood with Angel, an associate of mine. I didn't recall seeing them inside and doubted they would even look twice at a place like Smoothies. When Angel saw me, she called me over.

"Hey, they're looking for some dude named Smoke..."

"Or RaShawn," one of the men interrupted.

"You know him? I've never heard of him," she added.

I took a better look at the guys, recognizing two of them as the goons who came to Tameka's looking for TJ almost two years before. Isaac protectively pulled me close.

"His rotten ass is in the ground," I replied. The tall guy squinted as he looked at me. "Do I look familiar? You and you came to my house a couple years ago, tryin' to start some shit," I said, pointing at each of them.

"You know them?" Angel asked.

"These are the assholes who helped kill TJ, and their friend, Smoke, killed Meka."

"This bitch is tryin' to put us on blast!" the one with braids said.

"Let's go," Isaac said as he turned my body away from them.

198

Before we could take a step, the tall guy grabbed my arm, snatching me from Isaac's hold. "I don't take well to troublemakin' hoes like you. Tell me where Smoke is."

"At Cobblestone Cemetery, courtesy of my sister. MapQuest that shit if you need more details. Now get your fuckin' hands off of me." I yanked away and went to unzip my purse, but stopped. Blaze was in my car.

"You don't touch on no lady like that, my guy," Isaac said, stepping in front of me.

"What the fuck you gon' do, ol' D'Angelo-lookin'-ass nigga?" The men laughed among themselves.

"Go try to intimidate somebody who might actually be afraid of y'all sorry asses," I finished.

As we started to walk away, the guy with braids lifted his shirt, revealing his pistol. "Don't let your mouth get you in trouble, little lady."

I wished like hell I could show him my tool, too. Before I could snap back, though, Isaac pulled back his blazer.

"Is this show or tell? Because we can talk this out right now," he said with his hand resting on the shiny handle of his 9mm. His tone was calm and surprisingly unafraid.

Call me a dead woman, 'cause I would've bet my life that Isaac was totally against using weapons—especially after his request earlier in the evening. But when I thought about it, he had never criticized me for carrying my gun; he only teased me about my heavy purse. Though the incident could've happened with any of my exes, Isaac put a different spin on it. His gun wasn't tucked in his pants like a thug. It was situated in a holster beneath his left arm like only a sophisticated gentleman would carry it—the difference between holding for self defense and holding for recreational purposes. He was a classy man, all about business.

For a split second, I wondered if he was just trying to impress me by showing he could protect me, but his demeanor was too cool for that. He didn't raise his voice, didn't wave the gun around, and didn't step to the dudes.

They studied him for a few seconds, and Isaac glared back, his hand never leaving the handle.

Finally, the third guy spoke. "Let's get outta here before we hurt these lames."

"You gon' end up like your sister, talkin' to grown men like that," the tall dude said.

199

I reached for Isaac's gun, but he was too quick. He pinned my wrist against his chest. As I pleaded with him to let me use it, the guys walked away laughing. The guy with braids thrust his hips like he was having sex, while the tall one made a gun with his fingers and pretended to shoot me. We read their gestures with no problem. They thought it was funny how Smoke raped and killed Tameka. That was enough to piss Isaac off.

"Let me holla at y'all real quick," he said, starting down the street.

I was about to follow him when Tielle and Romeo came out.

"Where's Isaac going?" she asked. Then she heard the threats the threesome were shouting.

Though he was reluctant at first, Romeo jogged after Isaac while I filled Tielle in.

I think we all took extensive mental notes when the silver Audi the men rode in sped away. Tielle remembered details so she could give a description to the cops. I remembered so I could avenge Tameka's death. They were all a part of the ordeal from its origin to its ending, and since I wasn't able to help kill Smoke, it would be nice to make them pay. I studied the car so well that I could recite the license plate number backward or tell you how many dead bugs were on their windshield if you asked. If I saw them again, it would be on.

To unwind, Tielle suggested we go to Nightcap, a nightclub downtown. Everybody at work said it was hot, but I had never been there. I was used to supporting the hole-in-the-wall spots that made most people nervous.

Romeo warmed up to Isaac a little, despite his feelings of disloyalty toward Robert. Since they both were artsy guys, they found they had a lot in common. While they chatted, Tielle bought me a couple drinks. Eventually, my mood lightened and I hit the dance floor with Isaac.

I wasn't surprised at how well he moved. Our bodies moved in sync like each step was choreographed. We started close, but moved closer…closer. I wrapped my arms around his neck and worked him from the front. My rocking hips put him in a trance as he placed his hands on them and leaned into my neck.

"You're playin' right now," he said.

"I don't know what you're talkin' 'bout," I replied, turning around to give him a view of the back.

He pressed his hardness against me to signify that he wasn't backing down. He was turning me on—a process that started when he defended my honor earlier in the evening. Thank God the song ended, because I was about ready to take my clothes off.

200

When we got back to my apartment, that's what I did with Isaac's help. The combination of my horniness, his sexiness, and the newness of each other was a dangerous one. We both wondered how it would feel to dance naked, horizontally.

We began with kissing—lots of kissing. I can usually do without that, but I couldn't lay off of his feather-soft lips. I unbuckled his belt with the anxiousness of a five-year-old at Christmas. He stopped me when I went to unzip his jeans.

"Maybe we shouldn't. I didn't come down here for this. I don't want you to think I expect anything from you."

I knew it was small! He's punkin' out 'cause he has a small dick and doesn't want me to know. I was so horny by then that I could scream. Something was going to have to happen to let me release. As long as it broke the six-inch mark, I could work with it.

"Isaac," I whined, "you can't do that. You don't want it? Come here." I tugged on the waist of his jeans, then rubbed my hand from the top to the bottom of his zipper. His willpower weakened with each stroke, and I slowly pulled his zipper down. "You told me you wanted to make things better for me…as my friend. I figure since you're in the medical field, you can help me out with one more thing."

As I took him into my hand, I stood corrected. He was far from small, far more than six.

He licked his lips. "What hurts?"

I took his hand and tucked it into my panties. "I've got this throbbing down here and I don't know what to do about it."

He told me to lie down, and I obeyed. Before long, his tongue and fingers were inside of me, and I was squirming like crazy. When he was finished, he kissed my clit twice and then licked his fingers. *Freak*, I thought, while smiling at him. I was ready to return the favor, but he wouldn't let me. When I opened to prepare for his entry, he refused, saying, "All that will come in time."

***

The next day, we went shopping, rode go-carts, and played miniature golf. When night fell, we dressed for the club event WTIZ was hosting on the north side. Since I was running late, we had to park a few streets over.

"We might as well just cut through the alley here. It's faster," Isaac said as we neared an intersection.

I stopped. "I don't do alleys."

Portia A. Cosby

He was amused. "You mean to tell me you carry a pistol and you're afraid of alleys?" He held my hand and tried to pull me toward the entryway. "Come on. There's nobody down there."

I pulled the opposite way. "I'm not afraid. I just don't do alleys." We walked on the sidewalk, heading to the main street. "Did Meka ever tell you she was raped in an alley?"

"No. She never said where. My bad," he said.

"It's cool. Now you know why I don't do alleys." I smiled to put him at ease and turned on my tunnel vision. If I would've looked to my right, I would've seen the alley where it all took place two blocks down.

We had another great day together, but his visit ended too quickly. As soon as we laid down, it was time to get up. He had to catch a ten o'clock flight so he could be well rested for work at eleven that night.

"When are you gonna be my woman?" he asked before exiting the car.

"When you move back to Texas."

"You're killin' me."

"So you're stickin' with your story? You're not kickin' it with *anybody*?"

"It's not a story. It's the truth."

"Why me? We live so far apart."

"I have frequent flyer miles."

"And I'm not big on flying."

"Listen. We've been upfront with each other since we met almost a year ago. I told you then that I dig you. It's all good, though. Long-distance relationships aren't for everybody."

I could tell he wanted to say more, but he had to go. As I watched him walk away, I wanted to call out to him. I couldn't knock a long-distance relationship until I tried it. Since I waited too long to open my mouth, I opened my phone and texted him: *If the offer still stands, I'll be your woman today.*

He responded almost right away, *We'll make it work*. The "wink face" after his words sealed our deal. We were a couple.

***

WTIZ had teamed up with two local chapters of Zeta Phi Beta for a charity event. Our goal was to raise $5,000 to help keep the largest women's shelter in town open. We held an all-night bowl-a-thon that had something for everybody…games, food, drinks, celebrity appearances, and of course, a live broadcast.

It was packed. The crowd was mixed, ranging from the young to the old and the rich to the struggling. Other sororities and fraternities came out to support, as well. Since I didn't go to college, that wasn't my thing, but Tielle was representing her royal blue and "pure" white, as she put it, to the fullest. I always thought sorority chicks were stuck up, but her sorors were cool.

Since I rode with Tielle, I joined her and her crew at Lane 7. As I looked around to see who all I knew, a few faces stood out—none more than Robert's. I should've known he would be there with Romeo.

He wouldn't stop staring at me, which was pissing me off. I tried my best to stay focused on our game, but if he looked at me one more time, I was going to have to make a trip to Lane 12. His gaze wasn't one of longing. It was a crazy look, like the one I'd just seen on Court TV from the man who strangled his ex-wife.

I hadn't heard from him since the day he saw Isaac walking around my apartment, but I knew his ego was still bruised from that. People in love can go nuts sometimes when they can't have their way, so I kept my eye on my purse in case Blaze needed to come out and say hello.

"Steeee-rike!" I yelled as I danced to my seat. It was my third one in a row. "Take that! Y'all have y'all little call, so I'ma make that one mine. Stee-ee-ee-rike!" I said, throwing up some random fingers and making up an impromptu stroll. I was about to do the running man when Robert approached us.

"What's up?" he said brazenly and with a smirk.

"Don't come over here like we cool."

"I'm just tryin' to be cordial."

"Stop tryin'."

He nodded at Tielle, then turned to the other women. "Ladies," he acknowledged.

I looked him up and down, wondering what his agenda was. He was too cocky.

"Did you hear I got a callback from that team in Vegas?" he asked before licking his lips.

"Did somebody make the mistake of telling you I give a fuck?" My paper chasing days were over. I was far from a millionaire, but I had a solid job and real money coming in. The possibility of him getting paid to play ball meant nothing to me anymore. "Now can you go away so we can finish our game?"

"Are these your people now? Man, it must be cold livin' in Meka's shadow, huh? You ain't got no more friends, so you still clingin' to LT." He shook his head. "Did you get tired of Tiffany kissin' on you?"

I swallowed hard. "What? You thought I didn't hear about that?"

"Robert, don't come over here with that," Tielle said. "Lexis, don't let him take you there. Come on. You're up after Kym."

203

She was right. He was trying to push my buttons, and he'd gone straight for the flashing one. I turned to rejoin the group.

"Where's ya boy? He go back to his nursing duties?" He held his hand with a limp wrist, mocking Isaac's predominantly female profession.

"I don't know. I think he took a few more vacation days. He was worn out after licking all the wounds you gave me. He nursed me right back to health, though." Just then, it seemed like someone turned the volume down on everything in the bowling alley.

He laughed off his embarrassment. "So you let him hit it?"

"That's none of your business."

"You did. I know you. It'll never be better than this, so I ain't trippin'." He grabbed his crotch.

"Oh, it gets hard now? Or did you already pop your pill?"

He never dreamed I'd go there—ever. His Viagra secret was supposed to be just that—our secret. A year before, he listened to one of his dumb friends who told him steroids wouldn't mess with his erectile function, so Robert, being the vain ex-athlete he is, took the stupid things religiously. Within two months, we had problems. He blamed everything else but the steroids. He drank too much; he wasn't feeling good anyway; he was tired; I wasn't into it enough. When he ran out of excuses, he ran to his same idiot friend who hipped him to the blue pill. Although he didn't have to use them all the time, he kept a supply on hand for those inopportune moments.

"Alexis, do you realize people know who you are and you're standing here making a scene?" Tielle said in my ear.

With no real comeback left, Robert backed off. "Alright, Big Time, I'll let you get back to your game before you make up any more lies. It's kinda sad that you've let this little gig blow your head up. You're on the radio, not BET."

"Not yet, hater," I said before returning to the group.

***

On the morning of the DNA test, my dad called a little before eight o'clock. I answered, expecting to hear his last plea for me to change my mind. Instead, he told me he had changed his. Though he didn't want to let me down, he said he was not participating in the test and didn't want to know the results. I was okay with that. Between me, my mom, and Darryl, I'd still get answers.

The waiting area in the lab was as bright as I imagine heaven would be. The powerful fluorescent lights served more as spotlights than anything else, displaying the doubt on everyone's face in the room, mocking the shame in the clueless mothers' eyes. Three women and four men occupied the chairs farthest from the door when I entered. I glanced to see if I knew any of them, then proceeded to the check-in desk.

Where is the receptionist? I thought, while searching the counter for a sign-in sheet. Soon, a petite lady rushed to the desk, smiling uncomfortably. She greeted me, then nervously opened and closed drawers as if she were looking for something specific.

"I'm sorry," she said. "I'm one of the technicians. I know nothing about our front office, and our receptionist is running late this morning. Bear with me."

Just when the lady located a clipboard, Dap hurried into the office. "Sorry, Justine. There was a bad accident on the off ramp."

She was too busy hanging her jacket and putting her purse away to notice me standing there. I'd heard she wasn't working at the bank anymore, but I never thought she'd work in a front office. Once she was situated, she looked up and opened her mouth, but said nothing.

I spoke up. "I'm the ten o'clock appointment."

Dap's widened eyes looked down at my stomach, then back at me.

"No," I simply said.

She looked at the schedule, then bucked her eyes again. "Miss Regina?"

I nodded. "It's crazy."

"Mr. James ain't your dad?"

"If I knew that, I wouldn't be here, right?"

"I thought you were joking when you used to say you and Meka—"

Much like she'd abruptly stopped herself, I abruptly walked away and sat near the magazine rack. Pulling out my phone, I proceeded to play Solitaire to avoid acknowledging Dap's attempts to get my attention. Yeah, I used to say Tameka and I had different parents, but I was just talking shit.

Darryl and my mom arrived shortly after that. She almost pissed on herself when she saw Dap at the desk. Her reprimanding glare affirmed that she thought I set her up. Once they joined me in the waiting area, we resembled the uncomfortable bunch that was there before us. Darryl cracked jokes occasionally in an attempt to lighten the mood, but there was too much at stake for me to laugh. I caught my mom looking at the two of us, checking for similarities. I caught her agreeing with me.

We took turns entering the room, having our cheeks stretched out and swabbed from within. Darryl came out smiling, and my mom came out adjusting her sunglasses and lowering her hat. I came out wondering if I had made a mistake.

16

Tiffany:
Nosey

Tiffany leaned on the baluster on Marlon's mother's porch and hung her head as she listened to Aunt Retha on the other end of the phone.

"I've lived here twenty years, and I've never had to call the police," Aunt Retha fussed.

I knew I shouldn't have answered right now, Tiffany thought. She wanted to make her drop-off with Marlon a quick one, and her aunt's story was sure to prolong it. She moved the phone's receiver a few inches from her ear and shifted her weight to her right leg.

Aunt Retha had been complaining about the vehicle in her neighborhood for days. A month before, it was the stray cat that was getting too close to her flowers. "Well, what made you call them? What was the car doing this time?"

"It keeps riding back and forth, making me nervous. They stopped in front of my house today!"

"Maybe they're lost."

"They ain't been lost for a week! If they are, I'm sure the officers can help them get unlost."

Unlost? Aunt Retha was becoming too nosey for her own good. She stayed in the window looking out at the street. Every neighborhood needed someone like her, but she was taking this incident too far.

"They're probably some drug dealers, and I'm not havin' that on my street."

"Everybody's not a drug dealer, Auntie."

"I don't know a twenty-year-old with a fancy car and a career that helps 'em pay the note."

"What kind of car is it?"

"Some silver something with circles on the front. Even when I have my glasses on, I can't see the name of it. And they keep playing that loud music, shaking my house off the foundation."

"Just don't let them see you, Auntie. If they're troublemakers and think you're on to them, they could try to hurt you. Stay away from the windows."

Aunt Retha agreed, but Tiffany was sure she wouldn't take her advice. When they hung up, Marlon looked concerned.

"Is she alright?"

"She's just being herself. Anyway, I packed Tony's breathing machine because he's been wheezing at night. Make sure he's not running around too much. The cut on Bryant's foot has healed, so don't let him talk you out of taking a bath. He's been overdramatic, saying it burns when it's in the water. It doesn't."

"Baby girl is straight?"

"Bria's fine. Oh, but Billy is gonna have to come over here with them starting next week. I'm tired of running to the house on the weekends to let him out. I have too much going on." Tiffany looked at her watch. "Alright, I'm outta here."

"Meetin' up with Venni?"

"Why?"

"You don't have to tell me, but I'm tellin' you this: Keep my kids away from her."

"You couldn't tell me what to do when we were together. What makes you think you can now?"

"This isn't up for discussion. I don't want them around her. If you can't respect that, I'll get the courts involved."

Tiffany laughed with disbelief. "I'd love to see that."

"Don't test me. They'll declare you unfit in a heartbeat."

"And then you woke up. Please, Marlon. You don't want to go that route. I'm quite sure they frown upon street pharmacists like you in the court of law. And for your information, our children look at Venni just like they did Alexis. They went shopping with us. There is nothing inappropriate going on and I resent that you would think otherwise."

Bryant ran over to Marlon. "Can I have a snack, Daddy?"

"Anything else?" Tiffany asked. Marlon gritted his teeth. "I didn't think so." She kissed Bryant on his forehead, then turned to her ex. "Let me know when our court date is."

She left the stench of her arrogance behind as she strutted away. She was off to meet Venni, Frenchie, Lawrence, and his cousin, Cedric, at the winery for a tasting.

Tiffany was in red wine heaven. She tasted every variety available, from her usual cabernet and pinot noir to the unfamiliar but tasty Lambrusco. By the end of the evening, she was feeling good…all over.

However, she woke up early the next morning with a pounding headache. She raided Venni's medicine cabinet and gulped down two ibuprofen tablets with orange juice. Going back to bed sounded wonderful, but she had work to do. She sat at Venni's breakfast bar, overwhelmed with envelopes that still had to be addressed and stuffed with invitations for the twins' birthday party.

Venni entered the kitchen and stopped behind Tiffany's barstool. "Dang! How many of those are you sending out?" She leaned over Tiffany's shoulder. "That doesn't say 'Alexis,' does it?"

Tiffany sealed the envelope and placed it on top of the "Done" pile, then started addressing the next envelope.

"Did I miss something? Did you two make up since she humiliated you at the salon?" Venni continued.

"She's Bria's godmother. She wants her there."

"Bria's a child. She'll get over it. You want her there."

"Why do you care? She was my friend. So what if I want her there? You're right. I would be ecstatic if she came…for Bria."

"And if she doesn't come?"

Tiffany didn't respond.

"You'll be upset, right?"

This time, Tiffany shrugged.

"You're amazing. You were the same way with Marlon. I don't let anyone become important enough to determine my happiness," Venni stated.

"That's cold."

"That's real. Why should anyone matter that much? And Bria will enjoy herself just the same if Alexis doesn't show."

"You say that because you don't have children."

"I say it because you're using your daughter to reach out to a *friend* who doesn't give a damn about you. Real friends don't want to see you make a fool out of yourself."

As Venni walked to the refrigerator, Tiffany stared at Alexis' envelope. Maybe she was stupid for sending the invite. Alexis didn't even call, text, or email to acknowledge the flowers she'd left at Tameka's grave…but did she really expect her to?

"Are you ready to go?" Tiffany asked, leaving the kitchen to sit on the couch. She'd told Venni she would help her find some art for her bare walls and she wanted to get it over with.

"I can be. Let me change clothes and call Lawrence. We were supposed to go to the gym, but I'll tell him we'll go later."

Tiffany stopped her before she started up the stairs. "Do you have a phonebook?"

"Yeah. Look in the drawer of that end table next to you."

Tiffany found the book on top of a stack of old bills and newspaper clippings. The clipping on top caught her eye. The crisp paper was obviously more recent than the flimsy, discolored pieces beneath it. After looking more closely, she saw that the article with the handsome man's picture was really an obituary.

Vincent A. Miles, 55, passed away March 16, 2004 at his residence. Born February 28, 1949 in Nassau, Bahamas, he was the son of the late Dmitri and Vivian Miles. Vincent was the proud owner of VM Construction Company and a member of St. Paul Catholic Church.

In addition to his parents, he was preceded in death by his loving wife, Rita (Parish) Miles in 1989 and brother, Donovan Miles in 2000. Surviving are his son, Vincent Miles, Jr. (wife Kendra) of Burbank, CA; two daughters, Tangela Fields (husband Brian), District of Columbia, and Venita Miles; a grandson, Vance Fields, and a host of nieces and nephews...

Venni's resemblance to her father was uncanny. He couldn't have denied her to a blind man. Tiffany found it odd that her location wasn't listed like her brother and sister's. Were the two not speaking? Even more odd was Venni not mentioning her father's death. Sure, she was a private person, but something like that comes up at least once in conversation. Tiffany chalked it up to denial, a part of the grieving process that some go through longer than others, and flipped through the phonebook to get the number for the art gallery.

When she opened the drawer to put the book back, she couldn't help but notice the headline of another article, "Teen Found Slain." The morbidity theme of the articles was too intense for her, so she closed the drawer. When Venni said she had experienced more pain than joy in life, she sure wasn't lying. Her mother died when she was twelve, her dad was now deceased, and she was evidently close to the slain teen in the newspaper article. Her attitude toward others had a justifiable origin. She didn't place importance on relationships because so many people she cared about had passed away.

***

When Thursday rolled around, Venni couldn't have been more anxious. Tangela and Vance were flying in from D.C., and she would be picking them up at four. The day seemed to move at a snail's pace, but when 3:30 hit, she shut down her computer and hightailed it to the elevators.

Her phone rang while she waited. "Where are you?" Tangela asked once Venni answered.

"I'm leaving my office. Where are you?"

"Waiting for you. Our plane landed a half hour ago."

Venni could've sworn Tangela told her four o'clock. "Maybe the time difference threw me off. I thought you meant four o'clock my time. It won't take me long. Give me twenty minutes."

Tangela kept fussing at her, but Venni's phone signal was lost once she stepped in the elevator. When she reached the main lobby, her high heels click-clacked loudly, indicating her rush. Suddenly, she stopped. Fifty feet away, she could see Tangela and Vance entering the building and a white taxi waiting at the curb.

Tangela was a little on the heavy side, but she wore her weight well. Though her face was fuller and her eyes were much darker, her beauty matched her younger sister's. She walked with a rhythm, like music was playing in her head, exhibiting confidence worthy of envy.

Vance walked a few feet behind her with his hands in his pockets. From the neck down, he looked much older than thirteen, but his face displayed the innocence of a child. He looked mixed, like maybe he'd inherited the bulk of his grandfather's Caribbean genes. Even a glance could confirm that he didn't look like his father, who was a very unattractive man with opposite features.

"April Fool's!" Tangela said when they reached Venni.

"You ass," Venni replied. "You had me thinking I was crazy."

After they hugged, Vance took a step toward his aunt. "Hey, Aunt V."

"Look at you," Venni said. She ran her hand across his hair, then hugged him. Though his demeanor was more subdued, the warmth in his eyes showed how much he loved her. "You brought your shoes, right?" she asked.

He nodded. Vance knew there would be a few one-on-one games of basketball in his aunt's backyard every time he visited. He looked forward to them. Venni bought his first basketball when he was six, and it served as a physical representation of his inner gift. She gave him what his father had denied him. Theodore was a stuck-up intellectual

211

who refused to believe athletes could also be scholars. He tried his best to discourage Vance from playing sports at a young age, but Venni's influence proved to be much stronger.

She was glad she had made that contribution to his life. It was a simple one that was sure to turn into something much more profound. Vance had "it"—what it takes to be a superstar—even though he was barely a teenager. She had no doubt that his skills would eventually land him at a Division I college and in the NBA.

"Did you bring your game this year?" she teased. "I see you grew. That doesn't mean nothin'." He stood 6'3", five inches taller than her. "You'll just be more embarrassed when I rain those threes on you."

"Please. Just make sure you don't call a charge when I dunk on you," Vance replied.

Tiffany stood just outside of the daycare center and witnessed their greetings. Days before, Venni had stated she didn't let anyone determine her happiness, but she looked the happiest Tiffany had ever seen when she interacted with Vance. It was refreshing to see her contradict herself, because everybody needs someone to love. For Venni's sake, she prayed Vance would remain in her life. He was the "someone" she cared about; her reminder that it was okay to feel, okay to be human.

In an effort to keep their moment as intimate as possible, Tiffany took the long route to the elevators. When she reached her office, the light on her phone was flashing. She'd missed a call from Morgan, who needed Bryant and Bria's updated shoe sizes so she could send their birthday gifts on time. A shoe fanatic at heart, she always bought the twins matching customized sneakers in the boy and girl versions. When she called Morgan back, Tiffany ran down the itinerary for the party, expressing extra excitement about booking the best magician in the state.

"I wish I could be there," Morgan said. Without thinking, she had booked a trip to The Hamptons on the weekend of the party.

"I wish I could be where you're going!"

"On the bright side, I don't have to look at your baby daddy. Oh, I forgot he's your fiancé now. Either way, he's still pitiful."

It was time to tell her sister the truth. "We're not together. We haven't been together for a couple months."

Morgan tried not to shout with joy. "So are you seeing anybody?"

Tiffany remained silent.

"Wait. Who broke up with who?"

"It was mutual." She then went on to tell Morgan about the roofies.

212

"Why didn't you tell me when all this happened? I knew that raggedy fool was doin' something crooked. It's best that you learned now. I hate you had to find out like that, though. At least it explains the whole Venni thing, though. Do you still see her at work?"

"I just saw her a minute ago. I see her all the time."

"Does she speak?"

"I see her *all* the time. We talk every day."

"Wait. What do y'all have to talk about?"

"Everything. We're friends."

"What kind of friends? Are you…?"

"I'm having fun."

After a pregnant pause, Morgan burst into laughter. "You almost got me. I just remembered what today is."

Tiffany looked at her phone and saw the date…April 1st.

"That'll be a good one to get Mom with. Call her on three-way."

Morgan finally stopped laughing after she noticed she was laughing alone.

Tiffany wished she could please her sister with a boisterous "April Fool's," but all she could say was, "I'll call you later. My patient is here."

Portia A. Cosby

17

Alexis:
You ARE the Father

Tielle asked me to go with her to the caterer to taste food for the wedding after Romeo backed out at the last minute. He told her that he trusted her to make the right choices, which only heightened her indecisiveness. She needed a practical person who would pay attention to the taste and not get caught up in the fanciness of the ingredients.

She told me to be ready in a half hour, but she was banging on my door in fifteen minutes. I was practically dressed, but still had to brush my teeth.

"You're early," I said after letting her in.

"You'll live. Hurry up. I still have to stop by Craig's before we go." She leaned against the kitchen counter, knocking a stack of mail onto the floor. The last piece she retrieved was an invitation to Bria and Bryant's birthday party.

I jogged into the dining area with my sneakers in one hand and socks in the other.

"When's the last time you talked to Tiffany?" Tielle asked.

"At the beauty shop. Why?" I replied. She held up the invitation and I rolled my eyes. "Yeah, and she sent a note with it saying how Bria really wants me to come."

"You're her godmother."

I sighed.

"You haven't ripped this up, so you must be thinking about going. Tiffany has a damn good heart. I wouldn't fool with you after you publicly humiliated me. I wouldn't care if it was for my child or not."

"Right! Any normal person would feel like that. Tiff is messed up, I'm tellin' you. She's a smart girl and all, but she has a couple loose screws. She's clingy, even now!"

"I know you ain't talkin' about somebody with loose screws. Did you ever think she just values your friendship that much? Really, you need to make amends with her."

"You smokin'."

"That girl ain't gon' kiss you again, Lexis. She ain't crazy. Y'all hung out all the time before, and she didn't come at you like that."

"That was before Venni."

"You mean to tell me you don't miss her?"

I shrugged. Maybe a little. And I still felt bad about embarrassing her at the shop. Tielle asked if I even bothered to thank Tiffany for remembering Tameka's birthday. Of course, I hadn't.

She shook her head. "I thought your sister was stubborn, but you have her beat."

When we pulled up to Craig's, we had to park on the street because he already had company. A topaz Jaguar was parked in the driveway.

"You're getting out," she said.

"I am not."

"What's the deal with y'all?"

The car looked more and more familiar as I argued with Tielle. I exited her car to further inspect the Jaguar just as Craig's door was opening. When I reached the edge of the driveway, I found just what I was looking for—the "ECON QN" license plate. I then looked up and saw a teary-eyed Jacqueline rushing to the car.

"Do you have that much nerve to come to the scene of your brother's crime, or are you just stupid?" I asked as I tore after her.

Our short game of "Chase Me Around the Car" was interrupted when Craig and Tielle grabbed my arms and pulled me inside.

"Y'all always comin' to that broad's rescue," I yelled, while snatching away.

I reminded them of when she showed up to Tameka's baby shower uninvited. She thought it was okay because she was with Craig, but when the shower was over, Tameka was ready to make it clear that it wasn't. Tielle told Tameka to lay off of her, while Craig heroically sent her to the car for safety.

"We're looking out for your hotheaded behind." Tielle's finger was in my face.

I swatted her hand away. "I don't need your help."

"Why are y'all even here?" Craig interjected.

"You asked me to drop off these tickets. Don't come at me like that," Tielle replied. "I'll just put them on the mantle and leave you the hell alone. Both of y'all got me twisted with these funky attitudes." She walked into the living room. "Did she do this?" she asked, while stepping over pieces of a broken vase. "Do we need to call the cops?"

"You ain't gotta call nobody. I've been waitin' for another reason to dig into her ass," I said as I flung the door open and looked to see if she was still lingering around outside. The only traces of her were the black markings her tires left on the driveway's cement.

"I did it," Craig answered solemnly.

"Why? What happened?" Tielle asked.

He told us he threw the vase in a fit of anger. I automatically assumed he'd finally snapped on her for sending Smoke Tameka's way. Soon after, Craig shot down my assumption.

"She's pregnant." His head tipped backward, and the thud from its collision with the wall echoed through the quiet room.

"By who?" I asked, but he didn't answer.

"Craig, no," Tielle pleaded.

"By *who*?" I repeated.

"Who do you think?" he yelled as he finally looked at me.

My blood felt cold as ice as I stared at him. I felt betrayed. I didn't know who I was more pissed off for—my sister or myself. I thought more of him. In my eyes, he wouldn't have disrespected Tameka's memory by screwing the ho that was partly responsible for her murder. Guess I needed glasses.

"So when did you start seeing her again?" Tielle asked.

"We weren't seeing each other," Craig corrected.

"When did you start fucking her, then?" I looked up. "Sorry, Jesus," I said under my breath.

"Y'all don't think I feel bad enough? I don't need this right now."

"What you don't need is another baby," Tielle said.

"By an obsessed broad with two other kids," I added as I headed back into the foyer. "You didn't waste no time, huh? Meka ain't even cold in the ground," I said over my shoulder as I walked out. "I'll be in the car, LT."

Tielle came out to the car with Darius. She said he heard our voices and woke up wanting to go with her. We didn't discuss Craig during the rest of our time together, probably because there was nothing else to say.

Darius stayed the night with me, and I spent most of the night watching him sleep. I wondered what he was dreaming about as he smiled occasionally. I wondered if Tameka was an angel that appeared to him nightly. If so, I could've used a visit from her, but I couldn't keep my eyes closed long enough to dream.

***

Just after our eight o'clock diaper change the next morning, Craig called. He was at the gate of my apartment complex and needed me to let him in. I was annoyed that he had come unannounced, but it was all good. My real issue with him was much deeper than that.

I packed Darius' diaper bag and placed it by the door. At the last second, I stuffed one of Tameka's journals inside the bag. It was the one I had been reading off and on, the one in which Tameka professed her love and hate for Craig.

He knocked on the door as I situated Darius in his car seat. "It's open," I yelled.

Craig looked dumb as hell when he walked in. When he spoke, his eyes never left the floor. "Before I leave, we need to talk."

"I don't have nothin' to say to you. Darius' stuff is over there in the corner. Make sure you lock my door." When I turned to go to my room, he stopped me. I looked down at my arm. "Are you touching me?"

"Lexis, you might as well get it out the way. Say it. I messed up."

"I've got a better verb."

"Then say it. Let it out, 'cause at the end of the day, we have to get along for Darius' sake."

"I don't have to tell you that you a dirty dic—" Deep breath. "You dirty and you know it. Want me to let it out? I hope your dumb ass made sure Jacqueline doesn't have HIV like her brother. God don't just hand out miracles everyday. You and Darius not gettin' it from Meka was enough. I bet you didn't ask her shit about that while y'all was reunitin'. What's your excuse for bonin' her anyway? Did she remind you of Meka, too? What was it? Her nail polish? Earrings?"

"I made a mistake."

"*We* made a mistake. You and Jacqueline made a baby. A mistake happens once. You've been fuckin' her since I stayed with you 'cause that was her coffee mug you tried to put off on Ms. Rosie.

"Do you really understand how my sister felt about you? She chose *you* over TJ—your lame ass! She was writing in her journal about you like it was her middle school diary, leaning on your every word and loving you past the pain you caused her, and you just shitted on that.

I'm glad she didn't give my nephew your last name. When he's old enough to hear this story, I'm sure he won't want a damn thing to do with you."

"That's not fair."

"It's not fair that this little boy doesn't have a mother, and your new baby mama helped make it all happen. What's the plan now? Marriage? If you gon' do it, you might as well do it to death. Wanna dig up Meka's grave so you can retrieve her ring? Is Darius gon' be callin' Jacqueline 'Mommy'?"

"That's low."

"You're low. I know you have to get on with your life at some point, but five months later? Five months, and you have another kid on the way. Congrats, Big Daddy, if you really are the daddy. Her car sure spends a lot of time in U-Turn's parking lot before they open. You might wanna check that out."

He kept his head down.

"You wanted to know how I feel, right? That's how I feel. I feel like you ain't shit. Meka's lookin' down on you right now, feelin' like you ain't shit."

I waited a few seconds for a response. "Nothin' to say? I thought *we* needed to talk?" More silence. "Right. Get outta my house."

This time, I stuck around to see him leave. Dejected and speechless, Craig slowly gathered Darius' car seat and diaper bag and left.

***

Why do I miss you like this? I thought, while staring at the picture Isaac and I took at Dave and Buster's. I had called to tell him how sorry of a man Craig was and we'd just hung up.

In the month since we had declared ourselves a couple, I'd gone through a whirlwind of emotions. Yari was convinced I was in love, but I wasn't. It was too soon. I felt *something* for him, though, because I dreamed about him almost every night, I glanced at my phone every ten minutes to make sure I hadn't missed a text message from him, and I couldn't get Tyrese's song, "Sweet Lady" out of my head. It was on the Quiet Storm radio program one night while he was visiting, and he sang bits of it, jokingly dedicating it to me. Even though we both laughed, many parts of the song rang true and his delivery was strikingly similar to Tyrese's. To me, the moment was more romantic than humorous. Robert's tone-deaf ass never made me feel like that when he sang along to the radio. While Isaac was only trying to tickle my funny bone, I was ready to jump all of his bones. There was no question that he was a special man. The question was whether he was supposed to be *my* man. Opposites attract, but for how long? I couldn't help but think about what would happen after our infatuation wore off.

Darryl called in the middle of my daydream. We were expecting to get the DNA test results in three days, and we still hadn't met again for lunch. I declined his offer to treat me to wings and drinks at his bar. There was nothing more to know about each other unless he was my biological father. I would feel like I was betraying my daddy if I met with my mother's piece-on-the-side again.

The three days flew by. I had just come home from work, when a large envelope arrived by courier a little after one. The red "F.Y.I. Diagnostics" logo stood out on the white background, leaving no doubt where the package came from. I thought I would want to rip it open as soon as it was in my hands, but my heart was holding me back.

For forty-five minutes, I welcomed every distraction. I checked my email, did some research for work, picked at a hangnail, and started a load of laundry. When I ran out of things to do, I returned to the front room and sat on the couch. The envelope lay on the coffee table, waiting to give me the answers that neither party involved could give me.

I slid my thumb under the sealed flap and inhaled. Then I pulled out six sheets of paper and thumbed through until I found the one with "Parentage Testing Results (Inclusion)" in bold lettering. My eyes scanned the document. Case number, tested man, mother, child, blah, blah, blah, SUMMARY OF FINDINGS.

I exhaled as I read. *Darryl Middleton is not included as the biological father of Alexis N. James...*

There were a lot of numbers and letters and calculations of chromosomes and other biological data that I didn't understand, but those paragraphs didn't matter. All I needed to see was that one sentence. I threw my head back and smiled. Then, just for kicks, I read the other paperwork.

One sheet was an explanation of how the tests were done. It explained how I would find only two kinds of reports in my results packet—an inclusion and/or exclusion report—and no matter how many men were tested, there would only be one inclusion report because only one man could be the father. Since Daddy didn't get tested, I only received one report...

I froze. Though I only skimmed through the results page, I was sure the header read "Inclusion." *Please let me be wrong,* I thought, as I pulled the report from the bottom of the stack. I wasn't.

I read at the pace of a third grader, being careful to interpret each word as it was typed. *Darryl Middleton is not excluded as the biological father of Alexis N. James*. I even read the scientific data as if I knew what it meant, then read further and saw the text version of what I saw when I first met Darryl. *The alleged father, Darryl Middleton… probability of paternity is 99.99994%…*

Clearly, I read what I *wanted* to read the first time around. This time, I read what my heart already knew. Darryl and I didn't favor each other; we looked alike, and it was finally clear why. He was 99.9% included as a major part of me, and in one sentence, the father I've known all my life was reduced to a zero in the realm of science.

As soon as I tossed the papers onto the couch, the phone rang. It was my mother. Her copy of the results had arrived, too.

"Lexi, I'm sorry," was all she kept saying.

When I'd had enough, I said, "If you're really sorry, you'll keep your mouth shut. I'm tellin' Daddy that Darryl's test excludes him as my father. If you talk to him, that's the story you need to go with. It shouldn't be hard. You've been lying for years."

"Ouch. Okay, I deserve that," Mom replied. "But, Lexi, the lying has to stop sometime, right?"

"How convenient for you to want to tell the truth now. I get it. This is about you. You are so fuckin' selfish. You want to tell Daddy the truth so you can walk away from this like you planned it all out to hurt him."

"You don't know what you want, Alexis. You've preached about the truth ever since you read Tameka's diary, and now you want me to lie."

"Well, since you're so into telling the truth now, are you gonna call all your friends and tell 'em I'm your love child with your lawyer friend?" I asked.

She cleared her throat, but didn't speak.

"Let me ask you somethin'. Have you known all along?"

"I had a feeling," she answered smugly.

"Did you care how I would feel if I found out?"

"You weren't supposed to find out."

Self-righteous bitch. "Has Daddy ever seen him?"

"No. Why would he want to? And why all the questions? You have your answers and I have apologized. Any more details will only upset you more."

I had no wish to show mercy on her, but I wouldn't have been able to refrain from cussing her out if I didn't get off the phone. I reiterated my position to her. If she didn't go along with my story, she would lose me as a daughter forever. If she agreed to spare my dad's feelings, she would only lose me until I healed. She chose the latter, and we hung up uncertain of when we'd talk again.

When I insisted on getting the test, I thought the results would give me answers. Instead, I wound up with more questions. I wound up with more anger, hurt, and confusion. Was I supposed to call Darryl and set a day and time for lunch now?

He could never be my dad for all intents and purposes. He didn't teach me how to ride a bike or take me to my first concert; Darnell James did. Where was Darryl when I went on my first real date with JC Glover? My dad, Darnell, was in JC's face on the front porch, threatening his life. He was standing beside me in my high school graduation pictures. Those were the things that really mattered, that really determined paternity, so I should've found comfort in them. I would've if Darryl had chosen not to be in my life. He was never given the option, though, so I couldn't hate him for not being around. I couldn't bring myself to love him, though, nor give him the chance to earn my love.

The three dominant feelings were fighting within me, each competing for special attention, and my mind wouldn't slow down enough to let me handle them. All the anger, hurt, and confusion I felt was longing to come out by any means necessary. My first instinct was to kick the coffee table, but the vision of a huge shard of glass sticking out of my sock stopped me. Instead, I stood up and released a frustrated moan. When that didn't help, I punched the wall, which instantly caused me to forget about the paternity results because my hand felt like it had been crushed by a steamroller. I slid down the wall and fell to my knees. I wanted to punch something again, but I was sure to lose another battle with an inanimate object.

I realized I couldn't move my hand when Isaac called and I reached for the phone. He wanted to know if I'd received the results yet. My shaky voice adequately relayed my physical and emotional pain, but my words presented with pure anger. Isaac was unfortunately experiencing the worst of me.

"Take some time to let it all soak in. I'm here if you need me," he replied to my indignant rant. As expected, he handled himself as a gentleman, and that only pissed me off more.

"No, you're *not* here," I replied.

"Not physically, and I'm sorry. I wish I could be."

"You have all the right answers, huh?"

"I'm gonna let you go. You're understandably in a bad mood, and I respect that. I'll call you later."

"Don't. I can't do this, Isaac. It's nice that you called and all, but you can't help me over the phone. This is a prime example of why long-distance relationships don't work. Your phone call won't be any different than Tielle's or Yari's. Everybody's gonna have the same thing to say. They're sorry. You're sorry, my mother is sorry, Robert is sorry, Dap is sorry, Tiffany is sorry. Fuck sorry! That's everybody's default statement when shit goes wrong.

"Sorry can't sit with me and my broken hand in the E.R. for the rest of the damn afternoon. I know you care, but I need a man who can say, 'I'm outside, let's go,' not 'I'm sorry.'"

"Alexis…"

"I have to go. I can't feel my hand anymore."

"Call me and let me know what they say."

***

Just after midnight, I woke up to Jay-Z's "Excuse Me Miss," Isaac's ringtone. I texted him after I left the hospital at six to let him know my hand was broken in two places and that I chose a bright orange cast, but we hadn't communicated since. I lifted my heavy arm and flung it onto the other side of the bed, nearly crushing my poor phone with the cast.

"Were you sleeping?" Isaac asked once I answered.

"Yeah, but I have to get up. It's time for another pain pill."

"While you're up, open the door. I'm outside."

A quick look through the peephole confirmed he was. When I opened the door, he waved the taxi driver off.

"You said I couldn't help you over the phone. I'm here."

I wanted to cry, but I couldn't. I gnawed at the inside of my jaw instead. No one had ever gone to such an extreme for me. Either he was a psycho or he was just that into me.

As we hugged, he eased my mind. "Don't think I'm gon' be your little bitch. I'm not flying down here every time you throw a tantrum."

We laughed, and I planted a kiss of gratitude on his soft lips. "I didn't expect you to come."

"I know, 'cause you're used to dealing with lames. How does your hand feel?" he asked, as he followed me into the kitchen.

"Like I punched a wall." I shook a pain pill onto the counter, then picked it up with my left hand.

"Bet you won't try that again. Don't be overdosing on these pills, either. You haven't smoked in a while, so that feeling might be a little too familiar."

I tried to hit him with a left hook, but he moved.

223

"Keep playin' and you gon' break your other hand. I'm all steel, baby." He pounded on his chest a couple times.

Just like that, he had me laughing. We went back and forth a few more times before the conversation took on a more serious tone.

"You feel like going somewhere?" he asked as he came behind me and wrapped his arms around my waist.

"Where are we goin' at 12:30? Wal-Mart?"

"Nah. Come on. There's something you need to do."

Twenty minutes later, we pulled into the cemetery. Isaac followed the road to Tameka's grave and parked. We both sat motionless in my car.

"Are you gettin' out or somethin'?" I asked.

He shook his head. "Go talk to your sister." When I wrinkled my forehead, he said, "I visit my grandfather's grave from time to time just to vent. I'll listen to whatever you have to say, but there's only so much you'll tell me. You can give her the unedited version."

I opened the door, then paused. Isaac could sense I felt awkward and assured me that he would be handling business on his Palm Pilot while I was doing my thing. Except for occasional glances for security purposes, he promised not to look at me.

Crickets chirped eerie little songs, and I swatted at gnats as they swarmed near my head. I leaned against Tameka's headstone and looked around at the others. Some were surrounded with flowers. Others looked like they'd never been visited. I glanced to see if Isaac was looking, and he wasn't.

"I know I look crazy as hell. It's one o'clock in the morning and I'm chillin' at the cemetery," I said. "This is like a scene straight from a horror movie. All we need is some scary music and a dude in a Jason mask. I don't know if ghosts exist, but if any of your friends around here are into scarin' folks, you better tell 'em I'm not the one." I couldn't help but chuckle.

"Real talk, I miss you. I miss talking to you, so that's what I came to do. Every other time I've been here, somebody else was here, so I kept it short and sweet. This was Isaac's idea. I think he took my one-round fight with the wall as my cry for help." At that point, a wave of comfort came over me and I tuned out every sight and sound around. I wasn't sitting in a cemetery talking to a tombstone. I was outside talking to my sister. Maybe that could've been attributed in part to my pill kicking in.

"Well, I know the big secret. I read your journals and found out about Darryl…and had a DNA test done. You worked with Darryl for years, so you should know the outcome. I'm sure you saw how much I

224

look like him. I know you didn't tell me 'cause you wanted to protect me, and maybe you figured there was a chance that Daddy was really my dad, too. If you were still here, I would still be protected because I never would've read your stupid journals." Though I tried to sniff them away, out came the tears. "Remember when I used to call 'em that?

"So much has been goin' on since you left. Let me think. Robert's a daddy and I'm not a mommy, so solve that riddle. Remember how you used to tell me he was the best thing that ever happened to me? Remind me to punch you if I make it to where you are. Me and Tiff ain't cool no more. She got turned out by a chick at her birthday party, then tried to pull that mess on me. She kissed me!

"Oh, I have bad news about your boy, Craig. I don't know if this is possible, but I need you to throw that engagement ring out of your casket and I'll spit on it 'cause he's trippin'. Guess who he got pregnant?"

I went on and on, telling her the new things Darius was doing and how much he had grown, how happy I was with my job at WTIZ, and how Isaac and I had grown closer. When I was done, I felt fifty pounds lighter.

Isaac and I returned to my apartment and went straight to the bedroom. I was exhausted—more mentally than physically—and so was he. We were sleep as soon as we hit the sheets.

He sat on the side of the bed the next morning as I changed clothes. "So are you still dumping me?" he asked with a smile. I laughed and shook my head. "Do you trust me now when I tell you how I feel about you?"

I looked into his eyes. "I *believe* you, but I don't trust anybody."

"I just flew in on a red-eye with only eight hours notice and you don't trust my feelings for you?"

"In case you haven't tuned in for the last four months of my life, the two people I should've been able to trust just strengthened my case for not trusting. Why would you be an exception to my rule?"

"Look at me. I'm not Robert. I'm not your mother," Isaac replied as he stood. I averted my eyes. "Look at me," he repeated.

I didn't want to. I didn't want to be drawn in by his sincerity and blindsided later by his dishonesty. With his finger under my chin, he redirected my face his way.

"I don't do or say anything for the sake of flattery. I don't have time or money to waste, coming down here to impress you. I care. You have my heart. That's why I'm here. You can trust me because I've been nothing but consistent from the day we met. Don't compare me to them. I have no ulterior motives and no reason to feed you bullshit.

There are thousands of beautiful women in Ohio, but I'm puttin' in work all the way in Texas."

"What do you want me to say?"

"All I want to hear is the truth. Do we need to go back to being friends? If you can't be open to one day trusting me, we can't have anything more than a platonic relationship." He sat on the bed again, then leaned back, propping himself up with his elbows.

What am I so afraid of? I thought. He was the perfect man. Maybe that was it. He was too perfect. I thought about my theory of a person only being as trustworthy as their least revealing secret.

"I have a question for you," I started. "What's your deepest secret, something you wouldn't share with just anybody?" I waited to hear him say he didn't have a secret.

A minute or so passed before he spoke. "I should have an eleven-year-old child, but I paid for my girlfriend to get an abortion during my junior year of high school." He cracked his knuckles and stared at the carpet. "My mom doesn't even know that."

I sat beside him, not sure of what to do. I didn't want to insult his manhood by hugging him, and there's not much to say to that unless you've been through a similar situation.

"I don't know if you heard Robert that evening before we went to Smoothies, but when he said he should already have a child, he meant with me. I should have a two-year-old." My cast became my distraction as I, too, stared at the carpet. I had vowed not to share that information with anyone because it was a hasty decision I made out of selfishness, and there I was telling him what only Robert and I knew.

The mistake we shared and shame we felt placed us on common ground. It was refreshing to hear that my Golden Boy wasn't so perfect. I no longer felt like he was superior to me and stopped doubting that a guy like him could truly be interested in a chick like me. I realized I wouldn't have told him about the abortion if I didn't trust him, and though he didn't acknowledge it with words, he realized the same.

That night when we laid down and he took me in his arms, I felt what Tameka described in her journal as "love's energy." Untainted with lust, its power pulled at my reigns of stubbornness and allowed me to simply enjoy the moment, enjoy what my future could hold. Isaac had shown up and given me what I needed when I didn't know what I needed.

While I was up taking my pain pill in the middle of the night, I called Yari. I knew she was sleep, but I had to leave her a quick message.

226

"Hey. I just called to say maybe you were right about the fairytale thing. Isaac showed up unexpectedly. He didn't come on a white horse, but he flew in on a white plane. I think I'm starting to believe. Peace."

***

Though I was only operating off of a couple hours of sleep, I couldn't wait to get to work the next morning. "What's the Word?" was going to be hotter than hot. Toni Valentine had texted me some breaking news-slash-gossip about her ex-boyfriend and actor, Kwame Phillips. Everybody had been speculating the reason behind their split, but I had the story from the horse's mouth. She caught him in the shower with a male actor who she didn't want to name. If she was smart, she was waiting to see how much he'd pay her to keep her mouth shut. Dammit, I loved my job! After I reported that and a few other bits, I ended with my usual recap of reality TV.

"…I don't know how many of y'all watched, but I am officially boycotting *American Idol*. Well, technically, I can't because I won't be able to give y'all the updates in the entertainment report, but can y'all believe the madness that went on last night? The three divas, LaToya London, Jennifer Hudson, and Fantasia Barrino, were in the bottom three. I thought they were playin'! Those girls can out sing every other contestant on the show, all the judges, and most of the folks we play on this station. The judges wanna say it's America's fault, but I'm not feeling that. When it boils down to it, I believe the producers control who wins. How can they prove to us that they count every phone call and text message? Now there have been reports about a power outage in Chicago, Jennifer Hudson's hometown. That prevented those viewers from calling in, but once again, y'all, I'm not feelin' it. Somethin' ain't right and *that's* the word."

Eli stood on the other side of the glass with some guy I had never seen. I wanted to know who he was, though. He looked important with his expensive Italian suit, flashy watch, and slicked back hair that would probably extend beyond his shoulders if it didn't curl. I wondered who he was texting on his Sidekick while he talked on his Blackberry, and why the hell he had two phones in the first place.

It looked like they were pointing at me when I removed my headphones, which made me nervous. Tielle and her co-host, Big Easy, were back on the air, so I couldn't ask them who the bigwig was. I prayed he wasn't the head of our broadcasting company, disgusted with my delivery of entertainment news. I tried to wait for them to leave before I exited the studio, but my bladder wasn't having it.

227

I said a quick hello as I did the tight-leg shuffle to the bathroom. When I came back, they were still there, and Eli motioned for me to join them.

"I want you to meet Harvey."

Harvey placed his call on hold and extended his hand. "Harvey Russo."

"Alexis James," I replied.

"Yeah, I hear." His tone was mysterious.

"Harvey is one of my buddies from Atlanta. He's a TV producer down there," Eli informed me.

"Nice to meet you."

"You, too," he said with a wink, before returning to his phone call. Still, his eyes never left me as I walked away.

I was nervous for nothing. Eli only wanted to show his boy "the black girl he was tryin' to get with at work." I couldn't help but smile at the thought of both vanilla boys wanting a taste of chocolate syrup.

18

Tiffany:
20 Questions

The twins' big day had come and Tiffany's backyard looked like it was infested with hyperactive children. They were overwhelmed with fun, not knowing what they should do first. The clown was a big hit and so was the ball pit. Marlon's mother coordinated a hardcore game of musical chairs, and Karen from church entertained a small bunch with Simon Says. Marlon manned the grill, while Tiffany and a couple of the parents poured the chips in bowls and gathered the paper products to set the picnic tables.

When they were done, Tiffany took a minute to watch Bryant and Bria fight for a chair when Bow Wow's song went off. To her surprise, Bria pushed her brother onto the grass and became the musical chairs champion. Tiffany and Marlon made eye contact and laughed. They didn't know their little princess could be aggressive.

After the kids finished the hot dogs and hamburgers, it was time to sing and cut the cakes. Ever since their first birthday, Tiffany felt it was important they have their own. Side by side, she and Marlon carried out Bryant and Bria's cakes and set them in front of the giddy pair. Bria's eyes widened like she hadn't seen the cake earlier that morning. When Tiffany noticed she wasn't looking at her cake, she followed Bria's eyes, which were focused on Alexis.

"You came!" Bria exclaimed, leaving the table to run to her godmother.

Alexis set her gift on the ground and squatted in preparation for Bria's hug. Wanting to capture the moment, Tiffany snapped a picture of the two. Deep down, she knew Alexis would show up. She loved Bria.

"Go back to your cake so you can blow your candles out," Alexis said. "I'll be here when you're done." She stood where she could see, but kept her distance from the other guests as they sang "Happy Birthday" and watched the twins make their wishes.

Before she cut the cake, Tiffany dipped her finger in the icing and smeared it onto Bria's nose and forehead. When she tried to do the same to Bryant, he moved and she ended up smearing it onto Marlon's cheek. They paused for a moment, then laughed along with the kids who were already hysterical with laughter. Marlon got even, borrowing from the glob on his face and placing it on Tiffany's forehead.

Once everyone calmed down, they ate cake and ice cream and prepared for the magic show. While the magician wowed the group with his tricks, Tiffany ran into the house to get another memory card for her digital camera. On her way back out, she noticed Marlon talking with Alexis by the fence. He'd set up the perfect scenario for her to speak to her former friend.

She wanted to hear the story behind the cast on Alexis' arm and hand, but chose to keep their interaction short and to the point instead. She approached Alexis from behind and placed her hand on her shoulder blade.

"Thanks for coming. She kept asking me if I sent you an invite," she said, never stopping her stride.

Before she got too far, Marlon stopped her. "Are they opening their presents while everybody's here?"

"No. I think the kids are getting restless. They'll be ready to go after the magician is finished," she replied. As she headed toward the group again, Alexis spoke up.

"Hey, I'm sorry for clownin' you at the shop that day. You just caught me at a bad time. There's been a lot goin' on."

Tiffany nodded. "I was just trying to help. I knew it was a stretch to think you would listen."

"Did you really have somethin' to tell me?" Alexis asked.

Marlon took the camera from Tiffany. "Y'all talk. I'll take the pictures." He walked away.

"Yeah. I was just gonna tell you that Craig's been spending a lot of time at Jacqueline's house. I don't know what they're doing, but they're doing an awful lot of it."

Alexis grunted. "Making babies."

"Huh?"

"You heard me."

"He told you?" Tiffany asked.

She nodded. "And I called him everything but a child of God."

"We can add him to the list. Guess he ain't from shit either."

"So does that mean you and Marlon aren't…Are you and Venni…?"

"I'm single and unattached."

"You need to keep it one hundred with me. I know your freaky ass hasn't gone this long without sex. You and Venni been doin' somethin'. People talk. I know y'all been hangin' tough."

Tiffany chose her words carefully, but admitted to continuing her sexual involvement with Venni. "That's not why we're tight, though. We just click. We're practically carbon copies of each other."

"So, what? You feel like you're masturbating when you're with her?" She laughed at her own joke.

Tiffany smiled. Only Alexis would say something like that. "No, it's just not what you think."

"Why ain't she here?"

"Because I don't want the kids to see their daddy act a fool."

"If she's just your friend, it's not a big deal, right?"

Tiffany smirked and flicked her friend off.

"Okay. I have one more question and then I'm leaving this subject alone. Do you…participate in the pleasuring?"

"You wanna know if I've performed oral sex on her?"

Alexis turned to make sure none of the children were in earshot. "I was tryin' not to say that, but yeah."

Tiffany shook her head.

"What? So you just lay back and let her go to work?"

"Wow. We're really having this conversation," Tiffany replied, her smile tinged with embarrassment. "I guess you can say that."

"How the hell do you get away with that?" She held up her hands. "Rhetorical question. I still can't believe you gettin' it in with a broad, though. I thought you and Marlon were back together from the way y'all acted today."

"I think this is the first time we've occupied the same space for more than fifteen or twenty minutes. It's been nice."

When Alexis asked her if she missed Marlon, her answer was yes. They didn't break up because he was beating on her or because he cheated. She was the unfaithful one, unsuspectingly led into a relationship unlike she'd ever had before with a woman. There were times when she wanted to reconcile, but when she thought about his lack of decorum and stagnant mindset and remembered their last sexual encounter, she gained an appreciation for her new, carefree lifestyle.

Eager to change the subject, she asked Alexis about her status. "You said a lot's been going on. You didn't get back with Robert, did you?"

"Do I have 'Desperate Idiot' written on my forehead? You know I don't dig in the recycling bin. There ain't that much forgiveness in the world."

"Do you still talk to Isaac?"

"He's been down to visit twice…"

"And?" Tiffany said with a grin.

Alexis couldn't hold her grin back either. "And we're together."

Tiffany ran in place, elated for her friend. "Shut up! You're a couple?" After Alexis finished telling her all about their visits, Tiffany said, "You're in love."

Alexis frowned. "Please."

"I hear it in your voice and see it in your eyes. Girl, I'm so happy for you."

It felt so good to talk to Alexis again. She hated that she had just learned about Mr. James not being Alexis' father, but was glad Alexis still felt comfortable opening up to her after their fallout.

Alexis stayed for a while after the party was over to play with Bria, and had to sneak away while she was in the bathroom. Tiffany walked her to the door and thanked her again for coming.

"I've missed you, you little bitch," Tiffany joked. "Can I have a hug?"

"You know I don't do mushy stuff like that, but I guess."

Tiffany embraced her friend briefly, then let go. "Two or three seconds, right?"

Alexis chuckled softly. "Yeah, and keep your lips to yourself."

"That's something you don't have to worry about."

"Then we'll be alright. I'll holla at you later," Alexis said before she left.

Tiffany almost ran into Marlon as she reentered the house. "They're beggin' me to stay, so be prepared for tears. I'm about to dip now before they get their hopes up," he said.

"Why can't you stay?" she asked.

"You don't mind?"

"It's their birthday. Grant their last wish."

As Marlon watched her walk to the bedroom, he felt his nature rise. Before he could play with the kids, he escaped to the bathroom to allow time for shrinkage. While he kept the kids occupied, Tiffany took time out for a long soak in her Jacuzzi tub, and let her fingers remind her of the good times she once shared with the man just outside of her bedroom door.

Once they tucked everyone in, Marlon headed for the couch. "Where are the extra blankets?" he asked.

Tiffany stopped at her bedroom door. "In here."

Marlon frowned. "Why did you move 'em in there?"

"They're in the guest closet, but your blanket is in my room."

"Tiff, I don't think that's a good idea," he replied after catching on to what she was saying.

"You don't wanna come inside?"

Her question could be interpreted two ways, and either way, his answer was yes.

Their night together was nothing less than magical. It was everything it never was before. It was the pinnacle of their intimacy. It was beautiful, and it was emotional. Then, it was over…and awkward. Cuddling was reserved for couples; talking only worked when there were meaningful words to speak; and sleeping on opposite sides of a king-size bed was much like sleeping on opposite sides of the room. It was one-night-stand-ish, impersonal.

So, they lay within inches of each other. Close, but not close enough to cuddle; full of questions, but too timid to ask; full of emotions, but too afraid to feel. Their lovemaking was significant and trivial at the same time; acted upon because of the desires of their flesh but climaxing from the history of their love. In the morning, they would wake and become distant again, unsure of their boundaries and unaware of each other's feelings.

***

The next Friday after lunch, Tiffany and Venni chatted with one of the maintenance men by the elevators, when they were approached by a man and woman.

"Venita Miles?" the man asked as Venni turned to face him. He pulled out a police badge. "Detective Malloy. I'd like to talk to you briefly about a matter."

Tiffany looked at her friend for answers, but Venni didn't acknowledge her. "What's this about?" she asked, walking away from the elevators.

"We need you to come to the station with us. A young lady was found dead in Elgin, and we think you may be able to help us find the man who is responsible for her murder."

"I haven't lived in Illinois since I was a teenager. I can't help you."

233

Both officers stood in her way as she tried to walk away.

"This questioning isn't optional, Ms. Miles," the female detective said. "We're trying to make this as low key as possible. We don't want to make a scene at your job. However, we will handcuff you in front of your coworkers and escort you out if we need to. You seem like a dignified woman. Are you gonna use your two legs to walk to our car?"

Venni stared the woman down. The woman stared back, curious as to how such a beautiful young lady could be part of such an ugly operation.

Venni turned and motioned for Tiffany to join her. "Can you stop on my floor and tell them something came up and I'm leaving the office for the day?"

"Of course. Is everything okay, though?"

She cut her eyes toward the officers. "Yeah, but do you think you can pick me up from the station once they're done with me? Oh, never mind. I forgot about the kids."

"I can do it. I'm done at two. Marlon's picking up the twins, so I just have to take Tony to Miss Tina's."

"I should be done by the time you do all that," Venni said calmly.

As Tiffany watched her leave with the detectives, she wondered if Venni would indeed be released. When she read the man's lips, she was positive he said something about a murder. Had her mysterious past caught up with her?

***

Venni sat with perfect posture in the uncomfortable chair. She was eighteen when she'd first stepped inside a police station and she was there voluntarily. Nine years later, she was sure this visit was connected to her first.

"Do you remember Cassidy Rinehart, Ms. Miles?"

"The name sounds familiar," Venni replied.

"You've witnessed so many murders that you can't remember hers?"

Keep your mouth shut and your legs open.

Venni slowly turned her head and looked over both shoulders. She heard Cole's voice so clearly, but he wasn't there. He was still in her head. That motto had been drilled into her from the time she was fourteen and had gotten her out of a lot of trouble. Since Cole was no longer her source for life lessons, though, she only obeyed half of the rule. She didn't talk.

After the interrogating officer stated his desire to reopen Cassidy's case, she had to say something. "I've seen a lot of things in my lifetime, but I don't remember the majority of them."

"Selective memory?"

"Post-traumatic stress disorder."

"How convenient," the woman detective mumbled.

"You wanna check my medical records, *Detective*?"

It was the first time she'd admitted to having the disorder aloud. Nine years prior, the diagnosis seemed like an excuse for her behavior, a label that marked her as a victim; but it was her lifesaver this day.

They were grilling her to get to one person: Cole. She hated him with every fiber of her being, but she couldn't rat him out. When Detective Malloy said his name, she acted as if she'd never heard it before. When he presented a poor sketch of his face, she fought to hold in her laughter. When he showed her a picture of the teenage girl's bloody body, she tried not to gag.

Her pledge of loyalty to Cole was involuntarily strong. In spite of their constant power struggle, he looked out for her in his own twisted way. In a sense, her experiences with him helped hone her financial savvy. That's why she attended his seminar in the first place. Her bank account was loaded because of him—from the hush money he paid her before she left town to the tips he never knew about.

Years ago, she wouldn't have hesitated to whisper something in the male officer's ear, wait for him to dismiss the other officer, and have her way. And though she hated to admit it, if her straight-laced approach didn't work, she'd abide by the other half of Cole's motto again and reclaim her title as the master of distraction.

"You're asking me to recall a traumatic time in my life for the sake of getting a promotion or bonus, whatever you get for playing super detective. Cassidy was killed almost ten years ago. Don't expect me to warm up your cold case."

"You're protecting the monster that traumatized you!" the woman detective yelled.

"Experience what I did. Then come back and tell me if you want to talk about it over coffee. My subconscious is protecting *me*. Y'all want me to force some memories in hopes that you find a missing puzzle piece. I'm not reliving hell for you."

Detective Malloy leaned across the table and stopped about three inches from Venni's face. "I know you at least remember his name. You haven't blocked out everything."

"I never said I didn't remember my guy's name. I'm telling you I don't know the man in the picture. That's who's responsible for her murder, right? You're wasting taxpayers' money dragging me into this. I'm sorry to hear about the girl, but I can't help you. I moved here to escape that life. You need to take your case back to Illinois if you want answers."

"Your 'guy'?" he asked. "Tell us who he is then."

"He has nothing to do with this case. I know the law."

"Can you live with this again? Another young girl has been killed and you won't do your part for justice's sake?"

The overbearing detective let up after Venni asked to call a lawyer. Their shot in the dark was just that, and they were back at square one.

Tiffany beeped twice when she saw Venni exit the station.

"Thank you so much for waiting," Venni said calmly. "There was no need for them to have me in there that long."

"What was that all about?" Tiffany asked.

"Something from a long time ago. They wanted to ask me some questions. It's nothing." She took a clip from her purse and pulled her hair up.

"So…are you in trouble?"

Venni shook her head. "They just thought I knew somebody."

Tiffany shrugged and drove in silence. Venni asked Tiffany to take her straight home instead of to the parking garage at work, saying she would get to her car in the morning. When they reached Venni's house, Tiffany stayed in the car while Venni exited. Venni noticed she was alone just before she put the key in the door. She turned and threw her hands up as if to question why Tiffany was still behind the wheel.

After turning off the engine, Tiffany joined Venni inside. She didn't know how long she would stay, though. The police questioning Venni made her uncomfortable, and Venni's nonchalant reaction didn't help. She explained this as she stood in the doorway.

"Are you afraid to be here now?" Venni joked. "Do you think the cops are going to raid my place?"

Finding no humor in the situation, Tiffany didn't laugh.

"Let me put it to you like this: I live this life now, but I've lived the polar opposite, as well. During that time, a lot of things happened. Today, my past tried to reincarnate itself as my present," Venni explained.

"What things happened?"

"I haven't killed anybody if that puts you at ease. I just don't talk about my past."

"That's obvious." Tiffany wanted to believe her, but it seemed awfully strange that Venni used murder as her example. "If I go to jail…"

"You'll be in trouble. They can smell the good stuff from miles away." Venni winked. "I have to make an important phone call, but I can't use my phone. Do you mind? I'll trade you," she said, holding her Blackberry out for Tiffany to take.

Before she thought about it, Tiffany had surrendered her phone. Venni saw the concern in her eyes.

"It's for privacy reasons. Nothing illegal," she explained, then excused herself and walked into the laundry room. Once inside, she pulled a business card from her purse and dialed the number written on the back. The phone rang five times before a woman answered.

"Holly?" Venni asked.

"Who is this?"

"Naomi. I mean, Venni."

The woman sighed with relief. "I didn't recognize the number. I usually don't answer unknowns, but you never know when Oprah may call and tell me she's added my book to her list." They laughed. "Oh, and call me Keyonna. Holly was another person. I don't go by Noel anymore either."

"I hear you." Venni went on to tell Keyonna about her visit with the police.

"They've been looking for you all this time?"

"I think they only thought of me because it's a similar crime. They're convinced Cole has something to do with it."

"They know his name now?" Keyonna's voice raised an octave.

"Yep. The girl's sister is singing like a canary. She just doesn't know many details because her sister had just told her she was selling the day before."

"Stupid."

"Or smart. Shit, maybe we were the stupid ones for staying loyal to him. I don't think he killed her, though. He's done a lot of shit—sick shit—but I don't believe he has the balls to murder anyone."

Their conversation segued into their unexpected reunion at Flamingo Rose. Both women never thought they would see each other again.

"That was an overwhelming two hours," Keyonna started. "We saw you, then I ran into Craig of all people. I just knew Cole would be next."

"Who's Craig?" Venni asked.

"You remember when we went into the city for the basketball tournaments that one summer?"

"Yeah. I thought you were the biggest bitch because you got first pick and you took the star."

"Right. Number twenty-two. I ran into him in the lobby. He lives there."

"Deuces? No way! Did he remember you?"

"He called me out!"

"Is he still fine?"

"Grown-man fine, girl." They laughed.

"Did you exchange numbers?" Venni probed.

"He gave me his card, but there's nothing to talk about. I have two kids and a husband, honey. I've thought about him over the years, so it was good to see that he's doing well. That's where it ends, though."

Venni vaguely remembered Keyonna getting in trouble for seeing "Deuces" too much. Cole had become jealous, thinking she was meeting up with him for pleasure rather than business. Turns out he was right. Keyonna fell in love with the mild-mannered jock and they were making plans for the future.

"So what happened with y'all? I didn't know y'all were sweet on each other like that."

"I got pregnant."

"And he denied it?"

"She wasn't his."

After Keyonna recounted the complicated story of her oldest daughter's paternity, Venni finally understood why she was deathly afraid of Cole finding her.

"Well, you don't ever have to worry about me telling anybody where you are. As far as I'm concerned, your name is Holly and I haven't seen you since our entrepreneurship days."

"Don't you have a son?" Keyonna asked.

"Yeah. My sister still has him. He's thirteen now."

It was tough having Tangela raise her only child, but she still couldn't look at Vance without seeing her high school principal's face. Many times she considered telling him the truth and giving him the option to come live with her, but looking at his thick eyebrows and wavy hair 365 days a year would be equivalent to torture. She applauded Keyonna for raising her child in spite of the circumstances.

"You can't beat yourself up. Your situation was different than mine. As sick as it was, I loved him. She was conceived untraditionally, but out of love."

"I love Vance. He's my son, you know? It's just better this way."

Tiffany tipped away from the door and took a moment to digest what she'd heard. At this point, her miscarriage theory had been disproved and the murdered ex-boyfriend theory was looking better. She even wondered if Venni's ex was cheating on her and she killed him and the woman after she found them together. *Somebody* was murdered. And somehow, Craig was involved with these women. If she was eavesdropping correctly, he was not only the father of Jacqueline's unborn and Darius; he was also the father of Holly/Noel's child.

Hearing that Vance was Venni's son and not her nephew was the ultimate shocker, but in retrospect, oh so obvious. He looked nothing like Tangela or her husband, and he and Venni seemed connected on a much deeper level than aunt and nephew.

Whatever the case, Tiffany was done playing the guessing game. Her affiliation with Venni was now under serious review. She had been loosely referring to her as her friend, when she really knew nothing about the woman. She was too caught up in how much they had in common that she didn't see how much they differed.

***

Tiffany stopped by the gym the next day to give Marlon his I.D. It had fallen out of his pants when he stayed the night the week before, and she'd finally found it. On her way to his office, she saw Craig doing bicep curls near the mirrors.

She took a detour and approached him. "Hey, I'm glad I ran into you. Can I ask you something?" He nodded. "Remember when I saw you at Flamingo Rose with—"

"Tiffany, mind your business. I'm not in the mood to hear what you have to say about Jacqueline."

"I'm asking about the female you were talking to before Jacqueline came out of the restroom. Holly, was it?"

His eyes narrowed slightly as he lowered the weights. "How do you know her?"

"She had dinner with me and Venni."

"Who is Venni? Oh, that's your…"

"Friend. We work in the same building. She and Holly have known each other for years. How do you know her?"

"I knew her in high school. Why?"

"So she's from Chicago?"

"She's from a place and time I don't discuss. Why do you want to know about her?"

"I was just trying to get her and Naomi together for—"

"You know Naomi?"

Got him! He knew Venni, just not by her real name. She smiled. "Small world. Oh, and since you brought up Jacqueline, congratulations. I hear you're gonna be a daddy all over again." Her snide smile infuriated Craig. She ended the conversation there, claiming she didn't want to further disrupt his workout. He hadn't given her much information, but his recognition of the strange nicknames made her even more curious to find the origin of his tangled connection with Venni and Holly. There was only one way to find out.

While she was dialing Venni, Marlon came out of his office. She quickly disconnected the call and greeted him with a warm smile.

"Guess what I found?" she said as she pulled his I.D. from her purse.

"Where was it?"

"In Bria's Little Mermaid purse. She must've found it in my room. You know how she is."

"I still don't know how it fell out."

"We weren't paying attention to how your jeans landed on the floor when you threw 'em down there." She placed his license in his front pocket, being sure to touch what she'd been longing for since the morning after Bryant and Bria's party.

Marlon pulled her hand from his pocket. "Alright. Well, thank you. I gotta go see what's up with the pool. Everybody's sayin' the water's too cold." He was gone before she could respond.

***

That evening, Tiffany went to Venni's house on a mission to crack her code. Figuring people out was what she did for a living, what she was good at, but Venni was a challenge. Her evasive nature, strange alias, and minor references to her past were sure signs that she had lived a life she'd rather no one know about, but what could be so bad?

She tried to weave questions into their conversation as they dined on steak and shrimp. They touched on almost every subject, sharing stories from high school, college, and even their younger years. None of Venni's stories included Holly or G, though they seemed to have shared a significant amount of time together at some point. There was no mention of Vance, and she barely mentioned Tangela.

Tiffany had gotten nowhere with Venni as far as specifics, but one of her statements remained fresh on her brain when they talked about Venni's childhood. *If my mom hadn't died when she did, I'd be a different person.*

She didn't ask her to elaborate. Venni's weary eyes said enough. Her mother's death was still affecting her. She passed away right before Venni turned thirteen, and there was no other woman around to guide her through her pubertal years into adulthood. It was clear that she felt she would have made different decisions if her mother was alive then.

240

As the night went on, Tiffany found that she couldn't rest. It bothered her that Venni was hurting and wouldn't open up to her. So, she waited until Venni was fast asleep, and tipped down the steps to the living room. What better place to find information than in a newspaper? She sat on the edge of the couch cushion and pulled out the end table drawer. Working only with the light from her cell phone, she moved the phonebook and pulled out the newspaper clippings.

TEEN FOUND SLAIN
An investigation has begun into the death of a 16-year-old girl found dead behind the Ashbury Inn. Workers discovered her body while taking out the garbage late Saturday night. The body was I.D.'d as Cassidy Rinehart, a student at Lakeside Preparatory School. Friends and family say she was a good girl who didn't have any enemies…The police currently do not have any suspects, though they are sure of foul play.

WITNESS COMES FORWARD: TEEN GIRL WAS A PROSTITUTE?
A 19-year-old woman came forward to police yesterday, claiming she saw a man lure Cassidy Rinehart into his green Chevrolet Blazer on Saturday night. She later found the two a couple blocks away, with Cassidy being held at knifepoint in the back of the SUV. The girl says Cassidy wouldn't perform a sexual favor to the man's liking, so he slit her throat. For fear that the man saw her, the girl ran to a nearby restaurant for safety. The suspect is described as a Hispanic man in his mid 20's with black hair, dark eyes, and a thin beard. He was last seen wearing a gray hooded sweatshirt.

WITNESS DISAPPEARS
The only known witness to the murder of Cassidy Rinehart has vanished just three days before the trial. The girl, who only identified herself as Naomi, is the D.A.'s nail that would seal the coffin in the case. Police now believe she is also a prostitute and is afraid of being harmed, also. Stories have been circulating about an underground prostitution ring, though no one had any information on who is running it. Unlike typical teens that turn to the streets for survival, these girls are said to be from the well-to-do neighborhoods in northern Chicago's suburbs, and are in it for the thrill rather than the money…

Her snooping was interrupted by the loud ring of her phone. Startled, she fumbled the device, then answered with a whisper. It was Alexis calling to see why she didn't show up at the club event she promised she would attend.

"It's a long story," Tiffany whispered.

"Why are you whispering?"

"I'm at Venni's and I'm looking for something. Don't want her to hear me."

"Looking for what?"

"I'll tell you later. I gotta go before she wakes up and catches me."

"I don't know why you talk shit on Aunt Retha. You're just as nosey as she is. Bye, fool."

Tiffany wasn't sure if it was Alexis' loud voice or the ringtone that was set at its highest level, but something woke Venni and she was heading down the stairs. She quickly replaced the papers and closed the drawer. Her hand was still on the handle when Venni rounded the corner.

"What are you doing down here?" she asked with her eyes fixated on Tiffany's guilty hand.

"One of my patients just called," Tiffany replied, holding up the phone to show the screen that was still lit. "I had to use your phonebook to look up a number for a battered women's shelter for her and her mom."

She yawned. "She called your personal phone?"

Tiffany shrugged. "You know I turn my work phone off after nine. I gave her that number because I know she has a lot of problems. I guess you can say she's one of my favorites."

"So is everything squared away?"

"Hopefully." She stole a few glances at Venni. Her theories were no longer needed. She was Naomi, and Naomi was a prostitute—a suburban prostitute.

Poor thing, Tiffany thought. Venni's mother couldn't shape her as a person during her detrimental years of self-image and her father didn't have time to, so a pimp molded her into lust's vessel and conditioned her to satisfy without being satisfied. She was the good girl gone bad, who was able to reinvent herself in every way except the one that mattered. Her thick skin was impenetrable, making her incapable of feeling and trusting, limiting her happiness to only come from that which is tangible.

As Venni stretched, her low-riding boy shorts barely showed the top of her tattoo. Tiffany's eyes zeroed in on the area. "Father Forgive Me" had so much more meaning now.

19

Alexis:
Say What?

After over two weeks of avoidance, I finally had to face facts; I had to face Darryl. He was waiting by my car when I got off work one Wednesday afternoon. I spoke non-verbally with a head nod.

"I didn't want to go to this extreme, hounding you at your job, but it's the only way I knew I'd get to talk to you," Darryl said.

"Really, Darryl, what is there to talk about?"

"You're my child. I just met you. There's quite a bit to talk about."

"I'm an adult, and I'm not up for getting-to-know-you sessions."

"I'm not trying to take your father's place, if that's what you're worried about," Darryl said. "I have relationships with all my children, though, and I don't want you to be any different."

I lightened up a little. Truthfully, I knew Darryl and I could get along because our personalities were very similar.

"Okay, so you're my biological father. Now what?"

"Now if you need me, I can be there for you."

When I gave him a sarcastic thumbs-up, he noticed my cast and asked how I broke my hand. That's when I blamed him and asked how much money he was pulling toward my emergency room and prescription co-pays. I almost turned him down when he pulled out two hundred-dollar bills, but it was the least he could do. Though I was polite, I gladly accepted the money that only covered a fraction of my pain and suffering.

He laughed as I placed the bills in my wallet. "I gotta watch you. You're a little hustler."

The next time I saw him, it was May 19th, my birthday. He treated me to lunch at Flamingo Rose, the ritzy restaurant Tiffany was in love with. It was alright, but I could've done without the special wine sauce on my chicken. I enjoyed the meal mostly because it was the first time I had been out to eat since having my cast taken off, and I didn't have to try to be graceful with my left hand.

When we finished eating, I had to rush home. Isaac told me to expect a package to arrive by 2 p.m., and at 2:04, I received a wooden box that was about ten inches long and heavy. Inside, I found a bottle that contained seashells, sand, and a scroll. Before I removed the cork, I brainstormed about what the message could be on the scroll. I narrowed it down to either a poem or a scavenger hunt list that would lead me to my gift.

Instead, I found a printout of an airline ticket confirmation and a note that read: *I know you don't like the distance, so I'm closing the gap for the weekend. Your job already cleared you to prerecord Friday's show Thursday night, so we're good on that. Happy Birthday, baby! See you Friday.*

Since he was on duty, I could only text to thank him. After I did, I read the itinerary in detail to see what time I was leaving for Columbus. That's when I saw I was leaving for New York!

I didn't check my mailbox until I left for the club that night. I sat in my car by the cluster of metal boxes and sorted through the envelopes, only opening the cards. The last one I read was from my mother and she included a check. I was sure going to cash it before my trip so I could add it to my spending money. She wrote a short note saying she would be in town in a week, looking at houses. Apparently, she felt the need to be closer to me and her "only grandchild." She would have better luck reeling Darius in, because there was no redeeming herself with me.

I met Tiffany and Tielle at The Ice Bar, a club in the heart of downtown, and we partied in the V.I.P. section all night. I monitored Tiffany's alcohol consumption to make sure she didn't destroy our newly repaired friendship. She was fine, though. She spent more time getting loose on the dance floor than anything else, and she was only entertaining men. Tielle and I shared a bottle of Martel, and chilled with coworkers most of the night.

Yari called at 2:15 a.m. while we were at the Waffle House. She had just wrapped up filming for the day and knew I'd still be awake. She wanted to know how I celebrated my birthday, so I recapped my club experience, noting my annoyance with all the dudes who approached me.

244

"I pretty much stayed in V.I.P., girl. Those dudes were a little too thirsty for me. All I was tryin' to do was dance, but they wouldn't shut the hell up. If they weren't asking my name, they were asking if I had a man, what side of town I live on, how they could get to know me better, or how did I get 'all that ass.' Nobody asked where I work, what I like to do, or if I even wanted a damn drink!"

"That's 'cause you're used to Isaac. You were diggin' that kind of attention not too long ago," Yari said, laughing.

"I didn't ask you to bring up the past," I replied with a mouthful of hash browns.

"I'm just saying, once you realize your worth, you stop accepting coupons. Those bustas can't even pretend to offer what Isaac is bringing to the table."

"I think I love him," I blurted.

Tielle and Tiffany stopped eating and simultaneously said, "What?"

Yari gasped. "Have you told him?"

"No! I'm not even sure if that's what I'm feelin'."

"It is," Tiffany said. "I told you!"

"Why do you *think* you love him then?" Yari asked.

It was how he looked at me, how he smiled, how he called everyday, how he spoiled me. He bought me a plane ticket to New York! Who does that?

I tried to explain away my feelings for him, blaming my profession of love on the Martel, but the girls weren't going for it. They gave me hell, teasing me because Isaac had broken down my walls. Ultimately, they were happy that someone was making me happy during such a difficult time in my life.

I made it through the rest of my work week, which ended Thursday night after I prerecorded Friday's segment. At six o'clock Friday morning, Tank was dropping me off at the curb near Continental Airlines.

While checking my bags at the counter, I felt butterflies in my stomach. It was going to be my third time on a plane, and the first two times, I never opened my eyes while we were in-flight. This time, I was nervous, but excited. I kept my eyes open the whole time so I could take in every second of Isaac's beautiful gift to me.

His plane landed first, so he met me at my flight's baggage carousel and greeted me with a kiss and hug. "See? You're still alive and in one piece," he said, kissing me again on my forehead.

"Yeah, but I almost hurled four times."

"Oh. Well, I guess we'll just hang out in the room. I had some stuff planned, but…"

"I didn't say I was sick *now.* Don't play with me! I'm tryin' to be all over New York," I replied.

After we pulled my bag from the conveyor belt, Isaac promised to make it my most memorable birthday ever. Little did he know, it already was.

We took a cab to Manhattan and stopped at a tall building on the corner. I realized we were on Broadway when I looked up and read the street sign. I dug through my purse, looking for my camera and not noticing Isaac paying our driver.

"Did you forget something?" he asked.

I turned the camera on and snapped a quick picture of the Broadway sign. "Nah, I just wanted to get the street sign before we pulled away."

"You have all the time in the world for pictures, sweetie." He pointed to the red awning with "On The Ave Hotel" printed on it, and I felt so stupid. Since it was too late to redeem myself after looking like the ultimate tourist, I slid the camera back into my purse and opened my door without saying a word.

Isaac retrieved our bags from the trunk while I stretched my neck to count the hotel's floors. *If this is where we're staying, I won't mind hanging out in the room all day,* I thought.

Our room was the shit, for lack of a better word. The king-size bed, loveseat, 42" TV, desk, Italian black marble bathroom, and complimentary bathrobes made a statement of elegance; but the private outdoor balcony with an amazing view of Central Park put the exclamation mark at the end.

"Do you sell drugs?" I asked Isaac.

"What?"

"This room has to be a couple hundred dollars a night."

"And I have a job to handle it."

"I know. I'm just playin'. This is just…a lot. You're spoilin' me."

"It's about time somebody spoiled you."

When he first told me he takes care of his woman and therefore had no insecurities about a long-distance relationship, I didn't grasp what he meant. However, it sunk in as we sat on the balcony that overlooked New York City. Isaac was handling his business. He was giving me experiences that weren't restricted to a bedroom, though I was looking forward to one of those. All in all, he was giving me experiences no other man could compete with.

We spent the afternoon shopping and hanging out in Times Square, then returned to the room to drop off our bags. Isaac said we were going out, so I broke out my get-'em-girl dress and the stilettos that were a half size too small but on-sale. By 9:30 p.m., we were riding in the cab, going to an undisclosed location. When we neared the place, Isaac told me to close my eyes. I obeyed with reluctance, hoping I wouldn't open them and see a diamond ring, hoping he hadn't fallen that hard so quickly.

The car stopped and he told me it was safe to look. I did find a diamond—the one that was a part of the 40/40 Club logo. My scream startled the driver and satisfied Isaac.

The place was hot. I felt like a star as we walked amongst the crowd of heavy hitters and go-getters. And there *were* stars there, but not the one I wanted to see. Apparently, Jay-Z was overseas on vacation. It was my job to have exclusive entertainment scoop, though, so I took mental notes as I passed a few spoken-for celebrities who weren't with those who were speaking for them. Isaac and I chilled on one of the seats on the steps, ate appetizers, and sipped Remy Martin until we felt good.

Our next stop was the club, where we partied until 4 a.m. We were so tired when we made it to our room, we didn't even undress before we got in the bed.

I woke up at eleven to the smell of French toast. I heard Isaac thank someone and shut the door. "Morning," he said as he brought a tray of food over. "First things first."

He handed me a package of Tylenol and took one for himself. We then ate breakfast on the patio, hoping our headaches would be relieved by the time we were finished.

"What's on the agenda today?" I asked.

He pointed to Central Park, and my face lit up. After taking our showers, we were out the door. May's warm breeze flowed gently through our clothes as we entered the picturesque landmark. Though it was totally unplanned, we both wore white tops and denim bottoms with white sneakers.

I took in all the scenery around me. There were people everywhere—all ages, races, sizes, and personality types—and everybody seemed to be enjoying themselves. For the first time ever, I paid attention to trees and flowers, because the ones surrounding us were so gorgeous. Isaac and I took pictures near the Bethesda Fountain and on the terrace, looking fly as can be.

"I still can't believe you did this for me," I said as we walked through the mall lined with park benches and American Elm trees.

"I can't believe this is your first time in New York."

"I'm not well-traveled like you, Mr. Gray."

"Well, you will be, Ms. James."

I laughed. "Yeah, if I can stomach another plane ride."

Later, we discussed more of our future plans while eating dinner lakeside at The Boathouse restaurant. He was attentive as I talked about my career and the possibilities my future held. I imagined working in New York for Hot 97 or moving to L.A. and finding my niche there. Isaac challenged me to dream even bigger, to not limit myself. He asked why I wasn't thinking of having a segment that would be aired nationwide or crossing over to writing the entertainment portion of a major magazine.

"Because six months ago, I didn't even know what I wanted to do for a living."

"Now you do. Now it's time to build."

We shared a slice of warm chocolate-raspberry cake for dessert. I was hogging it, so Isaac playfully grabbed my wrist. "Don't make me break your hand again. Share."

I cracked up laughing, and he just smiled as held my hand, rubbing his thumb over my healed bones.

"If I told you I love you, what would you say?" he asked.

I chose my words carefully, hoping I wouldn't ruin the mood. "I'd say I don't know if I'm ready to love again," I said slowly.

He nodded as if he understood where I was coming from, but I wondered if I'd broken his heart. We finished our dessert in silence, focusing our attention on the rowboats floating by. After he paid for our meals, he led me to a nearby dock.

"Evening," a man said. He could barely speak through his thick mustache. "Gondola ride?"

"Yes, sir. That's what we're here for. It's under Gray."

He looked over the list in front of him and checked Isaac's name off. Just as I started to ask what a gondola is, another man appeared in the long, black boat, wearing a white and black striped shirt and a straw hat. For a half hour, we relaxed in the gondola while the oarsman pointed out some of the park's major attractions and sang songs in Italian.

After our romantic day together, I figured we were due for some physical contact. I couldn't wait to get to our room so we could celebrate my birthday the right way...in our birthday suits.

The elevator ride seemed to take forever, but we finally reached our destination. Isaac patted his pockets, then asked if I had my room key. I did, so I opened the door and was blinded by a sea of white. The room was filled with white flowers. There were calla lilies in vases on the desk and nightstand. A single white rose lie on the bed, surrounded by white rose petals shaped like a heart. More petals covered the floor, forming a pathway through the room. The flames from the dozens of white candles provided our light and warmed the space, and the slow jams playing clarified just what would be going down.

Isaac leaned over and kissed me on the cheek. "You've experienced hell. Welcome to heaven," he said, escorting me to the middle of the room.

I stood with my mouth open. "Are you for real?"

"I told you you're not ready for me," he said, kissing me again.

He doesn't waste time, I thought as he carefully undressed me.

When I was down to nothing, he took my hand and led me to the bathroom. The tub was full of piping hot water, just how I like it, and bubbles.

"How did you pull this off?" I asked as I lowered my body into the water.

"A phone call to the concierge," he replied as he lifted my leg from the water and kissed my calf.

He massaged both of my feet and then undressed so he could join me. As I looked at his already-erect piece, I had no objections to skipping foreplay and getting to the main event. Our trip up until that point was plenty foreplay for me.

After bathing me, he dried me off and helped me into one of the complimentary robes. He then instructed me to wait for him on the loveseat. Within minutes, he came out of the bathroom wearing the other robe, holding a platter of strawberries and a bowl of chocolate. He sat next to me and lifted my legs so they could rest in his lap. After dipping his finger in the chocolate, he placed it near my lips and let me lick it off, inciting a provocative game of seduction. For the next few minutes, we tried to break each other down, creatively incorporating the food and champagne.

The more we drank, the hotter things got. We first shared a strawberry he held between his teeth, and soon he was eating one from my cleavage. With strategically placed chocolate, we feasted on each other like it was our last meal.

He carried me to the bed and then stood over my naked body. "You are so beautiful," he said before he bent down and kissed my collar bone. "I've been waiting for this."

You didn't have to wait! I thought, as I savored the tingle I felt much lower.

He moved to my forehead and worked his way to my feet, planting kisses on every inch between. His warm breath tickling my skin before his lips made contact created a sensation that nearly drove me crazy.

When he reached my feet, he dipped my big toe in the chocolate and sucked all my toes, sending me into orgasmic heaven.

There was nothing nasty about his actions. He treated my body like it was precious, often stopping to stare at it for seconds on end. No one had ever made me feel so beautiful, so sexy. He was showing me even more of how he felt about me, leaving no room for doubt.

We rolled over and I straddled his body. "Thank you," I said, looking down at him with disbelief in my eyes.

"You don't have to keep thanking me for the trip, sweetie."

"No. Thank you," I repeated. "Thank you for seeing a different side of me and for letting me see it, too." I played with the few chest hairs that were beneath my fingers. "I feel like this is fake; like I'm gonna wake up any minute and be in my bed at home."

As he caressed my hips, his nature pressed firmly against mine. "Come here," he said. Right at that moment, he claimed the title for the best kisser ever. If a child could be conceived through a kiss, I would've been knocked up with sextuplets.

When we stopped, I played with his sensitive spot, just behind his left ear. "If I told you I love you, what would you say?" I whispered.

His hands stopped moving and I adjusted so I could see his face.

He smiled slightly. "I loved you first."

I anticipated his entry, envisioning what he would feel like, fantasizing about how he would move; but nothing could've prepared me for him. His movements were even more fluid, his touch was more electrifying, and his focus on pleasuring me was more of a turn-on.

Using Isaac's chest for leverage, I lifted my pelvis and welcomed all of him into me, my body involuntarily quivering as I lowered myself onto him. We paused to relish the "first time feeling" as our genitalia's pulses went through the roof. We were in sync from the moment I rolled my hips, eliciting an unadulterated expression of love.

I thought he was going to bite off a chunk of his lip while I was giving him the business, but when he flipped me over to hit it from the back, I was afraid I'd do the same. Before I drew blood, I pulled a pillow close and bit into it.

During our intermission, he snacked on me from my salad to my main course. He let me return the favor this time. I poured the remainder of the chocolate onto his piece, slid a strawberry along its shaft, and bit into it. He finished it off, trying not to choke while I sucked away every trace of the remaining syrup. When I was done, his mind was officially blown. I purposely stopped just before his climax, and we reached it together, chest to chest, missionary style. At that point, I had given myself to Isaac—all of me.

As we cuddled, I felt mellowed—like if I could sing, I would bust out a Jill Scott song or something, or write a poem longer than a haiku about this unbelievable man. I felt like I was living my dream in my personal and professional lives; but it was all real, and it was all right.

Before our flights left Sunday evening, we hung out in Harlem. As soon as we were done eating at the Lenox Lounge, we were in a cab and off to the airport. Saying goodbye was even harder this time. I was tempted to get on his flight to Columbus because I didn't want our time together to end. Yes, I had fallen—hard—and I was okay with it.

***

Tielle called me at about nine o'clock Thursday night. She said Craig was supposed to pick up his brother, Chauncey, from the airport at six, but never showed. Chauncey had finally gotten in touch with her, and she was on her way to get him.

"You know I wouldn't ask you to do this if I could handle it myself," Tielle started.

"Oh shit," I mumbled. "Does this involve me going to his house?"

"Lexis, we can't get in touch with him. Chauncey hasn't talked to him since last night, and you know I haven't talked to him in weeks. Just say you wanted to see Darius."

I really did want to see him, but it sucked that I had to see his father. Nevertheless, I went to Craig's and rang the doorbell. *Here we go with this again*, I thought, as I shifted all my weight to my right leg and waited. I banged on the door and called his name, but still got no answer. When I heard Darius crying, I used my key to get in.

"She's Out of My Life" was playing from the stereo in the living room. I slowly walked into the room and found Darius in his pack n' play. He stopped screaming as soon as he saw me, and I picked him up. His diaper was soaked, and his sippy cup was empty.

"Where's your daddy?" I asked. When I turned to my left, I saw Craig crouched over, facedown, in the spot where I found Tameka. Her journal lay open beside him.

"Craig!" I called. He didn't answer, but I knew he heard me. I walked toward him and stood near his head. "You didn't hear this baby crying?"

"It should've been me. She should've lived and I should've died," he said. When he looked up at me, his face was wet with tears. "You were right. She told me she hates me. She says I'm not shit. She tells me that every night. But I love her. I keep trying to tell her, but she won't believe me. I love her," he repeated, as he stroked the carpet beneath him.

251

I stood with lowered eyebrows and an open mouth, unsure of what to say.

"She said I was trying to replace her, but I wasn't. I promise I wasn't. She's not just mad about Jacqueline. She said I wasn't supposed to replace the carpet or get the walls fixed. She asked why I took her stuff out the closet. What was I supposed to do, Lexis?"

"I don't know," I said softly. "Hold on."

I walked to the couch and changed Darius' diaper. While I was cleaning him up, I called Tielle, who listened carefully to my whispering. "You have to get here now," I said.

"I just picked up Chauncey. We'll be there in twenty minutes," she replied.

"I need you to make it in ten," I said as I watched Craig hold Tameka's journal to his chest and apologize repeatedly. "I think he's lost it. He's acting like he's had a conversation with Meka, sayin' she's mad at him."

"Oh, Lord."

"Right. Hurry up. I don't fool with crazy people," I said before we hung up.

While I waited for them to arrive, I fed Darius and entertained him with two of his favorite toys. Craig never budged. In twelve minutes flat, Tielle and Chauncey were entering the house.

"Hey, man, what you doin' on the floor?" Chauncey asked, squatting beside him.

"She's gone, man. She don't want me no more," Craig answered matter-of-factly.

"Who?"

"Meka. After she heard Jackie was pregnant, that was it."

Chauncey looked at me, and I shrugged. "Told you," I mouthed.

When Craig looked up and saw Tielle, he said, "She won't talk to me, Tielle. She'll listen to you. Tell her to just hear me out."

Tielle leaned over. "Have you been drinking?"

"I haven't been eating or drinking."

"Have you been feeding this little boy?" I snapped. Before he responded, I grabbed my purse and turned to Tielle. "I gotta go, 'cause if he says no, I'm fuckin' him up."

Tielle called me later to tell me they took Craig to the hospital and he was admitted to the psych ward. "He cracked after reading Meka's journal entries. She had some harsh stuff written in there, and I think he tortured himself, reading them over and over."

She said the passages he must've read last were the ones in which Tameka stated how much she loathed Craig for starting a relationship with Jacqueline shortly after she moved to Columbus to escape Smoke. I didn't tell Tielle, but those were the passages I wanted him to read when I stuffed the journal into Darius' diaper bag. And though I didn't expect him to go crazy, I had no remorse about what I'd done. He, on the other hand, had plenty, and I was as satisfied as I could possibly be.

Tielle and I worked out a schedule so we could share the duties as Darius' caregivers. Since I already had a lot of his things at my place, we decided he would stay with me. I would be responsible for getting him to daycare in the morning, and Tielle would pick him up in the afternoon. We were suddenly mothers with no children, bogged down with a little more responsibility than we bargained for, and whenever Craig got out, we weren't sure if we'd be relieved of our duties. For Darius' protection, Craig would need to prove he was stable again before Darius left our care. It was the right thing to do, and it was what Tameka would want.

After I finished the second segment of "What's the Word?" the next day, Eli called me into his office. Harvey was sitting in one of the chairs when I walked in. He smiled as I joined him at Eli's desk.

"How you doin', sweetheart?" he asked, his New York accent thick with appeal. Though he had made his home in Atlanta, there was no question where he was born and raised.

"I'm alright. You?" I asked, unable to hide the suspicion in my voice. I was getting the feeling he had listened to my segment again and had something to say. Either that or they wanted to have a threesome.

I was right about the former. After unfulfilling small talk, Harvey asked how I had become a local celebrity so quickly.

"I'm not a celebrity. People just like my show because I'm not afraid to ask questions about somethin' I wanna know, and I don't put celebrities on a pedestal like everybody else," I said.

"I think you're a celebrity. You've got somethin'."

"Okay. I'm not gon' argue with you. It's not an insult," I replied with a smile. "I guess I don't feel like I'm a big deal because I don't make a big deal out of my job. I'm raw, Harvey. I didn't go to school for this, so everything about me is genuine and my listeners can relate to that. I don't ask what's politically correct because I don't believe in that politically correct garbage. People love me 'cause I'm just like them. I follow entertainment news and gossip, and I've got questions. I don't ask bullshit questions, and I don't accept bullshit answers."

His raised eyebrows let me know he was impressed. "Well, I can't blame them for loving you. I think I may be in love, too," he responded. "I was just tellin' Eli I'm gonna steal you away from him."

I looked at Eli's stone face, then turned back to Harvey. His slick smile was kind of cute until his bleached teeth blinded me. As I studied the gangster lean he rocked, with his arm hanging off the side of the chair, I laughed to myself. He didn't look like a "Harvey." He looked more like "Tony," a Brooklyn boy with mob connections.

"You need to take your show to the screen. Have you ever thought about doing TV?" Harvey asked.

"Not really. I don't see shows like "What's the Word?" on TV."

"There's a market for one."

"Harvey, don't try to gas me up, having me think I can have a TV show."

"You ever been to Atlanta, sweetheart?" he asked.

"Naw. I have a cousin who lives there now, but I haven't had enough time to visit."

"Come check it out, and while you're there, come check me out at the studio. I'll show you I'm not full of shit." He handed me his business card. "Give me a call if you ever make it to my town. I'll make sure you have a good time."

***

I arrived at U-Turn at four o'clock, just like Darryl asked. He said he had something important to talk to me about. We met in his office and talked about a bunch of nothing for a while. Just when he was about to tell me the purpose of my visit, his assistant manager knocked on the door. Darryl excused himself and then came back five minutes later.

"Sorry about that. There's a new girl who needs a pep talk every night."

I looked at my watch. "Oh, it's *that* time?" I asked. "That's my cue to leave."

"I've got a few more minutes before I have to get out there. We have to finish talking."

"We'll talk another time. People gon' see my car and think I'm in here lookin' at titties. Unless you've got some dudes droppin' their pants up in here, I'm out."

His phone rang as I headed out. He asked me to wait while he took the call, but I waved goodbye and kept stepping. I stopped in the hallway to check a missed voice message, but didn't hear a thing. I was distracted by another woman who'd just walked in the door, talking on her cell phone. Before I looked her way, I knew who she was. Her voice, her footsteps, and her Burberry perfume were programmed into my memory. It was Jacqueline.

254

I didn't waste time warning her to get away from me. Instead, I cornered her. "Nobody's here to save you now," I said.

"I'm pregnant. You better not touch me," Jacqueline replied.

"Are you proud of that, bitch? You gon' add that to your list of accomplishments next to gettin' my sister killed?"

"Hey, hey, hey! What's all the commotion about out here?" Darryl asked as he flung open his office door and wedged between us.

Saved again, I thought, never once considering maybe I was the one being saved. With all the animosity built up in me, I was sure to go to prison for first degree murder if I was left alone with her for more than three or four minutes.

"Your little fling here helped murder my sister," I said.

"My what? Jackie, you did what?"

"I did no such thing! I didn't know he raped her," Jacqueline defended.

"Your lunchtime ho led her brother to Tameka so he could kill her," I said to Darryl as he struggled to control my arms.

"You don't know the story," she screeched.

"You use that prissy, innocent act as a cover. You ain't nothin' but a fuckin' snake. Bet you didn't know you'd get pregnant if you boned Craig without a condom either, right?"

With my open hand, I reached around Darryl and smacked her forehead so hard that the back of her head almost touched her spine.

"Enough!" Darryl yelled. "I can't let you do that."

"Why, 'cause she's pregnant? Do you think she's carrying your child? You better sign up for another DNA test. See if they'll give you a buy-one-get-one-free deal." I pushed past him and snatched Jacqueline by her weave. Pregnant or not, she was going to take one to the face.

"Because she's your sister."

Jacqueline braced for impact as my fist paused in mid air. Again, Darryl stood between us. I unraveled her locks from my wrist and looked to him for an explanation.

"Jacqueline is my daughter. Jackie, that's what I wanted to talk to you about today. Alexis is my daughter, too."

I'm sure Jacqueline's look of horror mirrored mine. We looked at each other with mutual disgust. I literally saw red as the crimson walls around us sucked the air out of the corridor and took our breath away.

"I only have one sister—Tameka; and I only have one father," I said, retrieving my purse from the corner near the door.

Darryl was stuck between a rock and a hard place. Was he to stay near his terrified, pregnant daughter, or was he supposed to stop me from exiting after I'd just entered his life? He chose Door Number One as I opened Two and walked out.

20

Tiffany:
The Other Side: Second Thoughts

Morgan called Tiffany to have a heart-to-heart. Her little sister was acting out of character, and someone had to intervene. Their family had always granted Tiffany a generous amount of leeway because she was a free thinker who was willing to try anything once. But even after the skydiving adventure on her eighteenth birthday, the applications to be on MTV's *Real World*, and the stories of her and Marlon's sexcapades, they never expected she would become involved with a woman. Morgan was sure Tiffany was taking her open-minded nature too far.

She started their conversation asking about the kids, who were at gymnastics class. Tiffany bragged about Bryant's trampoline flips, calling him the daredevil of the bunch.

"How's Venni?" Morgan asked.

"Morgan…"

"I was just asking a question!"

"I know what this is about. You can call off your intervention dogs. I really don't hang with Venni any more."

"Do we call this a breakup….or…?" Morgan asked.

"You have to be a couple to break up. Let's just say we've untied our social strings," Tiffany replied.

"Alrighty then." Morgan paused before asking, "You wanna talk about it?"

"I won't get into details, but I found out some things about her past that she wasn't upfront about. She's not upfront about anything, really, and I don't have friends like that. Besides, I want my family

257

back," Tiffany said.

"With Marlon?" Morgan asked, her tone not hiding her disgust.

"Uh…yeah!"

Morgan grumbled, then said, "The lesser of two evils, huh?"

"That's my boo. Shut up. I just feel stupid for letting that one night change everything."

"Don't forget *his* role in that one night. You're not stupid. You just immerse yourself in other people's lives and become almost obsessed with their details. How many times have I told you to stop talking like Alexis and stop reacting to situations like she would?"

Tiffany agreed. She loved the uniqueness of people and therefore cared about their inner workings—what made them different, what experiences shaped their thought processes. Unfortunately, if there wasn't a desk separating her from someone, she would invite herself into their world at her own expense. This time, the price was too high. Venni had a little too much going on in her life.

"You should consider moving here with me," Morgan continued. "I think it could be healthy to get away for a while—at least for the next school year. That way you won't have to uproot my babies too many times."

"It's too cold up north."

"But we have the hottest leather coats! And maybe you'll have a real reason to wear your Burberry scarf," Morgan joked. "Just think about it and get back to me."

"There's nothing to think about. Marlon isn't gonna want to move up there, either."

"Tiff, do you really think he'll take you back? You left him for a woman."

In Tiffany's mind, she didn't leave him; they needed a long overdue break from each other, and the Venni incident just happened to speed up the process.

"Do you understand who I am?" she asked. "Marlon knows he still loves me. I'm not saying we'll go back to normal right away, but we're meant to be together."

***

On Friday, she stopped by Venni's to pick up a few things she'd left behind the last time she slept over. She took a casual approach by making small talk with the associate she'd once called her friend as she filled her bag. Her heart was heavy with worry, though. Regardless of whether they had a valid friendship, they had been close, and the information in the articles she'd read still left her unsettled.

Venni thought nothing ill of Tiffany's item removal. They hadn't held a lengthy conversation or gone to lunch together in over a week and a half, so she figured Marlon had been scratching at Tiffany's door, trying to get back in.

After Tiffany packed her final item and prepared to leave, she caught the tail end of Venni's phone conversation with Lawrence. It sounded like they were planning a trip to San Juan, and Tiffany couldn't help herself once they hung up.

"What's really up with you and Lawrence?" she asked. "Have you two ever…?" The day before, she saw him kiss Venni goodbye—on the lips—after they returned from lunch.

"Ever had sex? Un unh. Everybody thinks we have."

"You definitely have chemistry."

"Jealous?" Venni asked with a sly smile.

Tiffany ignored her. "Do you think about having sex with men? Have you considered it since you became a lesbian?"

"What am I, your case study? I didn't *become* a lesbian. I became disgusted with men."

"You and your wordplay," Tiffany replied with a chuckle.

"I never claimed to be a lesbian. That's what you assumed."

"So you're bisexual."

"No, I'm Venita Miles. You're into titles; I'm not."

"Sounds like you're into being screwed up," Tiffany said under her breath.

Venni prompted Tiffany to repeat herself so she could hear, and she did. Venni's laughter taunted her.

"Your issues are no laughing matter. Lawrence is in love with you, and you don't even see it. You don't think you can be loved," Tiffany said.

"Tiffany, relax your analytical muscles. You don't know what you're talking about," Venni said, smirking.

"I wish you would give yourself a chance at happiness. This house and your car won't satisfy you forever. I may not *know* you, but I'll tell you what I think; I think you're a broken woman. I can't imagine what you must have gone through when you were prostituting. One of my clients—"

Venni held her hand up, signaling for Tiffany to stop. "When I was *what*?" she asked, slowly rising to her feet.

Tiffany admitted to reading the articles and eavesdropping on Venni's conversation, justifying it because Venni was using her phone. "It's so clear now why Holly didn't want me to know her identity. A past like that has to be embarrassing. Her penname is her new start. KeKe Red is her true self minus the years of exploitation."

Venni stood toe to toe with Tiffany. "This is why I don't get close to females. You had no business going through my stuff. I told you not to worry about that situation, and you still dug for information," she snapped.

"You don't think I have the right to know about your past?"

"My past has nothing to do with you. Regardless of what you think you heard or read, you don't know shit about me or Holly."

"So you didn't witness a murder and Vance isn't your son?" Tiffany asked, taking a few steps backward. "He looks just like you, Venni. How can you not want him with you all the time? You're so good with him, too."

"You're playing a dangerous game. We've been tight for a few months, but this isn't a bone you want to pick. Don't let the BMW and this nice house fool you. I spent my formative years in Gary and Chicago and handled plenty bitches who thought they could talk to me any kind of way. If you were really as knowledgeable as you think you are, you would've never crossed me like this. Let me hear you've repeated any of what you saw or heard, and you'll see the not-so-professional side of me."

"Maybe that came out wrong. I wasn't trying to offend you. It's just frustrating when you won't let me help you. You're a broken woman."

"What, and you've been sent to fix me? I'm one of the strongest women you'll ever meet. You think those little paragraphs you read tell my story? Tiffany, you are not my psychologist. I haven't asked for your help. I'm good. I don't need a textbook understanding of life. I get it. I accept it for what it is. It's unpredictable, and I've learned to live with that."

"Have you really?"

"You know what? You need to stop focusing on me, and focus on yourself. If you did, you'd realize you have issues of your own that you need to resolve before you hand out free advice. Start thinking about why you really left Marlon when you still dream of the white picket fence and two-car garage. And I heard what really happened with you and Alexis. Ask yourself why you lied and acted like she was a homophobe instead of admitting that you kissed her."

"I only brought this conversation up because I care."

"You don't, so stop acting like you do. I thought you were a cool person because we had so much in common, but this so-called friendship was fueled by your curiosity. You're only around because you're fascinated with me."

"That's not true," Tiffany replied.

"Get out of my house before this talk takes a turn for the worse."

Tiffany was glad to. She didn't need that drama from her. If Venni wanted to carry her load alone, so be it.

***

Marlon arrived at Tiffany's house at 4:15 p.m. He apologized for being fifteen minutes late, blaming his tardiness on Tony's last-minute trip to the potty. She held her baby boy while the twins ran into the house.

Marlon looked good. He had on a red and white striped Sean John button-down with French cuffs, dark wash jeans, and white and red Reeboks. He looked freshly shaven, and his lineup was tight. Tiffany had been contemplating their reconciliation ever since they'd had sex, but she wasn't sure how she would approach him. If he was going to look that fine every time she saw him, though, she needed to get her plan together ASAP—before someone else snatched him up.

She ran her hand over the first few buttons of his shirt. "You look nice. Where are you headed?"

His subtle embarrassment was obvious to Tiffany. He was never good at taking compliments. "I'm just goin' to play cards at Dap's."

"Oh, that's nice." She continued to enjoy the view as she leaned against the doorframe.

He stood there for a few moments. The comfort they felt was peculiar, yet familiar from years passed. She wanted to invite him in and fix him a plate of the smothered pork chops she had made for dinner—his favorite—but he'd be sitting in the same chairs he turned upside down months before. He wanted to bend down and kiss her, but he'd be kissing the lips that had most likely been kissing Venni since they ended their engagement.

Saved by his phone, both were able to escape their inner battles. A quick "See you later" and wave goodbye ended their exchange as Marlon took the call and walked to his car. Tiffany closed the door and smelled her hand. *Curve.* Her nostrils celebrated its aroma. She missed her Marly Bear. Dare she tell him now?

After feeding the kids, Tiffany dozed off on the couch. She was awakened by Bria's whining an hour later. "Mommy, will you play princesses with me? Bryant won't play," she said.

"That's because he's not supposed to be a princess. He's a boy, Poochie," Tiffany said as she sat up. "Mommy will play. What do I need to do?"

Bria placed a plastic crown on her mom's head. "Perfect! It fits. First, I have to do your makeup." She dug in her Barbie makeup bag.

As she rubbed strawberry-flavored gloss on Tiffany's lips, something sparkled in the bag, catching Tiffany's eye. "What all do you have in there, girl?"

"Wait, silly!" She giggled and proceeded with the makeover.

Tiffany wanted to laugh when Bria handed her a mirror. Her face looked like a color palette. Instead, she said, "I didn't know I could look so beautiful, Pooch!"

"Now for the finishing touches," Bria said with a smile.

Tiffany sat patiently as her daughter draped plastic necklaces on her and placed a bracelet on her wrist. She then took a ring out of the bag and placed it on Tiffany's finger. It was the engagement ring Marlon had bought.

"There!" Bria stepped back and admired her work.

"Where did you get this from?" Tiffany asked, pointing to the ring.

"Daddy's house. It's yours."

"Did he tell you to give it to me?"

Sensing that she was in trouble, she didn't answer for a while. "No," she finally replied, "but it's yours."

Tiffany lectured Bria on taking things without permission, warning that if she was a grownup, she could go to jail for something like that. When Bria broke into tears, she consoled her and apologized for scaring her.

Though she continued to play with Bria, her mind was a thousand miles away. Marlon still had the ring. She couldn't help but smile. Her man hadn't given up on her, and knowing her custom made ring wasn't sitting in some store's display case made her confident that her family would become one again.

She called Marlon after she tucked their little ones in, and he was just leaving Dap's house. When he showed up twenty-five minutes later, he barely looked her in the eye. He stood just inside the door as she handed him the ring.

"Why do you still have it?" Tiffany asked.

"I never got around to takin' it back," Marlon said.

"We broke up in February; it's May, Marlon. I thought you would've been more than happy to get that money back."

"Did I come here for an interrogation?" he asked, rolling the ring between his fingers.

"You can come here for whatever you like," Tiffany replied, flashing her most charming smile. "The kids are sleep."

"Nah…no more of that."

Tiffany's smile faded. She wasn't used to rejection, and having it come from Marlon was devastating. He hated to hurt her, but he had to protect his heart. As a man, he still hadn't gotten over Tiffany's stabbing revelation that Venni was better at pleasing her.

"What we did the other week meant nothing to you?" Tiffany asked.

"Why should it? What did it mean to you? Ain't you still hangin' wit' ya girl?"

"No. And really, Marlon, we were friends above anything else. Yes, some sexual things happened between us, but that's the past. I want you to be my present, my future."

Marlon chuckled. "I don't want a bisexual woman."

"I'm not into women. It was never about Venni being a woman. I was attracted to her personality. Sexually, I was attracted to her confidence. She knew she was good at what she did," Tiffany explained.

That made him laugh even harder.

Tiffany continued. "Marlon, I can't recall one time when I was intimate with her without being drunk. I had to be in another state of mind to go there with her; and despite popular belief, we didn't go there often."

As Marlon twisted his lips, she continued. "I know it's almost impossible to understand, but I've learned my lesson. I was chasing a thrill. I was exposed to something new and fell right into it."

"And now you want boring ol' Marlon."

"I want my love back. You're my love. You know that. Remember how you used to say you'd always have a special spot in your heart for my spoiled ass? Is it still there?" Marlon's face was emotionless as Tiffany waved her hand in front of it. "Hellooo!"

"What do you want me to say?" he asked.

"Right now, I want you to act like you see me standing in front of you. You're acting like I'm invisible," she replied.

"I'm looking at you."

"You're looking *through* me. Besides that, I just asked you a question."

"I'm not answering it."

"Why did you come here if you're unwilling to talk?" Tiffany asked.

"I came to get this ring. Ain't that why you called?"

"You really thought I *only* wanted to give you this ring at this time of night? I'm trying to get my Marly Bear back," she said, reaching out to touch him.

He backed away to avoid contact. "You're right. I made a mistake. I shouldn't be here right now," he said. He went on, advising her to stop throwing herself at him before she made a fool of herself. "You think you can get your way, no matter what. Those days are over. Listen to yourself. You wouldn't play that shit if I left you for some girl and came back to you when the thrill was gone. I'll see you next weekend."

Tiffany was left unfulfilled as her tear-glazed eyes watched Marlon walk out. She was tired of being confused, tired of not knowing the direction in which her life was heading. She was morphing into a person she didn't want to be, depending on someone else for her happiness. Venni accused her of that shortly after they became friends and turned out to be right. Still, her heart wouldn't let her throw in the towel. Marlon meant too much to her, and until he could look her straight in the eye and say he didn't want her, she wouldn't give up hope.

Anxious to get another take on Marlon's attitude, she called Alexis. Like Morgan, she asked Tiffany if she really thought Marlon would get past his feelings about her relationship with Venni.

"You got past me kissing you," Tiffany said.

"I'm *getting* past that. The difference is I don't have to be around you every day. Marlon would, if he takes you back," Alexis rebutted.

"I'm sick of hearing about that, like he's such a victim. If you really break it down, I'm the victim. That damn pill in my drink made me a victim. Yes, later I chose to further associate with Venni. Does that take away from the wrongdoing that occurred first? Imagine somebody saying Meka wasn't a victim because she chose to get in the car with TJ that night. Was it her fault that she got raped? Does it mean she deserved to get HIV?"

Alexis was silent while Tiffany continued talking. Finally, she said, "You're comparing your shit to what my sister went through?"

This time, without being drunk, Tiffany had used her lips to push Alexis away...again.

***

A week and a half had passed, and Tiffany had successfully avoided seeing Venni at work. She used the east wing entrance and exit instead of those in the front of the building, ordered lunch from rinky dink delivery spots with the girls on her floor, and took the stairs instead of the elevator, which was toning her legs quite remarkably. Yes, it was that deep. She was willing to climb fourteen flights of stairs to evade discomfiture.

Her coworkers often teased her about coming to "the other side." They questioned why she was eating with "the common folk" and not "Miss Money Bags." Each time, she would jab back, reminding them that the majority of them had never spoken to her until her third month on the job. She could take that form of teasing. She just hoped they never found out about her and Venni. If that happened, she would lose their respect and be categorized as something she wasn't.

After lunch with the girls one afternoon, she had a craving for an iced coffee. Since she had a few minutes to spare, she made a quick run to the Coffee Hut located on the main floor. She stood in the unusually long line, shifting side to side and occasionally looking at her watch.

"Are you about to be late for an appointment?" Venni stood to her left, iced coffee in-hand.

"Not really," Tiffany replied as her eyes frantically searched for something or someone else to focus on.

"How have you been?" Venni asked.

"Good. You?"

"I'm dealing. I've been thinking about some of the things you said. Insert big reveal about me and Lawrence being a couple now, right?" she said, laughing. "All jokes aside, you're right. I'm broken, and I won't let anyone in. So, no, I probably won't love or loved, and that's okay with me. It's what I've known for years."

Tiffany nodded dismissively, wondering why Venni was opting to have such a conversation in the presence of others. "As long as you're okay with that..." she said.

"I am. Take care of yourself," Venni said before walking away.

There was a sense of finality in their words—a cracked door that was now completely closed. Tiffany could only hope the door to Marlon's heart would now be opened.

When the time arrived for her to determine if that door was open, she was optimistic. It was a gorgeous June day, a perfect day for a wedding. Tielle would be marrying Romeo in two hours, and Tiffany had just pulled into the church parking lot. Her truck was among just a few vehicles—those belonging to members of the wedding party. Three spaces away, Marlon's car glistened in the sunlight. He would be standing up for his cousin on Romeo's side as his groomsman. Tony and Bryant were ring bearers, and Bria was the flower girl. They were all excited about being in Cousin Tielle's wedding, though Bria was the happiest. She was convinced *she* was the bride.

They were greeted by the wedding planner as they entered the church. She checked the children's names off of her paper and complimented them on how nice they looked. Like a proud mother, Tiffany snapped about a dozen pictures before she turned them over to the lady.

She peeked into the sanctuary and smiled at the beautiful sight. The setup was very similar to what she imagined hers would be, back when she actually had someone to marry. Careful not to mess up her mascara, she blinked her tears away. As she paced in the hallway wondering if the kids would follow through with their duties, Marlon rounded the corner, stopping when he saw her. They exchanged uncomfortable hellos, and he fussed with his vest.

"You need help?" Tiffany asked.

"I'm all right," he said.

"You don't look it," Tiffany said, laughing.

Just then, a female exited the bathroom in front of them. "Do I just go sit in there now? I know it's still early," she asked.

"It's up to you," he replied, nervously cutting his eyes toward Tiffany.

The lady saw that he was still struggling with his vest and went to his rescue. Tiffany sized her up as she watched her smooth the material on his back. She was dark-skinned with full lips, at least four inches taller than Tiffany, and thick all over—the exact opposite of Tiffany.

"Did your kids make it yet? I can't wait to meet them," the mystery lady asked.

Tiffany's head jerked in their direction. "You need to meet me first," she said, as the lady gave her the once-over.

"Tiffany, this is Sabrina. Sabrina, that's Tiffany, their mother," Marlon intervened.

The ladies' eyes did the only speaking, saying words no one should say in the Lord's house. Marlon walked his date into the sanctuary and then came back out.

"Is that your girlfriend?" Tiffany asked.

"Now isn't the time or place," he replied.

"I believe I deserve an answer. This woman spoke of our kids as if she knows them. Does she know them?"

"She knows I have kids and she knew they would be here. This is Tielle's day. Don't start."

"I'm not starting a thing. I'll just tell you this: Remember how we used to fight when we were together? Remember how strongly we felt about our positions and how adamantly we defended them? Knowingly bringing your little plaything in front of me just jumped off the biggest

266

battle ever. I'm gonna fight for you with the same energy I used to fight against you. I know your game, and I feel sorry for Miss Sabrina. Tell her to enjoy you while she can, 'cause you know I don't lose."

She ended her speech as other guests entered the building, filing in line with them and never looking back.

21

Alexis:
The Other Side: Second Chances

Tielle's wedding was starting in a half hour, and there was a problem in the bridesmaid room. The maid of honor's zipper was broken, so she couldn't close her dress. To make matters worse (for me, at least), the wedding planner said she changed the order of the groomsmen for the procession and I was walking with Robert down the aisle. It was bad enough we were both in the wedding, but Tielle knew better than to put us together. Since she was nowhere around when the last-minute decision was made, I had to suck it up and prepare to link arms with the man I hated with a passion.

By 1:55 p.m., Miss Rosie had worked a miracle on the maid of honor's dress with her stash of safety pins, and we were lining up in the hallway. When the men came out, I quickly pulled Marlon aside and asked him to be my escort. The wedding coordinator interrupted my plea, hastily placing us in our positions while the pianist played "Endless Love." Robert didn't acknowledge me as we stood side-by-side, and that was just fine.

After the coordinator handed the bridesmaids our roses, Robert held out his arm. I intertwined mine with his, struggling to find a happy medium between familiarity and uneasiness.

"Ain't this ironic?" he said under his breath as we stood in the doorway of the sanctuary, waiting our turn to enter. I clenched my teeth and squeezed my lips tightly in an effort to not speak. I only opened my mouth to smile when we were cued to stroll toward the altar.

The church was decorated beautifully. Two live doves were perched in their cages—one on each side of the white arch Romeo and Tielle would stand under. Blue bows hung on the pews, almost an exact match to our serene blue dresses, and blue and white flowers lined the altar and the aisle. Tielle swore blue was her favorite color and that her selection had nothing to do with her sorority.

When she appeared in the doorway, Romeo teared up. She looked like a queen in her strapless satin corset ball gown. The corset was garnished with lace and beading, and her chapel train trailed about five feet behind her. I felt tears welling up in *my* eyes, thinking of how happy she was going to be, spending her life with a man who adored her. Isaac winked at me from the fifth pew as I dabbed my eye.

Romeo recalled the day they first met as he stated his vows. I chuckled at the memory, remembering how Tameka first thought Romeo was trying to get with her. Life is fascinating. That day was the beginning of Tameka's end, but had also become the start of Romeo and Tielle's life together.

After their "I do's," they rode away in a horse-drawn carriage and the wedding party rode to the reception hall in limos. I partied all night with Isaac, ignoring the holes Robert's staring eyes were burning into me. I felt sorry for his date, who was desperately fighting for his attention. It seemed there were multiple pairs of eyes watching us. As Dap looked on from a nearby table, I could tell she was wondering who Isaac was. I even caught Tiffany smiling at us, but she wouldn't approach me. She knew she'd messed up after she compared herself to Tameka.

When the night ended, I held Isaac around his neck on the dance floor and said, "I'm tired of saying goodbye to you."

"I'm not leaving until tomorrow night, baby."

"I know, but you're leaving."

"Come back with me."

"Find me a job," I said before laughing.

"I knew you were just talking," he said.

"I'm serious. I'm just laughing because that's probably the first time I've talked about moving somewhere and said I needed a job first."

He leaned over and kissed me. "You sure you wanna be where I am?"

"No, I just bitch at you about being long-distance because I feel like it," I replied sarcastically.

He looked at me with contemplative eyes, never saying a word. When I asked what he was thinking, he kissed me again and said, "About how much I love your sexy self."

Just then, Bria, Bryant, and Tony ran over to me. Bria hugged my legs, and the boys waved. "Y'all 'bout to leave?" I asked.

"Umm hmm," Bria said. "When you gonna come play with me again?"

"I'll tell you what. I'm supposed to go to Six Flags with my job in a few weeks, and you can come with me. Is that a deal?"

"Yeah!" she said, giving me a high-five.

Tiffany approached us and rounded up her crew. "It's time to go, guys," she said. Before walking away, she turned to me and Isaac. "You make a beautiful couple. If people didn't know any better, they'd think you were the bride and groom."

Isaac thanked her, then asked why I rolled my eyes.

"Because Tiffany is extra. She only said that to see if I would talk to her," I said.

"I think she said it because it's true."

"She knows damn well we ain't gettin' married."

"Damn! So you wouldn't marry me?"

"I'm not sayin' that. You would have to know Tiffany to understand what I mean," I replied as we walked to his rental car. "And don't try to call me out about marriage. We haven't even been together that long. You just made it past your ninety-day trial period," I joked.

"I've got your ninety-day trial period," he said, while throwing a Tic-Tac at my head.

I swatted it away and doubled over with laughter as he retrieved another and put it in his mouth.

***

Tielle returned from her honeymoon the following Sunday, and on Monday night, we were off to Hollywood for the BET Awards. I had overheard Eli and Harvey discussing them before I left Eli's office weeks before, and managed to snag two tickets from Harvey. I invited Tielle to go as a late "thank you" gift for getting me the job in the first place.

I felt so accomplished sitting in the Kodak Theatre, rows away from superstars. Mo'Nique killed the opening of the show with her rendition of Beyoncé's "Crazy in Love." She and her big girl crew brought the house down as they did the "Uh Oh" dance.

During commercial breaks while people were walking around, I seized every opportunity to mingle with the celebrities closest to me.

After all, it was my job. I talked with Big Boi from OutKast and Flavor Flav, waved at Toni Valentine from afar, and was able to get a head nod from Lil' John. I didn't get close enough to speak to Jay-Z, but it was probably for the best. His bodyguards wouldn't have been able to stop me from snatching his Yankee hat or pinching his booty. I was just as pleased watching his performance of "99 Problems" with a star-studded band.

Rick James and Teena Marie presented the award for "Best Female R&B Artist", but performed before doing so. I think everybody in the building sang along to "Fire and Desire" from Rick's first note to Teena's last wail. They did a lot of off-key screaming, but it was cool seeing them back together. I think they were just happy to be on-stage again. I turned to Tielle and said, "That's my cellmate!" We laughed, recalling the night we played "Who Would You Rather?" back in December. Just when I thought I was satisfied for the night, Rick stepped to the mic after Beyoncé's acceptance speech and ended his own speech with, "I'm Rick James, bitch!" I stood with the thousands of others and cheered with everything in me.

I recapped every major moment on "What's the Word?" when we returned to the studio Thursday morning. My listeners loved my segment on the good, the bad, and the ugly of the entertainment business. I put some stars on Front Street, warning my audience not to trust what they see in magazines and on TV. Half the men were five inches shorter, and some of the women were five inches wider. Tielle invited me to stick around for a few more minutes because callers were blowing up the phone lines with questions.

After the show was over, Tielle and I had more work to do. Craig had been released from the mental hospital, and we were taking Darius to see him for the first time. Craig refused to go back to his condo for fear he'd have another breakdown, so Chauncey had flown in to help him get settled into his new apartment.

The place was decorated nicely, though it was missing the woman's touch Tameka added to the condo. Craig had gained some of his weight back and was looking closer to normal. Tielle hugged both of her cousins when we entered, but when Craig went to hug me, I put Darius between us and handed him over.

Every second we were there felt like ten minutes as I leaned against the front door. Tielle walked through the apartment with Craig, while Chauncey and I discussed the severity of Craig's mental state. He assured me that Craig was much better, though he wasn't sure if he was capable of having full custody of Darius yet.

"Me and Tielle figured that. I'm not about to leave D-Baby with him no time soon."

"He'll get back on track," Chauncey said.

"Has Jacqueline been over here yet?" I asked.

"She stopped by last week," Craig answered as he and Tielle exited the bedroom in the back of the apartment. "Have you talked to her?"

"Why would I talk to her?"

"Lexis, I know. She told me. Sounds like Darryl was a busy man in his day," he said.

"And you're a busy man now."

Tielle nudged me.

"Maybe I should just go," I said, gathering my sunglasses and purse. "I'm sorry, LT. I'm not family. I can't stand here and be supportive like y'all."

I kissed Darius, and I was out.

***

Darryl invited me to his house for dinner. He wanted to hear the story behind my hatred for Jacqueline, minus all the screaming and yelling. I planned to also use the visit as my opportunity to tell him I was leaving town.

I had visited Atlanta at Harvey's expense during the Fourth of July weekend and was sold on the idea of moving there as soon as I toured the city with Yari. As promised, Harvey showed me around his television studio and introduced me to a few of the other producers. After executing an impromptu mock interview with a crew member who impersonated Usher, Harvey and his executive producer offered me a half-hour entertainment news segment on their morning show, *Wake Up, Atlanta*...and I took it.

When I entered Darryl's dining room, Jacqueline was already seated. "I'm not into games, Darryl. You know you should've told me she was gon' be here."

"Would you have come if I told you she was here?"

"Hell no!"

"I really would like to speak with you, Alexis. I think my name has been slung through the mud enough," Jacqueline said.

"This is gonna be good," I said as I sat at my place setting.

Darryl smiled and fixed my plate. We ate the majority of the meal in silence until Darryl asked Jacqueline when her next in-service day was.

"She's an economics teacher," he said in an effort to fill me in.

"I know. Me and ol' Jackie here go way back," I replied.

He prolonged the inevitable blowout by telling Jacqueline what I did for a living.

"I *used* to do that," I corrected, then told Darryl about my new job in Atlanta.

Jacqueline gasped and said, "You're *that* Alexis? I listen to your show every morning."

I almost smiled, but the urge to vomit overpowered that emotion when I noticed how much her stomach had grown since I'd last seen her.

"Please. You probably don't even listen to WTIZ," I said.

"I told you I can't win, Daddy," Jacqueline said.

I put my fork down and turned to Darryl. "Can we cut the small talk? It's really not working. What do you need to know about your fake daughter so I can get outta here?" I asked.

"Let's start with why you call her fake," he said.

"Because she's sitting here like she didn't stalk Craig and send her brother to kill my sister."

"Whoa," Darryl said, turning to Jacqueline. "Rashawn killed Tameka? *He's* Smoke?"

"And your sister killed my brother," Jacqueline replied.

"She sure did, and he deserved to die."

"That's a low blow," Darryl said.

When I asked how he would feel if someone raped any of his daughters, gave them HIV, and killed them, he changed his tune.

"I didn't know he'd done that until I saw the news broadcast," Jacqueline said. "I couldn't believe it, because he wasn't like that."

"He was a fuckin' monster."

"Shawn had issues, but that didn't make him a monster. What he did was wrong, but you don't know what his childhood was like," Jacqueline defended.

Before I could respond, Darryl mediated, asking me to let her finish. I sat back and crossed my arms.

"The doctors diagnosed Shawn with HIV when he was ten, but my mom didn't tell him until he was sixteen. She found out he was having sex, and she was forced to make a choice between morality and motherly instinct. She fought between whether she should tell him the truth and protect his partners or say nothing and protect him. If it were up to her, he would have never found out. I heard her cry to her friends on the phone at night. I saw her sneak the medicine in his food for years. The pills she couldn't crush, she lied and told him they were vitamins. So, yes, when he found out he was HIV-positive, his world fell apart. I believe he only turned to the streets because his father wasn't in his life and he didn't want to talk to me or my mother about his feelings. He was misunderstood—withdrawn and insensitive at times—but never monstrous."

"So rape isn't monstrous? Ejaculating on her face wasn't monstrous?" I asked.

She lowered her head.

"You claim to be so educated, but you're just as ignorant as his ass. I can't sympathize with a motherfucker who gives somebody a deadly virus on purpose. He raped my sister *twice*. Justify that."

"Alexis, you want answers that I don't have."

"Exactly! So, stop tryin' to come up with some. Your dad is sittin' here, wantin' answers that you do have, though," I said as I walked to the front door.

Darryl followed me, and Jacqueline walked a few steps behind him.

"Okay," she called out.

I took my hand off the doorknob and listened while she admitted to Darryl that she stalked Craig and asked her brother to scare him.

"Never mind that he wasn't the only one living there. Thank God Darius wasn't with Meka," I added.

"I really didn't know she would be there, and I told Shawn not to do a thing if Darius was there."

"Right, but you never gave him instructions regarding Meka. Then you wonder why I find you just as guilty. Tell me you didn't want her to die. Tell me you weren't hoping something would happen to her so you could get back with Craig," I said.

Her phone rang while she hesitated. "Excuse me. I have to take this. It's a private number—might be one of my sons." After she answered, she looked like she'd seen a ghost. "What do you want?" she asked. "That was not the agreement...I can't discuss this right now...Yes, I understand that...Fine, but this is the last time," she said before snapping her phone closed.

"Is everything alright, baby?" Darryl asked.

"It's fine," Jacqueline snapped.

"I'm outta here," I said, strolling to my car.

"Wait! Do you know Jye and Waylon?"

I stopped when I reached passenger door. "Are you serious? We were talking about my dead sister and now you wanna bring up some random names? Do they have anything to do with you sending your brother to Craig's?"

"Well, no, but they—" Jacqueline started.

"This is stupid. I don't know why I came here. I don't want a relationship with you, so we don't have to get along. Darryl, it's the thought that counts. Sorry you didn't get results," I said as I walked to the driver's side.

Though I heard Darryl call out to me, I sped away, hoping neither of them would contact me again.

***

Time was not on my side. I had been running around for two weeks, tying up all the loose ends I could before I made my big move. I'd already signed the paperwork to break my lease, made arrangements with a moving company, and called to have the utilities taken out of my name. Will bought my car for $4,700 cash, which was going to be a decent down payment for my Nissan 350Z. I'd been eyeing it for a while, and since I was stepping up my game with my job, it was only right that I do the same with my ride. My flight was scheduled to land in Atlanta at 9:10 a.m. on Saturday, and I was planning to drive off a lot in my LeMans Sunset Metallic roadster by 3:00 p.m.

With only three days left, I had to handle personal business. I hadn't talked to Tielle much since I stopped working at the radio station. Miss Rosie had taken over my caregiver duties for Darius since my schedule had unexpectedly become hectic, so Tielle and I no longer had our drop-off briefings about the latest happenings in our lives. I didn't bother calling her once she was home with Romeo because I didn't want to interrupt their newlywed activities. To make sure I caught up with her, I stopped by the station just before her show ended on Wednesday, and we set a lunch date for Friday.

Isaac was extremely supportive of my move to Atlanta. When I called from the TV studio to tell him about the job offer, he reminded me of our conversation in New York when he motivated me to think big and said I'd be a fool if I didn't pursue my destiny. I appreciated his backing, but one major drawback remained. When he called Wednesday night, I spoke with him the only way I knew how—honestly.

"I've been thinkin' about us a whole lot during these past few days," I began, "and I'm havin' a hard time believing our relationship can survive my move."

"Why is that?" Isaac asked.

Atlanta was full of fine men, and though Isaac was just as fine and I loved him, I couldn't promise that I would turn down every offer for dinner and a movie after too many lonely nights.

"Companionship is part of a relationship, baby, and I want to have that every day," I said.

"So what are you sayin'?"

"Do you think we should just let go now?"

276

"Why would we let go? Planes fly to Georgia just like they flew to Texas."

"You ain't tired of flyin'?"

"I told you I'm looking at jobs down there. If the right one comes along, I'm taking it."

"And if it doesn't?" I asked.

"I'll tell you what, Alexis. I'm done tryin' to override your pessimism with my optimism. Since we got together, I've busted my ass to see you at least once a month despite the demands of my job, and you're givin' me a bullshit excuse about companionship. If you weren't so busy throwin' tantrums, you would've considered that I was about to uproot my life to be in yours. You wanna let go? It's all good. Enjoy yourself in the A," he said before hanging up.

I started to call back, but what the hell was I gonna say? Maybe I was wrong for bringing up the subject so soon, but early in our relationship, he made it clear that he wanted us to be straight up with each other.

I tried to go to sleep, but I couldn't rest. By 3 a.m., I was tired of tossing and turning, tired of fronting. Isaac needed to know I wasn't trying to break up with him. I just wanted us to talk—needed a little more reassurance that we would work. I texted him: *I know ur busy at work, but call me when u get off. Sorry for earlier. Done wit my tantrum. Luv u.*

***

It was Thursday afternoon, and I still hadn't heard from Isaac. I called, but got no answer. I texted him a few more times, but got no reply. *Maybe he's working over and his battery is dead,* I thought. I'd have to try him later.

In the meantime, I headed to "Bourgeois-ville" to see my mother's new place. She'd been back in town for weeks, but this was going to be our first time seeing each other since the DNA testing. I still wasn't ready to see her, but since she was all broken up about me moving away after she'd moved back, I agreed to stop by briefly to say goodbye.

Stony Brook Estates was set in a secluded area on the north side; so secluded that I didn't know the subdivision existed until my mother gave me her new address. *My little Accord looks like a bucket,* I thought as I drove past driveways with Lexus trucks and Benzes. When I reached her house, I looked down to double-check the address. *538 Pebble Throw Lane.* I was at the right place. When I pulled into her driveway, her garage door opened. She appeared and directed me to park inside, next to her new burgundy Range Rover.

"When did you get this?" I asked, exiting my car and walking to hers.

"Yesterday," she said, while I checked out its interior through the driver's side window.

Wow, I mouthed as we entered the house that looked way too big for one person. The kitchen was bigger than my living room and was furnished with stainless steel appliances.

"Did you have another kid or something?" I asked, pointing to the blue and yellow sippy cup that stood out like a sore thumb on the island.

She rolled her eyes. "That's Darius', Alexis."

"He's here?" I asked, peeking into the TV room nearby.

"No, but he will be in another hour," she said after looking at her watch.

Since I wasn't talking to Craig any more and hadn't talked to Tielle yet, I was out of the loop. My mother was going to keep Darius during the week, and Tielle or Miss Rosie would supervise Craig's visits on weekends.

She led me upstairs so I could see his room. As soon as she opened the door, I smiled. He was going to love it. It had a "Trucks" theme, and she stocked it with every type of truck you could think of. The carpet was a city layout with roads everywhere—perfect for him to roll the trucks on when he got older. There was a crib set up and even a Tonka truck toddler bed.

"You have this set up like he's gonna be here for a few years," I said as I looked through the closet stocked with clothes. "Did I miss Craig giving up custody?"

"Darius is my grandson. He'll always have a place here. I retired early so I could focus on what was important—my family. Since you're leaving, he's all I have. If Craig chooses to give up his rights, which I wouldn't object to, that baby won't miss a beat. Gram will be right here," she said.

Her eyes sparkled when she talked about him, and I hadn't seen her face light up like that since I was in middle school. Though she didn't say it, he was her second chance. She failed me and Tameka in major ways, and I believe she wanted to redeem herself by being the best grandmother she could be. I could only hope she would get it right with Darius.

Before I left, she apologized again for lying about my paternity—this time, with tears. Without a hint of bitterness, I stopped her. "Apologies don't change what happened, and they don't take away my pain. You did what you did. It is what it is."

278

I blew up Isaac's phone the rest of the day, to no avail. By ten o'clock p.m., I was done apologizing—done begging him to communicate with me. It was clear that he didn't want to be bothered with me, and I needed to heed the words I'd shared with my mother just hours before.

***

I met with Pastor Johnson after my lunch date with Tielle. He was happy to hear about my new job, and gave me words of encouragement to use if I ever questioned my life's path. His most memorable words took place in an alley behind the church. As we stood in the narrow space shaded by buildings on each side, I wondered why in the world he chose such a place to minister to me.

"Describe where we are," Pastor Johnson said.

"An alley," I replied, clenching my fists.

He laughed and then said, "*Describe* it to me. Act like I'm blind."

"I don't do alleys, Pastor. Tameka was raped in an alley."

"I know, Sister Alexis, but I need you to trust me." He grabbed my hand and said, "Now tell me what you see."

I detailed the scenery from the rusting blue dumpster on our left and loose trash scattered all around us, to the uneven pavement we stood on and the pigeon that was walking away from us.

"And I notice it's a little cool in here, and it stinks," Pastor Johnson said. Since he was stating the obvious, I didn't respond. "Let's walk," he continued, as we headed toward Grace Boulevard.

I walked to the rhythm of my heartbeat, almost leaving the pastor behind. He stopped me at the midpoint. "This alley represents your life experience thus far. You had to go through all this mess to get to the good stuff. What can you accomplish here? How can you flourish in such a restricted environment? How do you shine amongst the shady? How do you stay clean after being amongst the grimy?"

"You keep doin' you—don't stay in it," I replied with a shrug.

"That's right. You acknowledge the present for what it is, and persevere to experience what your future could be. The longer you stay around the mess, the more accustomed you get to it—it doesn't smell as bad, and you don't jump when you see rats any more. You feel me?"

When we reached the street, we stood on the sidewalk, free of walls, bright with sunlight, and full of possibilities. Pastor Johnson stretched his arms to the sky and said, "What a difference."

I looked at him and smiled. I liked how he laid that out for me.

"Remember this: Some of life's tests are designed for you to fail. If you ace every one, what appreciation do you gain from your accomplishments—the failures you've overcome?" He pointed to the alley that was then behind us. "Don't be ashamed of that. If you hadn't been there, you wouldn't recognize the true value of where you are now. Just don't find an excuse to revisit it."

At that moment, I realized I had gained much more than I had lost. I gained understanding—an understanding of responsibility, family, friendship, and real love, though I messed that one up.

"It'll be okay," was the annoying mantra that everyone's lips chanted to me on the day of Tameka's funeral. Ten months later, I could say they were right. It *was* okay…and so was I.

22

Tiffany:
Moving On

Tiffany sat in the massage chair at New Nails and talked on the phone with Morgan while Steve Wong massaged her feet. "So how are we gonna do this? I'm not gonna be without Big Boo," she said, referring to her Escalade.

"I'm confused. Do what?" Morgan asked.

"You said I could come there, right?"

"Yeah, but you—"

"I put in my two-week notice today," Tiffany said.

She was supposed to give a four-week notice, but she couldn't stick around that long. She was tired. Marlon was not only keeping her at arm's length, but he was cold toward her every time he dropped off the children. Over the past few weeks, he had conveniently worked over, and his mother had been picking them up. He was avoiding her, and Tiffany was done fighting for him. Furthermore, she was tired of passing up lunch at her favorite restaurants for fear she'd see Venni, tired of pretending her life was intact when it wasn't.

"Okay. If you want your car here, drive it, genius!" Morgan replied.

"I for damn sure ain't drivin' with two five-year-olds and a two-and-a-half-year-old terror," Tiffany said. "Are you crazy?"

Morgan sighed. "Let me think of who I can tolerate for two days…"

"Huh?"

"I could fly down there and drive your truck back, but I need a riding partner. That's a long trip, even if I split it into two days."

"You would do that for me?" Tiffany asked.

"Yeah, yeah. You better hope my traveling buddy doesn't bug the hell outta me, because you'll owe me big."

They set a date for Tiffany's move, and Morgan said she'd call back with logistics.

As Steve painted her toenails, Tiffany debated whether she should call Marlon or talk to him in person. He wasn't going to like her news no matter how she delivered it, though. She called him at work, and he spoke with an attitude once he heard her voice.

"Tiffany, I'm at work. This better be important," Marlon said.

She'd had enough. "Marlon, get over yourself. You are *not* the shit. I'm not calling to sweat you. I said I would fight, not make a fool of myself. I got your message loud and clear, and I'm moving on. Excuse me if I'm interrupting you wiping off the weight machines, but I'm not calling to beg you to take me back. This is about our kids."

Marlon corrected his tone as he absorbed the sting of Tiffany's words. "What's the problem?"

"There is no problem. We're leaving town."

"You can't make decisions like that without talking to me," he said after she elaborated.

"There's nothing to discuss with a man who is always unavailable."

"You could've told my mother about this."

"I didn't lay down with your mother!" Tiffany snapped. She looked up and saw she had the attention of everyone in the shop. She lowered her voice and continued. "If you can't communicate with me like an adult, that's your problem. Why would I go out of my way to accommodate you? You don't even have the decency to get out the car when you drop them off any more, and you peel out before they can shut the door good."

"I knew I should've taken you to court for partial custody."

"It's never too late, sweetheart. In the meantime, we'll be in Jersey," Tiffany said before hanging up.

***

Tiffany stood in line at the UPS Store, frustrated with the elderly gentleman who had a hearing problem and couldn't understand why the clerk wouldn't let him ship his great-granddaughter's favorite ice cream. *Where else can I get boxes*, she thought. If she hadn't procrastinated already, she would've had the option to return for the boxes the following day. However, with the movers coming in four days, she had some hardcore packing to do. She wasn't taking everything to Morgan's, but her essentials were unlike those of most households.

Just when she thought she couldn't become more annoyed, the lady behind her started humming a tune in her ear. She turned around, and it was Frenchie.

"Girl, I was about to go off on you!" Tiffany said.

Frenchie laughed. "I'm sorry. I was just listening to that song in the car. What you doin' in here?"

Tiffany turned to show her the folded boxes propped against her other leg. "I'm moving."

"And you're buying boxes? Girl, you better go to the grocery stores at night and ask the stock boys for some."

"They'll just give them to me?"

"Yeah!" She laughed at her friend who didn't have a clue.

"Did anyone get back to you about the jobs?" Tiffany asked.

Frenchie had been searching for a job in their field ever since they graduated, but had no luck. She had settled for a job as an admissions counselor at a college in the meantime.

Frenchie held up a poster board. "That's why I'm here now. I got the job at the high school, girl! I know school doesn't start for over a month, but I have all these ideas. I've been working on all kinds of things to post in the room to get them pumped about psychology. As a matter of fact, I need to ask if they have my banner done since I'm here."

Tiffany smiled and shook her head. Frenchie was so excited. She was sure she would be a great teacher. Her students would love her once they understood her dynamic personality.

"So are you moving closer to Safe Haven?"

"I'm moving to New Jersey with my sister. I guess it's *my* safe haven," Tiffany said with a smirk.

"Is everything okay?" Frenchie asked.

"I've lost focus, so I need to regroup," Tiffany replied. "I'll be fine, though. I'm Tiffany Price, honey." They laughed.

Frenchie knew Venni was partly responsible for Tiffany's loss of focus, so there was no need to ask questions. She only hoped Tiffany would find what she was looking for and be happy. As the clerk looked in the back room to see if her banner was ready, the ladies checked their phones to make sure they had correct phone numbers for each other.

After a brief hug, Frenchie said, "I really hope everything works out for you. Keep in touch."

Marlon called as Tiffany pulled out of the parking lot. He had been singing a new tune since she put him in his place the week before. They had worked out a short-term compromise that would allow the children to stay with him until school started in New Jersey. That way, he would get a full month with them before resorting to buying plane tickets for weekend visits.

In an effort to make the children's transition a smooth one, they had already been staying with him for the past week. Marlon tried to talk Tiffany into letting him move back into her house with the children, but she shot that down. Sure, their rooms were already set up and they were more comfortable there, but she knew his real angle: He didn't want to be cooped up in his mother's small house with them for more than a weekend. As far as she was concerned, if he wanted more space, he needed to stop being cheap and move into his *own* place.

She asked how their little ones were doing, then rushed him off the phone because she had just arrived at Aunt Retha's house. Since she was going to be busy packing the next few days, she figured she'd say goodbye early. Her aunt answered the door with a tear in her eye.

"Don't start, Auntie," Tiffany said.

"I ain't," Aunt Retha said, dabbing her eye with a handkerchief. "I know it's for the best." She thought Tiffany was moving because she accepted a new job offer.

"Don't worry. I'll be calling to check on you. I'ma find you a boyfriend to occupy your time. Maybe he can keep you out of that window," she joked.

"I like to see what's goin' on around my house," she said. "Jackie says she knows those little thugs, but they don't look like her kind of people. Those little trifling rascals can barely walk with their britches hanging off of 'em."

"Well, if she knows them, there's no problem, right?"

Aunt Retha grunted with dissatisfaction as Tiffany changed the subject.

***

The next day, Morgan flew into town with her new boo, Kaleb. He was a six-foot, two-inch dark chocolate dream. His bald head and clean-shaven face gave him a look of distinction, but his gray Nike sweat suit also showed a sporty and relaxed side. He had just moved to New Jersey from Atlanta, and Morgan had already taken him off the market.

This one needs to be a keeper, Tiffany thought as Morgan introduced them.

Morgan looked stunning as usual. She had let her hair grow out and wore it in a roller wrapped style. Her Kenneth Cole frames complemented her narrow eyes, and the diamonds in her ear bragged of how well her real estate agency was doing. Besides those things, she was glowing. Tiffany couldn't help but wonder if Kaleb had something to do with that.

She hugged her big sis. "You look good. I thought you got in at eleven?"

"We did. We stopped by Aunt Retha's for a little while."

"Say no more. What's the latest neighborhood scoop?"

"She was talking about her neighbor being pregnant. I don't know. I was only half-listening."

"And she was complaining about that car. Remember, babe?" Kaleb added.

Tiffany released an annoyed sigh. "The silver one?"

"Yeah. When we went outside, there was an Audi in front of her neighbor's house," Morgan replied.

"Was there anyone in it?" Tiffany asked.

"No. Some guy was arguing with the lady on the porch. I guess it was his. Why?"

Tiffany explained how their aunt had involved the police at one time, all because the car was making her nervous. "I keep telling her to get with one of those widowed deacons so she can have some business of her own."

Kaleb's phone rang. He excused himself, saying he had to take the call from his brother. Morgan sat on the sofa and removed her shoes.

"So, he's the insurance agent, right?" Tiffany asked.

"Kaleb? No, he's a lawyer."

A lawyer from Atlanta. Why do I feel like I should know him? Tiffany thought. "And he has a brother, huh? Does he look like him?"

Morgan laughed. "I've never seen him. He lives here, actually."

Kaleb returned to the den where Morgan and Tiffany were. "Sorry, ladies." He turned to Morgan. "Rob was trying to convince me to shoot by there before we leave."

"Did you tell him you're here on business?" Morgan asked.

Tiffany tuned them out as Kaleb's identity hit her. He was Robert's brother. He had to be. As soon as she had the chance, she pulled Morgan into another room and asked if Kaleb had a nephew named Shemar. When she answered yes, Tiffany told Morgan the Alexis-Robert-Monica story. She made it clear to her sister that she didn't want Kaleb to know her identity. She and Alexis were no longer friends, so the little co-ink-i-dink wasn't worth mentioning.

"Robert can't stand me, and he'll associate you with me if he finds out we're sisters. If you like this one, don't say a word," Tiffany said.

Morgan agreed. Her sister wasn't a head case, but she had sure been acting like one lately. Kaleb didn't need to know she used to be Alexis' nosey/crazy/annoying best friend.

After an hour-long nap, Morgan and Kaleb were ready to hit the road in Tiffany's truck. Tiffany sighed as she stood at the driver's side window where Morgan was sitting.

"You alright, kiddo?" her big sister asked.

This is really happening, Tiffany thought as she nodded.

"You can't say something is in your past until you get past it. It's time to work on you," Morgan said with a smile.

It was, and when Tiffany woke up July 24th, she was ready to say goodbye to the "Lone Star State" and hello to the "Garden State". The movers had already made it to Morgan's house with the majority of her belongings, so she only traveled with a carry-on suitcase, her laptop bag, and her favorite purse.

The cab driver pulled in front of Miss Tina's house and blew the horn twice. She teared up a little as Bryant, Bria, and Tony ran out in their pajamas. They bombarded her with hugs and kisses as Marlon stood in the doorway.

She walked them back to the house and faced Marlon. "Well, this is gonna be different. I'm gonna be so far away from them."

"Why don't you stay?" Marlon asked.

"Because I need this."

"And our kids need *you.* I've never known you to run from your problems."

"Don't put this on them. They have me. And I'm not running from my problems; I'm running toward a solution."

"Your solution is all the way in Jersey?" he asked.

"My sister is in Jersey—someone who really knows me, has never turned her back on me, and who has been guilty of judging me, but has never convicted me. She's been there for me all my life, and she'll be there when I land at 2:40. My solution starts with being around someone who loves me unconditionally, and that's what she does. She's the *only* person who does besides our parents."

"What if I told you I broke up with Sabrina?"

"I'd say, 'Congratulations, she wasn't your type.'" She touched him lightly on the arm. "Take care of yourself."

She waved goodbye to her children as she slid into the back seat of the taxi cab. She turned her head to wipe her tears, then waved again. She was proud of her little munchkins. Neither of them cried unless she counted the short-lived whimpering Bria did after their last hug. As the driver pulled away from the curb, she knew she was making the right choice.

Forty-five minutes later, she was rolling her suitcase through the airport's security checkpoint. Once she reached her gate, she still had a ten-minute wait before boarding time. Instead of sitting, she leaned against the wall and people-watched.

They better not be in first class, she thought, observing a weary mother with a screaming and kicking little boy ten feet away. Beside him, an older lady was shamelessly scratching her crotch. A text message from Marlon came across her phone's screen, diverting her attention from the disturbing sights.

Remember when u asked if that spot was still there a long time ago? The answer is yes.

She responded with a smiley face and placed her phone in her purse. When she lifted her head, she noticed a lady carrying a red Coach purse. Though she could barely see anything but the purse, the woman's stride was familiar. Determined to confirm her suspicions, Tiffany stared at the woman until she came into view. Alexis hurriedly broke through the crowd and spoke with the gate agent across the walkway.

Tiffany looked on with a closed mouth and a hesitant spirit. Her good friend was standing just a few feet away, but the gap seemed much larger. It was a gap that was once bridged, but the bridge had been burned. She wanted to ask Alexis where she was going, if she had made amends with her mother…wanted to tell her about Kaleb and Morgan…give her Morgan's number in case she ever wanted to talk to Bria.

Alexis looked annoyed as she placed her ID in her purse and waited for the agent to look up something in the computer. Instead of calling out to her, Tiffany silently wished her well and faced her gate again. The agent would be calling all passengers in first class soon, and in the end, there was really nothing to say. Aunt Retha always told her not to burn bridges because you can't rebuild with ashes. She was right.

Portia A. Cosby

Epilogue

Alexis' Decisions

Atlanta was treating me well. Everything was in place from the moment my plane landed. My go-to person/personal assistant, Simone, picked me up from the airport and took me straight to a Nissan dealer to get my 350Z. From there, I followed her to my loft in the heart of downtown. Yari was parked across the street from my building, waiting with my key. I had given her sole permission to let the movers in, so she already knew what my place looked like and had admittedly done some decorating. She met me and Simone at the door with a grin.

"What the hell is wrong with you?" I asked, taking the key from her.

Yari shrugged. "I'm just excited for you."

When I opened the door, Isaac was kneeling on his right knee and holding an open ring box. "I figured this was better than texting you back," he said.

I didn't know how to feel. I'd poured my heart out in my texts, begging him to answer me, and he hadn't. I put my heart on the line and left Texas accepting that he rejected me.

Sensing my confusion, he continued. "I read all your texts and listened to all your voicemails. Is this enough reassurance?" he asked.

"A ring?" I finally muttered.

"I'm not saying we have to get married in a few months or even next year; but I'm not gon' let you walk around this city without somethin' on your finger to let these cats know you're taken."

Not wanting to embarrass him, I knelt down and spoke softly. "I can't. I'm not sayin' no, but I can't say yes until you're here."

"I live in Buckhead," Isaac replied. "Soon as you said you were moving, I called my old professor and he put me on to a few jobs here. I was gonna tell you the last time we talked, but when you took our conversation to another level, I got pissed. I had already quit my job and planned my relocation." He revealed that he'd been in town for a week and would begin work as an HIV/AIDS nurse at a private clinic in a few days.

"How do you go from being that pissed off to proposing?"

"I know what I want. Do you?"

From that moment on, I proudly sported the radiant-cut diamond on my hand and you couldn't tell me I wasn't the shit.

4 Months Later...

"They were able to arrange the *Set It Off* reunion show!" Simone exclaimed as she walked into my dressing room.

"My girl!" I replied. "That's why I like you. You get stuff done."

"You only watch that movie once a week. Who would imagine you'd want to interview them," she joked.

"Once a month," I corrected. "And think about it. When those actresses starred in that movie, they were barely known across the board. Now look at 'em. Tell me that won't be a hot show."

Before Simone replied, my cell phone rang. She handed me the phone displaying an unknown number. When I answered, Darryl asked if I was busy, saying he had to ask me something. "Well, actually, Jacqueline insists on asking you herself."

"If it's what you asked the other day, my answer hasn't changed."

"Do me a favor and hear her out, please. She's not even supposed to be talking right now."

I sighed as Jacqueline came on the line. "Alexis, I'm in the hospital." Her feeble voice strained to be heard.

I knew. Darryl had called a few days before to tell me, and my mother called, too. The same assholes that Isaac and I got into it with at Smoothies had been extorting money from her, saying Smoke owed them. When she refused to give them any more money, they retaliated, running her car down and causing a fatal accident—the only fatality being Craig's unborn daughter who was due in three days. Luckily, Jacqueline's sons were at a school event and were unharmed. It was a sad story, but I couldn't find much sympathy in my heart.

Jacqueline had lost a tremendous amount of blood and was going to need a transfusion. Darryl couldn't donate because he was on antibiotics; her mother was doing missionary work in Africa; and the two half-siblings she was able to reach weren't compatible. Then there was me, the universal donor, type O.

"How did I know you would call?" I asked. "Didn't Darryl already tell you I said no?"

"Did he tell you who did this?" I said nothing. "We'll pay for your flight. I'll pay for your blood. Whatever it takes," she bargained. "I know you hate me, and you have every reason to feel that way, but can you put that aside out of compassion? They say I can't wait much longer. Please, Alexis. I'll owe you my life."

Still, I sat silently and listened to the buzzing and beeping machines in the background—sounds that took my mind to a place I didn't plan on visiting until the next day, the one year anniversary of Tameka's death.

"I'm sorry to put you in an awkward position, but whether we like it or not, we're family. I can be the sister you can save."

A few more seconds went by, and then I broke the silence by pushing the "End" button. "Lord, forgive me," I said.

I was glad I didn't have on a "WWJD" bracelet, because Jesus wouldn't have done that. I was a work-in-progress, though, not far enough in my Christian journey to run to Jacqueline's aid. A part of me felt bad, but the other part was on the phone with Sprint, arranging for my number to be changed.

Jacqueline's Karma

The loud hum of the dial tone sounded in Jacqueline's ear. She didn't really expect Alexis to say yes, but her harsh refusal was disheartening. As Darryl looked on, she shook her head. "Any more ideas?"

She blamed herself. All she had to do was come up with $5,000, but she lied and said she didn't have it. She could've easily cashed in a CD to keep Jye and Waylon out of her hair for good, but she was tired of paying Rashawn's debt. If she hadn't started paying the thugs in the first place, she probably wouldn't have been in that predicament; but what did she know? They threatened her life from the moment they first showed up at her house in Waylon's silver Audi. She recognized them immediately as the men who dropped her brother off when he came to get the Acura on the night he attacked Tameka again.

She had played with fire and was now feeling the burn. As she watched the hands on the clock, she wondered how much time she had left. The doctors couldn't guarantee more than a few days if they couldn't find any more donor blood.

Karma's a bitch, she thought. Bearing Craig's child was her way in. Sure, she'd made it into his bed, but she was aiming for his heart. As she stared at the empty chair beside Darryl, it was evident her plan didn't work. Now that Taylor was dead, there was nothing to keep Craig around, nothing to help him forget the pain she'd caused in the past.

Portia A. Cosby

Tiffany's Appointment

Tiffany kissed Bryant and Bria on their cheeks. "Behave," she said, while watching them get on the bus. As soon as the bus pulled off, she ran inside to escape the November chill.

The phone rang while she hung her coat in the closet. It was her mother…again. She had been calling every day since she moved to Newark. Though she tried to act like she was making small talk, it was the same thing every time. After asking if Tony's stomach virus was any better, she said, "I found another great scripture in the *Daily Bread* today." She had suddenly become a Bible freak since she found out the specifics of her relationship with Venni.

Tiffany made a cup of cappuccino as she listened to the short verse. Like the others, it had nothing to do with sexuality, but somehow her mother would relate it to "exorcizing the homosexuality demons" that were fighting for her soul. After all, that's why she didn't want Tiffany working. She wanted her to focus on finding herself again, so she sent her money every month.

To Tiffany, it felt like an allowance. She would get it as long as she was a good girl and stayed away from other girls. Little did her parents know, that was the farthest thing from her mind. She and Marlon were reconciling and would most likely resume their relationship when she returned to Texas. She played the game, though. If it took going on the stupid dates her parents had Morgan set up to prove she still liked men, she'd do it. That check from Mom and Dad ensured she would be able to maintain her fabulous lifestyle.

"How did your date go last night?" Mrs. Price asked.

Tiffany had gone to a museum with a psychologist Morgan knew from church. "It would've been wonderful if I felt like talking about Freud all night."

"That should have been interesting. Morgan thought you two had a lot in common."

"I don't want someone who is just like me. I was just fine with Marlon."

"Evidently you weren't."

"Well, now I am. I will be," Tiffany corrected, "if we get back together."

"So you've learned from your mistake, I'll assume."

"I don't make mistakes. I make progress. I don't regret my time with Venni, if that's what you're looking for me to say. I learned a lot from her."

Mrs. Price groaned with disgust.

292

"Not like that, Ma. Saying that part of my life was a mistake attaches a negative connotation to our friendship. I needed those experiences with her in order to grow."

"Well, I most certainly hope you're finished growing."

"And on that note, I'm getting off the phone. Goodbye, Mother."

Her parents worried for nothing. She and Venni hadn't been in contact since her last day at Safe Haven. Their short-lived acquaintance could have been a lifelong friendship if they hadn't crossed crucial boundaries, but its demise was for the best. Venni was damaged goods, and her baggage far exceeded the weight limit of Tiffany's heart. It was unfortunate, though. Tiffany often felt like she abandoned Venni when she could've helped her. The connection was still there. Venni was her sister soul mate from their expensive taste in food to their addiction to *Who Wants to be a Millionaire*. They were destined to meet, just not under the terms that were in place.

Marlon called with exciting news just as Tiffany prepared to leave. After signing all the paperwork, he was no longer just a manager at Fit Club; he was now the owner. While they discussed his plans for renovation and expansion, Tiffany beamed with pride. Marlon had been waiting three years for this day to come.

"Well, I hate to cut you off, but I have to get outta here," she said, as she bundled Tony up. "I'm gonna be late for my appointment."

Instead of rushing off to a nail shop, she was dropping Tony off at preschool and going to see her counselor. For three months, she had been on the couch rather than in the chair—the patient instead of the practitioner.

On her way out, she noticed the date on the calendar, November 26th. *Wow. It's already been a year*, she thought, taking a moment to reflect. She wondered how Alexis was doing and what she was doing. One more day would mark a year ago when Tiffany was sitting with her at the hospital, telling her everything would be okay. She could only pray that it was now.

Though she didn't have any contact information for her, she knew she could visit a few people search engines on the internet to get it. Her heart would have. Her mind told her to leave that door closed, though, refusing to be pegged as a stalker again. If she'd learned nothing else, she learned she can't love everyone the same way. The former best friend who taught her every song on Tupac's "All Eyez on Me" and took her to her first house party would forever be in her heart and remain out of her life.

When she attended church on Sunday, everyone in the sanctuary seemed invisible. They had to be, because the pastor was talking directly to her. His sermon was entitled, "Reason, Season, or Lifetime: Pick a Column." Neither category was good or bad; they each had a purpose. The overall message answered why people come into each others' lives. As he elaborated on each category, Tiffany's proverbial sky parted, the angels sang, and a bright light shone down.

Alexis entered her life for a reason. She helped her fit in, in a fast-paced, urban high school when she was just a weird military brat relocating from rural North Carolina; Alexis led by example, showing Tiffany how to be a stronger woman. For that, she would be eternally grateful.

Venni was in her life for a season, to knock her down a few notches. Through their dealings, she was humbled, forced to respect boundaries—her own and others'. She had also gained greater respect for women with sordid pasts, realizing there's a story behind every book. The next time she had a session with a troubled teenager, she would listen with a more in-tune ear and advise using not just her textbooks, but her heart.

Marlon kept her grounded. He was practical when she was unrealistic and easygoing when she was uptight. Though she hated their differences at times, he was good for her. She was hard to love, but he was up for the challenge. Because of their children, he would be around for a lifetime. If she could win him back, they could spend that lifetime together.

Discussion Questions

1. When Alexis was questioning Robert's fidelity, should she have just left, or was she justified in going through his belongings to get answers?

2. If you were in Alexis' position, how would you have reacted to Tiffany's advance? Would you have befriended her again?

3. Alexis made an important decision concerning the paternity results once she received them. Would you have kept the truth from Darnell?

4. Do you feel Alexis was responsible for Craig's breakdown?

5. Tiffany was obsessed with Marlon proposing to her. Do you think she sincerely wanted to be his wife, or was she just in love with the idea of marriage?

6. How do you feel about Tiffany's explanation of her relationship with and feelings for Venni?

7. What did you think of Venni? Were you shocked to read of her past?

8. In your opinion, does Tiffany deserve another chance with Marlon?

9. Craig wasn't at Jacqueline's bedside at the end. Why do you think that is? Should he have been?

10. Alexis hung up on Jacqueline at a critical time. Just from a human perspective, should she have had more sympathy?

11. Considering both of the ladies' journeys, do you feel they learned their lessons?

LIFE LESSONS

Lesson One: People can only play games with you when you opt to participate.

Lesson Two: A liar only wants a second chance to come up with a better lie.

Lesson Three: When you only think of yourself, you end up by yourself.

Lesson Four: Love doesn't hurt. Please refer to your scripture for more understanding, students (1 Corinthians 13: 4-7). Any questions?

Lesson Five: The truth may hurt, but like an immunization given to us with a needle, it is very necessary.

Lesson Six: Once you realize your worth, you'll stop accepting coupons.

Lesson Seven: You'll never be satisfied with how someone loves you if you don't love yourself.

Lesson Eight: The purpose of being tested is to see if you've learned your lesson. Don't be mad at the teacher if you fail.

Lesson Nine: Never look for someone who will complete you; find someone who will complement you.

Lesson Ten: We all have choices in life. In the end, it is usually safe to choose true happiness…if, of course, you know what that is.

Lesson Eleven: God doesn't need help. Stop trying to be his vice president and let HIM do his thing in your life.

Lesson Twelve: Wanna know one of the quickest ways to get hurt? Place expectations on others.

Lesson Thirteen: Food for thought: If you can live without your significant other, just how significant are they?

Have you learned a valuable lesson you would like to share?

Visit www.myspace.com/haveyoulearned
and leave it in the "Comments" section

COMING SOON...

Books Three and Four in the Situations & Circumstances Series

AIN'T NOTHIN' FREE

Think Venni's story is over? It's just beginning, and Keyonna is ready to tell it. From their first meeting to their first goodbye, Keyonna shares her and Venni's story of life in the suburbs, where adventure turned into danger, having fun was a business, and freedom came at a price that Mommy & Daddy couldn't afford. They were sent to Lakeside Preparatory School to become successful young women, but no one said what they had to be successful doing...

...BUT NOW I SEE

Dallas is happy that Yari's movie career is going well, but being one of the hottest new actresses in the business comes with a demanding schedule and an automatic induction into the rumor mill. As filming begins for her second movie, Dallas feels slighted and begins to resent Yari's new career. When rumors swirl of a budding romance between her and a co-star, Dallas begins to entertain advances from one of his clients, inciting a fiery affair with critical repercussions. When the smoke clears, Yari suffers the consequences of her husband playing with fire.

ALSO BY PORTIA A. COSBY:

TOO LITTLE, TOO LATE

ISBN: 978-0-9823013-0-2 (Second Edition)
ISBN: 978-0-9718920-6-4 (Collector s Edition)

Where it all begins...

TAMEKA JAMES has always been a confident, outspoken, strong-willed woman with her one weakness being her ex-boyfriend, TJ. That weakness soon becomes the catalyst to a new life of fear, disease, and pain when one of TJ's enemies rapes her and threatens to kill her if she goes to the police.

Now with a police report on file, an HIV diagnosis in her medical records, and the rapist running free, Tameka fights to maintain normalcy and save her new relationship. As tensions mount and stakes are raised, some lives are threatened while others are taken.

The phrase "too little, too late" becomes a reality instead of a cliché when last minute efforts are made in vain.

With hundreds of new books flooding the market every week selling a gimmick, it is refreshing to find a novel that delivers substance and quality. That is what you will find in Portia Cosby's TOO LITTLE, TOO LATE. A book that is all-too-real for so many people today, it chronicles a journey that no one would choose to take but so many are forced to tread. Cosby shows both maturity and sophistication in her debut novel, and by the end of the story she lets you know one thing: this is by no means the last time you will be hearing from her.
-Cyrus A. Webb, Conversations Book Club

Exciting and theatrical from start to finish; it is a page-turner and a tear jerker...TOO LITTLE, TOO LATE is a must read, and is very, very good for a first time novel. I'm looking forward to next book.
-Toni Bonita, RAWSISTAZ Reviewers

Contact the author at: feedback@portiacosby.com

For general questions or to be added to Portia A. Cosby's mailing list: info@portiacosby.com

Visit www.portiacosby.com and
www.myspace.com/portiacosby
to leave feedback about Portia A. Cosby's novels, get the latest news about events and books, and to order additional copies

Portia A. Cosby

www.ingramcontent.com/pod-product-compliance
Lightning Source LLC
Chambersburg PA
CBHW071112250626
47159CB00002B/703